MEDITERRANEAN WEDDINGS

Marriage under the hot
Mediterranean sun…

Three passionate novels!

GW00382681

*In April 2007 Mills & Boon bring back
two of their classic collections, each
featuring three favourite
romances by our bestselling authors…*

MEDITERRANEAN
WEDDINGS

A Mediterranean Marriage
by Lynne Graham
The Greek's Virgin Bride by Julia James
The Italian Prince's Proposal
by Susan Stephens

WHOSE BABY?

With This Baby…
by Caroline Anderson
The Italian's Baby by Lucy Gordon
Assignment: Baby by Jessica Hart

MEDITERRANEAN WEDDINGS

A MEDITERRANEAN MARRIAGE
by
Lynne Graham

THE GREEK'S VIRGIN BRIDE
by
Julia James

THE ITALIAN PRINCE'S PROPOSAL
by
Susan Stephens

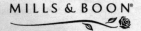

MILLS & BOON®

MILLS & BOON and MILLS & BOON with the Rose Device are registered trademarks of the publisher.
Harlequin Mills & Boon Limited,
Eton House, 18-24 Paradise Road, Richmond, Surrey, TW9 1SR

MEDITERRANEAN WEDDINGS
© by Harlequin Enterprises II B.V. 2007

A Mediterranean Marriage, The Greek's Virgin Bride and *The Italian Prince's Proposal* were first published in Great Britain by Harlequin Mills & Boon Limited in separate, single volumes.

A Mediterranean Marriage © Lynne Graham 2002
The Greek's Virgin Bride © Julia James 2003
The Italian Prince's Proposal © Susan Stephens 2003

ISBN: 978 0 263 85513 5

05-0407

Printed and bound in Spain
by Litografia Rosés S.A., Barcelona

A MEDITERRANEAN MARRIAGE

by

Lynne Graham

Lynne Graham was born in Northern Ireland and has been a keen Mills & Boon reader since her teens. She is very happily married with an understanding husband, who has learned to cook since she started to write! Her five children keep her on her toes. She has a very large dog, which knocks everything over, a very small terrier which barks a lot, and two cats. When time allows, Lynne is a keen gardener.

Don't miss Lynne Graham's exciting new novel, *The Italian's Inexperienced Mistress,* out now from Mills & Boon Modern Romance™

For my editor, Tessa Shapcott, in fond
appreciation of her creative support beyond
the call of duty

CHAPTER ONE

WHEN his new investment consultant had finished speaking, Rauf Kasabian gazed out across the Bosphorus strait towards the city of Istanbul, his lean, handsome features grim.

For once, Rauf was impervious to the magical spell cast by his waterside home. The ever-changing play of light and shadow over the shimmering water and the gentle lapping of the tide usually relaxed him. But his bitter memories triumphed over his surroundings and now his anger had been roused as well. So, the Harris family had played ducks and drakes with his money and Lily was flying out to Turkey in person to ask for what? Special treatment? On what grounds? That her family should choose *her* as messenger had to be the ultimate insult!

In receipt of that bewildering lack of response from a tycoon whose ruthless intolerance for dishonest business practice was legendary, Serhan Mirosh regarded his employer with anxious eyes. Had he himself overreached his powers in taking instant punitive action in the affair? True, the funds involved were mere pocket change to a media mogul as wealthy as Rauf Kasabian, but Serhan took keen pride in his attention to detail. Uncovering the disturbing history of Rauf's unprofitable investment in the small English travel firm concerned had seemed a laudable effort for he had been dismayed that his predecessor should have allowed such flagrant irregularities to continue without intervention.

'That in over two years you should have earned no financial return for your backing is outrageous,' Serhan recapped with measured care, in case he had omitted some salient point in his previous explanation. 'In line with the contract you agreed with Douglas Harris, I have demanded the repayment of the original sum invested plus the percentage of profits which you should have received during that period.'

'I'm grateful that you have brought this matter to my attention,' Rauf asserted with a cool nod of acknowledgement.

Praised, Serhan relaxed and spread speaking hands. 'I cannot understand why this Harris woman should now seek a meeting with you but my faxed response to that effect and indeed my refusal on your behalf has been ignored. Yesterday I received a second request for an appointment between the fourth and the fifteenth.'

As it was now the second of the month that could only mean that Lily would soon be on Turkish soil, Rauf registered, his lean, lithe, powerful length tautening at that awareness. 'The English can be stubborn.'

'But such persistence is rude,' Serhan lamented. 'What is the point of this woman coming here? The time when explanations might have been considered is past. Furthermore, it is her father who owns the firm.'

Rauf decided not to add to the other man's confusion with the additional news that Lily Harris was, or had been three years earlier, training as a nursery school teacher. 'Leave the file with me and I will deal with it,' he instructed. 'I would also like to know where Miss Harris is staying.'

'In an Aegean coastal resort,' Serhan advanced drily, but he was unable to quite conceal his astonishment that Rauf should be prepared to give his personal attention to such an undeserving cause. 'Perhaps Miss Harris believes Gumbet is next door to your head office in Istanbul!'

'It's possible.' In a mood of rare abstraction, Rauf was studying the file that he had already opened with hard dark golden eyes. 'When I knew her, geography wasn't her strong point.'

When I knew her? A startled exclamation on his lips at that revealing comment, Serhan thought better of voicing it and departed. At the same time, he wondered how his employer would react to the discovery that Harris Travel had treated the Turkish builders engaged to build villas for them in a dishonest and disgraceful manner.

Some minutes later, Rauf cast aside the file, a cold gleam in his dark gaze, his handsome mouth clenched hard. He was outraged by what he had read: Lily would receive no mercy from him. He remembered her eyes blue as the summer sky telling him that he was the centre of her world. A cynical laugh fell from Rauf's wide, sensual mouth. Yes, he had believed her to be both sincere and innocent. Like countless men before him, in burning to possess one particular woman, he had, momentarily, shelved intelligence and caution. Mercifully, it *had* only been the weakness of a moment from which he had soon recovered.

But then, long before he had met Lily, Rauf had recognised what had once been his own essential flaw and had tracked it back to its unfortunate source. He had great respect and affection for his mother but she had indoctrinated him with a lot of foolish romantic notions about her own sex that had caused him nothing but grief. But then his naive parent had no concept of the much more basic level at which men and women of Rauf's generation interacted, and regarded his womanising reputation as a source of deep shame.

Whereas Rauf rejoiced in the knowledge that what he had once got wrong, he now always got right. Women passed through his bedroom without causing him any concern that he was taking cruel advantage of their supposedly weaker and more trusting natures. Having shaken off the dangerous misconception that good, old-fashioned lust was love, he enjoyed his male freedom of choice. He would get a kick out of seeing Lily Harris again, he decided. No doubt Lily imagined that her beauty allied with some soppy recollection of their brief relationship might blunt his business acumen and soften his heart towards her: she would soon find out her mistake...

Lily came downstairs lugging her case step by step.

Her three nieces, Penny, Gemma and Joy, were playing in the sitting-room and the sound of their giggles brought a smile to her tense mouth. It said a lot for her older sister, Hilary, that her children were able to laugh like that in the wake of events that might have destroyed a less close-knit family. It was only a year since Hilary's husband, Brett, had walked out to move in with her sister's former best friend.

At the time, Brett and Hilary's youngest daughter, Joy, had been undergoing the last phase of her treatment for leukaemia. Mercifully, Lily's four-year-old niece had since made a full recovery but then, right from the moment Joy's condition had been diagnosed, Hilary had refused to contemplate any other possibility. Lily's sister was a great believer in the power of positive thinking and she had needed every atom of that strength to keep up her spirits in the testing times that had followed.

Lily's father, Douglas Harris, had signed over his comfortable detached house to Hilary and Brett lock, stock and barrel soon after their marriage and had continued to live with them. In the divorce settlement, Brett had been awarded half the value of the marital home, which he had never put a penny into either buying or maintaining, and as a result it had had to be sold. Not long after that development, it had emerged that Lily's father's travel agency, Harris Travel, which Brett had until recently continued to manage, was also in trouble. Just a month ago Douglas Harris, Hilary and her little girls had moved into the tiny terraced house that was now their home for the foreseeable future.

'You should have let me help you with that case!' Hilary scolded from the kitchen doorway. She was a tall, slender woman with short light brown hair, but even her ready smile could not conceal the tiredness of her eyes for she ran herself ragged struggling to keep up her many commitments. 'We have time for a cup of tea before we leave for the airport. Have you said goodbye to Dad yet?'

'Yes, and once we head off he's going to take the girls down to the park—'

'That's great...I was beginning to think we needed a tin-opener to prise him out of that bedroom upstairs!' In spite of her look of relief at the news of that planned outing, Hilary's light-hearted response wobbled a little. 'Once Dad starts taking an interest in life again, he'll be fine. There's no point looking back to what might have been, is there?'

'No,' Lily agreed, averting her gaze from the bright shimmer of tears Hilary was attempting to conceal, for she was well aware that her elder sister held herself responsible for their father having been forced out of the house he had lived in all his life and his subsequent depression. 'Shouldn't we run through my schedule for Turkey again before I leave? My first priority is to see Rauf about—'

'Are you still worrying about that stupid letter his accountant sent?' Hilary gave her a reproachful glance. 'There's no need. As I told you, I've checked the agency books and those payments *were* made. In fact we've kept every part of that agreement and the accounts are in apple-pie order. This business with Rauf Kasabian is a ridiculous storm in a teacup. When he realises that his new accountant has made a gigantic embarrassing mistake, I'm sure he'll be very apologetic.'

Lily's imagination refused to put Rauf in that guise and her thoughts shied away from him again in discomfiture. Hilary always thought the best of people, always assumed that a genuine mistake or simple misunderstanding lay at the foot of problems, she reflected anxiously while her sister poured the tea. Lily, however, was less trusting and more of a worrier. When she had seen that very official letter from Rauf's high-powered accountant she had been shocked by that blunt demand for the return of Rauf's investment, not to mention a request for payments that had already been made.

Indeed, Lily would have been happier if her sister had consulted a solicitor or even another accountant over that demand. However, having seen large sums of money she could ill afford consumed by such professionals during her divorce, Hilary was determined only to request legal or financial advice as an absolute last resort. In addition, Hilary believed that the contract that Rauf Kasabian had signed with their father was watertight. But what if it weren't? What if there *were* a loophole and Rauf just wanted his stake back out of what had proved to be a far from profitable enterprise?

Lily felt very much personally involved. Had she not brought Rauf home to meet her father that investment would never have been made, for at the time Douglas Harris had already dismissed Brett's suggestion that he should borrow from the bank at high rates of interest. Cautious as he had always been in business matters, her father had, however, been tempted by the offer of financial backing from a silent partner that would spread the risk of the ambitious expansion plans his son-in-law had persuaded him into considering.

'Stop worrying about that silly letter,' her sister urged, reading Lily's troubled air with the ease of a woman who had virtually raised her from birth, and then addressing herself to the task of serving out juice and biscuits to her trio of daughters. 'Getting those two villas Brett had built at Dalyan into the hands of a decent estate agent is more of a priority. Once they're sold, the cash-flow problems I'm having at Harris Travel will be at an end. Just make sure a reasonable price is set on them. I can't afford to hang out for the best possible offer.'

'Will do and, if they're looking a bit shabby after lying empty for so long, I'll do what I can with them,' Lily promised, wondering if Hilary was aware that her face still shadowed whenever she mentioned her ex-husband's name, and then feeling horribly guilty that the divorce had been a secret source of intense relief where she herself was concerned.

'The budget would run to a lick of paint but that's about all.' Hilary grimaced, breaking off to settle a sudden squabble between Penny, who was nine, and Gemma, who was eight, both girls carbon copies of their mother with their fine, flyaway brown hair and hazel eyes. 'Aside of that, concentrate on getting in all the sightseeing trips you can and I'll use your feedback to work out some all-inclusive tour packages to Turkey for next spring. I'm determined to take the agency back to its roots. We can't compete with the big travel chains but we *can* offer a personalised exclusive service to up-market travellers.'

'I'll sign up for every tour available.' Lily let her youngest niece Joy climb up onto her knee and hugged her close. She was a little blonde sprite of a child and very slight in build. For endless months she had been weak as a kitten and the sparkling energy that she had regained was a delight to them all.

Leaving the children in the care of their grandfather, Hilary drove Lily to the airport. 'I know you don't want me to say it...but thanks from the bottom of my heart for everything you've done to help out these last few months,' the older woman said abruptly.

'I've done next to nothing and here I am getting a free holiday off you into the bargain!' Lily teased.

'Solo holidays aren't exactly fun and I know that you could've spent the whole summer in Spain if you hadn't turned down that invite from your college friend on our behalf—'

'How did you find out about that?' Lily demanded in surprise.

'Dad heard you on the phone to Maria and, let's face it, I'm sure you're in no hurry to meet that rat, Rauf Kasabian, again.' Hilary sighed with audible regret. 'But there's just no way I can leave the kids and Dad and the travel agency right now.'

Eyes staring dully straight ahead, Lily forced a laugh of disagreement in determined dismissal of her sister's concern. 'This long after the event, I'd be a sorry case if I was still *that* sensitive about Rauf. And don't call him a rat. I mean...what did he do?'

'He was a gorgeous, arrogant louse and he broke your heart!' Hilary countered with an unfamiliar harshness that shook Lily. 'If he wanted female company to wile away his stay in London that summer, he should have picked someone older and wiser. Instead he led you up the garden path and then ditched you without a word of warning.'

At that angry response, Lily turned startled blue eyes to her sister's taut profile. 'I never realised that you felt like that.'

'I hate his guts,' Hilary confided with a shocking lack of hesitation. 'More so since I've realised the damage he did to your confidence. It's unnatural for a girl of your age not to date. You've always been a little shy and reserved but, after what he did, it was like you locked yourself up tight and threw the key away! I'm sorry...I should mind my own business.'

'No, it's all right.' Lily swallowed the aching thickness in her throat, touched by Hilary's loyalty and love but pained by her perception.

Although her sister remained unaware of the reality, she *had* pushed herself out on dates over the past year, hoping to meet someone who might make her feel as Rauf once had and enable her to finally shake free of the past. Only it hadn't happened. But, very fortunately, her sibling had got the actual identity of the man who had most damaged Lily's trust in his sex quite wrong and Lily knew that she would never tell the sister she loved the truth for there would be no gain to be made from causing Hilary such pain now.

Yes, Rauf's sudden defection had hurt her terribly, but then he had never mentioned love or the future and indeed had told her that he had no intention of *ever* getting married. On his terms, what they had shared had only been a minor flirtation. She was not bitter about it. Was it Rauf's fault that she had managed to convince herself that he thought more of her than he in fact had? No, she answered for herself. She had been young, inexperienced and so much in love that she had not wanted to face the unfortunate reality that these days a gorgeous, sophisticated guy expected sex to be part of any relationship, serious *or* casual. Most probably, Rauf had dumped her because she had failed to deliver on that score.

'No, it's not all right,' Hilary muttered unhappily. 'You're almost twenty-four and I really shouldn't be talking to you and interfering in your life as though you're still a teenager.'

An involuntary grin lit Lily's tense face for Hilary was like a mother hen and never stopped interfering. 'Don't worry about it.'

Almost fourteen years older than Lily, Hilary often treated her more like a daughter than a sister. Their mother had died from post-natal complications within days of Lily's birth and from then on Hilary had shouldered a lot of responsibility within their home. Childcare had been arranged for the daylight hours but it had been Hilary who had fed her newborn sister during the night and rocked her to sleep. It had also been Hilary who had sacrificed her chance to go to university sooner than leave her toddler sibling to the charge of an ever-changing series of carers and a father, who had often acted as guide for the tours that had once been the core element of Harris Travel's prosperity.

She was very conscious of how much she owed Hilary, and there was little that Lily would not have done to lighten her sister's current load in life. Between family commitments and the endless challenge of battling to prop up a failing business and live on a shoestring, her sister already had too much on her plate and Lily only wished that she were in a position to do more to help. Unfortunately, during term time, she worked in a nursery school a couple of hundred miles away.

In a few short weeks, when the new school term started,

she would be returning to work and nowhere within reach when Hilary needed an extra pair of hands or even a supportive hug. Unhappily, flying out to Turkey in Hilary's stead was all that lay within Lily's power and, although she dreaded seeing Rauf again, accepting that necessity without dramatising the event felt like the very least she could do in return.

'There's a message for you,' Lily was informed when she finally got to check into her small hotel at two the following morning.

As she trekked after the porter showing her to her room, Lily shook open the folded sheet of paper and then sucked in a sharp sustaining breath.

'Mr Kasabian will meet you at eleven a.m. on the fourth at the Aegean Court Hotel.'

For what remained of the night, she dozed in stretches, wakening several times with a start and the fading memory of vivid dreams that unsettled and embarrassed her. Dreams about Rauf and the summer she had turned twenty-one. Rauf Kasabian, the guy who had convinced her that a woman could actually *die* from unrequited love and longing. How had he done that to her? How had he got past her defences in the first instance? It still bewildered Lily that she, who had until then backed off in helpless distaste from masculine overtures, had somehow felt only the most shocking, soaring happiness and satisfaction when Rauf had been the offender.

When she walked out of her hotel later that morning to climb into a taxi, she felt hot and bothered and so nervous she literally felt sick. The document case she carried contained copies of all the relevant account-book entries and bank statements that Hilary had given her as proof that all dues had been paid over to Rauf's company, MMI, on the correct dates. She was dropped off at an enormous, opulent hotel complex with a long line of international flags flying outside the imposing main doors.

Rauf had not paraded his great wealth in London. In fact she had had no grasp whatsoever of his true standing in the business world until her father had made discreet enquiries through his bank about the male offering him financial backing. Her father's bank manager had suggested that Douglas Harris break out the champagne to celebrate such a generous offer from a business tycoon whom he had described as being one of the richest and most powerful media moguls in Europe.

In the vast reception lounge inside the Aegean Court, Rauf sank back into his comfortable seat, a glass of mineral water cradled between his lean brown fingers for he never touched alcohol during business hours. He was secure in the knowledge that the staff were hovering at a discreet distance to ensure that nobody else sat down anywhere within hearing for it was *his* hotel. Conducting his meeting with Lily in a public area would ensure that formal distance was maintained and keep it brief.

But then he might have staged their encounter in his penthouse apartment on the top floor had it not been for the fact that it was already very much occupied by family members expecting him to join them for lunch. The pushy but lovable trio of matriarchs in the Kasabian family had that very morning elected without invitation to come for a heady spin in his private jet. Rauf suppressed a rueful groan, for his ninety-two-year-old great-grandmother, his seventy-four-year-old grandmother and his mother could in combination be somewhat trying guests. Was it *his* fault that he was an only child and the sole unappreciative focus of their hopes of the next generation?

Shelving that reflection with a wry grimace, he concentrated his thoughts back on Lily. He fully expected, indeed he was even looking forward to, being disappointed when he saw her again. No woman could possibly be as beautiful as he had once believed her to be.

So, it was most ironic that, when Rauf saw the two middle-aged doormen compete in an undignified race to throw the doors wide for the woman entering the hotel, it should be Lily in receipt of that exaggerated male attention that only a very real degree of beauty evoked. Lily, who still seemed to drift rather than walk, her long dress flowing with her fluid movements and baring only slim arms, narrow wrists and slender ankles. As Lily approached the desk, Rauf watched the young clerk rush to greet her and his wide, sensual mouth compressed into a line harder than steel.

Hair the colour of a sunlit cornfield fell all the way to Lily's waist, even longer than it had been that summer. Her modest appearance, though, was pure, calculated provocation, Rauf thought in raw derision. The plain dress only accentuated her classic beauty and anchoring that mane of fabulous golden hair into prim restraint merely imbued most men with a strong desire to see those pale silken strands loose and spread across a pillow.

In fact it was an education for Rauf to watch every man in her vicinity swivel to watch her move past and note how she affected not to notice the stir she caused. But no woman blessed with her perfect features could remain unaware of the gifts she had been born with. Had he not let himself be fooled by that same air of innocence, had he just taken her to his bed and enjoyed her body, he would surely have realised then that she was not only nothing that special, but also a practised little tart.

* * *

As Lily headed in the direction that the desk clerk had indicated her heart started to beat very, very fast, indeed so fast that she could hardly catch her breath. She still could not believe that she was about to see Rauf Kasabian again. But then across the wide empty space that separated them she actually saw Rauf rise from his table. Her whole body leapt with almost painful tension and she froze, paralysed to the spot by that first glimpse of him.

He was so very tall. He stood six feet four inches with the wide shoulders, narrow hips and lithe, muscular build of a male in the peak of physical condition. And gorgeous did not *begin* to describe that lean, bronzed face, Lily conceded in dazed acknowledgement. Rauf was so startlingly handsome that even on the crowded streets of London women had noticed him and turned their heads to stare. Lustrous, luxuriant black hair was cropped to his proud head. He had a riveting bone structure overlaid with vibrant skin and tawny eyes that could be dark as bitter chocolate or as pure a gold as the sinking sun.

Her legs behaved like sticks without the ability to bend as she forced herself to move towards him. Her colour was high at the lowering awareness that she had stopped dead to look at him like an impressionable schoolgirl. He did not make the moment easier for her by striding forward to meet her halfway. Instead he stayed where he was, making her come to him. How had she forgotten how he dominated everything around him? How he could entrap her with one mesmerising look from those thick-lashed, brilliant eyes?

Rauf watched her approach. She was a perfect doll, dainty and exquisite as a Meissen ornament. On even that very basic level she had once appealed to every masculine protective instinct he possessed. Rauf drew in a stark short breath. Memory hadn't lied, memory had only dimmed his recollection of her wonderful skin, not to mention those deep blue eyes wide as a child's and fringed by soft brown lashes a baby deer would have envied. The cool intellect that outright rejected the temptation she presented warred with the much more primitive urges of his all-too-male body. When lust triumphed, stirring him into aching sexual tension, Rauf was infuriated by his own weakness.

Lily hovered several feet away, alarmed by the jangling state of her nerves, the terrifying blankness of her mind and the even more demeaning truth that she could not drag her attention from him. 'It's been a long time,' she said breathlessly, almost wincing at the nervous sound of her own voice.

'Yes. Would you like something to drink?'

'Er…pure orange, please.'

Rauf passed on the order to the waiter nearby and turned back to her. 'Let's get down to business, then,' he drawled with intimidating cool. 'I don't have much time to spare.'

CHAPTER TWO

TAKEN aback by the coldness of that greeting, Lily was grateful for the small hiatus created by the waiter, who stepped forward to swing out a high-backed armchair for her occupation. 'Thank you.'

'My pleasure, *hanim*,' the young man asserted with an admiring smile until a cool word of Turkish uttered by Rauf sent him into hasty retreat.

'You may have noticed that my countrymen go for English blondes in a big way,' Rauf remarked in his dark, deep drawl.

'Yes,' Lily confided ruefully, thinking of the taxi driver who had tried to chat her up and all the discomfiting male attention that she had attracted since her recent arrival.

Yet she was conscious of Rauf's masculine proximity with every fibre of her being and even more aware of the weird tight little knot low in her pelvis of something that felt dangerously like suppressed excitement. Her tension increased for she was as unsettled by her own reactions as she had been at twenty-one, because no other man had ever had that effect on her.

Rauf lifted a broad shoulder in a casual shrug. 'Here, I'm afraid, and in certain other resorts, British female tourists have the reputation of being the easiest to bed in the shortest possible space of time.'

Lily's face flamed. 'I beg your pardon?'

Rauf dealt her a cool golden glance laden with mockery. Being downright offensive was not the norm for him but he was determined to blow her I'm-so-sweet-and-shockable front right out of the water. 'Some Englishwomen go mad for Turkish men, so don't blame the guys for hassling you.'

'I wasn't aware that I was blaming anybody.' Lily's fingers tightened round the document case on her lap. She just could not credit that he was talking to her in such a way and, bewildered by the antagonism she sensed, she allowed her scrutiny to linger on the scornful slant to his beautifully shaped mouth.

Without the slightest warning, she found herself remembering the wicked, unforgettable excitement of those firm, hard male lips on her own. A deep inner quiver slivered through her slight frame and her skin heated. Mortified by the intimate nature of her wandering thoughts, she could not even recall what they had been talking about. Forcing her head up, she encountered intent tawny eyes and stopped breathing altogether.

His lush black lashes dipped to a slumbrous level over his stunning gaze and she shifted on her seat, every muscle tightening, every nerve-ending flaring with agonising immediacy into sensitised awareness. Desperate to break free of the raw magnetic power he exerted over her and shattered that she could still be susceptible to a male who had once rejected her, she tore her eyes from him and muttered with an abruptness that only increased her discomfiture, 'You said that you didn't have much time…so can we discuss this misunderstanding over the contract that you agreed with my father?'

Rauf's shimmering golden scrutiny rested on her evasive gaze with grim amusement and no small amount of satisfaction. So she did want him and that, at least, had not been a total lie like all the rest. He elevated a challenging black brow. 'There *is* no misunderstanding.'

'There *has* to be.' With hands that were betraying a

dismaying tendency to tremble, Lily dug into the document case and dragged out the sheaf of papers that Hilary had put together.

Wondering what on earth she could hope to achieve by going to such pointless lengths in an effort to convince him that his highly qualified investment consultant was incapable of spotting a rip-off when he came across one, Rauf released his breath in an impatient hiss. 'I have no intention of studying those documents. By failing to make the agreed sharing of annual profits your father has been in breach of our contract for more than two years. That's the base line and the only one that counts.'

'Dad would never default on any contract.' Alarm gripping her at Rauf's stubborn refusal even to direct his attention at the papers that she had set on the table, Lily leant forward, frantically swept up the first sheet and extended it herself. 'This is last year's account-book entry. A sizeable sum of money was wire-transferred to an account known as Marmaris Media Incorporated at your Turkish bank in London. I have every identifying detail of that transfer. For goodness' sake, if that's not proof that a major misunderstanding has occurred, what is?'

His interest now fully engaged by what she had said, for he did not use a Turkish bank in London, but making no attempt to accept the proffered document, Rauf gazed at her flushed and anxious face. 'This sounds remarkably like a *misunderstanding* destined to end up in the hands of an international fraud squad.'

Her natural colour draining away, her blue eyes rounding, Lily let the sheet of paper drop back on the pile and gasped, 'What on earth are you trying to suggest?'

'That it seems very suspicious that the trading name Marmaris Media Incorporated should bear such a very close resemblance to the name under which my own companies operate—'

'Which *is* MMI…Marmaris Media Incorporated!' Lily argued in bewilderment.

'No, I rather think that you must know that that is untrue,' Rauf countered with sardonic cool, for he was now convinced that she was attempting to mount some kind of clumsy belated cover-up. 'MMI stands for Marmaris Media International and no part of my holdings trades under any similar name. Any cash paid into an account in the name of Marmaris Media Incorporated has nothing to do with me.'

'Then the money must still *be* there in that wretched account!' Lily exclaimed, immediately believing that she had found out where a fatal error might have occurred in Harris Travel's dealings with Rauf. 'Don't you see? Nobody at Harris Travel realised they'd got the name wrong and the payments have gone into someone else's account…oh, my goodness, suppose they've *spent* it?'

Against his own volition, Rauf was becoming more entertained with every second he spent listening to her spiel. She looked like a live angel and, had he not known what he did know about her, the appeal in her beautiful eyes might have penetrated even his armour-plated cynicism. He lowered his dense black lashes over his appreciative gaze. She ought to be on television creating kiddy-orientated whodunnits of shattering simplicity. That climax of a punchline, 'Suppose they've spent it?' was priceless and he would long cherish its utterance for he had an excellent, if dark, sense of humour.

Nobody with any wit could have been taken in by so unlikely a tale. He was willing to bet a good half of his vast wealth that were he willing to go through the laborious motions she was trying to prompt him into making, willing to act like her trusting ally in pursuit of an un-known criminal, he would find out…guess what? Surprise, surprise, he *didn't* think! The fake account called Marmaris Media Incorporated would be as empty as the old lady's cupboard in the English nursery rhyme. Switching money between accounts to conceal where it was heading next and false entries in the account books were one of the most rudimentary and common methods of concealing fraud.

'Didn't you hear what I said?' Lily prompted, incredu-lous at his lack of reaction and actually jumping to her feet to stress her enthusiasm for that possible explanation. It seemed obvious that a stupid but simple mistake had sent the payments that Rauf should have received into the wrong bank account. 'Either all those payments have been piling up in one of those dormant accounts that you read about or someone's been having a merry old time for the last two years on money that was rightfully *yours!*'

'Thankfully it's not my problem,' Rauf responded smooth as silk, but he was operating on two levels again, his brain attempting to disengage from his libido as he tensed with growing annoyance. As she automatically an-gled her slender body towards him he was maddeningly aware of the tantalising thrust of her lush little breasts be-neath the shrouding dress and his body hardened on a surge of instant sexual hunger that inflamed his pride.

'But it's your money…don't you care about that?' Deflated and bemused by his apparent disinterest, Lily dared to look at him direct and clashed with smouldering golden eyes.

Her heart skipped a beat and in the interim she felt her full breasts shift inside her cotton bra, the soft tips pinching into sudden taut sensitivity. Rigid with shamed awareness of what was happening to her, she lowered her head and dropped back down into her seat again at speed. Could he still sense the appalling effect he had on her? A crawling sense of humiliation engulfed her, for she had never dreamt that, three years on, she might still be vulnerable around Rauf Kasabian. After all, she wasn't in love with him any more, and he might be a good-looking guy—all right a *very* good-looking guy—but that was no excuse, was it?

Sheer anger having overwhelmed his arousal, Rauf was reminding himself of what a cruel little tease Lily had always been. Once she had drawn him in with the same languishing looks and responsive body language, only to treat him to shrinking reluctance when he had dared to react to those invitations. But her most effective ploy of all had been three quite unforgettable and very clever little words. ''You scare me,'' she had once confided in a breathy little voice of apparent apology, shocking and shaming him into the kind of total physical restraint that he had never had to practise round any other woman.

Still raw from the memory of that unjust and wounding accusation, Rauf squared his wide shoulders, his formidable intelligence now fully back in the ascendant. 'Harris Travel would *still* be in breach of contract and I do wish you luck in pursuing the dormant account scenario. However, all that is owed to me must be repaid—'

Tense as a bowstring, Lily parted dry lips. 'Yes, of course I accept that, but—'

'I don't like being ripped off.' The chill in Rauf's hard dark-as-midnight eyes was now pronounced. 'In fact, with very little encouragement, I can be a total unforgiving bastard.'

'I'm just asking you to be reasonable and examine these papers and you won't even do *that* for me.' Lily regarded him with reproachful blue eyes. 'That's not so much to ask…surely? Why are you treating me like this?'

'Like…what?' Rauf asked in the same cool tone.

'Like we're enemies or something….' Lily muttered uneasily.

'There's nothing deader than a dead love affair, except perhaps an affair that never was,' Rauf spelt out with cutting clarity.

Lily went very still and paled as though she had been struck. She stared with strained intensity at the papers he had refused to scrutinise while she fought to hold back the lowering tears stinging the back of her eyes. There it was, confessed in his own words: the truth of why he had lost all interest in her. *An affair that never was.* It was so belittling to appreciate that what she had believed they'd shared had meant nothing to him without sex. She had always suspected it but that direct confirmation truly hurt. She snatched up her glass of pure orange and took several sips to ease the aching fullness in her throat. Reminding herself that she had much more important matters to concentrate on, she struggled to pull herself back together again.

'Time's running out.' Rauf steeled himself against the artful way she was sitting bolt upright in the chair with the brave but vulnerable aspect of a punished child. As he had already learnt to his cost in the past, she was a very convincing actress and her sole objective then as now had been his wallet, not the wedding ring he had once naively assumed.

Swallowing hard, Lily lifted her head and breathed in deep. 'I'm willing to admit that since we last met, Harris Travel may not have been run quite the way it ought to have been. Two years ago, after a spate of ill health, my father retired and Brett took over. Now he's gone and it's my sister, Hilary, who is managing the business. You say that the contract has been broken and you won't allow any leeway for human error. But if you insist on reclaiming your stake in the agency right now, it may well bankrupt it.'

'Business can be tough. I'm sorry but I'm not prepared to sit through the plucking of a thousand violin strings,' Rauf said very drily, wondering with revulsion where Brett Gilman had 'gone'. The grave? To employment elsewhere? He would not allow himself to ask.

'Brett went off with Hilary's best friend, Janice,' Lily extended heavily and he noted that, just as he recalled from the past, even now when she referred to her sister's husband her eyes were carefully screened in a secretive way. 'Hilary and Brett are divorced now.'

So *that* was why Lily had come all the way out to Turkey to beg his indulgence and bat her fawn-like eyelashes in his direction! Smarmy Brett had scarpered with yet another foolish woman. His lean, strong face taut, Rauf's handsome mouth compressed with distaste. Look beyond the illusory purity of her beauty and Lily was revealed for what she was: an unscrupulous, greedy little schemer, ever ready to tell lies when it suited her to do so. Once, she had been stupid enough to lie to him and in lying had convicted herself with her own tongue.

'I get this feeling that you're really not listening to anything that I say, but what I'm saying is *so* very important,' Lily emphasised in a low intense plea. 'If those payments which you say were never made—'

'I know for a fact that they were never made.' Rafe's aggressive jawline squared. 'Do we have to keep on going over the same ground?'

'Well, if they weren't made, then it was a case of a genuine mistake. Surely you have enough understanding and patience to allow Harris Travel to sort it out?'

'Why should I be patient?' Rauf dealt her an enquiring

glance in which the milk of human kindness was most noticeable by its unapologetic absence. The Turkish builders defrauded by Harris Travel had also practised patience and much good it had done them!

'I don't know you like this...' Lily mumbled sickly, sinking ever deeper into a sense of shock over the extent to which he seemed to have changed. Had Rauf always been so cold, callous and unfeeling? Had she only imagined that she'd seen other finer and more sensitive qualities in him?

She tried afresh to reach him. 'I'm only asking for some more time—'

'No.' Rauf uttered the word in a tone of crushing finality. 'You've wasted enough of my time.'

'Look, I didn't come out here prepared for this awful situation!' Lily protested, her voice rising in spite of her attempt to keep it level, and a flush of embarrassment covered her face as Rauf elevated an ebony brow in meaningful rebuke. 'Couldn't you help me with this? I don't have the resources to check out this bank account mix-up from here.'

Lily down on her knees and begging. Rauf liked the idea even though he knew that he would still pull the plug on the travel agency and cut that last reminder of her out of his life. For his own amusement, would he play along for a little while with her absurd stories and excuses? What would he discover? That she and her family were a set of outright thieves? Reckless thieves too, unable to look ahead and spot the obvious fact that their dishonesty would inevitably be exposed. Then he reminded himself that his own newspapers were full of tales of such foolish fraudsters, who, regardless of the obvious consequences, were quite unable to resist temptation.

Sensing that she finally had his attention, Lily pushed

the documents across the table again. 'Please look these over…and I *can* offer one concrete promise—whatever happens, you will be compensated. Brett built two luxury villas near Dalyan and I have to arrange for them to be sold. Harris Travel does have some assets,' she proclaimed in desperation.

But the biggest asset of all was seated just feet away from him, Rauf conceded, looking direct into her pleading violet-blue eyes, a kind of wonderment laced with cold, deep anger rising at volatile force inside him. He could not credit her gall! How *dared* she feed him such falsehoods? How could she think that he would have agreed to their meeting without having all the facts at his disposal? That Lily should face him with outright lies proved beyond all doubt that she was involved up to her throat in blatant deception! That was the moment that Rauf decided to take a harder line with Lily.

Anxiety holding her taut, Lily noted how very still Rauf had become and her attention lingered on the semi-screened shimmer of his unreadable gaze. Then even as she watched Rauf reached out and swept up the Harris Travel documents he had earlier disdained, sending a surge of hope travelling through her. 'I'm not making any promises,' he asserted in a dark, deep, honeyed drawl that sent the oddest little shiver down her spine.

'Oh, no, of course not…I wouldn't expect that at this point,' Lily hastened to assure him, almost sick with relief at his change of heart and certain that he would be more sympathetic once he had gone over those papers.

'But the amount of time that this tangled affair will consume only comes at a price.' Rauf moved in for the kill, knowing just how much he would revel in making Lily dance to his tune while he kept her in suspense. Hadn't she once done the same to him in a much more primitive way? With raw contempt, he recalled the pseudo-nervous squeaks he had been made to suffer that summer while she had swerved between brief bouts of melting enthusiasm to keep him hooked and sudden attacks of timidity. She had played him like a violin virtuoso, convincing him one hundred per cent that he'd been dealing with a very nervous virgin. But on this occasion, he had the whip hand.

'A…price?' In confusion, Lily frowned, her heart hammering as she noted the gleam of gold in his arresting gaze.

Rauf angled his arrogant dark head back with the measured and confident timing of a hunter about to spring a trap. 'In this world everything comes at a price…haven't you learnt that yet?'

'I'm not sure I follow…' Her oval face taut, a frown marked her smooth brow.

A faint sardonic smile lightened Rauf's lean, dark features. 'It's very simple. If I have to go through these documents in detail, I need your help.'

Her frown evaporating at that statement, Lily sat forward with an air of eagerness, soft blue eyes brightening. 'Certainly…that's not a problem. How could you think it would be?'

'I'm only here in Bodrum for a few hours. Since I have a board meeting in Istanbul tomorrow, I'll be flying back there this evening. Later tomorrow, however, I'm going to my country estate and I suggest that you join me there and stay for a few days,' Rauf murmured levelly. 'It would be more convenient to have you on hand to answer any queries I might have and assist in my inquiries.'

As Rauf delivered that bombshell Lily had parted her lips several times as if she'd been about to speak, but on each occasion caution had made her bite her tongue. She was unnerved by the prospect of staying as a guest in Rauf's country home. However, in the circumstances, his request was a reasonable one. She could hardly expect him to fly back to the coast just for her benefit.

'Yes, all right,' Lily conceded tautly.

Rauf had had no doubt that she would agree and her obvious discomfiture surprised him not at all. Naturally, she could not refuse the opportunity to keep an eye on the course of his inquiries because she would be afraid that he might turn up evidence that would incriminate her and might even be hoping for the chance to bury it again. At the same time, however, she had to continue to play the innocent. Before he took her to Sonngul, he would ensure that they made an unannounced detour to view the 'villas' she had proffered as assets. Even the cleverest liar could not hope to lie her way out of what he intended to confront her with!

'When would you like me to come to your home?' Lily prompted uncomfortably. 'Is it far from here?'

'Quite some distance. I'll make arrangements for you to be picked up at your hotel tomorrow morning at eleven. I'll meet you at the airport, so that we can travel on to Sonngul together.' Studying the soft pink fullness of her lips, Rauf was picturing her splayed like a wanton temptress across his magnificent bed at the old house where he had, out of respect for his family, never taken a woman. Would he…or wouldn't he take advantage of her present eagerness to please? *No,* he decided with fierce determination, he would not. He would take no woman to his bed on such sordid terms.

'Thank you. I appreciate your kindness in making time for this.' Lily felt her lips tingle from his glinting scrutiny and a wave of slow, painful colour warmed her fair complexion. In the pulsing atmosphere, her mouth ran dry and her breathing pattern quickened. She recognised her own excitement, her longing for him to touch her, was shamed by it but not to the degree she had once been when her own contrary physical responses had scared and confused her. But that had not been Rauf's fault or, indeed, even her *own* fault, she conceded with pained regret.

Rauf was offended by that unsought and forbidden image of Lily ornamenting his bed, and his lean, strong face was grim. He could not give credence to the smallest doubt of her guilt now: she had played her part in defrauding him. Once he had assembled the necessary evidence, he would hand her over to the police. He would do what was right and would not be swayed by her desirability or his own lust into compromising either his own ethical code or the honour of the Kasabian family. There should be no distinction between his treatment of Lily and any other wrongdoer. In daring to approach him with her lies and invite his investigation of the facts, she would discover that she had merely precipitated her own punishment and, even worse, had done so in a country with a judicial system far less liberal than that of her own.

That decision etched in stone on his soul, Rauf rose upright, his brilliant dark eyes cool and bright as a mountain spring. 'I'm afraid I must close our meeting here—I have a lunch engagement to keep.'

Disconcerted by that sudden conclusion to their meeting, Lily scrambled up in even greater haste, but by then she had already lost Rauf's attention. Following his frowning gaze, she saw a tiny silver-haired old lady with a stick moving towards them, a helpful young man by her side.

Rauf ground his teeth together as his great-grandmother approached with all the unstoppable determination of a stick-propelled missile. One of the hotel staff must have let drop that his appointment was with a young and beautiful foreigner. That exciting disclosure would have been all it would have taken to shoot Nelispah Kasabian into the penthouse lift and down to the ground floor to satisfy her lively curiosity.

'Mrs Kasabian says…' The hotel executive acting as Nelispah's guide and translator skimmed Rauf a strained glance of apology before turning to address Lily. 'Mrs Kasabian says…what a lovely dress you are wearing!'

Rauf blinked and then scrutinised the billowing folds of Lily's shroud. Yes, he supposed a dress that only hinted that an actual female body existed beneath it was right down his very modest great-grandmother's street. The entire family and their staff conspired to ensure that Nelispah's delicate sensibilities were protected from the shocking moral laxity of a world that would distress her for her heart was weak. Fortunately, she did not watch television or even read the family newspapers because she believed that her late husband would not have approved of her engaging in either activity.

'I have the honour of introducing you to my great-grandmother, Nelispah Kasabian…Lily Harris.' Rauf performed the introduction with gritty reluctance but spoke in soft, gentle Turkish to the little woman, who barely reached his chest in height.

'Please tell her how very happy I am to meet her.' Lily returned Mrs Kasabian's big, beaming smile with warm appreciation.

Resting a frail hand on Rauf's supportive arm, Nelispah chattered on in Turkish while Rauf employed a fast covert signal to send her translator into silenced retreat. 'Lily *hanim* has a sweet smile. I like what I see in this young woman's face,' his great-grandmother confided with alarming enthusiasm. 'Would she like to join us for lunch and tell us about herself and her family?'

Striving not to wince at the threat of what might emerge were Lily to come into contact with the matriarchal interrogation team, Rauf depressed that hope and, with a quiet word of apology to Lily, he walked the old lady back towards the lift. Seeing the affection that had softened his stunning eyes, Lily glanced away again, pained by that contrast to Rauf's abrasive treatment of her.

But then this was a business matter, not a personal one, she reminded herself doggedly. Evidently, Harris Travel had messed up big time when it came to that contract. Had Brett been responsible for that? Although Lily loathed her sister's ex-husband, she knew that both Hilary and her father had been very impressed, not only by the efficient way in which Brett had run the family business, but also by the long hours he had worked. Profits might have sunk to a dismal level but nobody had blamed Brett for that reality. After all, it was hardly his fault that another travel agency had opened up in competition in the same town.

Whatever, Lily was uneasily aware that Rauf had only been willing to relent after she had mentioned the villas that were to be sold. What was going to happen if those payments made into the wrong account could not be tracked down and retrieved? And if the cash from the sale of the villas had to go to Rauf rather than Harris Travel, would Hilary still be able to stay in business? Deciding to wait until she had concrete facts at her disposal before passing on any bad news to her sister, Lily tensed as Rauf returned to her side.

'My limo will take you back to your hotel,' Rauf imparted, shortening his long, fluid stride to her slower pace to walk her outside.

On the pavement, she hovered and stole a strained glance up at him, intimidated and troubled by his continuing detachment. 'This business stuff aside…can't we still be friends?' she heard herself ask in a rush.

As he met her beautiful blue eyes seething derision at

that appeal flamed through Rauf's big, powerful frame, hardening his superb bone structure, firing his fantastic eyes to raw, shimmering gold. It infuriated him that once upon a time he had swallowed her every mushy sentence. 'I'm not five years old and neither are you.'

Lily flushed in embarrassment and cringed for her own impulsive tongue.

'On the other hand, *güzelim*,' Rauf growled soft and low as he reached for her with two lean, purposeful hands and pulled her to him on a surge of anger so strong he did not even question what he was doing, 'I hate to disappoint a woman.'

Pinned into startling connection with six feet four inches of hard, masculine muscle and power, her heart pounding like crazy, Lily gasped, 'Rauf—?'

His wide, sensual mouth came down on hers with explosive force, all the passion of the volatile nature he usually kept in check powering to the surface to drive that kiss. For an instant Lily froze in total shock and then, without any mental prompting she recognised, she stretched up on tiptoe and wrapped her slim arms round his neck. As the first wild wave of response rocked through her trembling length, she loosed a low moan, angling her head back, letting the erotic plunge of his tongue feed from the sweetness of her mouth.

With an abruptness that left Lily in a turmoil of confusion, Rauf set her free again. A dark line of febrile colour scoring his taut cheekbones, he was appalled both by his own reckless disregard of his surroundings and by her unexpected encouragement. Trust Lily to change her game plan when he could least afford her to do so! Such public displays were frowned on by his people. What the hell had come over him?

Her lush mouth reddened from the fiery imprint of his,

Lily focused on Rauf with dazed eyes and a helpless surge of pride in herself. She had stayed in his arms without succumbing to an attack of unreasonable fear. Finally making herself acknowledge those disturbing feelings and openly discuss what had caused them with a counsellor the previous year had worked.

'That will *not* be repeated,' Rauf breathed with icy emphasis, yanking open the door of the long silver limo waiting by the kerb with his own hand. 'There is nothing between us now.'

Then why had he touched her in the first place? Stiff with hurt bewilderment, Lily climbed into the opulent car. She wished she had pushed him away, indeed done anything other than thrown her arms round him in encouragement. She was furious with herself. Here she was almost twenty-four years old, still a virgin and still, it seemed, as immature as an adolescent. Obviously Rauf had reacted to the willing signals that *she* must have been putting out! On the strength of that demeaning conviction, Lily stopped being angry and felt that she had asked to be humiliated.

But then who would ever have forecast that she of all women might ever be guilty of forward behaviour around a male of the species? As Rauf's limousine drove Lily back to her hotel in Gumbet she was pale and taut and already mental miles away from their recent meeting. Memories that she only rarely allowed herself to take out and examine had engulfed her...

Hilary had married Brett when Lily had been only twelve. Delighted to be their bridesmaid, Lily had been thrilled that Hilary had been so much in love and even happier that Brett had been willing to move into their family home rather than take Hilary to live somewhere else. Their father had been equally impressed with Hilary's bridegroom for Brett had always awarded the older man

pronounced respect and deference. A year later, Douglas
Harris had signed his house over to his daughter and son-
in-law.

Just two years after that, when she'd been only fifteen,
Lily had had her first sight of Brett with another woman.
Heading home from a friend's house, she had cut across a
car park on the outskirts of town. Seeing Brett's sports car
parked there and the shadow of movement within, she had
hurried towards it thinking that she would get a lift with
him. Instead she had seen her brother-in-law locked in a
passionate embrace with a stranger. Devastated by that
sight but grateful that the guilty couple hadn't noticed her,
she had been so upset that she had wandered round town
for several hours before she'd been able to face going
home.

All her life up until that point, Lily had told Hilary virtually everything. But what she had seen that day had deprived her of her only true confidante for she had been
painfully conscious that her big sister had worshipped the
ground her handsome husband had walked on and had also
been heavily pregnant with their second child. Lily had
agonised for weeks over what she ought to have done before finally deciding to confide in her father and put the
responsibility of that knowledge in his hands.

But in no way had Douglas Harris reacted as his teenage
daughter had imagined he might have done. 'You were
mistaken,' her father told her in instant angry rebuttal.

'But I saw them…it was Brett and it was his car!' Lily
protested.

'Don't you *ever* mention this again and don't you
breathe a word of this nonsense to your sister!' the older
man censured in even greater fury. 'Brett and Hilary have
a very happy marriage. What's got into you that you can

make up such a wicked and dangerous story about your own brother-in-law?'

In her turn, Lily was shattered that her usually mild-mannered father could react in such a disbelieving and unjust way to her trusting confession. She had to get older before she could appreciate that her unfortunate parent had too much invested in the stability of Hilary's marriage to easily face the threat that Brett might not be the fine, up-standing young man he had believed him to be. And how could she have foreseen that worry over what she had told him would eventually drive her father to make the very great mistake of warning Brett that he had been seen in that car park?

Faster than the speed of light, for there was nothing slow about Brett's survival instincts, Brett added two and two together and worked out *who* had seen him. That same afternoon he picked Lily up from school and frightened the living daylights out of her with his rage and his threats. Then and there Lily's happy home life and her faith in the adults around her came to a harsh and final end.

'You sneaky little bitch!' Brett roared at her, after shooting his car into the *same* car park in an act of intimidation that she soon learned was pure Brett Gilman. 'From here on in, you'd better mind your own bloody business. Haven't you ever heard of the three wise monkeys? Speak no evil, hear no evil and see no evil. Tell tales on me again and you won't *have* a home any more…I'll tell Hilary that her precocious little sister has been trying it on with me and she'll believe me long before she'll believe you!'

Lily then learnt what it was to live in fear. Resenting her, and determined to punish her for exposing his wom-anising ways to Douglas Harris, Brett gloried in his power over Lily and soon worked out the kind of treatment that would make her feel most threatened. Out of her sister's sight and hearing, he began to look at Lily's developing curves in a way that made her skin crawl and taunt her with crude familiar comments. He never actually touched her but she lived in terror that some day he *might*.

By the time Lily escaped her home to start her teacher-training course at a college a long way away, Brett had turned Lily into a silent, secretive and timid teenager, who covered every possible inch of her body and who went in genuine fear of male aggression and sexuality.

Surfacing from her recollections of that traumatic period of her life, Lily found a sheen of perspiration on her skin. When she went for a shower in her room, she reminded herself that that nightmare was in the past. Yet her most bitter regret was still that the damage Brett had inflicted had almost inevitably destroyed any hope of her having a normal relationship with Rauf Kasabian when she had first met him.

Three years on, Rauf was hostile, cold and detached in a way that Lily had never dreamt he could be and she was much too vulnerable. Lily recognised with shamed self-honesty that she would still do just about anything to get a second chance with Rauf. But he had made it clear that he had no intention of getting involved with her again.

Could she even blame him for that? Lily asked herself as she lay in bed that night. If anything, Rauf had been kind when he'd described what they had had as the affair that never was. With pained hindsight, Lily knew that Rauf might have utilised more hurtful candour. He might have told her that blowing hot and cold with a man was a huge turn-off and that treating a decent guy like a ravenous sex beast was an even less enthralling experience…

CHAPTER THREE

THE summer after she finished her second year at college, Lily had taken a temporary job working as a waitress in a fashionable London bar while she looked for a suitable position as a nursery nurse.

Within the first week, Lily had begun dreading going into work for she hadn't been able to easily handle the sort of teasing and touching that the other waitresses had withstood from the male customers. However, her salary plus the generous tips she'd received had met the rent on the tiny apartment she'd been sharing and had made it possible for her to avoid having to return home and live under the same roof as Brett.

Rauf had come in with a female in tow one lunchtime.

'Why are all the *really* gorgeous men already spoken for?' Annabel, her flatmate since first year and fellow waitress, lamented while she and Lily waited at the counter for their orders.

'Who have you noticed now?' Lily groaned, accustomed to Annabel's frequent complaints about the extreme rarity of the free and fanciable male.

'He's sitting down with the brunette in the sexy white dress.'

Lily glanced over. His commanding height and build, the slashing angle of his high cheekbones, strong nose and wide, passionate male mouth combined with his lustrous black hair made him stand out from the common herd all right. But she would have looked away again had not Rauf thrown his arrogant dark head back as he sat down and let

her see his extraordinary eyes. Tawny gold as polished
tiger's-eye stones reflecting the light, riveting, beautiful,
utterly hypnotic. Involuntarily she stared, heartbeat kicking
up pace, breathing fractured, her whole body tight and
tense as if she was waiting for something indescribably
exciting to happen. Then his narrowed gaze clashed with
hers and it was as if somebody had switched on Christmas
lights inside her. Suddenly she was electric, wired, alive
for the very first time.

'And wouldn't you just know it?' Annabel muttered re-
sentfully as she watched Rauf appraise Lily's glowing
blonde beauty with predictable male intensity. 'I might as
well be invisible but he's *yours* for the asking. You should
wear a little "I'm gay" badge, Lily…at least it would stop
the guys wasting their time and let the rest of us get a
look-in!'

Aghast at the startling content of that disgruntled little
speech, Lily shot her attention back to Annabel. 'Say that
again?'

Annabel just shrugged. 'Well, you *are*, aren't you? You
might still be in the closet but the way you feel about men
makes it pretty obvious. I guessed ages ago.'

'I'm *not* gay…' Lily countered in whispered but em-
phatic denial as Annabel lifted her laden tray.

'Look, it's none of my business.' Annabel grimaced. 'I
was only being a jealous cow about your looks.'

Shaken that someone she had known for two years could
have got her so wrong, Lily went to serve Rauf. Not once
did she look directly at him or his companion but, even in
the ennervated state she was in, she noted his rich, dark
drawl and the faint exotic accent that edged his excellent
English. Disaster only struck when she delivered their
drinks. As she tried to set the glass of red wine down the
brunette made a sudden snatch at it mid-air and their hands

collided. The glass fell, spilling a cascade of ruby-red liquid down onto the woman's lap.

'You stupid girl!' the irate brunette screeched, behaving as though she had been subjected to a deliberate assault. 'Wasn't coming on to my man enough for you? Did you have to ruin my dress too?'

As Lily's boss hurried to the scene and Lily proffered napkins and apologies that were ignored while really wanting to sink through the floor in chagrin, Rauf dropped a banknote on the table and herded his hysterical lunch date out at speed. Lily didn't expect ever to see him again. But the next day when she turned up for her shift a beautiful bouquet was waiting for her along with a card.

'Sorry that you were embarrassed yesterday. Rauf'

'When a bloke spends about a hundred quid on flowers, it certainly tells me *who* was coming on to *who*,' her female boss quipped with considerable amusement.

Emerging from the powerful pull of the past, Lily needed enormous effort to shut down the surging tide of memory keeping her awake. What did it say about her that she should still be so obsessed with a relationship that Rauf had long since left behind him? Angry at her lack of self-discipline, Lily told herself to grow up.

The next morning, Rauf flew in on a sleek private jet half an hour after Lily arrived at the airport. In the brilliant sunlight of midday, she watched him emerge and descend the steps with the fluid, measured pace of a very self-assured male. Sheathed in a beautifully tailored dove-grey business suit, he looked stunningly handsome and, even at a distance, his bold bronzed features emanated all the decisive authority of his forceful personality. Exchanging a laughing word with the official waiting to greet him, he paused, lean, strong face settling back into striking gravity again as he aimed a cool-eyed glance at Lily where she waited just inside the building.

'You can go through now, Miss Harris,' she was told.

Rauf watched her walk towards him. Clad in a pale blue dress and a cardigan that had to be roasting her alive in the heat of midsummer, golden hair glittering in the bright light, Lily looked apprehensive and very young.

An insane impulse to urge her to turn back and board the first available flight home assailed Rauf. Faint colour demarcating his hard cheekbones, his jawline clenched hard. Had she been a man, he would have harboured no second thoughts. So who was being sexist? He was only doing to her what she had once done to him: luring her down a path that would look safe until the very last moment. How would she react when she found herself staring into the abyss with the police waiting to make an arrest on the other side?

As yet, he hadn't called in the police, hadn't identified her to them. But the gendarme in the village where the villa project had misfired already had a file prepared on the case. Furthermore, Lily, Rauf had discovered, was now listed as a director of Harris Travel on the firm notepaper and as such could be held liable. But what Rauf wanted most of all was Brett Gilman's head on a plate.

'It's hot,' Lily murmured as she drew level with him.

'And likely to get hotter,' Rauf imparted in his distinctive drawl, a light hand touching her spine just enough to turn her in the direction of the helicopter sitting parked.

'Will it be a long flight?'

'About an hour or so in all. We're making a stop on the way.' Without hesitation, Rauf made a smooth change of subject. 'How are you enjoying your stay so far?'

'I'm still getting acclimatised. Next week, I'm going to sign up for all the trips and see the sights. Hilary's hoping to organise special tours for the spring...' Lily said, her voice petering out as Rauf closed his hands round her waist and lifted her up into the helicopter as if she weighed no more than a child. 'Thanks.'

As he settled in beside her and signalled the pilot, the rotor blades began to whir. Lily struggled to tighten the seat belt, which had been loosened to hold a much larger frame than her own. Rauf leant over to assist and she tensed, soft brown lashes flying up on uncertain blue eyes to connect with reflective gold. Her hands fell from the clasp and let his take over. As he bent his dark head his luxuriant black hair brushed her chin. Breathing in the warm, achingly familiar scent of him, she trembled, feeling her breasts lift and stir beneath her dress and the tender tips swell into prominence, and biting her soft lower lip in an agony of discomfiture.

She wanted to plunge her fingers into his silky black hair and drag his mouth up to hers again and she was shocked rigid by the depth of her own longing. In the midst of such crazy promptings, she didn't know herself. What was it about him that he could reduce her to such a level without even trying? Mouth bone-dry, her fingers curled in on themselves lest they too developed a will of their own, she only breathed again when he had settled back into his own seat.

For the entire flight, she stared out the window. She had a fantastic view of the bright turquoise sea studded with islands and edged by tall crags and sandy beaches before the helicopter went into a turn and headed inland. When the coastal development was left behind, she saw the ruin of a castle built on bare rock, hazy tracts of soft green pine forest, the occasional dust road leading out miles through tiny cultivated fields and orchards to small clusters of re-mote dwellings. She remembered Rauf telling her that virtually every family had links with a village and would often maintain contact with their roots there generations after they had taken up residence in a town.

After the tranquil, soothing scenes of beautiful unspoilt countryside, it was something of a surprise to Lily to see a coalmine come into view as the helicopter started to land. Coalmining was a business, she reminded herself, and Rauf *had* mentioned a stop on the way. Perhaps one of his newspapers or magazines was doing a feature on the mine, she thought dimly.

Springing out of the craft, Rauf swung back to extend a hand to her. Lily stepped out onto waste ground and saw a dust road several yards ahead of them.

Level dark golden eyes zeroed in on her. 'Do you know where you are?'

Lily shook her golden head and wondered how on earth he could imagine she would know. 'I haven't a clue.'

'I think you'll solve the mystery soon enough,' Rauf asserted, leading her across the road towards a steep paved driveway edged with fancy carriage lamps and really the very last kind of opulent entrance one would have expected to see within yards of the fencing that surrounded the mine.

Lily frowned. 'Is this where you live?'

'Even the locals don't live in this neck of the woods. Who wants to look out the windows and see the slagheaps?' Rauf derided.

Some sixth sense she had finally picked up on the scorn that edged his every sentence, the strange challenge in his watchful gaze. A wave of tension infiltrated her. She stared back at him, her slender body very taut. He withstood that appraisal with unflinching assurance and her cheeks warmed with self-conscious colour, for he might look intimidating in his current mood but he also looked drop-dead gorgeous. Unhappily that reality kept on playing havoc with her concentration.

'So if you don't live here, where are we going?' Lily prompted, dry-mouthed.

'I decided to surprise you with a flying visit to the villas built by Harris Travel,' Rauf responded drily.

Lily blinked and then a startled laugh fell from her lips. 'Then I'm afraid you've got the address wrong. The villas are near Dalyan, which I understand is quite a beauty spot.'

As she came to a halt Rauf closed a hand over hers. Disconcerted by that move, she flexed her fingers in his and then stilled as a sensation of warmth travelled up her arm, making her outrageously aware of him. He drew her on up the long, winding driveway and then came to a halt, releasing her fingers at the same moment. 'This is the land Brett Gilman bought for a song because nobody else wanted it.'

Closing both of her hands together in front of her, Lily stared at him. 'It can't be...for goodness' sake, this doesn't even look like a tourist area. I'm telling you this is definitely *not* where our villas were built—'

'Since it was my money that financed the project, do you honestly believe I could make such a mistake?'

Lily sucked in a slow, steadying breath of the hot still air and struggled to think straight. 'You were only a silent partner—'

'That was my mistake. Had I insisted on tighter control and greater input, what Harris Travel did here would not have happened because I would not have *allowed* it to happen,' Rauf spelt out with fulminating emphasis.

'What do you mean by..."what Harris Travel *did here*"?' Lily questioned uneasily, her tension mounting with every second that passed. 'Why aren't you listening to me? This isn't where the villas were built.'

'Stop feeding me that bull!' Rauf ground out with raw impatience, lean, powerful face taut and unyielding. 'I have a copy of the contract that Brett signed with the builders in my pocket and a copy of the land purchase deed as well.'

'I don't care if you've got your entire filing cabinet in your pocket!' Lily slung back an entire octave higher, her temper flaring without warning because nothing he had said or done since the helicopter had landed had made sense to her. 'I have photographs of the villas when they were almost complete and the view from the front of the villas was fantastic...there was no wretched coalmine in it!'

'You couldn't possibly have photographs.' Rauf subjected her to a raking appraisal, furious at her stubborn refusal to stop lying even in the face of the overwhelming evidence confronting her.

The driveway had petered out on the brow of the hill, Lily noted somewhat belatedly. A driveway that led to nowhere and nothing? In the act of fumbling in her bag for the wallet of photos that Hilary had told her Brett had brought back from his final visit to Turkey the previous winter, Lily stilled in momentary bewilderment to scan the empty, overgrown ground surrounding her on all sides.

Suddenly Lily laughed, relief coiling through her. 'There are no villas here even to make a mistake *about*! Why won't you just admit that we're in the wrong place?'

While Rauf continued to watch her much as though she had made a sudden claim that she could fly without wings, Lily walked over to him with some satisfaction to extend the photos. 'Our villas, Rauf.'

In seething frustration, Rauf gave the half dozen snaps a cursory appraisal. 'Which proves *what*, Lily? That someone with a camera can take pretty pictures of someone

else's building site? Now either you start telling the truth
or I let the police handle this investigation.'

Freezing where she stood at that threat, Lily gazed back
at him wide-eyed. 'The...*police*?'

'Harris Travel ripped off the local builders and sup-
pliers. The builders were given a fake name and address
for the firm and a fake phone number.'

Pale as she stood there under the relentless sun, a trickle
of nervous perspiration running down between her breasts,
Lily parted her soft lips, but it was a second or two before
her voice picked up sufficient strength to emerge. 'Harris
Travel ripped off people? I...I don't know what you're
talking about.'

Rauf expelled his breath in an impatient hiss. 'There *are*
no villas. Nothing was ever built beyond that entrance and
you have to know that.'

Lily gulped. Only then did she recall him saying that he
had a copy of the land purchase agreement. Surely that
was indisputable proof that she was standing on the site
that Brett had bought? But this was not the land that Brett
had photographed and there were no buildings within
view.

'Are you sure the villas aren't just down the road?' she
mumbled, peering round herself with frowning incomprehension. 'I want to see that purchase agreement.'

Rauf extended it and Lily grabbed at it. The document
trembled along with her hand. It was written in Turkish
but when she scanned down the sheet she recognised
Brett's signature and an official seal. Her brain was now
functioning in very slow motion. Shock was setting in hard
and she could not accept the enormity of what Rauf was
telling her. 'I still think these villas have got to be around
here somewhere...if we look. I mean, maybe we're on the
wrong road or something,' she suggested shakily. 'You

were always telling me how vast this country is…you can't know *every* road around here!'

She was shaking like a leaf in a high wind. But Rauf was determined not to fall victim to what innate cynicism warned was most likely to be a performance aimed at convincing him that she was a misunderstood innocent. At the same time, however, he could not help but be impressed by the rendering of stupefied shock and disbelief that Lily was giving him.

'There are no villas,' he said again.

'There's *got* to be!' Lily launched at him in feverish protest.

'The land was bought, the builders engaged,' Rauf advanced in a grim undertone. 'But after a small first-stage payment was received, they neither heard from your sister's ex-husband again, nor were they able to establish contact with him.'

Lily tottered backwards and sank down on a low rock in the shade of a spreading chestnut tree. Her legs felt all wobbly and hollow.

'Before the builders discovered that they had been had, they put in the driveway and the foundations. Since the mine shut down, there isn't much employment round here and the builders were promised bonuses for fast results. Gilman had a big car and they thought he was rich, so they went ahead and bought more supplies on credit with a relative, trusting that the next, much larger payment was in the pipeline. Two families were plunged into poverty and debt by this.'

Lily's tummy gave a sick lurch, shame enveloping her. What had happened? What had Brett done? Could he have used the cash earmarked for the villas just to keep the agency in business? She hated Brett, could not initially comprehend her own reluctance to accept the obvious until she acknowledged that the security of her entire family rested in that same balance.

Evidently, Brett had lied over and over again about the villas. He had shown Hilary and their father photographs of another site and had later given them more pictures of that same site and the two big villas that had been erected there. Neither her sister nor her father could have had any suspicion that there was anything suspect about the enterprise because that building project had been Brett's baby from the outset. By then, her father had retired and Hilary had only gone back to work in Harris Travel after Brett had stepped down from managing it just a few months ago...until then, Brett had had an entirely free hand.

So what had happened to all the money that should have gone into building the villas? Brett could only have taken all those thousands of pounds for himself. There were no villas, just a piece of scrubby land with no outlook in the back end of nowhere. Yet Brett had contrived to argue during his divorce settlement with her sister that he was entitled to half of the marital home because Harris Travel would be retaining the sizeable asset of two luxury villas abroad. In addition, Brett had managed to satisfy an admittedly unsuspicious pair of solicitors that those two villas *did* exist. Her poor sister had ended up being grateful that her estranged husband had not also claimed a right to a share of the family firm after all his years working there!

Lily stared into space with shattered eyes. *There were no villas.* That meant that Rauf's investment had gone missing altogether. What chance now was there that that supposed mix-up over those bank account names was genuine? She shuddered and, lifting nerveless hands, she pressed them to her clammy face. Brett had been embezzling from the business and, by the looks of it, he had sucked Harris Travel dry. Her family was going to be left penniless and in debt.

Rauf studied Lily, who was seated like a traumatised pixie on her rock, transfixed by shock. She kept on looking at the overgrown foundations as if she were still hoping that two villas would spring into literal being right there before her very eyes.

'I can't credit this…' she muttered, shaking her head. 'How could Brett do this to his own family? I mean, they've already lost so much since the divorce.'

Smouldering dark golden eyes pinned to her ashen face as she uttered that first-ever disparaging comment on Brett Gilman, Rauf growled, 'You had no idea?'

Blinking, Lily lifted her golden head and looked at him for the first time in several minutes, blue eyes stricken pools as she endeavoured to come to terms with the sheer scale of Brett's lies. 'How can you ask me that? One of the main reasons I'm here in Turkey was to *sell* those villas! I can hardly get my mind round the concept that they were never built in the first place…'

'That's understandable.' So, on the count of the non-existent villas at least, he had misjudged her, Rauf conceded grudgingly, his wide, taut shoulders squaring below the fine, expensive cloth of his jacket. It seemed that Brett Gilman, regardless of his former liaison with Lily, had acted alone and without her knowledge. That would be a shock for her too though: the wounding discovery that her one-time secret lover had lied to her as well, while he'd plunged the family business into fraudulent dealings. But then over the past year, Lily had already suffered a certain amount of punishment, he reminded himself grimly. Brett choosing to divorce her sister for a woman other than herself must have been quite a slap in the face too. But a very well-deserved slap, Rauf reflected without hesitation.

The thick fullness of tears in her throat, Lily compressed her tremulous lips. 'But you *knew*, didn't you? You knew there were no villas when we met up yesterday.'

'I only learned of this scandalous affair forty-eight hours ago when my investment consultant finally brought it to my attention. As I too have a stake in Harris Travel, I have already instructed that the two Turkish families who sustained losses through this venture are to be fully compensated.'

Lily stared at him through swimming eyes. He was so detached from her, so controlled. A helpless sob bubbled in her throat. 'That's good,' she said in a wobbly voice. 'But I doubt very much that you're about to compensate *my* family for their losses!'

Striding forward, Rauf bent down to curve his lean hands round her shaking shoulders and raise her upright. 'Let's get out of here.'

'I feel so awful…like it's somehow my fault!' Lily sobbed, her distress taking her over for a couple of seconds before she contrived to get a grip on herself again. 'But I've never had anything much to do with the business and I still can't understand how Brett could literally steal from his own kids. Goodness knows, I hate him, but Hilary and Dad always had a *very* high opinion of his business acumen!'

Rauf smiled a not very nice smile above her down-bent golden head and closed a supportive arm round her slender back. Her tears would not soften him. Having cracked her façade, he had her on the run and he would keep up the pressure until he knew everything there was to know. He supposed a lot of women would embrace a selective memory when it came to an indefensible affair that should never have happened, but he felt that she owed him, at least, the truth. 'You didn't always *hate* your brother-in-law—'

'Not when he and Hilary first married—'

'And *not* when you brought me home to invest in the family firm at Brett's instigation either,' Rauf slotted in with harsh clarity.

'Sorry?' Lily whipped round to throw him a startled glance. Brett's instigation? How had he known that Brett *had* played a part in her decision to finally take Rauf home to meet her family? But what Rauf said next soon wiped that seeming irrelevancy back out of her mind again.

'Do you think I didn't eventually work out that that was a set-up?' Rauf dealt her contemptuous appraisal from shimmering golden eyes. 'Harris Travel needed an investor and I was rich. Are you trying to say that it was pure coincidence that you decided to introduce me to your family at that particular time? I don't think so!'

'Is that what you believed?' Lily was appalled at that accusation coming out of nowhere at her. How could he have thought that she could be that mercenary and calculating?

'Despite what you seem to think, I didn't come down in the last shower of rain,' Rauf derided, utilising the colloquial speech he had acquired attending an English public school.

'Back then I had no idea how wealthy you were!' Lily slung at him in angry reproach. 'Nor did I find out about the expansion plans for the business until after we arrived that weekend and we both heard Brett and Dad talking. The only reason I took you home was because my sister was dying to meet you!'

'I wish I could believe you,' Rauf breathed in a fierce undertone.

'So you decided that I had been after your money all

along…' Lily framed shakily, stinging tears burning in her darkened eyes. 'And how do you justify believing that when that same weekend I took you aside and suggested you think very carefully before you invested in Harris Travel? And what did you tell me? "This is business, Lily, not something you know much about"!'

Thrown by that unsettling reminder, Rauf opened his mouth to point out that her apparent lack of self-interest might also have been a very effective means of spurring him on to demonstrate his generosity towards her family. But in the end, he said nothing. After all, he was seeing a side of Lily that she had never allowed him to see before and he had no desire to silence her. There she was, practically jumping up and down with rage in front of him, the ultra-feminine, vulnerable front nowhere to be seen, and he was fascinated by that sight.

'You knew it *all*, didn't you?' Lily accused in her furious turmoil, little pearly teeth visibly gritted. 'But now it's all gone wrong, you're blaming me! Well, I'm sorry, but the only mistake I ever made with you, the only thing I have to regret, is that I was ever *stupid* enough to fall in love with you!'

Brushing past him on that final ringing assurance, Lily sped back across the dust road and fairly leapt into the helicopter, no assistance required. She turned her head away when Rauf boarded. She was convinced that she would never look him in the face again after losing control to the extent of admitting that she had been in love with him that summer. How could she have lowered herself to that level? He hadn't been entitled to that ego-boosting confession.

The helicopter lifted into the air. Rauf snatched in a slow, steadying breath. No way could he have got everything so wrong. He was too clever to have misread the evidence. But maybe Lily's tacky affair with Gilman had been on the wane by the time he himself had entered her life, maybe it had even been over...yeah, sure, she had been slinking shiftily out of that hotel with Gilman that afternoon for entirely innocent reasons and had lied about where she had been for entirely innocent reasons too? That was about as likely a possibility as her being the virgin she had sworn she was at the time!

His lean, devastating features set into aggressive lines. He was furious with himself. He was letting her get to him and work her wiles on him again. All she had had to do was tell him she had been in love with him and he had started doubting his own intelligence! But not for nothing had Rauf's own mother deemed her son to be as stubborn in his convictions as a steel-wrapped rock set in concrete. Rauf knew exactly why Lily was tempting him again. His hormones had no discrimination and her draw was pure sex. Even in that prim cardigan, she sent his temperature rocketing!

But then Lily still had that pulling power only because she was incredibly beautiful and he had never been her lover. While she had been screaming at him through gritted teeth, he had been watching the sun gild her glorious hair, noting the delectable prominence of her breasts when she threw her slim shoulders back and wondering if she would unleash that same passion in his bed. Shifting in an effort to ease the tormenting ache of his lingering arousal, Rauf veiled reflective dark golden eyes. Why shouldn't he find out?

After all, it was pretty obvious that if she was innocent of all blame when it came to the villas that never were, she was hardly likely to be involved in the accounts scam either. Gilman had moved on and doubtless taken his ill-gotten gains with him and Rauf would track him down and hang him high with pleasure for his sins...

CHAPTER FOUR

WITH pointed deliberation, Lily ignored Rauf's proffered hand when the helicopter landed for the second time and stepped out alone.

Lily wouldn't look at Rauf either, felt she couldn't trust herself that far. That unfamiliar rage had emptied her, shaking her to her very depths with its ferocity. Yet after the revelations that Rauf had dropped on her without warning, she was only reeling into a state of deeper shock.

'Where are we?' she asked, focusing on his blue silk tie, and her mind in such conflict that she was thinking half a dozen other thoughts all at once. That he had decided she was a gold-digger without any justification. That, with even less reason, he had been prepared to believe she and presumably her entire family had conspired to defraud him along with Brett. That he had with a cool deliberation that chilled her to the marrow flown her out to that abandoned building site to confront her with Brett's crooked dealings. That he also seemed to believe not a single word that she said.

Therefore she didn't need to ask, indeed she already knew without being told that Rauf Kasabian had not the tiniest shred of sympathy for her or her sister or her sister's children or her father.

'Sonngul, my country estate…and I don't know about you,' Rauf imparted, 'but I could do with a drink.'

A slight tremor ran through Lily's whip-taut frame. She was terrified of breaking down in tears. She knew that that was the natural outcome of shock but she didn't want to let herself down in front of him. In every way that mattered, Rauf seemed to be the enemy and a very ruthless one too. He would set the police on Brett and, although Lily would have loved to see Brett banged up in a prison cell, she could only shudder at the prospect of what that same reality would mean to Hilary and her daughters.

Her family lived in a small town and people were never kind when it came to fraud or bankruptcy. Hilary might be divorced from Brett but Harris Travel was still their father's business and that was what people would remember longest. Having been betrayed by her husband and lost her former home into the bargain, Hilary would now have to face not only the scandal and shame of Brett's prosecution, but also the loss of her family's only means of support. It would break Lily's father too, for the sole source of pride the older man still possessed was his good name. They would all be lambs to the slaughter.

As Lily accompanied Rauf down a path screened in and shaded by a wealth of lush overhanging foliage she broke the silence. 'I must phone Hilary. She needs to be told about the villas.'

'I can't agree to you informing your sister at this point. In fact I don't want you communicating with anyone back in England.'

Glancing up in astonishment at that forbidding assurance, Lily met the unashamed challenge in Rauf's steady gaze.

'Your sister may be divorced from Gilman but I doubt that she could be trusted to keep so much bad news to herself. She's much more likely to demand an explanation from Gilman and I don't want him to realise that he's been found out until all the facts have been established,' Rauf explained.

Lily snatched in a sustaining breath. 'What *you* want may not be what I think best for my family!'

'But if you want me to ease your family's passage through this, you'll do as I ask. If you choose to go up against me, remember that you were warned.' Golden eyes hard as a polished wall rested on her shaken face.

'You're threatening me,' Lily whispered sickly.

'No, I'm not,' Rauf contradicted with cool conviction. 'I'm just pointing out the facts. At this moment, I have no reason to trust your sister or your father but I'm willing to withhold judgement in the short term. However, if one of you were to tip off Gilman, accidentally or otherwise, he might disappear and I would then have good cause to wonder whether or not he really was the *only* thief in your family.'

'Thanks a bundle…' Lily muttered, flags of chagrined colour blooming across her taut cheekbones as she absorbed that telling speech.

'You need to know where you stand.'

Between his foot and the ground and in danger of being crushed. Oh, yes, she understood the message she was receiving. Either she left her sister in ignorance or she invited Rauf to suspect either Hilary or their father of having been in league with Brett. 'Am I your hostage now?' Lily demanded.

Rauf paused and from below dense black lashes cast her a molten-gold glance that was as erotic as a caress. 'Would you like to be?' he asked huskily.

That easily he churned up the atmosphere between them. She was disconcerted and trapped by those stunning eyes of his, and a tiny flame of awareness lit low in Lily's tummy; it happened so fast it left her breathless. Tearing her gaze in dismay from his, she focused in a daze on the extraordinary house that had come into view. It sat like a fantasy painting surrounded by venerable oak trees and Lily just stared. With a domed roof and an overhanging first floor, it had all the appearance of a medieval building for, unless she was very much mistaken, it also seemed to be made entirely of wood.

'Sonngul,' Rauf said with perceptible pride. 'The Kasabian *yali*…that means summer home. I had it restored two years ago as a surprise for my great-grandmother.'

A summer home the size of a mansion. Lily breathed in deep.

'Of course, I also built a large extension at the rear,' Rauf continued. 'In the original house, cooking and washing were done in the courtyard. There were no bedrooms either. The family slept in the same areas where they lived by day.'

The arched front door stood wide. It was an airy house of open spaces, tall windows with shutters, soaring ceilings, plays of filtered light and shadow. At the entrance he removed his shoes and a second later she followed suit. Up the sweeping carved staircase on the first floor was a huge room with doorways leading off in several directions and Rauf told her that it was called the *basoda*. Each corner of the room was a distinct and different area, one furnished for dining, another with bookshelves and a desk. Rauf strode up the single shallow step into the furthest corner and opened a drinks cabinet. There opulent cushioned divans edged the walls and created a charming window-seat into the tall bay that overlooked a tranquil river and the dense woods beyond. Slipping off her cardigan, Lily sat down there, soothed by that beauty and the silence.

Unasked, Rauf brought her a brandy. Lily sipped and grimaced, for she had never liked the taste of alcohol, but the fiery spirit helped to disperse the chilled knot of apprehension still keeping all her muscles taut.

Rauf set his own glass down untouched and studied her with level dark golden eyes. 'I misjudged you yesterday,' he murmured with wry honesty. 'I was also very rude. That is unlike me but the whole time that I was with you, I was angry and I wanted to hurt you.'

Surprised by his candour, Lily nodded jerkily, compressed her lips and then dropped her head because the over-emotional tears were threatening her again. Finally she was getting a glimpse of the male she had once fallen hopelessly in love with. A guy who was incredibly proud and very stubborn but who would acknowledge when he was in the wrong even though it killed him to own up to being anything less than perfect. A passionate and very masculine male, who could be domineering and arrogant but who had still been capable of melting her heart with one rueful charismatic smile. But then mercifully, she thought crazily as she fought the moisture dammed up behind her aching eyes, Rauf had *not* smiled since her arrival in Turkey.

'Why would you want to hurt me?' she muttered unevenly, for she could think of no good reason in the world why he should have experienced such a need. He had been the one to walk out of her life. He had not looked back either, but it had been a very long time before she had answered the phone in her student flat without a prayer in her heart that it would be him calling her. But then wasn't she forgetting his current suspicions about her, or at least her family, having been involved in Brett's dishonesty? She shut out that unwelcome recollection for, as matters stood, she had neither control nor influence over the events that would enfold.

Rauf vented a roughened laugh. 'How can you ask me that?'

Lily looked at him, recognised the raw tension in that

lean, strong face that had once haunted her dreams and her heart skipped a beat.

'You must *feel* the hunger you rouse in me,' Rauf breathed with driven emphasis. 'I neither expected that nor sought its return, but that desire for you is still there inside me just as it was that summer.'

Through the open sash-window behind her, Lily could hear the soft rushing sound of the river flowing and rippling over stones and, in the silence that fell, it seemed to fill her eardrums while she tried to absorb what he had just admitted. Was he saying that he wanted her back? Why else would he admit to still desiring her? Slowly, she lifted her head high, faint pink chasing the pallor from her lovely face, astonished blue eyes finally connecting with his fierce measuring appraisal.

'Do you always want most what you think you can't have?' Lily whispered shakily.

'*Evet*…yes,' Rauf admitted in Turkish with a fatalistic shrug as if that state of affairs went without saying as the norm for him.

'So I say no and get wanted even more…you shouldn't have told me that,' Lily tried to tease, wanting to laugh and cry at the same time, and then the tears pounced when her guard was down and streamed in rivulets down her cheeks, startling her as much as they seemed to startle him.

'Lily…*no*…' After an instant of hesitation, Rauf found himself sinking down by her side to draw her into his arms, only to still the motion when she was mere inches away.

'I'm s-sorry…' she gulped, but that confession of his had set free the pent-up tears as nothing else could have done.

'I've been tough on you,' Rauf conceded, and then he questioned why he had said that, but he did not question why he was holding her for that development struck him as inevitable.

'It's hardly your fault that Brett's a total creep,' Lily bit out unsteadily, giving way to what every natural sense prompted and pushing forward into the support of his broad muscled chest to bury her damp face in his shoulder. 'But I don't want to think about him right now.'

'I expect not.' Rauf held her back from him and used one lean hand to tip her lovely face back up to his.

It was the optimum moment to demand answers. His other hand closed into the fall of her hair where a clip held it confined. His intent golden eyes melded with her damp blue gaze for a long, timeless moment while he reminded himself that she had slept with her sister's husband, that she was an accomplished liar. But *still* he stared down into those glorious blue eyes that he recognised were the exact same shade he had chosen for the bedroom ceiling in his Istanbul apartment. A what-the-hell feeling that was totally out of character hit Rauf in a raw, energising wave.

'Why are you looking at me like that?' Lily whispered half under her breath, for he was so close she could see the gold lights in his amazing eyes and a different tension, an edge-of-seat, thrilling sense of suspense, held her taut.

'I'm appreciating you.' Rauf tilted her back over one strong arm as he freed the clip confining the long, thick fall of her hair and tossed it aside. He made every move with exaggerated slowness, instinctively waiting for her to protest or retreat as she had once done whenever he got too close. Her response in his arms the day before still struck him as unreal, for that was not how he remembered her.

Beneath the burning probe of Rauf's measuring appraisal, she felt her breath feather in her throat for she could hardly wait to feel his mouth on hers again. 'Are you?'

'Very much…' Rauf husked, a bitter sort of amusement lancing through him, for there was no doubt in his mind now that the reluctance he had met with before could only have been a deliberate ploy to make him all the keener. 'Especially as you don't seem quite so nervous as you used to be around me.'

Hot pink surged into Lily cheeks and her uneasy gaze dropped from his in embarrassment at that unexpected reminder. 'I got over that.'

But *when* had she magically got over it? Just yesterday when she'd appreciated that he held the future of Harris Travel in his hand? Dark, dangerous thoughts threatening, Rauf tuned them out with single-minded purpose and let his fingers slide into her gorgeous hair to tug the golden weight of glossy strands round her taut shoulders where it coiled and slid downward again in a tumbling mass. 'I always wanted to see you wear it loose like this.'

'It's too long…gets in the way.' The smouldering entrapment of his golden gaze kept her still. She could hardly breathe and her heart was thumping as though she had run a marathon, making it difficult for her to speak. Her breasts ached and a liquid sensation of heat was stirring at the very heart of her so that she pressed her thighs together in sudden guilty mortification.

'I love it…' Rauf confided thickly, dropping his lean, strong hands to her slender hips to raise her to him. 'I promise you…it won't get in *my* way.'

He captured her lips in a slow, searching onslaught that sent her senses spinning. The very taste of him was pure intoxication and the feel of his sensual mouth sublime. All that still approached rational thought was stolen from her in the first few seconds and then the sheer pleasure of what he was doing to her took over. He explored the tender interior of her mouth with a seductive expertise that made her gasp and cling, fingers biting into his broad shoulders with helpless impatience, tiny little tremors assailing her quivering length while she melted and burned for more.

Rauf lifted his dark head. 'Time to make a move…' he growled, springing upright.

Before she had even surfaced from the effects of that last lingering kiss, he had bent and swept her up into his arms to stride across the *basoda* and into a connecting hallway.

Lily stole a confused ennervated look up at Rauf. 'I can walk…'

'I like carrying you,' Rauf imparted with a slashing smile that brought his lean, devastating features to vibrant, charismatic life.

Her heart leapt inside her at the appeal of that smile.

Rauf shot a charged glance down at her. 'I'm taking you to my bed, *güzelim*. If you don't like that idea, say so now…'

Something akin to panic seized Lily in initial response to that invitation. His bed. Wasn't it much too soon for that development? But was she about to refuse the only male who had *ever* managed to make her want him? Taking into account his strong pride and their past history, he would never approach her again. This time around he expected an adult relationship and evidently he saw no reason why they shouldn't just go straight to bed. Having stuck by her moral principles would be cold consolation if she lost Rauf again at their expense. And, all nerves and shyness aside, if she was truly honest with herself, the mere idea of finding out what real passion was like with Rauf just left her limp and weak with wanton, wicked longing.

'Lily…?' Rauf prompted, strung high on the suspicion that he had fallen for yet another come-on destined to end in a freezing-cold shower.

Lily collided with sizzling golden eyes and butterflies broke loose in her tummy. By dint of clutching his shoulder, she lifted herself up to find his tempting mouth again for herself and gave him her answer that way. He succumbed with a roughened groan of appreciation and flattering immediacy. It was at least a minute before Lily got a single brain cell operating again and by that stage she was being set down on a superb gilded and carved bed. Instant tension froze her there.

Rauf backed off just to fully enjoy the sight of her there on his bed, her wonderful hair draped round her in a rippling sheet of gold, fairy-tale-princess style. She looked breathtaking. As he shed his jacket where he stood, quite unable as yet to actually imagine touching her, his tawny gaze rested on her and narrowed with sudden decisive force.

He was going to *keep* her! No way was he letting her go again. Why should his moral code sentence him to self-denial in his private life? He would take her back to Istanbul and set her up there in an apartment. In a cosmopolitan city, such arrangements were understood. If a faint current of unease assailed Rauf on the score that his female relatives were about as sophisticated as home-baked bread and as quick to pick up on gossip about him as high-tech listening devices, he blocked it out fast. At the age of thirty, he told himself that he had an indisputable right to live his life as he saw fit.

'I can't take my eyes off you…' Rauf confessed with roughened appreciation.

Lily watched him jerk loose his silk tie and let it fall and her tension level hit another high. She could not take her eyes from him either, but then nor could she quite believe that she was on his bed so soon after her arrival in Turkey. She felt terrifyingly shy and self-conscious yet being with Rauf still felt so right to her. But then he had stayed in her heart, hadn't he? Her memory of him locked there with magnetic determination and ferocious staying power. Taken aback by a truth that she had denied for so long, Lily focused on Rauf with dawning comprehension and understood why her resistance was nil around him. She had never got over loving him.

'Do you do this all the time?' Lily heard herself ask without even being aware that she was about to frame such a leading question.

Halfway through unbuttoning his shirt, Rauf stilled in surprise.

'I mean…' Lily continued unsteadily, her tongue reacting to her anxious thoughts faster than caution could instigate a hold on it. '…just kiss and go straight to…er… bed?'

'Not since I was a teenager.' Somehow, Rafe acknowledged a second later, that was not the most comforting of thoughts.

Her cheeks flushed, Lily bent her golden head. 'I just wondered.'

Without hesitation, Rauf gathered her up and kissed her with drugging intensity. 'This is *us*…that's different,' he pointed out.

Stepping back from her, he peeled off his shirt. Lips tingling but mouth running dry, Lily stared: he was all sleek, rippling muscles and bronzed skin. He was magnificent. A haze of dark curls outlined his pectorals and arrowed down into a faint furrow over his flat, taut abdomen. As he embarked on removing his well-cut trousers, treating her to a view of his narrow waist, lean hips and a disturbing glimpse of long, powerful, hair-roughened thighs, Lily actually thought she might have a heart attack then and there. Dragging in a stark sudden breath, she dredged her attention from him, but his disturbing image stayed stamped behind her eyelids: incredibly male, big, dominating. Rampantly sexy too, just rather panic-inducing.

'I forgot to offer you lunch...' Rauf commented without warning.

'Lunch?' Lily echoed as the mattress gave beneath his added weight. Without glancing in his direction, she endeavoured to look less like a reclining statue. Having watched his boxer shorts hit the rug, she wasn't quite ready as yet to embrace the visual challenge of him in all his unadorned glory.

'Later...' Rauf promised, closing a long, confident arm round her to tug her back towards him, shift her hair out of his path and reach for the zip on her dress.

Lily almost told him she was too hungry to wait for lunch. Only will-power kept her on the bed. Hadn't she passed the kissing category with flying colours? Why else had they reached the bed so fast? Only Rauf was now expecting her to jump several categories all at once and without any prior practice. This was Rauf she was with, though, she reminded herself bracingly. He would make the experience as good as it could be. Adverse circumstances challenged him, brought out the very best in his competitive character.

'This feels so sexy...' he purred, inching down her zip only inch by inch, dragging out the moment as befitted what felt like an historic occasion, for he had never seen an inch of Lily exposed between throat and knee.

'Does it?' Lily muttered tautly as cooler air touched her spine.

'You have incredibly soft skin.' Lean fingers brushing

over her narrow back, Rauf let his lips zero in on the pale perfection of one slender shoulder and linger there.

His knowing mouth felt like a brand on her and she trembled, suddenly plunged back into aching awareness. Weak with longing, she leant back into him for support. But instead, he turned her round to face him, took her lush mouth with hungry urgency and drove every thought from her mind. Her dress and her bra fell to the carpet without her even being aware of their smooth removal. Every inch of her skin felt supersensitive, thrumming with wild anticipation to the passionate melding of his mouth on hers and the even more erotic plunge of his tongue. Nothing else existed for her, nothing else mattered, and she laced her fingers into the springy depths of his hair to hold him to her.

But when Rauf drew back and lifted her to pull the bedspread back from beneath her and settle her on the cool crisp sheet instead, the real world reclaimed Lily again. As she tumbled back against the feather pillows she was startled to find herself clad in only her panties and embarrassment inflamed her at the sight of her own bare breasts.

But Rauf wasted no time in coming back to her again, smouldering golden eyes raking over her with very male appreciation.

'You're gorgeous,' he breathed with roughened conviction as he absorbed the picture she made against the white linen: blue eyes bright as stars, her lips reddened from his, her glorious hair semi-veiling her in sensual disarray, allowing only a tantalising glimpse of one pouting, pink-tipped breast. With Lily in his life, getting out of bed to make an early meeting would prove to be the toughest challenge he had ever faced. But also the most enjoyable.

Heart hammering at the charged appraisal she was receiving, Lily parted dry lips. 'I should warn you…I still haven't…er…done this before.'

Taken aback by that unlikely claim, Rauf screened his sardonic gaze and tried not to wince for her. Surely she didn't *still* expect him to believe that she was pure as driven snow? But then, as he had chosen not to confront her about her liaison with Gilman, she might feel that she had to keep up that pretence. But even after several years had passed?

In the taut silence, Lily worried anxiously at her lower lip. 'Does that put you off?'

'Nothing could do that.' Relieved that she had said something he could answer with honesty, Rauf took the easy way out. Bringing her back to him again, he crushed her inviting mouth under his own and kissed her breathless.

Reeling from that impassioned onslaught, Lily lay back in his arms, quivering at the hot, hard weight and lure of his muscular body lying half over hers. She collided with shimmering golden eyes as he moulded the tender swell of her breasts and her spine arched, pushing her sensitised flesh up into shameless, satisfying contact with his palms. Sweet sensation fired her with a wicked, restive impatience that embarrassed her. Without pause, he captured a straining pink nipple between his lips and an audible gasp was dragged from her. An insistent throb had begun at the very heart of her. Suddenly her body was in control of her, desperate and hungry for more of that tormenting pleasure and unable to conceal the fact.

'Never have I wanted a woman as I want you now,' Rauf admitted with a ragged edge to his dark drawl. It was the truth, but a truth he bitterly resented.

But that confession thrilled Lily and her eyes shone and she had not a doubt in her head from that moment that she was doing the right thing: giving where once she had been afraid to give and sharing in the same way. 'It's the same for me,' Lily whispered, looking up at him with complete trust.

Only it had not always been the way and Rauf was all too well aware of that fact. A dangerous smile curved his expressive mouth. 'Now that Brett's gone?'

Lily blinked, unable to grasp the connection and then suddenly wondering in shrinking dismay if Rauf had suspected all along that there was something odd about her relationship with her sister's ex-husband. But she shrank from the idea of telling Rauf about Brett's loathsome behaviour towards her when she had been a teenager. Brett might never have touched her, but he had left her feeling soiled and she was convinced that Rauf would be disgusted, repulsed...or, worse, that he might even wonder if in some way she might have invited or encouraged that attention from the other man. Either way, she believed that Rauf would think very much less of her.

'Sorry...I don't follow,' Lily muttered in a discomfited rush.

She was pale, blue eyes awash with strain and conflict that Rauf interpreted as guilt. A guilt that gave him no satisfaction but that sent sudden ferocious anger flaring through him. If he ever got his hands on Gilman, he knew he would hammer the bastard into a pulp.

Veiling his fierce, glittering scrutiny, he just pushed himself up and reached out to yank Lily back across the small space that separated them into his arms again.

'It may be a big bed,' Rauf quipped, 'but that doesn't mean you're allowed to stray.'

It was pure caveman but she melted into the lean, hard heat and strength of his muscular frame. Even as relief that he had not said any more about Brett washed over her every nerve-ending she possessed went on red alert at the renewed force of desire that overwhelmed her that close to him.

She burned with a helpless mix of nerves and anticipation as she felt the hot, hard length of his arousal against her belly. He rearranged her, teased the throbbing peaks of her breasts with his tongue until she writhed and gasped, and she was lost in sensation again long before he sought out the slick dampness between her slender thighs. He caressed the most sensitive spot of all and she moaned out loud, startled by her own feverish response. The intensity kept on building until she was panting for breath, pitched to a torment of wanting by his merest touch.

'Rauf…' she gasped, and she didn't even know what she wanted to say, only that the hunger was almost unbearable, the ache consuming her a growing torture to withstand.

Scorching desire blazed in the golden eyes that scanned her as he donned protection. He sank his hands beneath her squirming hips and came over her in one lithe move. He entered her with a smooth, expert thrust and wanton little tremors of pleasure assailed her at that initial sensation of his fullness stretching her tight.

Then he said something in his own language, surprise darkening his heated gaze as he had to lift her and tip her up further to sheathe himself in her fully. A sharp stab of pain jolted Lily at the height of that manoeuvre and for a split second she went rigid and wasn't quite quick enough to bite back a startled yelp of complaint.

Rauf felt that resistance too late. He stopped, in fact he froze as if a fire alarm had gone off, but his own powerful momentum had already carried him through that delicate barrier. 'Lily…?' and his voice just failed him for the first time in his life.

'It's all right,' Lily mumbled dizzily, adjusting with admirable speed, ease and appreciation to a category of sensation that her body sensed harboured the promise of possibilities she had not even dreamt might exist. 'I'm getting used to it…*oh*…oh, yes…'

Eyes tight shut, Lily wrapped both arms round him, shifted her hips experimentally and was seized by such a blinding wave of delicious sensation that she was left breathless and craving more. Hunger for her reignited to fever pitch but, fighting it, Rauf moved to withdraw, but she arched up to him in encouragement and at that point he succumbed by sinking back into her with an earthy groan. Her excitement mounted with every fluid thrust of his lithe body into hers, his primal rhythm driving her pleasure to uncontrollable heights. Then she hit a glorious peak and broke up into a million tiny, ecstatically happy little pieces. She coasted down from that dazzling experience with a sense of profound wonderment.

Tension would not allow Rauf to reach the same rewarding climax. He withdrew and stared down at her happy, *innocent* face and it was like having a knife plunged into him to the hilt. Releasing her from his weight, he rolled over. Lily scooted back into connection with him, dropped a kiss on the bunched muscles of one wide shoulder, drank in the sexy scent of his damp, hot skin with dizzy satisfaction and the heady sense of being a *real* woman. Rauf flipped back, curved an arm round her slight length and drew her close again.

'I feel so…so happy,' Lily finally admitted, still on a self-preoccupied high unlike any she had ever experienced. The world at just that moment encompassed Rauf and there it stopped. She was in his arms. She loved him. She had finally made it into bed with him and been rewarded beyond her wildest hopes.

'I need a shower…' Rauf breathed grittily.

And as Lily opened her eyes to watch Rauf stride towards the door on the far wall she noticed, really could not have helped noticing, that *he* was still…unsatisfied. The sheer extent of her own alarming ignorance of why that should be preoccupied her. Her sunny sense of achievement died there. Only then did she recall that in the aftermath of their lovemaking he had initially pulled away from her, had not spoken, had indeed only put his arms round her after she had swarmed all over him first.

A hollow, sick sensation in her tummy, Lily sat up and hugged her knees, anxious eyes dark with pain and mortification. Obviously, Rauf hadn't got much of a thrill from taking her to bed and, even though he had still been aroused, he hadn't wanted to continue either. That latter fact seemed the lowest blow of all. The shower seemed to exert more charisma than she did. Why, though? What had she done wrong?

CHAPTER FIVE

RAUF was having a very long cold shower.

Lily had been a virgin. Rauf was still transfixed by the shock value of that discovery. In fact, he was so stunned by that revelation and by the equally disturbing experience of having been proven wrong in his every conviction that it was an intellectual challenge just to surmount that and move on into more practical mode of what to do next. He would have to be honest with her. That was his first decision.

He then attempted to picture a scene in which he would tell Lily that he had once believed that she was sleeping with her sister's husband. What was more, he had believed that of her right up until he had shared a bed with her himself. Rauf grimaced. No, he definitely didn't want to run with the unvarnished truth. She would be horrified and offended beyond forgiveness. How could he distress her by admitting that he had credited the existence of such a *very* sleazy affair? That he had ditched her because of that same belief? That he had believed she had betrayed not only his trust, but also her own sister's?

And all the time, Lily had been all that she herself claimed to be, everything she had seemed on first acquaintance and everything he had once accepted her as being. So, when she came off with things like, 'Can't we still be friends?', she really, truly *meant* it. In the cleanest sense. That had not been a subtle sexual hint that this time around she was willing to spread herself on his bed.

At that point, Rauf groaned out loud, raked long brown

fingers through his wet black hair. A dozen once strictly censored and cynically dissected and despoilt memories bombarded him in their restored and original form. Memories of Lily that summer before they broke up. In all of those recollections, Lily featured as being especially nice, especially soft-hearted and especially unmaterialistic.

For a start, she just adored little children and lavished phenomenal patience on even the irritating yappy ones. She was a pushover for every tramp or homeless person that came within twenty feet of her and she had cried when he'd told her about his dog dying when he was eleven. She had even worried that he was spending too much money on her and had kept on making up picnics so that they could eat alfresco. It was getting very cold in the shower but Rauf was looking back three years in time with an unfamiliar sense of appalled bewilderment at the colossal depth of his own misconceptions about Lily. Shivering, he finally grabbed a towel.

The more he examined his own behaviour, the worse it seemed. He got no brownie points on any score. At every juncture, he had assumed worst-case scenario and treated her accordingly. Therefore, candour really wasn't a viable option. Off that particularly challenging hook, Rauf breathed again. She never had known the way his mind had worked and now he knew that he never, ever wanted her to find out. He was a ruthless, cynical guy with, it seemed, a mind as naturally given over to intrigue and seething suspicion of his woman as that Shakespeare character who had done away with his wife. He didn't want any living soul knowing that and Lily, who scared easy, least of all!

Just one small inconsistency continued to nag at him. What *had* she been doing in that hotel with Brett Gilman? And why had she lied about being there? Furthermore, why had she stopped being so nervous around him? What miracle had brought about that refreshing change? Quit wondering stuff like that, Rauf's new caution control centre warned him. He strode through the connecting door to the dressing-room and yanked out fresh clothes. Lily looks like an angel, she *is* an angel, stop doubting your good fortune at landing the one woman you do not deserve to have!

As Lily listened to Rauf's shower running, she told herself that she would get up and get dressed in just a minute. Lying in his bed naked now felt shameless and all her intoxication with her own daring had shrivelled on the vine. Foolish love and even sillier hopes had led her astray and she hadn't had to wait long to pay a price for her stupidity. Why didn't she just face it? All Rauf had ever wanted from her was sex and, having finally got it, he had been disappointed.

But then, one way or another, hadn't she always disappointed him? Her mind roamed back to when she had first met Rauf Kasabian...

The glorious flowers he had sent in apology for the fracas over the red wine being spilt had merely heralded Rauf's reappearance at the bar later that same day. He'd wasted no time either in making his intentions clear. Throwing back his handsome dark head, he had treated her to that riveting smile of his and murmured, 'I think we both know I'm only here to see you again.'

'But you have a girlfriend—'

'No...I don't date women who scream at other women in public. I'll wait until you finish your shift.'

Never had she met a male less aware of the possibility of rejection. Automatic refusal trembled on her lips but remained unspoken, for when she met his gorgeous dark golden eyes the thought of him walking away and never coming back just silenced her. When she had to serve the table beside Rauf's, a drunk put his hand on her bottom and she brushed it away. When the drunk then asked her who the hell she thought she was, Rauf intervened.

'She's mine,' Rauf drawled with perfect equanimity. 'So hands off…'

He took her back to her apartment in a taxi to get changed and Annabel followed Lily into her tiny bedroom to snipe, 'All right, so you're *not* gay and you've snagged him. But that guy will expect more than a hug at the end of the night, so don't say you weren't warned!'

'Meaning?' Lily was apprehensive enough without that assurance.

'He's a real sexy stud. It's written all over him. Enjoy yourself tonight because you won't see him again,' Annabel forecast. 'You'll say no. He won't waste any more time on you…after all, why should he? Girls always come across for guys like him.'

He took her to dine in a wonderful Turkish restaurant and they talked for hours. Well, mostly he talked and she listened. He was working on the launch of a news magazine and he would be in London all summer. That first night he didn't even try to kiss her but he booked her every free hour for the entire week ahead.

The second night he did kiss her but she coped because it was broad daylight and in a public place and she did not feel threatened in any way. She also discovered that she liked it when he kissed her. The third night, he asked her to come back to his hotel and spend the night with him, as if sharing her body with a male she had only known a couple of days was the most natural thing in the world.

'I don't do stuff like that,' she told him.

'Of course you do,' Rauf traded. 'You're only trying to

play that time-honoured female game…make him desperate before you say yes. But I was desperate within seconds of first laying eyes on you.'

'I haven't ever slept with anyone,' Lily finally mumbled.

There was a very long silence. Startled tawny eyes gazed deep into hers. 'You're saying you're a…?'

Hurriedly she nodded, face flaming.

'I suppose I ought to say that seducing virgins isn't my style but, to be very frank,' Rauf husked, those smouldering eyes turning slumbrous with anticipation, 'I've never been in this situation before and the idea of being your first lover just blows my mind!'

That was not the understanding response she had been hoping to receive and she muttered in considerable embarrassment, 'What I'm trying to say is that I really want to wait until I'm married.'

'But I'm not looking for a wife. I doubt that I'll ever marry,' Rauf informed her steadily. 'I come from a family where for several generations marriage at a very young age was the norm. I've been fending off potential brides since I was eighteen. I like my freedom. So if you want more, I'm the wrong guy.'

She wished he had told her all that on the first date. By then it was too late to stop loving him. But the night died there and at the end of it she told him she didn't want to see him again. And, even now, she remembered the dark, incredulous fury in his lean, devastating features and the fright it had given her to see what a temper he had. He hadn't said or done anything to demonstrate that anger but that memory had lingered. For forty-eight hours, he didn't call and then he turned up at the bar, still furious with her but trying to hide it and, just looking at him, she knew that, even if their relationship had no future, he was still her fate. That same week he found her another job as a receptionist in a beauty salon owned by the wife of a friend of his and she was very grateful.

For a few weeks, they had a wonderful time together most of the time. Things only went wrong when sex entered the equation. On three separate occasions, she steeled herself to go back to his hotel with him. The first time, he said to her, 'You're not ready for this,' because when he tried to move beyond kissing she just froze on him. The second time she drank too much in the hope of losing her inhibitions and he took her home in brooding silence. The third time, she told him he made her feel scared sometimes and he looked so shaken she felt the most awful guilt because she knew that she was the one with the problem, not him.

But then, surprisingly, for a while, he just accepted how she was and he was very gentle and caring and she loved him more than ever. Yet when Hilary begged her to bring Rauf home, she continued to make excuses. Then Brett turned up at her student flat one night just before Rauf was due to pick her up.

'It's time we buried the hatchet,' Brett announced with a creepy smile while she shrank behind the door and kept it on the chain. 'Hilary is gasping to meet this Rauf Kasabian character and I swear I'll be on my best behaviour if you bring him home for the weekend.'

'Why? Why would you swear that?'

'Hilary's hurt that you hardly ever visit. That makes me feel bad.'

Rauf was amazingly keen to meet her family and, although she was surprised by his interest in investing in Harris Travel, it was a terrific weekend. A week later, they made a second visit because Rauf's accountant had flown over from Turkey to look at Harris Travel's accounts and the contract Rauf's London lawyer had already drawn up in readiness was then signed by Rauf and her father. But during those same forty-eight hours, everything that could go wrong *did* go wrong...

Lily was very much on edge with the knowledge that Rauf was within days of making a permanent return to Turkey. Her niece, Gemma, was ill when they arrived. Lily had to offer to stand in for a sick member of staff the following day at the travel agency. Then, Gemma was taken into hospital for emergency surgery and Hilary was frantic and unable to contact Brett. Shutting out that unappealing slice of memory, Lily remembered how she had seen Rauf off at the airport that same evening and not one word had he said about seeing her again or not seeing her again or indeed anything else. But that had been the last time she'd seen or heard from him. Once she had called his mobile phone just to check he was still alive and he had answered and she had not had the nerve to speak.

When Rauf strode back into the bedroom, Lily gave him an aghast look for she had lost track of time. Having intended to be dressed and elsewhere by the time he reappeared, she just dived under the sheet like a little kid, leaving nothing but some trailing hair showing.

Rauf was very encouraged by the fact that Lily was still in his bed an hour after the event. In particular, an event that had been a lot less of an event than it should have been. She was still naked too, which meant she was a captive audience.

'Lily...'

'Go away...I want to get dressed!' Lily launched from below the sheet, feeling exceedingly foolish.

Rauf hunkered down by the side of the bed, inched up the sheet about three inches and met frantic blue eyes. 'I've been a total inconsiderate bastard but I *do* care about you.'

'Prove it then…go away!' Lily urged chokily, thinking that that noncommittal word, 'care' had always come very readily to Rauf's lips around her. But that word promised nothing and while she'd waited on a phone that had never rung at the age of twenty-one she had learned the hard way that his concept of 'caring' could mean absolutely nothing too.

'I can't stand it when you're upset and you won't let me hold you!' Rauf fired back at her in immediate frustration.

At that, Lily lifted her head a little. He sounded so sincere. 'I just don't understand you….'

'Why would you even want to?' Rauf asked her, gathering strength by the second on that reassuring piece of news. 'I'm a guy. I'm supposed to be different.'

'You're *too* different,' Lily told him helplessly. 'I don't know where I am with you.'

'In my bed beneath my sheet and I'm going to rip you out of there if you don't come out under your own steam,' Rauf told her steadily.

Fierce resentment hurtled up through Lily. 'You do that…and I promise you, I'll thump you!'

Dark golden eyes arrowed over her angry face in astonishment at that threat. 'I was only teasing…'

No, she knew he hadn't been. On that level, she knew him well. Ripping off the sheet would not have cost Rauf a second of hesitation. He was a stranger to patience.

Lily shimmied up from under the sheet, carrying it carefully with her until her head hit the pillows again. She didn't even think about what she was doing because with every moment that passed a far more engrossing conviction had been growing on her. It was as if time had gone into reverse. It was spooky. Somehow, somewhere between vacating the bedroom and returning to it, Rauf had switched back into being the male she remembered him being in London. More relaxed, less abrasive, not a shade of coldness or scorn or reserve about him and there was warmth in his beautiful eyes again. So what had changed? No matter how hard she tried, she could not stop staring at him.

It was a bad move, she conceded dizzily because, as usual, Rauf looked drop-dead gorgeous. Sheathed in black jeans, he could have sold racks of them to besotted women and his grey tee shirt was designer casual and made him seem much more approachable than a business suit did. And then there was him, the guy in the clothes. Black hair still damp from the shower, the riveting attraction of that lean, hard-boned face and the dark, deepset eyes with only a restive glitter of gold pinned to her with an intensity she could feel.

Rauf sank down on the edge of the bed and spread two lean brown hands. 'I was *really* surprised that you were a virgin. I know you said you were but I didn't believe you.'

At that sudden confession, Lily blinked in slow motion. 'You mean…you *never* believed me?'

'I did when we first met…most of the time,' he qualified, opting for total truth on that score. 'But sometimes I did wonder if it was just a clever way of trying to wring a marriage proposal out of me.'

Lily lost colour and studied him in frank reproach even as resentment made her bridle. 'You told me how you felt about marriage. I knew that what we had was going nowhere.'

Strangely enough, that concluding statement annoyed the hell out of Rauf.

'There was nowhere for it *to* go,' Lily continued helplessly, wondering why his stubborn jawline had clenched as if she had said something offensive. 'I lived in England. You lived here. All that was on offer was a casual affair.'

'I don't do casual,' Rauf drawled, brilliant golden eyes challenging.

Her lush mouth tightened and her lashes screened her gaze, her lovely face shadowing. 'You just *did*…here, with me,' she breathed unsteadily, her throat tightening because talking about anything so intimate did not come easily to her. 'I don't know what I expected, but it wasn't the way you behaved afterwards—'

Rauf leant forward, closed one hand over hers. 'I told you that I—'

'That you were totally wrapped up in yourself as usual,' Lily sliced in helplessly.

Hugely disconcerted by that condemnation, Rauf tightened his lean brown fingers over hers. 'That's *not* what I said—'

'But what it comes down to. You didn't *care*…' Lily framed painfully. 'About how I felt that you were disappointed.'

'*Disappointed?* Is that what you think?' Rauf demanded in disbelief, 'totally wrapped up in yourself as usual' still lingering with a sting he couldn't believe and keen to shift the dialogue into safer channels. 'How could you think I was disappointed with you?'

'I don't want to discuss that…' Lily became very evasive when it came to the point of sharing how she had reached that conclusion.

Lacing his other hand into her hair, Rauf tugged her forward and devoured her mouth with a passionate hunger that had a megawatt effect on her startled system. Heart banging fit to burst, pulses racing, Lily looked up at Rauf with stunned eyes as he sprang upright, peeled off his tee shirt over his head and unzipped his jeans.

'Rauf…?' Lily whispered in a daze.

The boxer shorts landed in a heap beside the discarded jeans. Glorious as a Greek god, he had the additional appeal of being infinitely more hot-blooded for he sported a bold erection. Lily flushed to the roots of her hair but a wanton little throb thrummed deep down inside her in response.

'Could I persuade you to disappoint me again?' Rauf asked with sizzling effect.

Lily sort of slid down the bed into a more encouraging position without even thinking about it and ten seconds later Rauf was melded to her like a second skin. And if the first time had struck her as incredible, the second time qualified as wild. Afterwards, she fell asleep in his arms floating high above planet earth, got woken up to disappoint him again at some length. Then with a boundless energy that could only impress her when she honestly thought she would never move again, he answered a phone call, pulled on his clothes, said he'd order dinner for them and that he had to return that call. From the door, he gazed back at her, vibrant golden eyes centring on her again and he strode back, threw himself down on the bed to extract a last lingering kiss and groaned out loud at having to drag himself away.

'Later…' he promised huskily.

The sun was going down behind the shutters when Lily tottered out of bed to take advantage of his shower. She felt like a woman lost in an erotic dream. She felt sublime. He made her feel so loved. Wasn't that strange? It was only sexual love. She knew that, of course she did. She told herself that she was not naive enough to start thinking that Rauf's incredible passion for her body meant anything more. But she was awash with images of having been held close and showered in endless compliments too.

'You're exquisite…' he had said.

'You're perfect for me…' he had sighed.

'I find you irresistible…'

For the moment, Lily affixed, reflecting back to that last assurance. She was in love with a male who would never regard her as anything more than a small part of his life, who would never say the love word even under torture and who would always be very, very careful to promise nothing he could not deliver.

Rauf had once described the staunchly traditional Kasabian family to her and Lily sighed at the ironic damage that that trio of matriarchal figures—his great-grandmother, grandmother and mother—had done to their own fondest hopes of marrying him off. For a start, Rauf had been educated at an English public school and literally raised between two different cultures.

But when he was eighteen his family had begun inviting over the daughters of family friends and business acquaintances and telling him that he didn't need to get married for a few years but that there was no harm in choosing early and settling on a long engagement. Over-protective of him, no doubt aware that with his looks and wealth he would be targeted by designing women in droves, his female relatives had been desperate to get him safely welded to some suitable girl even before he'd gone to university. Of course, given Rauf's force of character and stubborn nature, all that pressure had had the exact opposite effect. Staying single had become a burning crusade.

When she returned to the bedroom, she discovered that her case had been brought up. Having dried her hair, she was in the act of clipping it back when she recalled Rauf's preference and then, smiling, she left it loose. As she put on a pale green cotton skirt and a fitted, short-sleeved white shirt she thought about how much stronger she had grown since she was sixteen. At sixteen, naively believing that her long blonde hair was responsible for drawing Brett's attention to her, she had gone out one Saturday and had it cut to within two inches of her skull. Hilary had been shocked but Brett had just laughed and had continued to target her. Apart from the occasional trim, Lily now wore her hair long in defiance of the timid teenager she had once been. But she would wear it loose only for Rauf's pleasure.

Rauf was in the main room in the old part of the house still talking on the phone. His lean, strong face flashed into a brilliant smile of welcome that left her giddy. He closed an arm round her, finished his call and led her outside to a charming old stone-built arbour lit with lanterns that overlooked the lush gardens. Drinks and an astonishing variety of appetisers on tiny plates were brought by a man-servant.

'*Mucver*…courgette. *Piyaz*…that is haricot and this one is *sigara boregi*…cheese pastries.' Explaining what each was, Rauf encouraged Lily to try a little of everything and he watched her enjoyment of Turkish cuisine with uncon-cealed pride.

It was a fantastic meal. Even Rauf seemed taken aback by the number of courses that appeared and the wide se-lection of dishes.

'Do you eat like this every night?' Lily could not help asking.

'Not unless it's a special occasion.' Rauf shook his proud dark head and laughed. 'This feast can only be in honour of my guest. As Sonngul is remote, it is rare for me to entertain here but to offer the ultimate in hospitality is a matter of pride to all Turkish people.'

He asked her about the nursery school where she worked and she told him about the children she taught. Having eaten, however, she began to feel guilty that even a few hours had passed without her pressing Rauf to a task that surely ought to be tackled as soon as possible. The sooner Rauf acquired the evidence he wanted to prove Brett's guilt, the sooner Hilary could be told about the disastrous financial losses about to engulf the travel agency.

'Perhaps we could take a look at Harris Travel's bank statements and stuff now,' Lily suggested rather awkwardly.

A wry smile curved his beautiful, sensual mouth. 'I have no need of your assistance in that line, *güzelim*.'

'But isn't that why you brought me here?' Lily queried in surprise. 'To *help*?'

'That was an excuse,' Rauf admitted. 'On my behalf, discreet enquiries are already being made through the head office of that Turkish bank in London. I have considerable influence and in due course the confidential information that I require will be given to me.'

That smooth explanation shook Lily, for she had never dreamt that his invitation to Sonngul might not be what it had seemed. 'You don't need me at all?'

'How can you ask me that when you met my *every* need this afternoon?' The irreverent look of shameless intimacy in Rauf's dark golden gaze fired hot pink across Lily's troubled and increasingly weary face. 'But as I have already told you, I didn't want you muddying the waters of my investigation either.'

'You're very clever at concealing your true motives,' Lily remarked tightly.

'Our situation has changed since our first meeting at the Aegean Court. I didn't trust you then,' Rauf reminded her levelly. 'But I still want the evidence that will nail Gilman's hide to the wall. I make no apology for that.'

Lily sighed heavily. 'I'd dearly like to see him punished too but…that's going to hurt my family a lot.'

'I'm afraid there's no room for negotiation on the prosecution front.' Rauf's jawline squared. 'But I see no reason why your family should suffer too.'

'But they *will* suffer,' Lily muttered painfully. 'There's nothing you can do about that.'

Rauf looked amused. 'Of course there is…I won't allow your family to be ruined. I'll just refinance Harris Travel.'

In receipt of that extraordinarily generous proposition, Lily stiffened in astonishment. She also found herself wondering if that offer was the direct result of her having met his 'every need' in bed. It was a demeaning thought, which made it impossible for her to continue meeting his eyes. 'Neither Dad or Hilary could accept that. You've lost money and they've lost money but Harris Travel is *our* business and responsibility and Brett was Hilary's husband.'

'I'll deal with it. You don't need to worry about anything.' With cool assurance, Rauf stroked a light forefinger in a soothing caress across the back of her clenched hand where it rested on the table. 'I'll take care of it all. Trust me.'

Still in turmoil from the shock of that offer of further cash support, Lily tugged her hand shakily free and stood up. 'If I promise not to contact anyone, will you have me taken back to my hotel?'

In one lithe movement, Rauf sprang upright. 'But why should you want to leave?'

'Because I feel that what happened between us today… and this horrible situation with Brett are getting much too tangled up together!'

But before she could walk back into the house, Rauf stepped into her path. A lean hand pushed up her chin.

Keen dark golden eyes searched her strained face. 'You don't want Brett prosecuted,' he condemned in a tone so chilling that Lily trembled.

'I do...it's you who doesn't understand—'

'*Make* me,' he urged.

As briefly as she could, Lily explained how much her family had already endured in recent times: Joy's long illness, which had worn Hilary to the bone, the loss of the Harris home in the divorce settlement, Douglas Harris's subsequent depression. Rauf's lean, handsome features grew even more grim as he listened to that recital of woes, all of them brought about or exacerbated by Brett Gilman's monstrous lack of concern for his own children.

'But there's no way that Hilary or my father would accept more money from you,' Lily reiterated in a driven undertone. 'And I don't want to listen to you offer that just because I...I slept with you! Can't you see how that makes me feel?'

'No. What you see is *not* what I see. You're my woman and I will look after you. There is no shame in that for you and what sort of man would I be if I didn't support you in such a crisis? I'll find a way to make my financial help acceptable to them. Call it pure selfishness, if you like. How could I stand by and do nothing while you worry about your family?'

The fierce sincerity with which Rauf voiced those arguments in his own defence and his supportive words touched Lily deep.

'You're not going back to your hotel,' he informed her, still inflamed that she could even have considered that as an option.

'But I *ought* to...' Lily groaned.

'To some degree, I'm also to blame for the freedom with which Gilman was able to steal from all of us.'

Lily frowned. 'How?'

'My last accountant was a family friend. I should've suggested that he retire much sooner than I did,' Rauf explained ruefully. 'His health was failing and the job was too demanding but still he clung to it. The very first contract payment that failed to arrive from Harris Travel should've been noted and questioned, but it wasn't.'

'That was unfortunate,' Lily conceded as Rauf walked her back indoors.

'That oversight must've encouraged Gilman to believe that he could get away with a lot more.'

Lily smothered a guilty yawn. She was so tired she might have been moving in a dream. All the unsettling events of the past forty-eight hours were weighing in on her at once.

'You're totally exhausted.' With a rueful laugh, Rauf swept her slight body up into his arms and carried her back to his bedroom, where he laid her on the bed.

The internal house phone rang and he answered it. The news that a senior officer from the *jandarma*, the section of the army responsible for law enforcement in rural areas, had driven over to Sonngul to request a meeting with him focused Rauf's thoughts fast...

CHAPTER SIX

THE older man introduced himself as Talip Hajjar and greeted Rauf with a polite apology for his intrusion.

Talip was the superior officer of the gendarme, who had prepared the file on Brett Gilman's dealings with the builders contracted to work on his villa project. From him, Rauf learned that the builders involved, having received what was owing to them from Rauf's representative, now wished to drop the charges they had laid.

'Although I understand that you have only just learned of this unpleasant business, you came forward immediately to compensate those defrauded by the Englishman. In doing so and in acknowledging your own interest in the firm who employed him, you have behaved with honour in every way. I doubt that we would ever have discovered that connection without your frank admission of it,' Talip Hajjar admitted with wry honesty. 'However, I also believe that it would be wrong to allow this dishonest foreigner to benefit from your acceptance of responsibility and escape the prosecution he deserves.'

'It is not and never was my wish that that should be the result either,' Rauf agreed with considerable gravity.

The older man regarded him with approval. 'Then I must ask you to persuade the victims of his crime to let those charges stand. They only wish to drop them out of respect for the Kasabian name. But in such circumstances, a businessman of your standing and reputation can have nothing to hide or fear.'

Unhappily, Rauf could not feel that, while he had Lily

lying in his bed, an as yet unacknowledged director of Harris Travel, that was quite true and, in instant defiance of a disturbing urge to keep quiet about her presence as a guest in his home, he offered the older man *çay*.

Over the tea that was brought, Rauf sat down to tell the gendarme officer the rest of the story. Having explained Lily's presence in Turkey, he went on to vouch for her complete ignorance of her former brother-in-law's unscrupulous activities as well as describing what her relatives had already endured at Gilman's hands.

'Her own family will face bankruptcy through this,' Rauf concluded ruefully. 'It was a sorry day indeed for the Harris family when Lily's sister married her toy-boy charmer.'

'Even their home taken from them! In placing so much trust in a son-in-law the father was sadly at fault,' Talip Hajjar contended with a grimacing shake of his head. 'And yet, which of us do not wish to place total faith in a family member?'

'If you wish to interview Lily, I would ask you to wait until tomorrow. She has already retired for the night.'

'The young woman must be very distressed at what she has discovered since her arrival. At present, I see no reason to trouble her with an official interview. However, should that situation change, I will know where to find her.'

When the officer had departed, Rauf strode back to his bedroom where he found Lily fast asleep, one hand tucked beneath the pillow, her lovely face serene above the lace neckline of the nightdress she wore. Had he not been so conscious of the faint purple shadows that lay beneath her eyes, however, he might have been tempted to waken her again. He had put his own honour on the line in standing as her character witness in an effort to shield her from being associated in any way with her corrupt former brother-in-law. He had done so gladly. But enough was enough, he told himself with decision. In turn, it was only right that Lily should explain what she had been doing at that hotel with Gilman three years earlier and, most of all, why she should've chosen to lie about it. He needed to have that last tiny shadow of doubt in her cleared away.

Around dawn after a long and restful sleep, Lily opened her eyes and focused on the light filtering in. One of the bay-window shutters had been drawn back. Rauf was sprawled along the window-seat, one powerful jean-clad thigh lifted, his attention on her as she sat up with a start.

'What's wrong?' she whispered, instantly aware of his brooding tension.

'I couldn't sleep. There's something on my mind, something I've always wanted to ask you about…'

As Rauf sprang off the seat and strolled across to the foot of the bed like a prowling lion ready to spring on the unwary, intent golden eyes zeroing in on her, Lily snatched in an anxious breath. 'I haven't quite woken up yet…but go ahead.'

'On the last occasion that I stayed at your home in England…I saw you leaving a hotel with your sister's husband.'

In stark disconcertion at that announcement, Lily lost colour and stiffened, her memory throwing her back in time to a very unpleasant experience. 'But how could you have seen me?'

'My accountant was staying at the same hotel that weekend and I had just dropped him off. I was in the car park. I watched you go in and I waited for you to come out again—'

'But if you saw me *why* didn't you mention it?' Lily studied him in growing bewilderment and annoyance. 'Why didn't you just approach me?'

'Yet you later claimed that you hadn't left the travel agency at all that morning,' Rauf completed, ignoring her interruption.

The awful silence that fell sawed at Lily's ragged nerves like a knife. But as she understood how Rauf had set her up, pure unvarnished anger lit her eyes with sapphire fire. 'So, you sat and watched me and you deliberately didn't let me know you were there. Then you encouraged me to believe that it was safe to tell a harmless fib…and all the time,' she condemned with rising volume, '*all* the time, it was a trap!'

'You lied to me…if you'd told the truth, the trap couldn't have touched you,' Rauf countered, outraged that she should dare to question his behaviour when she was the one who had been in the wrong.

Lily thrust back the sheet and threw herself out of the bed. 'Are you telling me that in your whole life you have never once told a lie to avoid embarrassment?'

His riveting golden eyes hardened. 'You're evading the issue—'

'As far as I'm concerned the real issue here is your downright devious lack of decency in setting me up to fall like that!' Lily flung. 'What about trust? What about honesty?'

'You proved yourself unworthy of my trust,' Rauf spelt out with a contempt that stung her sensitive skin like a whiplash.

As Lily snatched in a deep, quivering breath, his brilliant gaze lodged to the natural prominence and movement of her breasts as she filled her lungs with air. Her face flamed at that male sexual appraisal and, even as he looked, her weak flesh tingled and swelled and the tender peaks pinched shamefully tight. In a defensive movement, Lily folded her arms over her chest. 'Did I really?'

'Entertain me…' Rauf traded with derision. 'Give me an innocent reason for telling me that harmless little fib!'

Lily compressed her lips so hard on that invitation that pallor spread round her mouth. That day three years back she had mounted a cover-up for the sake of appearances. She had lied sooner than admit that her supposedly happy family had been, from her point of view at least, very far from being what it had seemed.

'Brett was having an affair,' Lily admitted with a bone-deep bitterness that made Rauf's gaze lock to her angry, defiant face with even keener attention. 'Not for the first time either. Unfortunately that day Hilary was desperate to get hold of him because Gemma had been rushed into hospital and he wasn't answering his mobile phone. But I had a fair idea where he would be. Local gossip suggested he always took his little tramps to the same hotel!'

'You're saying that, while you and others knew that he was a womaniser, your sister *didn't* and you chose to protect her from that knowledge?'

'Why not?' Lily tilted her chin, knowing that Rauf, whose principles had about as much bend as ice, would concede no excuse for her concealment of the truth. But she had been much too scared of what the consequences of betraying Brett might have been and of how Rauf might have reacted to the reality that Brett's threats had trapped her into keeping that silence.

'And protect him too?'

Lily sent him a furious look for daring to attack her from that angle. Her father's unswerving belief that what went on in Hilary's marriage was none of their business had been the first chain that had bound her to secrecy. 'Of course not…Brett didn't come into it…Gemma was crying for her daddy. That's *all* I cared about that day!'

'It was a hell of a long time before you came out of that hotel with Gilman,' Rauf reminded her with sardonic bite.

'Because I had Reception ring his room and nobody answered,' Lily explained with angry embarrassment. 'I checked the bar and the restaurant but he wasn't there. I didn't want to go up to the room myself and I hung about for ages, but in the end, I had to sneak past the receptionist into the lift and knock on the door of that room to get hold of him!'

Rauf found that account extraordinary, yet she told her story as though what she had done had been her only obvious choice. He could have believed that she might have chosen to stay silent the first time that she'd been confronted with her brother-in-law's infidelity. But to ask him to accept that she would turn a blind eye to more than one affair and indeed lower herself to the level of tracking Gilman down to the place where he'd been staging his adulterous tryst stretched his credulity too far. Yet he registered that Lily saw nothing strange in what she had just confessed, saw nothing questionable in her own behaviour. Yet in forewarning Gilman, she had engaged in a complicit act of protecting his position in her family circle and shielding him from the consequences that he had so richly deserved.

'Why don't you just tell me the *whole* truth? You were infatuated with Brett Gilman!' Rauf condemned with icy, derisive force.

At that shattering allegation, Lily stared back at Rauf in horror and it was a second or two before she could even get her vocal cords to work for her again. 'How can you accuse me of something that sick?'

'In what you've just told me that's the only explanation that makes sense!' Rauf shot back at her with chilling conviction, his eyes cold and dark as a winter pool. 'I'm going to the *hamam* before I lose my head with you!'

The *hamam*? The bath house, she recalled abstractedly, that big domed building that she had noticed in the old courtyard and assumed to be no longer in use. There he was, the ultimate contemporary sophisticated male, about to go and immerse himself in the kind of ancient cultural experience that Hilary had urged her to try out as a tourist. As the door thudded shut in Rauf's imperious wake, Lily lifted a trembling hand to her pounding brow and sucked in a jagged breath.

You were infatuated with Brett! She shuddered in angry recoil. How very wise she had been not to tell Rauf about the distasteful treatment she had had to withstand from Brett until she had left home to attend college! No doubt, Rauf would be all too happy to construe those facts as proof of an inappropriate sexual attraction and credit his own outrageous accusation as being founded in fact.

But even aside of that concern, Lily was still in considerable shock at what Rauf had revealed about his side of events three years ago. Rauf had seen her at that hotel, had known that she had lied to him and, after she had seen him off at the airport on his flight home that same day, she had never heard from Rauf again. Was it possible that Rauf had dumped her because of that lie? At that idea, a storm of powerful emotion seized hold of Lily: anger, fierce regret, incredulous frustration. Could Rauf not understand that she had not had a choice?

No way was he taking refuge in the *hamam* where he no doubt believed that she would leave him in peace! Snatching up her light robe and pulling it on, Lily left the bedroom. Sonngul was silent and dim behind the closed shutters. Entering the old whitewashed passage that appeared to lead out to the bath house, she opened the door at the foot of it and found herself in an opulent changing room with a line of shower and changing cubicles, luxurious built-in cupboards and shelves of fleecy towels waiting in readiness. It was obvious that the facilities were still very much in current use. Shedding her nightwear, Lily yanked a bath towel from the nearest shelf, wrapped it round herself and, having opened one door to discover that it led into a massage room complete with couch, stepped through the other into the bath house itself. There she fell still in astonishment at the magnificence of her surroundings.

The giant domed roof, supported on a circle of superb marble pillars, was studded with little star-shaped glass inserts that filtered the dimness with shards of golden dawn light. The walls were a glorious rich expanse of antique tiles beneath which sat marble washing wells into which water flowed in constant refreshment. Round the perimeter of the central raised and stepped platform ran a walkway and in a further expanse a flight of steps ran down into a sizeable pool.

A towel lay abandoned there and even as she watched, Rauf's dark head broke the surface of the pool and he swam over to the steps to mount them. Nude and magnificent, water streaming from his big, powerful bronzed length and quite unaware of her presence, Rauf swept up the towel.

Her mouth running dry, Lily stared at him, watched his sleek muscles flex taut as he towelled his hair, burning colour warming her cheeks. 'Rauf...?' she breathed, disconcerted embarrassment engulfing the angry sense of frustration that had made her follow him.

In all his life, Rauf had never heard a female voice in the *hamam* and he could only be shocked. Some tourists might be willing to bathe in mixed-sex groups, but his own people were a great deal more inhibited and would not have dreamt of using even a private bath house at the same time as a member of the opposite sex. 'What are you doing in here?' he demanded, shaking out the towel and securing it round his lean hips in angry, instinctive circumspection.

Her legs uncertain supports, Lily sank down on the side of the warm central platform. 'I needed to talk to you about what you said…and *explain*—'

'And that could not have waited?' Rauf fired back at her.

'OK…once I lied to you but I want you to understand the situation as it was back then,' Lily persisted, her hands closing together in a taut movement. 'The first time I saw Brett with another woman, I was only fifteen. I told Dad about it but Dad made it quite clear that he didn't want to know and he was very angry with me—'

Taken aback by that statement, Rauf strode forward and came down by her side. 'With you? Your father was angry with *you*? But how could he be angry with you?'

'Think of how things were in our family by then,' Lily urged him heavily. 'Dad liked and trusted Brett. He'd already signed over our home to Brett and Hilary. He had allowed Brett to take on more and more responsibility at Harris Travel—'

'Your father was afraid to rock the boat,' Rauf slotted in with instant grasp of why the older man had embraced such an attitude.

'Dad believed that their marriage was their private business,' Lily confided with a helpless sob catching at her throat as her overwrought emotions threatened to get the better of her. 'Maybe to some degree he was right about that because Hilary *was* happy with Brett. She just worshipped him…she thought he was perfect but he was never faithful to her!'

Angry that he had not appreciated the complexity of the situation and that Lily should have been exposed to Gilman's sleazy habits when she was still so young and vulnerable, Rauf closed a supportive arm round her slight frame. Lily had been caught up in a sordid family secret and taught that she had to keep it quiet. That her father could have laid such a burden on her outraged Rauf, but that she should have continued to blindly respect that embargo even at the age of twenty-one and lie even to him in her efforts to cover up for Brett continued to trouble him.

'With us all still living in the same house and me feeling guilty at what I knew and what Hilary didn't know, it was horrible... I *hated* Brett and once I got away to college I hardly ever went home because I couldn't bear to be anywhere near him!' Suddenly, Lily was sobbing incoherently against Rauf, her slim figure shaking with the force of her disturbed emotions.

On the brink of asking why, if that was true, he had, prior to ever meeting her family and without even realising who the man was at the time, himself once seen Brett Gilman leaving her London apartment building, Rauf almost groaned out loud at the analytical precision of his own keen brain. So there were a few minor inconsistencies still to be cleared up, but he could not doubt the genuine pain that his angry accusation had caused and it would be cruel to probe deeper.

'I'm sorry,' Lily exclaimed raggedly. 'I'm sorry I lied to you—'

Rauf framed her distraught face with firm but gentle hands. 'It doesn't matter now...it's not worth your tears. Nothing that bastard Gilman did is worth a single tear!' Keen to distract her from the unhappy memories he had roused, Rauf lowered her down full length onto the heated navel stone and a slow smile curved his wide, sensual mouth as she looked up at him in surprise. 'Now since you are here and the rest of the household is still asleep, you might as well stay and enjoy the *hamam*.'

Lily pressed her palms down onto the surface of the marble platform beneath her and finally realised why she had been getting so warm. 'It's like a sauna...' she remarked with a soft laugh of appreciation. 'In fact this entire place is just amazing!'

Rauf lay down several feet away.

'Do the whole family bathe here together?' Lily asked.

At the ignorance inherent in that question, Rauf drew in a startled breath. 'Men and women don't usually share the facilities. But this once, we'll break with the rules and relax together.'

Good, clean, wholesome relaxation, Rauf told himself at the exact same time as he recalled how he and his friends as young boys had once fantasised about what might happen if a sexually adventurous woman were ever to enter the *hamam* when one of them was there alone. A ridiculous fantasy, for as a rule attendants were present and no such event could ever have taken place. But even so, at that point, his golden eyes flared and zeroed in on Lily's prone length of their own seeming volition. Tiny beads of perspiration already mantled the satin stretch of delicate skin below her throat. Where his libido was concerned, even looking at Lily was a mistake and all the effects of the cold dip he had enjoyed minutes earlier evaporated fast.

With a stifled groan, Rauf flipped over onto his stomach and endeavoured to control an imagination that for all his maturity was outrageously keen to zoom to the forbidden heights of male fantasy. Served him bloody well right, he told himself as his aroused sex ached with the hunger she stirred in him with such ease. Lily had said he was always totally wrapped up in himself and he could now be tormented by the knowledge that, while telling himself he only wanted to take her thoughts off the distress he had caused, he had for an inexcusable instant considered an erotic bout of passion in the *hamam* as a cure. A cure for what or whom? Where was his respect?

Lily turned over and stretched out uncertain fingers to touch his. 'You're very quiet.'

'I am only hot.' Making that charged admission, Rauf barely lifted his proud dark head.

His own family would be ashamed of him. That he had treated an innocent young woman, who had once loved him, as though she were one of the many practised lovers who had slept with him to sate a desire as basic and fleeting as his own. Lily was different. Lily had always been different, yet he knew that even three years ago he had fought that truth with every fibre of his being.

Disturbed by his tension, Lily sat up and whispered worriedly, 'You do believe what I told you about Brett?'

'Yes,' Rauf ground out, struggling to achieve mastery over a wild tide of imaginative excesses and concentrate on less dangerous and more important issues.

Shifting to within inches of him, Lily studied him and tingled. His sleek brown back was taut with male power and muscle and the smooth, powerful expanse glistened with moisture. A wicked pulse stirred at the heart of her and she pressed her thighs together in mortified acknowledgement of the fierce hold he had on both her heart and her body and rested back down again by his side. In the rushing atmospheric silence, only broken by the soft sound of running water, she snatched in a shaken breath for already her breasts felt languorous and heavy, the tender buds stiff and sensitive. He had taught her to want him and now the wanting came on its own and she could not control it.

'Maybe I should go back to bed...' Lily muttered shamefacedly.

Rauf glanced across at her, shimmering golden eyes encountering hers and reading a guilty longing there that smashed his own self-command. In the space of a moment, he reacted with all the fire of his passionate temperament. One hand closing into her tumbled hair, he brought his mouth crashing down on hers with a fierce, driving hunger that made her gasp in surprise and then in helpless pleasure.

'I can't resist you...I look at you and I burn,' Rauf breathed thickly, his desire for her a fiery blaze in his possessive gaze.

Her heart hammered as lean brown fingers flicked loose the end of the towel she had tucked in and spread the two sides apart to bare her body for his appreciation. Quivering, Lily watched his heated gaze drop to the wanton sight of her straining nipples, and then he ran his tongue over the prominent buds at the same time as he stroked apart her thighs and touched her where she was so very desperate to be touched.

Excitement took her in a wave of such blinding intensity that she was lost from that instant on. He spread her out like a willing sacrifice for his enjoyment and worked his erotic way down over her shivering, gasping length until the only awareness she possessed centred on the incredible heights of sensation her own body was capable of reaching. No, she could never have guessed that anything could be as powerful as her own total absorption in what he could make her feel. When a shattering climax gripped her and hurled her even higher, she could only moan and cling to him in ecstasy, only afterwards realising in extreme em-

barrassment and confusion that she had reached that ultimate height without his having made love to her and that,
indeed, all the pleasure had been hers and none of it his.

'Why…? I mean—?' Lily began to mumble as she
grabbed frantically at the towel beneath her, desperate for
its concealment.

Holding her close, Rauf smoothed her hair back from
her damp brow with an unsteady hand. 'I couldn't protect
you…I won't risk getting you pregnant,' he admitted in a
ragged undertone, for even her bewilderment at his restraint was more than his conscience could stand at that
instant. 'Go back to my room and sleep, güzelim. Later,
we'll talk.'

At that reference to pregnancy Lily tensed, realising
with dismay that she ought to have had sufficient common
sense to have foreseen that danger for herself. Pulling the
towel round herself with hands that were all fingers and
thumbs, she slid off the platform onto limbs that were still
weak as water and hurried back into the changing room
without looking back. He made her feel like a wanton. He
made her realise that she had not known herself until he
had shown her what passion was.

Lean, strong face grim with the gravity of thoughts that
he could no longer avoid, Rauf plunged into the icy pool.
From the very outset of Lily's arrival in his country, he
saw that he had been selfish, in fact reckless in his treatment of her. He had brought her to Sonngul, taken her to
his own bed and within a very little while, for gossip was
the very food of life to his people, half the neighbourhood
would be scandalised by that news. The standards of moral
behaviour that prevailed in the countryside were very
much higher than those of the slick city society in which
he moved and he had no excuse to offer on his own behalf.
Were word of the intimacy of his relationship with Lily to

reach the ears of the army officer, Talip Hajjar, the older man's belief in her respectability would sink without trace.

Rauf squared his broad shoulders and swung back out of the pool. The anger of the past had powered his initial aggressive attitude and the strength of his hunger for her had led him on to a dishonourable path before he had even registered the danger and the wrong of what he'd been doing. There was only one way in which he could make appropriate amends and protect Lily: he would marry her. With as much haste and secrecy as his wealth could buy him, he would get a wedding ring on her finger before any damage could be done to her reputation. She deserved his respect and the protection of his name.

CHAPTER SEVEN

ALTHOUGH Lily had not believed that she could sleep again, the minute her head touched the pillow she sank into a deep slumber. She wakened when a maid entered bearing a laden tray and was startled to realise that it was almost two in the afternoon; the snatched and broken hours of rest she had suffered since her arrival in Turkey had finally taken their toll.

Even as she ate, all she could think about was Rauf. Everything had happened so incredibly fast and hadn't she encouraged that? Hadn't she been ready to do almost anything to get a second chance with Rauf? Her troubled face flamed with guilty colour. She remembered her total absorption in Rauf at dawn, the shameless speed with which she had succumbed to her own passionate need for him and abandoned all control. For a lowering instant, she wondered how he had transformed her into a wanton creature without apparent self-will.

But then wasn't that her old insecurity and lack of self-esteem creeping back up out of her subconscious again? For the very first time, Lily told herself, she had reached out and taken what she wanted and she had wanted Rauf. She had always wanted Rauf. Acknowledging that, she was proud that she had found the courage that she had once lacked. She felt alive again and it had been too long since she had felt like that. When had she last been so happy? That summer with Rauf three years back. For Lily, that single fact outweighed all else for simple happiness had been in too short a supply throughout her life.

When she heard the noisy clickety-clack of a helicopter coming in low to land, she was putting on a grey short-sleeved cotton dress that Hilary had loaned her and she hurried over to the window to push back the shutter. From there, she watched Rauf spring out of the craft and stride towards the house. Just looking at the arrogant angle of his dark head, the hard, masculine perfection of his bold profile and the lithe power and command of his tall, well-built frame made her heart leap.

Rauf had had an exceptionally busy morning. He had embarked on the arrangements for a civil wedding in a remote mountain town where his name was unlikely to be recognised and where nothing any journalist might consider worthy of note appeared ever to have happened. He had then flown over to the former mining village to meet with the builders ripped off by Brett Gilman. Over a very long, typically Turkish male-bonding session, he had contrived to dissuade them from dropping the charges against Gilman. He was justly proud that he had achieved that feat without offending their need to demonstrate gratitude for the compensation he had paid.

He stopped with deliberate intent to chat to Irmak, his middle-aged and devout housekeeper, who had been most noticeable by the low profile she had embraced since Lily's arrival at Sonngul. Asking where Lily was, he referred to her as his wife while affecting not to notice the surprise, excitement and sheer relief that Irmak was incapable of concealing from him. Although he hated to tell an untruth, he already thought of Lily as his wife and, when it came to protecting her and redressing the damage he had done, he could not regret it.

Rauf strode up the stairs into the *basoda* and saw Lily, her lovely face warm with self-conscious colour, rising from the window-seat in the far corner to greet him. In one glance, he took in her ill-fitting drab dress that even his great-grandmother would have been challenged to admire and knew that his first gift to Lily when she became his wife would be a new wardrobe.

'I slept for absolutely ages,' Lily remarked in a stilted rush, assailed by a tide of discomfiture as she recalled her own abandoned response to his expertise in the *hamam*.

'I had some business to take care of,' Rauf drawled, catching her slim, restive hands in the gentle hold of his to draw her forward.

As Lily tilted her head back to look up into his dark golden gaze, familiar butterflies broke loose in her tummy, followed by a coiling twist of wicked heat that made her breath catch in her throat. She wanted that hard, handsome mouth on her own so badly she could almost taste it, almost taste *him*. A wanton little frisson of pure, helpless longing slivered through her taut figure.

'No, we're not heading back to bed, *güzelim*,' Rauf murmured in rueful reproach as if she had spoken that invitation out loud. Pressing her back down onto the divan behind her, he withdrew a step. 'Yesterday you asked me if I was in the habit of rushing into sudden passionate encounters with women and I said, "Not since I was a teenager"…an answer that should have given me pause for serious thought.'

'I don't understand…' As Rauf released her hand, a chill of fear spread through Lily's tense body. Was he saying that making love to her had been a mistake? A mistake he regretted and did not intend to repeat?

'Here in my home land, women may be the equal of men in law but if a woman embraces sexual freedom, she will lose her good name,' Rauf admitted, assessing her pale set face and lowered eyes with concern. 'If I keep you here at Sonngul, if we continue as we have begun, you will be regarded as my mistress and, no matter what happens in the future, your reputation will be irreparably damaged.'

His mistress. It had a sexy, adventurous sound to it, Lily conceded with a certain amount of pride in that designation. She loved him. Her bland workaday world had been transformed into one of colour, passion, sunlight and emotion. She did not regret sharing his bed. If she could be with him, she told herself that she did not care either what label people might put on her.

'I understand…' Lily focused with self-conscious care on the gorgeous rug on the floor. 'That's not a problem.'

Thrown by that unforeseen response, Rauf settled incredulous and startled golden eyes on her down-bent head. 'It's *not*?'

Emerging from her sybaritic vision of being Rauf's mistress and lolling about like Cleopatra on imaginary satin couches, Lily came back down to earth with a bump the minute she thought about how her sister would react to that same label. Hilary would be outraged if Lily accepted that kind of role in Rauf's life. But if that was all that was on offer, how would walking away from the guy she loved benefit her? With the conviction that she was abiding by the principles that she had already compromised but ultimately done the right thing? At that moment, that did not seem much of a consolation prize for surrendering the wonder of being with Rauf.

'Actually, being a mistress is something I'd have to think over…very carefully,' Lily admitted in a strained conclusion, cringing at an all-too-real image of Hilary coming all the way to Turkey just to give Rauf, who was not her favourite person, a piece of her mind.

'Or we could go for the alternative option,' Rauf countered, vibrant amusement brimming in his eyes before he veiled them in haste and reminded himself never, ever again to consider accepting Lily's first answer to a thought-provoking question. 'We could pay the price for being impulsive and indiscreet and just get married.'

Blue eyes widening to their fullest extent, Lily lifted her golden head and stared at him in thunderstruck amazement.

'A choice we have to make right now, I'm afraid.' Lean, powerful face taut, Rauf compressed his wide, passionate mouth. 'My family could never accept a woman who has lived openly with me as my bride. I owe both them…*and* you more respect than I have so far shown.'

Slowly, Lily began breathing again. 'You're serious about this. But I can't believe it. I can't believe you're suggesting that we marry just because we've…well, you know—'

'I know very well. I still desire you more than any other woman I have ever met, *güzelim*.'

Her eyes shone overbright and she screened them, her throat aching. 'But that's not enough, is it? Especially not for someone like you who's always hated the very idea of getting married.'

That was the moment when Rauf appreciated that he had expected Lily to accept his proposal practically before he finished speaking. Was he really that arrogant? Faint colour darkened his superb cheekbones as he braced himself to find persuasive arguments when he had already given her the only reason he considered important and it was simple, straightforward and sensible: he wanted her within reach twenty-four hours a day.

'People change.'

'But you said you would *never* change,' Lily reminded him helplessly.

Rauf spread lean, impatient hands wide. 'You shouldn't

believe everything you're told. That was three years ago. I can now see many ways in which a wife would be useful to me—'

'Useful…' Lily studied his lean, devastatingly handsome features with a sinking heart.

'I own three homes here in Turkey, an apartment in New York and another in London. A wife could take charge of them and be my hostess when I entertain…and eventually I believe I would like a child.' It was an ambition that had never before occurred to Rauf and when those words emerged from him of their own apparent volition he was as taken aback as she was.

'Honestly?' Lily gave him what could only be described as a misty-eyed look of mingled surprise and hope.

Recognising that, while she had seemed seriously underwhelmed by the amount of property he owned, that reference to his own previously unsuspected desire to multiply had struck a pure-gold chord with her, Rauf did not hesitate. 'Honestly,' he confirmed. 'So, how will you answer me now?'

'I'd like about four,' Lily confided abstractedly, fighting to keep her head out of the clouds, thinking that she could settle for caring and affection and children without too much difficulty. All right, he wasn't offering love. It wasn't the whole fairy-tale fantasy she might once have cherished in her secret dreams, but if Rauf wanted to marry her she was not about to turn him down.

Rauf expelled his breath in a startled hiss. *'Four?'*

'Two?' Lily bargained, recognising that she had been too frank, too soon.

'We'll think that over. I should tell you that I've already made a preliminary booking for us to be married in a civil ceremony tomorrow afternoon.'

'Tomorrow?' Lily gasped, while noting that he had had

the assurance to go ahead and embark on those arrangements before he had even mentioned marriage to her. However, taking into account his prior aversion to connubial bliss, she was much inclined to believe that a demonstration of such enthusiasm was encouraging and ought to be rewarded rather than censured.

'I intend to allow it to be assumed that we married before we even arrived at Sonngul. In that scenario, we then stole a couple of days alone here together before we could bring ourselves to share our good news with the outside world,' Rauf imparted very drily. 'My family will be so delighted that I've finally found a bride, I don't envisage awkward questions on that score. You will be received by my relatives as if you are the Eighth Wonder of the World. Throw in the news that you want four children and a red carpet will be rolled out from here to Istanbul.'

Lily blushed and then just laughed. 'Tomorrow...' she repeated afresh, still not knowing whether she was on her head or her heels. 'What will I wear?'

'Nothing likely to attract too much attention to us,' Rauf advised.

Obviously even a hint of bridal apparel would be way out of line. Her shoulders drooped a little. 'Do we have to get married as if we're the SAS on a covert operation?'

'If we don't want to publish the fact that we have been intimate without that legal tie in place...*yes*.' Rauf dealt her troubled expression a grim look of acknowledgement. 'It's my fault that it has to be that way, but once tomorrow is over we can put this unfortunate beginning behind us.'

'When I tell Hilary about this, she'll think I've gone crazy.' Lily sighed in a daze.

'As your husband, I'll be able to sort out the mess Gilman left in his wake without too much argument from your family,' Rauf contended with satisfaction.

'As sons-in-law go, I expect you qualify as quite a catch,' Lily mused with a dizzy smile as she studied him. He was drop-dead gorgeous and he was going to be hers *for ever*. She wanted to dance round the room, do mad, silly, childish things. Wow, she was getting married. Wow, was this really happening to her? Ought she to be worrying about the reality that he was behaving out of character? She worried at her lower lip, conscience stirring. This was a once very cautious, very clever and very grounded guy suddenly acting in a very impetuous way.

'Are you feeling OK?' Lily prompted grudgingly.

'Why wouldn't I be? By the way, I need your passport to fill out the forms I obtained this morning,' Rauf responded, his thoughts clearly on more practical matters. 'A copy of your birth certificate would be even more welcome.'

'I brought a copy in case I lost my passport.' Lily rifled her bag for both items.

'Excellent. You will also need a brief medical examination before the ceremony can go ahead. I have organised that with a female doctor in the same town,' Rauf explained. 'I've already had my own check.'

Lily accompanied him into a charming sun-dappled room lined with bookshelves that nonetheless rejoiced in all the high-tech equipment of an office. 'How soon do you expect to find out anything about that bank account in London?'

Rauf sent her a keen glance. 'Why?'

'Because once that's sorted out, I assume I can then tell my sister what her ex-husband has been up to,' Lily muttered ruefully, watching a frownline draw his winged ebony brows together. 'Rauf...Hilary mightn't have been expecting to hear from me immediately, but if I don't get in touch soon she'll start worrying. I could just send her a text message on my mobile…what about that?'

Rauf stilled. 'You have a mobile phone with you?'

'Yes…'

'So great was my distrust that, had I known of its existence yesterday, I would have taken it from you,' Rauf admitted. 'I hope to get the information I requested within the next forty-eight hours. Text your sister and tell her that you're fine. When I've got all the facts, we'll fly over to England together and break the bad news and the good news face to face.'

'It would be much better that way…' Touched to the heart by that thoughtful suggestion, Lily gave him a luminous smile.

Like a male drawn by a spell of enchantment, Rauf leant down and let his sensual mouth come down with sweet, drugging intensity on hers. As she trembled and leant into him for support, her body thrumming with eagerness, Rauf loosed an earthy groan of frustration low in his throat and thrust her back from him again. Brilliant eyes ablaze with hunger, he snatched in a ragged breath.

'Tonight I sleep down here…from here on in, we're respecting the conventions—'

'But if you're planning to pretend that we were married anyway…' Lily heard herself mutter and then she flushed crimson.

'But we know we're *not*…' Lean, strong face set with stubborn determination, Rauf swept up her passport and birth certificate and began to fill out the forms he had mentioned.

He had turned her into a shameless hussy at breathtaking speed, Lily acknowledged when she later lay in solitary state in his bed, so happy and excited that she couldn't sleep.

*   *   *

At three the following afternoon, Lily fingered the intricate new wedding band adorning her finger, breathed in the heady scent of the glorious bouquet of white lilies that Rauf had given her and joined him in thanking the government official who had presided over the ceremony.

'What did he say?' Lily pressed for a translation of the older man's response as Rauf guided her back out to the sunny, deserted town square where a car waited to ferry them back to the helicopter.

'That without a doubt you are the most beautiful bride ever to grace his humble office.' Angling a look of unashamed admiration over her, Rauf swung into the car beside her. In her simple straw sun-hat and pale pink dress, she was a perfect vision and he closed his hand with possessive pride over hers.

Back at Sonngul, they dined in the arbour and lingered over the coffee. Finally Rauf went off to call his family and make his announcement about their marriage. 'I'll just tell my father. He can break the news to the rest of the family.'

After relaxing in the shade a little while longer, Lily heard a funny little tune play and sat for a few seconds wondering what it was before it dawned on her that it had to be her mobile phone.

Retrieving the phone in haste, she stabbed the answer button.

'It's Brett…'

At the sound of that eerily familiar voice, Lily sat bolt upright in her cushioned chair, goose-flesh prickling at the nape of her neck. '*Brett?* What do you want?'

In the act of walking back outdoors, having made his brief call, Rauf heard Lily speak Brett's name and initial surprise stilled him in the hallway.

'What are you doing over in Turkey?' Brett demanded rawly.

Cold with the fear that Hilary's ex-husband had always inspired in her, Lily drew in a steadying breath. As she thought of the thieving, lying and cheating Brett had utilised to rob her family blind, angry, bitter disgust overcame that fear. But on the very brink of lambasting Brett for his lack of conscience, Lily froze on the recollection that Rauf did not want Brett to be warned that his criminal activities had been exposed.

'If you're trying to make trouble for me again or sticking your nose in where it's not welcome, you're going to *pay* for it!' Brett bit out nastily.

Lily felt sick: she couldn't help it. 'I have no idea why you should talk like that,' she muttered unsteadily. 'I'm just checking out the tourist trail over here for Hilary—'

'Don't lie to me...'

'Rauf and I have just got married,' Lily heard herself say and she winced at her own cowardice for even as she spoke she knew she was throwing up Rauf like a defensive barrier, hoping that Brett would be intimidated by that news.

'Married?' Brett questioned in audible disbelief.

'*Yes*...married, so just leave me alone!' Lily told him fiercely. 'You can't threaten me now and I want nothing more to do with you—'

'Kasabian has married you...well, fancy that!' Suddenly, Brett laughed as if she had cracked the best joke of the year. 'Oh, what a wonderful world it is and oh, what grief there is going to be if the bridegroom goes digging!'

'What are you talking about?' Lily exclaimed in angry apprehension, wholly disconcerted by that facetious response.

'When the balloon goes up, you had better protect me

because if you don't that marriage of yours might just end up in the dustbin too. See you soon, Lily!' As Brett rang off Lily was left clutching the phone and staring into space.

See you soon? Her flesh crawled at that concluding threat. Surely Brett could not mean that he was actually in Turkey? She checked where his call had come from and was relieved to be able to verify from the number that he had phoned her from England. Brett had only been trying to scare her. Common sense suggested that the very last place Brett would want to visit would be the scene of his own crimes. But *what* balloon was he expecting to go up? The villas he had never built? Or the likely scam that Rauf suspected over that misnamed bank account? But why on earth would Brett think that she would protect him? For the sake of her own family? For the sake of appearances? Well, this time around, Brett had no hope, Lily thought angrily. Never again and no matter what the cost would she allow herself to go in fear of Brett's threats.

Shattered by the revealing dialogue he had just overheard, Rauf hauled in a jagged, shuddering breath. Swinging away, caution making him resist the instinctive need to immediately confront Lily, he headed for the sweeping staircase instead. Just when he had finally mastered any urge to doubt Lily's veracity, he had found out the truth and, ironically, from her own lips. It was in itself suspect that Brett should contact Lily. Why, after such a bitter divorce, would he phone his ex-wife's little sister unless they had had a relationship that went beyond the usual boundaries? And why would he call at all when Lily herself loudly professed to hate him?

Leave me alone! You can't threaten me now and I want nothing more to do with you! At some stage, Lily must've been in love with Brett Gilman. And why not? Gilman was a good five years younger than his ex-wife, blond and boyish, a lightweight charmer, but still the type a lot of women went for. Lily might not have slept with her sister's husband, but evidently Gilman had been well aware of Lily's feelings for him, might even have encouraged them and had no doubt tried to use her to his own advantage. Perhaps guilt had brought Lily to her senses, perhaps she had even wanted to confess all to her sister. Had Gilman then threatened to tell his wife that Lily had been trying to tempt him into an affair?

As Rauf reached the top of the stairs Irmak brought him a phone and he answered it. It was his mother, Seren, and she was very, very excited, having only just heard from his father that her son had got married. Rauf said not a word while his mother implied that civil marriage ceremonies were only for heathens and announced that he had to bring Lily straight home to Istanbul so that they could enjoy a *proper* family wedding.

His grandmother came on the line next and pointed out that, since he had already made his poor family wait half their lives for him to find a bride, he really had to do the deed the traditional way and in style. Rauf again said nothing for it would have been a very great challenge to get a word in edgeways.

At that point, his great-grandmother, Nelispah, took her turn on the phone. First she told him how overjoyed she was before reminiscing at some length about how her own wedding celebrations had lasted forty days and forty nights. But she then let a little sob escape as she pointed out how shocked everybody would be when they learnt that her great-grandson had wed his bride without his own family present. Of course, the simple way out of that painfully embarrassing predicament, Nelispah added in a pathetic whisper, would be to stage another wedding and act as if the civil ceremony had never happened.

'Whatever you want, anything…' Rauf muttered, barely able to keep what he was hearing in his head for longer than five seconds but aware that even more guilt was hovering heavily on his horizon.

'Are you well?' Nelispah Kasabian trilled in a more lively tone.

'I'm fine.' Rauf breathed in deep and knew he was lying.

'Bring Lily home to us tomorrow and we will see to everything,' the old lady told him chirpily and the call ended much faster than he would have expected it to end, but as it was a relief at that instant he brushed aside his faint surprise.

Rauf's next conscious move was in the direction of the drinks cabinet. The phone call was already forgotten. He poured himself a brandy. He couldn't keep his hand steady and the rage of shock was now coursing through him like molten lava. But what was he planning to say to Lily? Indeed could he even reasonably say anything?

For, three years ago, he himself had come a poor second-best to Brett Gilman! He broke out in a cold sweat at that humiliating acknowledgement. But it was obvious. Everything in his past relationship with Lily that had once puzzled Rauf now fell into place: her former aversion to being touched by him, her surprising reluctance to visit her own family. When he had first met Lily in London, she could only have been trying to get over her love for her sister's husband and dating Rauf had most likely been part of that effort.

In those days, Lily had neither wanted nor needed nor loved him. She might have recently said that she *had* loved him then, but he saw that as a case of wishful thinking, a case of wanting to forget an attachment that still made her feel guilty. How could she ever have loved him when it was so evident that it had been Brett she still cared about? However, Lily did want him *now*, Rauf reminded himself doggedly. But did she still languish after Gilman in some secret corner of her heart? The fact that she had broken off the relationship didn't mean that she had stopped loving the guy, didn't mean that she wouldn't still try to save his useless hide if she got the chance! Since time immemorial supposedly sane women had been falling in love with hardened criminals they longed to redeem.

Furthermore, Lily would not be impressed if he killed Gilman with his bare hands because, right then, Rauf felt more than equal to doing that. Dead competition had a lot less pulling power. After all, how would Lily react when Gilman went to prison? Rauf expelled his pent-up breath in a shaken surge for he felt as if he were coming apart at the seams with not a shade of his rational intellect left intact. But Lily was *his*, wasn't she? No other man, nothing was about to get in the way of that reality. He was not going to lose her. Lily was his wife. Possession would be ten tenths of the law in his household.

He embarked on a second brandy. He would say nothing…he *could* say nothing! Falling in love with the wrong person was not a crime. Indeed, it seemed clear that Lily had behaved exactly as she ought to have done in the circumstances: there had been no affair. She had left home, stayed away and resisted temptation. He ought to be proud of her for that, Rauf told himself fiercely. But that was a step too far for him at that moment. He was still too devastated by what he had learned.

Pale and taut, Lily went off in search of Rauf. He was in the *basoda*, his back turned to the room as he stared out the window. Even in the state she was in, she noted the rigidity of his stance, the bunched muscles evident in his wide shoulders as he flexed them in a sudden abrupt movement that lacked his usual fluid grace.

'I suppose your family was sure to be upset about you marrying a woman they've never met...' Lily sighed unhappily, assuming that that was why he had not returned to the arbour.

Rauf closed his eyes for a second and then swung round, dark eyes veiled. 'No...nothing of that nature and you did meet my great-grandmother briefly,' he reminded her.

'They probably think you've made the biggest mistake of your life...just suddenly plunging into marriage with a stranger,' Lily suggested next, determined to know the worst.

Conscious that she was staring at him, Rauf made a major effort to concentrate. 'I told my father that we first met a few years ago. It was the fact that we opted for a civil ceremony and went ahead without their presence which caused some distress...I think—'

Her brow indented. 'You...*think*?'

His beautifully shaped brows knit. 'I believe I may have promised to take you to Istanbul tomorrow.'

'Oh...' Lily worried at her lower lip and then pressed ahead. 'I've something I have to tell you. Brett just called me on my mobile phone.'

Impressed by that honesty, Rauf studied her with dark eyes beginning to flare gold.

'I didn't let him know you were on to him!' Lily hurried to reassure him. 'He takes my nieces out on Friday evenings—well, at least he's *supposed* to, but most weeks he doesn't turn up—only presumably he did show yesterday and I bet one of the girls mentioned that I was over here. I suspect that that must have put Brett in a panic...so I said I was just here doing the tourist trail for Hilary...I also mentioned us being married...'

At the very top of her voice, Rauf recalled, striding forward to gather her straight in his arms. In the midst of wondering why Rauf had made no comment whatsoever about Brett's call, Lily was engulfed in an embrace so passionate that every powerful, angular line of his hard, muscular physique imprinted on her softer, more yielding curves. His tongue slid between her lips and plundered the tender interior of her mouth until she shivered against him, buried her hands in his thick black hair and surrendered to being lifted right off her feet.

'It's OK for you to make a habit of this…' Lily mumbled through reddened lips as he carried her off towards their bedroom. 'In fact, I rather like it.'

A vague recollection of Brett's call slid back into her mind. 'Aren't you annoyed about Brett phoning me?' she asked abstractedly.

'Not at all…obvious move for him to make.' Rauf contrived to answer with only the very faintest edge in his rich, dark drawl. 'But let's not talk about him on our wedding night, *güzelim.*'

'Wedding evening,' Lily whispered, feeling truly wicked and loving it and so grateful he wasn't one whit bothered about Brett having called.

CHAPTER EIGHT

SETTING her down beside the bed, Rauf removed Lily's sun-hat and embarked on the dozen hairgrips she had used to pile most of her glorious mane up out of sight.

Blue eyes bright as jewels, she looked up at him. 'I'm really happy,' she told him.

Who was she keenest to convince? Herself? Rauf shut down on that thought as soon as it surfaced but it led right on in to another. Right now, was she trying not to think about Brett? Of course, she was! How could she not be thinking of the bastard after he had just phoned her? He *had* to get rid of that phone. What had happened once was not going to happen a second time.

Recognising the aggressive thrust of his jawline, troubled by his unusual silence, Lily whispered worriedly, 'Do you have regrets about marrying me already?'

'Are you crazy?' Rauf launched at her with a force of instant rebuttal that struck her as a not quite convincing overreaction.

'It's all right to admit it…I'd sooner know…we did go into this a bit fast,' Lily conceded tightly.

'I can't imagine my life without you,' Rauf breathed tautly.

'But I've only been back in your life four days…'

'Four days is long enough with a lifetime ahead of us,' Rauf swore, backing off a step to throw off his jacket and wrench at his silk tie. 'My great-grandfather asked for Nelispah's hand in marriage the first day he saw her…'

'Love at first sight.' Lily was impressed.

'Or the fact that the men in her family said he was a dead man if he *didn't* marry her,' Rauf traded with sudden grudging amusement.

'I don't believe you…'

'You should. He was on a walking tour of the mountain villages. Quite by accident he saw Nelispah bathing in a river in her underwear and she liked the look of him so she told her brothers about it. Her brothers liked the look of him too because a Turk prosperous enough to take a holiday seventy-five years ago was a rich man on their terms. So forty days later he came back down the mountain with a wife and *said* it was love at first sight—'

Lily was fascinated. 'Why forty days later?'

'Village weddings used to be extremely lengthy affairs.'

'And your grandmother…how did she meet your grandfather?'

'With a great deal of cunning because in those days only parents arranged marriages and daughters were never allowed out without a chaperone. She dropped her scarf in the street, he picked it up and then it was the love-at-first-sight story all over again,' Rauf delivered cynically. 'My parents were the same. They got one glimpse of each other at a wedding and my mother went into a decline until my grandfather agreed to her marrying him…at the time he wanted her to marry someone else.'

'You have a very romantic family tree.' Lily tried not to say what was on her mind but in the end could not hold her curiosity in. 'So why did you have to be different?'

'Because the girl I thought I loved at nineteen was in love with one of my best friends…but she would *still* have married me because I was a richer catch.' The minute he'd said it, Rauf admitted that he was irritated with himself, for even his family had no idea how close he had come then to fulfilling their fondest hopes.

'Oh, no...that must have been awful for you,' Lily exclaimed with the kind of ready sympathy that made him grit his teeth. 'How did you find out?'

'I found them rolling about a bed at a party.' Rauf shrugged with expressive finality and went back to unbuttoning his shirt. 'It was no big deal. I got over it. Don't get the idea that I went off marriage because of that one bad experience.'

'Of course not...' Lily swallowed hard but she could imagine how vulnerable he must have been as a teenager, especially after having been raised on a careful diet of romantic love-at-first-sight stories by his shrewd but over-protective family. 'Was she one of the girls your relatives were hoping you would marry?'

'Yes. How the hell did we get onto this subject?' Rauf demanded.

Lily did something she had never done before. Seeing that a distraction was called for, she reached behind herself and undid the zip on her dress. Then she let the sleeves drift down her extended arms and the entire garment finally dropped in a heap round her toes.

The strangest ache stirred in Rauf's chest. He couldn't understand why he didn't laugh when she shimmied out of her dress with that taut, flushed air of daring and stood there revealed *in*...a full-length white cotton petticoat that revealed very little more than the dress had. 'Love the frills,' he breathed huskily.

Lily had forgotten she was wearing the petticoat. 'That dress is a bit see-through,' she muttered awkwardly.

'I wouldn't have liked that at all,' Rauf asserted instantly, moving fluidly forward to spin her round and peel her out of the petticoat.

Lily shut her eyes tight and leant forward as he let his mouth drift down the exposed line of her spine and a faint moan parted her lips. He caught her back against him, the shirt he still wore falling open to bring the smooth skin of her back into contact with the hard muscularity of his hair-roughened chest. As she quivered he whispered, 'Want me?'

'Can't help it...' Lily admitted.

'That's how it should be.' *But how much did she want him?* a little demon in Rauf's conscious mind taunted. Enough to turn down Gilman had circumstances been different? If she was content to settle for sex and look for nothing more, wasn't that his *own* fault?

'Exactly as it should be.' Rauf breathed in deep to continue with a roughened sexy edge to his drawl that made Lily's toes curl. Unclipping her bra, he let it fall and his hands curved round to mould the creamy swell of her breasts. 'You're my wife.'

A long, sighing gasp broke from her as he toyed with her taut rose-tipped nipples. A little flame had already flickered into a slow burn low in her belly. She squeezed her eyes tight shut in shame because she couldn't keep herself still, couldn't prevent her hips from squirming back into connection with the bold thrust of his arousal, couldn't think of anything but the pleasure to come.

He nipped at a tiny pulse point below her ear with his teeth and she jerked, already well on the way to meltdown. Not a sound did she make as he caught her up in his arms and tumbled her down on the bed.

'Look at me,' Rauf commanded.

Lily opened dazed eyes feeling as if she had 'wanton' stamped all over her. Her total inability to do anything but revel in his every caress still seemed vaguely indecent to her.

'What are you thinking about?'

'You…' A wave of colour washed her fair complexion. 'What you do to me.'

A brilliant smile flashed across his mouth and she rested back limp with incredible longing and love. He discarded his shirt. She watched his every move from below the screen of her lashes, breath catching in her throat at his sleek male beauty, heart thumping a little faster each time.

'You didn't use to think of me like that…' Rauf said thickly.

'I *did*…' As he gave her a disbelieving look, Lily came up on one elbow, struggling to find the right words to explain. 'It's just when I tried to make the…dream real, I…I couldn't…'

And why had that been? Because Gilman had had her loyalty and her love, Rauf reflected with vicious anger, swinging away with scorching golden eyes to toss his Rolex watch down on the cabinet.

'But I can now,' Lily muttered, noticing the hard set of his masculine profile, feeling the dangerous vibes emanating from his lean, powerful frame, trying to understand what she had said that had had that effect.

'I'll make every dream real,' Rauf intoned as though she had thrown down a gauntlet.

'You already do…' Lily confided half under her breath, absorbed in the insidiously sexy way he stripped off his trousers, noting the way the light coming through the window glistened over the fine furrow of dark hair running down over his hard, flat stomach. As the boxer shorts came off her eyes widened and she blushed for herself. The tiny beat of need already pulsing at the very centre of her throbbed.

'You make me so hot…' Rauf confessed, coming down on the bed with all the easy grace of a prowling tiger, plundering her reddened lips and letting his tongue delve deep in a darting, erotic imitation of a more intimate penetration.

The meltdown point came back to Lily fast. She just looked at him and dizzy joy grabbed hold of her because, now that they were married, she felt that he was finally hers and that emotional high of loving heightened her every response. He stroked the sensitive pink tips of her breasts, employed his knowing mouth there, shaped her tender flesh, worked his expert path down over her slender, gasping body, discovering pulse points she had not known existed and lingering there with a quite devastating effect on her self-control.

'I want this to be superlative,' Rauf muttered fiercely when she was way beyond grasping words of more than two syllables with any degree of comprehension.

She tried to touch him, she was desperate to touch him, smooth worshipping hands over the sleek, tight skin of his muscles, discover the solid wall of his chest with her palms and let her own lips explore and taste him as he tasted her. But every time she got anywhere near to fulfilling that need he pinned her back flat to the bed and overwhelmed her with more sensation. She was panting for breath, half out of her mind with excitement, her hips writhing long before he deigned to seek out the damp, aching heat at the heart of her.

'Rauf…' she moaned.

'Don't be so impatient,' he husked.

And somewhere around then, all sense of time and place left Lily. She didn't know what was happening any more. The excitement would build and build and then he would let it fall again until she wanted to scream and almost did. It was like being tortured with pleasure and her body was driven from one excruciating high of frustration to the next.

'Please…' she gasped.

'Please what…?' Rauf teased in a suggestive growl, sizzling golden eyes intent on her, enjoying his power over her.

'Don't stop…please don't stop,' she practically sobbed, begging, helpless, desperate for that unbearable need to be quenched.

He came over her and into her then, in one forceful movement and she almost passed out on the shock wave of incredible pleasure. Intense excitement took over and finally sent her flying over the edge into ecstasy and into an explosive shower of sensation that seemed to last for ever. In the aftermath, she felt drained, shell-shocked, still out of her own body, but she fought off the drowsy relaxation threatening to claim her.

Rauf rolled over and took her with him, arranging her over his hot, damp, sprawled length with a possessive intimacy that warmed her even when she was angry with him. As he closed both arms tightly round her and claimed another kiss, part of her wanted to just lie there and make appreciative noises, but another part of her wanted to kick him for his arrogant need to control her.

Golden eyes slumbrous with very male satisfaction, Rauf murmured, 'That *was*—'

'You at your most domineering…' Lily slotted in helplessly, lifting her tousled head, face hot but eyes reproachful.

Rauf laced long lazy fingers into her tumbled hair. 'So you can go for domineering in a very big way, *güzelim*,' he countered silkily.

Lily trailed herself free of him and suppressed a sigh, knowing she ought not to say what she wanted to say, knowing she was going to say it anyway because it hurt so much not to be loved. 'Maybe I wanted romantic…'

'Was Brett romantic?' Rauf asked in a tone of derision.

Lily blinked and then turned her head in confusion. 'What's he got to do with anything?'

'I was just curious,' Rauf drawled smooth as honey.

'Well, how would I know?' Lily grimaced and turned away again, thinking of the way Rauf had made love to her. Wild, inventive, exciting, full marks, she guessed, for technique, expertise. Was it such a turn off when she touched him? Was she so inept? And had he had to demonstrate his superior control with such humiliating completeness that she had ended up virtually begging for him to make love to her?

'I can do romantic…' Rauf asserted, tugging her back to him.

Lily stiffened. 'No…you can do sex.'

'Don't be crude…I don't expect that from you.'

Lily had never attracted an accusation like that in her life before. Crude?

'Sex…sex…sex…*sex*!' Lily hissed back at him like a furious spitting cat.

In a sudden movement, Rauf leant over her, propped his blue-shadowed jawline on the heel of one lean hand and studied her with wickedly amused golden eyes and a lazy, electrifying smile. 'Petticoat…petticoat…petticoat.'

The volatile speed at which Rauf could change mood had always disconcerted her. As Lily gazed up at him in chagrin he lifted her hand and threaded an exquisite diamond ring onto her finger next to her wedding ring. 'Romantic,' he pointed out.

'Where did it come from?'

'I put it under the pillow before I got into bed.'

Dumbstruck, Lily surveyed the glorious diamond cluster from all angles.

Rauf shifted with lithe masculine intent into a more intimate position over her. 'What's my score now?'

'Eleven out of ten...it's a very beautiful ring.' Lily sighed, feeling incredibly tired and knowing that she should have guessed that he would excel at one-upmanship. He loathed being criticised and it was their wedding night. It wasn't the time to tell him that, no matter how incredible he was in bed, no matter how intense her own response, having to plead for him to make love to her made her feel small.

He gave her a challenging look and then freed her to sprawl back across the pillows, all lithe indolence and gorgeous masculinity. 'But I would *hate* to be thought domineering.'

Impervious to hints and with a sleepy smile, Lily just wriggled back across the divide he had opened up between them and snuggled up to him as if he were a large teddy bear. 'I can hardly keep my eyes open,' she mumbled round a stifled yawn. 'And I don't want to look like a hag when I meet your family tomorrow.'

'You couldn't look like a hag if you tried,' Rauf groaned and tucked her under his arm.

But he then lay there smouldering and trying not to wonder if she would have gone to sleep on Brett. It was not that he was jealous or competitive, just that he was sensitive. She might be his wife but he was not about to make a fool of himself over her. So why was he staying in bed at ten in the evening wide awake but holding her tight as if she might be about to make a break for freedom? She was his wife; she wasn't going anywhere. And if she ever did, he would soon fetch her back.

All things considered, he decided that he felt remarkably good in spite of overhearing that phone call. He relaxed and listed all the physical things he liked most about her.

The smell and the feel of her hair, the smoothness of her skin, the blue of her eyes and the sparkle there when she smiled, the trusting way she curved round him. Trusting her, though, was still a challenge. He would never tell her that that diamond ring was three years old.

The next morning, Lily ended up in a mad rush. Having breakfasted in bed and promised Rauf she would only be half an hour, she went through everything in her luggage before finally settling on wearing a lilac skirt and toning shirt that looked more formal and smart than anything else she had with her. But when she emerged breathlessly from her room, she found Rauf's housekeeper waiting to intercept her in company with one of the maids who spoke English and who explained that Irmak wanted to give Lily the official guided tour of the house. Reluctant to risk causing offence, Lily smiled and just hoped that Rauf would be patient.

She loved Sonngul. It was a timeless, special place where she and Rauf had found each other again without the intrusion of the outside world. She was duly admiring the tall, serried ranks of pristine bedding in the huge linen cupboard when Rauf appeared and gave her a pained masculine appraisal. 'We have to be at the airport in less than an hour…what are you looking at sheets for?'

'Irmak was pleased,' Lily chided.

As they passed the door of the room he used as an office he paused and strode in to wait for the fax that was spewing out papers. Tucking them at speed into the file lying on the desk, he lifted the file and rejoined her.

'If I hadn't had work demanding my attention, I would've stayed in bed later.' In the shaded privacy of the path that led out to the helipad, Rauf claimed a hungry kiss that made her senses sing.

At Bodrum airport, Lily could only be impressed by the

sleek private jet that bore an MMI logo on the tail fin that awaited them.

'This is definitely how to travel,' she confided after take-off, studying the big, luxurious cabin and the amount of space surrounding her cream leather seat.

There was no response from her bridegroom and she smiled. Rauf was settled by the built-in desk opposite, a laptop computer sitting open in readiness, and his entire attention appeared to be consumed by the contents of the file he had brought with him.

Rauf had not realised that one of the faxes that had arrived before he'd left Sonngul was a response from the Turkish bank he had requested information from. There-fore when he initially glanced at the sheet in the act of leafing through the file, he could not at first grasp why Lily's name was printed there. And then he saw Brett Gilman's name as well and comprehension dawned at an excessively slow speed, for Rauf did not want to believe the evidence before his eyes.

There *had* to be a mistake. He angled a sideways glance at Lily from below dense black lashes. She was watching him and she gave him a sunny smile as if she had not a care in the world.

'Lily…' Rauf breathed without any expression at all.

Something in his voice made her tense and she looked at him and connected with piercing dark eyes. 'What is it?'

Rauf rose upright in one forceful motion and stared down at her, not a muscle moving in his lean dark face. 'You must've known that I was going to find out. Is that why you married me?'

A frown line indented her brow. 'What on earth is the matter?'

Rauf lounged back against the side of the desk, raw

incredulity and rage beginning to flame inside him. He had made it so simple for her. He could not credit his own stupidity. She had run rings round him! Had he really believed that he was the one controlling events? In the space of four days, she had got his wedding ring on her finger and, with that single achievement, she had made herself safe from all threats.

After all, it really didn't matter what he found out *now*, did it? She could afford to sit there and look politely enquiring, for he wasn't likely to prosecute his own wife, was he? He had married a thief. A lying, greedy little thief, who had conspired with Brett Gilman to defraud him of over two-hundred-thousand pounds. He snatched up the fax he had been sent and slung it down in front of her.

Lily lifted the sheet and tried to read, only to say, 'But this is in Turkish—'

'I'm sure you're capable of reading your own name and Brett's,' Rauf derided.

Lily looked up at him, frightened by the dark bleakness of his accusing gaze. 'My name and Brett's? What is this? Where did you get it?'

'You and Gilman opened that bank account for Marmaris Media Incorporated *together*,' Rauf spelt out so softly that she almost strained to hear him. 'And guess what, the little bad fairies have been in and they have emptied the account just as I expected!'

CHAPTER NINE

LILY lost colour as she finally grasped what Rauf was talking about. 'I did not open any bank account with Brett!' she protested.

'Yes, you *did*. It's down here in black and white in this fax,' Rauf pointed out with a rawer edge to his deep, dark drawl, his fabulous bone structure rigid, his pallor below his bronzed skin pronounced.

'Well, then, someone's made a mistake...or Brett has set me up. That's the only possible explanation!' Lily flung back at him, and no longer able to bear him standing over her like a very tall building casting a menacing dark shadow, she jumped up out of her seat.

'Don't waste my time. I don't believe you. You conspired with Gilman to steal from me!'

Lily was shaking from the terrifying and frustrating awareness that she seemed to have been tried, judged and found guilty on the spot. Nor did Rauf appear to have the slightest intention of hearing a word she said in her own defence.

'That's not true. How can you even *think* that I could do such a thing?' she asked with shocked distaste. 'For goodness' sake, I'm your wife!'

Dark colour accentuated the taut angularity of Rauf's superb cheekbones and he spread both hands into a violent arc. 'Yes, you're my bride. That's quite a coup I gave you, isn't it? You must've been laughing all the way down the line at me—'

'I've had enough. I am not even going to try to talk to you in the mood you're in—'

'Oh, yes, you *are*,' Rauf bit out, closing strong hands to her wrists before she could complete her intent and drop back into her seat again. 'And I warn you…your usual, very effective ploy of turning on the waterworks won't silence me this time around!'

'At this moment, Rauf Kasabian…' as Lily wrenched her wrists free of his hold her blue eyes burned like the sapphire centre of a flame over his lean, darkly attractive features '…I wouldn't cry if you tied me to a stake and stood over me with a match!'

'At last a piece of *good* news. I also think you need to know when and where my suspicions about you and Brett began—'

'Inside your own very colourful imagination?' Lily sliced in.

Incensed by that scornful suggestion, Rauf flashed her a scorching look of pure intimidation. 'Tecer Godian…do you remember him?'

Disconcerted, Lily muttered, 'Mr Godian, your last accountant…the one who came over to England to check out Harris Travel three years ago?'

'Tecer was an astute man. That last day that I stayed at your home, you said you had to go into the travel agency to help out because an employee was ill. Tecer was there checking the accounts and so were you and Brett. Even though Tecer saw nothing that he could quite put his finger on, he saw enough to rouse his concern—'

'What do you mean?'

'Tecer had no idea that I was personally involved with you. Later that same morning, he said to me, "The son-in-law, Brett…and Lily, the wife's little sister, there's something wrong and disturbing about that relationship.

They don't behave like *normal* family members do with each other.'''

At that revelation, Lily tensed with surprise. Had Tecer Godian noted her fear and nervous tension at being alone, as she had initially believed, with her brother-in-law in the front office? Her considerable relief when she had first registered that the older man was in the back room going over the accounts and her chattiness once Brett had mercifully gone out? Yes, as Rauf so rightly said, Tecer had been a shrewd man, as an outsider seeing what those more closely involved did not see. But Rauf had taken those astute warning words and put them into a very different context.

'I paid no heed, asked no questions, but I understood what Tecer meant all right after I had waited in that car park until you finally emerged from that hotel with Gilman!' Rauf grated in contemptuous condemnation. 'Even though you refuse to admit it, all along you were in love with your sister's husband—'

'That's *not* what the man saw between Brett and I,' Lily argued with furious emphasis. 'It's a pity that you never asked Tecer to explain what he meant—'

'Do you think that I would've lowered myself to the level of discussing you with a man who was not only my employee, but also a family friend?' Rauf scorned.

'You might have saved us both a lot of unhappiness if you had,' Lily condemned with angry reproach, finally understanding what had first made Rauf suspect the nature of her relationship with her sister's ex-husband. 'But perhaps you took out of his words what you *wanted* to believe—'

'And what the hell is that supposed to mean? We're straying too far from the main issue here,' Rauf condemned with brooding force, shimmering golden eyes pinned to the flushed, taut oval of her face. 'My every worst suspicion about your integrity has been proved correct.'

'And that's a relief for you, isn't it?' Lily studied him with wondering eyes, bitter anger of a strength she had never before experienced building even higher inside her. 'To believe that I loved Brett, that I only took you home so that you could invest in Harris Travel and that all the time my sole motivation was to enrich Brett and get my own greedy hands on your wretched money?'

His aggressive jawline clenched, for it infuriated him that, even when he set the evidence before her, she was *still* striving to portray herself as a poor little victim. 'Yes...that is what I must believe.'

Lily loosed a jagged little laugh. 'Then I'm sure this can't come as a surprise to you either...I very much regret getting married to you yesterday!'

'Like hell you do!' Rauf countered in a lion's roar of rebuttal that shook her where she stood. 'If you weren't my wife, I'd be handing you straight over to the police!'

'Hopefully they would be a little better at investigating crime than you are...then that's their job,' Lily traded with dulcet sweetness of tone, her powerful sense of injustice mounting as she had considered all the sins that he seemed to believe her capable of committing. 'So go ahead and hand me over because I don't ever want to have anything more to do with you!'

'Let me tell you, after a few nights in a prison cell you wouldn't be half so bloody impertinent!' Rauf launched back at her, incensed by what he interpreted as a ridiculous declaration. 'And what's more, you married me knowing that you were protecting yourself from any threat of imprisonment—'

'My goodness...' Lily trilled, burning spots of furious

colour now highlighting her cheekbones. 'I ought to write a book about my life as a wicked, unscrupulous adventuress…only I don't seem to have been a very successful one, do I?'

'What's that supposed to mean?' Rauf demanded.

'Well, according to you, I loved Brett and cheated, lied and stole for him, but somehow never had the guts to be wicked enough to sleep with him,' Lily recounted with wide, questioning eyes. 'Then there's also the small fact that I'm virtually broke until my next month's salary arrives, so I appear to have been a total loser as an embezzler as well. And, lastly, my crowning error seems to have been to marry the guy I robbed…which hardly promises me the happiest of secure futures…does it?'

His devastatingly handsome features clenched hard. 'If I receive one more facetious response from you—'

'You'll what…divorce me?' Lily slung at him bitterly. 'Well, I'm ahead of you there…*I* want a divorce!'

Rauf went rigid at that threat and instantly asserted, 'You can forget that as an option—'

'*And* you can keep your lousy money too. I'll think myself lucky just to be free from the nightmare of being tied to a guy who has no faith in me at all!'

'You're married to me and, I'm afraid, there's no escape clause in this lifetime,' Rauf heard himself launch back at her in an even blacker rage.

'I'd rather take my chances with the police…I'll hand myself over, get this sorted out,' Lily declared again, her chin taking on a defiant tilt.

'Don't be stupid!' Rauf seethed, out of all patience with her.

'I did *not* put my name on that bank account—'

'Stop *lying* to me! Gilman needed your name on the account because you're a director in Harris Travel, which means that he can lie and say he opened up that account as an employee at *your* request! As a director, you can be held liable for the disappearance of the funds I invested in the firm!'

Without warning, Lily's knees betrayed a lowering need to knock together in fright and she sank down into a seat on the other side of the cabin. She had not realised that the awarding of that directorship by her father from which she had yet to earn a single penny meant that she could be put in such a position. Now at last she understood why Brett had smugly informed her that *she* would have to protect *him*. Very probably, Brett had put her name on the account with his own for the reasons that Rauf had just defined, and no wonder her sister's ex-husband had crowed when she had announced that she and Rauf had just got married! Brett would also have foreseen the unlikelihood of Rauf choosing to press charges over the stolen cash when to do so would cast doubt on his own wife's honesty. But Lily could not abide even the idea of Brett Gilman escaping his just deserts!

Having thought that through, having cast her mind back over the misery Brett had sentenced her to suffer when she'd been too young and naive to know how to fight back, Lily breathed in slow and deep to strengthen herself. She was very pale but she folded her trembling hands together on her lap and finally lifted her head high. 'Well, it's better that I should be held liable than either my sister, who has children, or my father, who has a string of health problems,' she pointed out with quiet determination.

'When are you going to stop talking nonsense?' Rauf demanded, throwing his arms wide in incredulous roaring frustration, for the dialogue was travelling into fanciful realms that made no sense at all to him. 'There will be *no* prosecution about the missing money for the very obvious reason that I am not prepared to label my wife a thief!'

'But that would mean that Brett got off scot-free...and *I* couldn't stand that,' Lily stated. 'He has caused my family and me so much unhappiness that I want him to pay for it even if it means that I have to tolerate suspicion being cast on me for a while. But I firmly believe that the truth will come out...and that in a law court his guilt would be proved.'

Rage beginning to dwindle in the face of such agonisingly naive statements, Rauf studied Lily with the inescapable conviction that once again, against all belief and the apparent facts, he had jumped to the wrong conclusion. From where he stood, he could practically feel the flames of idealistic, self-sacrificing fervour Lily exuded and he snatched up that fax from the Turkish bank's head office with a hand that was far from steady.

Her name was on the account but that was not actual evidence that she herself had put it there. After all, what was to have prevented Gilman from taking another blonde woman into the bank to open that account and supplying a piece of identification purloined from Lily without her knowledge? Nor had she been a co-signatory on the account, which meant that the withdrawals had been made solely by Gilman. In fact, Rauf registered at that second, calmer reappraisal, Lily's name being on that account bore all the hallmarks of a clumsy attempt by Gilman to cover his own tracks and spread the blame. Suddenly, he was certain that he would discover on further investigation that Lily's signature on opening the account had been forged. Lily had reacted with honest anger and she had no fear of talking to the police. Furthermore, no *sane* guilty woman would seek to defend herself and engage his support by angrily abusing him and threatening to divorce him!

'We're going to be meeting my family in little more than an hour,' Rauf drawled not quite levelly because, so shattered was he by the belief that he had again misjudged her, clinging to what he saw as a safe certainty felt comforting. He had fallen once more into the same chasm of doubting her and he cursed the jealousy that had clouded his judgement. He knew he had to redress the damage he had done and grovel…only grovelling was not a talent that had ever come to Rauf in any shape or form.

Lily gaped at him. 'I'm hardly going to go ahead with that now—'

'But you have convinced me that you are innocent of any blame. I wasn't prepared for that fax and I overreacted to it and I must apologise to you. A more level-headed examination of the facts does indeed suggest that Gilman has tried to frame you,' Rauf asserted levelly.

'But it's obvious that you've never been able to trust me,' Lily said tightly. 'Your suspicions about Brett and I have always been there and have never gone away—'

'But it's all out in the open now and I'm finally convinced that there was *never* anything inappropriate in your dealings with Gilman!' Rauf swore with fierce intensity, dark-as-midnight eyes glittering, revealing his steadily rising stress level, for he was not accustomed to Lily not listening to what he said or rejecting his pleas in his own defence. 'Right now, I don't give a damn about him…I'm much more concerned about *us*—'

'Why would that be? Even though you couldn't trust me, you still married me. I find that very strange and extremely hurtful,' Lily confessed a little unsteadily, for tears were prickling at the back of her aching eyes. 'But that's the way it is and what it means is that you have never *cared* for me as you ought to care for me—'

'You are totally wrong about that.' Getting tenser by the

second, for Lily was in a frame of mind he had never before had to deal with, Rauf strode forward and attempted to reach for her hands. However, Lily only shrank back and coiled her fingers even tighter together, resisting even his touch.

'No, I'm not…from start to finish, all you can ever have wanted from me was sex and all you still want from me is sex…and you're *so* obsessed with the sex that you were even willing to stay married to a woman whom you once believed not only carried on with her own sister's husband, but also stole from you!' Lily condemned in tight, jerky spurts of words. 'I don't think that's healthy. I don't think anyone would think *that* was healthy—'

'And put like that it doesn't sound healthy either.' Rauf groaned with a feeling grimace, dropping down into an athletic crouch beside her seat and striving to gain eye contact because he knew that always got results. 'But to write off everything that is between us as just sex is outrageous—'

'I think so too, but then I also think you're just orientated that way,' Lily muttered ruefully, finally looking up to connect with his beautiful dark golden eyes and the rather stunned light that was starting to take root there. 'You're also the most dreadfully suspicious guy I have ever met—'

'But only over this *one* single issue,' Rauf interrupted at speed, desperate for her to make that distinction. 'And that issue is that bastard, Gilman, and every single misunderstanding that has occurred between us has related to him in some way—'

'I really don't think you can call accusing your own wife of being a thief…a misunderstanding,' Lily interrupted heavily.

'I have a very quick temper and an obvious and very

regrettable propensity for leaping to the wrong conclusion when it comes to you.' Pouncing on her hands the instant her slender fingers loosened their grip on each other, Rauf tugged her upright out of her seat. 'But that is only because I care so *much* about you. I'm sorry, *güzelim*.'

But just then even the rare sight of Rauf looking drawn and taut with strain could not make Lily swerve in her convictions. She had always loved him and as a result felt she had been much too willing to overlook the flaws in their relationship. But now harsh reality had punctured her happiness and she believed all that she had said to him. She also reckoned that he was hopeless at working out what went on inside his own complex head. After all, he had looked very shocked when she had said that his sole interest in her was sex, but when had he ever mentioned anything else?

'I'm sure you can explain to your family that you made a mistake getting married to me in such haste—'

'They'd still expect me to bring the mistake home,' Rauf cut in with helpless irony as he settled her back in her seat and did up her belt because the jet was soon to land. 'In the Kasabian family, when you get married, you *stay* married—'

'Maybe the Harris women have a fatal habit of marrying the wrong men—'

'Putting me on a level with Gilman is hitting *way* below the belt—'

'If we've already split up, it would be less embarrassing for you when I'm helping the police with their enquiries,' Lily told him flatly.

'You won't be helping the police with *any* enquiries!' Rauf countered with savage determination, his adrenalin racing at the mere mention of such a development, and at the same time as he spoke he saw his entire system of values take a metaphorical lurch into new and dangerously disturbing territory. For hadn't he too once believed that it was always right to speak the truth? Only now intelligence was suggesting the direct opposite. That fax made Lily look like an embezzler and Gilman's co-conspirator.

Just then, Rauf registered that there was *nothing* that he would not do to protect Lily from potential harm. And if protecting Lily meant lying and burying the evidence to ensure that she could in no way be tainted or threatened by Gilman's crimes, he would do it without hesitation. He was shocked by that awareness but he only had to look at Lily and think of her in a prison cell and every one of his ethics and every one of his principles went into hiding and what was left immediately assured him that the ends justified the means.

As the jet landed Lily was in a complete daze at the far-reaching decisions she had made. Yet, Brett *had* to be stopped. Enough was enough. What other awful things might Brett do if he was left free? Was she to spend the rest of her days in secret fear of the man? And why should Rauf lose his money because he had married her? That would be wrong. It would be even more wrong if Rauf or his family were to suffer embarrassment through his having married a woman in danger of being arrested for fraud. After all, if she could be held liable as a director of Harris Travel for the disappearance of Rauf's investment that also meant that she could be held liable for the villa fraud as well…didn't he realise that she saw that now?

She shivered, cold, quaking dismay springing her from her daze. How could she even blame Rauf for his distrust when that fax had thrown up such seemingly convincing proof of her involvement in the matter of those missing funds? How could she blame him when she had yet to tell him the real truth about her relationship with Brett?

Possibly, Rauf had always sensed that he was not hearing the whole story and that was why he had stayed unconvinced. Yet what was the point of telling him now when they were parting? For of course they *had* to part; if Brett was to be prosecuted, if Rauf was to be protected from scandal, there was no option on that score.

So, she would hand herself over to the police, rather than wait for the police to catch up with her. Had she only fired off threats of divorce at Rauf because she was hurt and angry with him? When it came to crunch time, the thought of being without Rauf was like offering to have her heart removed without an anaesthetic. At the same time, when she thought of how proud Rauf was and how attached he was to his family, she could only cringe about how he must be feeling now at the knowledge that he had married a woman who could well be accused of criminal activity in the near future.

'I don't blame you for thinking I might be guilty,' Lily said miserably to Rauf as they walked through the airport at Istanbul. 'You had grounds—'

'No. No matter what life throws at me, I should *always* have faith in you—'

'How can you have when I come from a family who harboured Brett for so many years?' Lily mumbled, sunk in despair. 'It's better that we get a divorce and you just don't mention me to anyone. If your family was unhappy because you'd got married without them present, with a bit of luck they won't have discussed our marriage with any friends yet and it can all be hushed up.'

In a sudden move, Rauf closed a lean hand hard over hers as if divorce were so imminent he had to retain a bodily hold on her to prevent it. 'I've upset you a great deal but there is no reason whatsoever for you to be talking about divorce—'

'I don't think you'll feel that way if I'm arrested—'

'Should there be the slightest risk of that, I'll get you out of the country,' Rauf declared with a lack of hesitation that unnerved Lily, for it seemed to suggest that there was indeed a fair chance of such a situation developing. 'But as I will not be pressing charges against Gilman for the payments I didn't receive, that cannot happen—'

'But you really *wanted* to prosecute him—'

'You matter to me a great deal more than revenge,' Rauf confessed, brilliant golden eyes clinging to her delicate profile. 'Your peace of mind is also of paramount importance to me.'

Unwilling, it seemed, to cede him the ability to have even that amount of tender feeling for her, Lily sighed. 'Of course, you don't want to risk this whole horrible mess coming out in public and upsetting your family.'

In frustration, Rauf herded her into the waiting limousine.

'You can just take me to the police station and I'll get it all over with,' Lily muttered as he swung in beside her. 'It's not right that Brett should be let off—'

'It's not right that my wife should talk about divorcing me!' Rauf bit out rawly, tawny eyes shimmering over her startled face as he closed two strong hands round her tiny waist and propelled her toward him. 'Or that when you're innocent you should even consider approaching the police with a very complicated and confusing story which they might not understand as well as I do. Both subjects are closed. *For ever* closed—'

Held only inches away from him, Lily quivered, her tense body leaping with wicked immediacy to the proximity of his, her mind a bemused sea of anxious thoughts. '*But*—'

'Turkish wives don't argue with their men. Ask my

great-grandmother, Nelispah,' Rauf advised silkily. 'You can try to manipulate me in a thousand much more devious ways…that's OK, that's perfectly acceptable and even expected of you. But you *never* argue outright with me—'

'You quite like it when I argue with you—'

'Not on this issue, *güzelim*. Take it from me…I know best on this subject—'

'But when the police find out I'm a director in Harris Travel and Brett's prosecuted for what he did with those villas—'

'You're Lily Kasabian. You have done nothing wrong, therefore you can have nothing to fear,' Rauf murmured in a soothing and yet subtle forceful tone, striving to get through to her with every fibre of his extremely determined personality and seeing no reason to concern her with the reality that the police were already aware of her directorship in the firm. 'As my wife, your place is by my side and if any problems arise you can rest assured that *I* will move immediately to deal with them on your behalf.'

'I wish life was like that,' Lily mumbled, almost laughing in spite of her anxiety, for he really, truly believed that there was nothing he could not handle, nothing he could not make right.

'Life with me *is* and will be like that, I promise you,' Rauf intoned, golden gaze dropping to her sweet lush mouth, and then he tensed, fighting an almost irresistible urge to kiss her with all the pent-up passion that the mere mention of losing her had roused in him. *All you have ever wanted from me is sex*, however, was one of those Lily-type accusations calculated, Rauf knew, to come back and haunt him at the worst possible moments. The very last thing he wanted to risk was stoking that impression any higher. Tonight, when they went to bed in his riverside home, he would just *hold* her, nothing else. Maybe for at least a week he should hold her…

As if she were being tugged by elastic, Lily leant slowly forward in an inviting way, heart banging hard up against her ribs, lips tingling, but Rauf set her back from him with a preoccupied air. Truly embarrassed by her own disappointed expectations, Lily sank back into the far corner of the seat and endeavoured to concentrate instead on the exotic busy streets of Istanbul. Would everything be all right as he had sworn it would be? Ought she to listen to him? Then there was no point kidding herself that she wanted a divorce, was there?

Was he obsessed with sex? Rauf was engaged in a rare phase of the uneasy self-examination of the type that only overcame him in Lily's vicinity. He would have said he was obsessed with *her* but she had to have worked that out for herself by now. When a man married a woman within the space of four days, it was hardly a sign of sophisticated cool and restraint, was it? Especially when the same guy had spent all of his adult existence swearing that he was never, ever going to get married. Did Lily think sexual restraint was a demonstration of romantic and considerate caring even in marriage? Suddenly sexual restraint was looming on his horizon like a very big black cloud.

Apprehensive about meeting his family, Lily preceded Rauf into the enormous mansion where three generations of Kasabians lived. 'I bet you anything they don't like me—'

'Nelispah liked you on sight and my father will be very grateful that he won't have to listen ever again to the three of them bewailing the shame of me still being single,' Rauf informed her cheerfully.

From the minute the maid opened the door of the big, gracious drawing-room and Rauf's mother, Seren, a small, rounded brunette in her fifties emerged proffering an animated welcome in English, Lily did not have the time to be nervous. His father, a tall, craggier version of Rauf with greying hair, smiled at her. His grandmother, Manolya, was the quietest of the three older women. Nelispah Kasabian grasped Lily's hand in her frail fingers and just looked at her with tears in her bright old eyes and nodded to herself with satisfaction.

'You and I are to fly over to England tomorrow,' Rauf's father, Ersin, murmured to his son under the cover of the feminine chatter filling the room.

'Say that again,' Rauf invited.

'This promises to be a *very* traditional wedding,' Ersin stressed. 'We must ask Lily's father if he will accept you as a bridegroom—'

'He's already got me whether he likes it or not,' Rauf pointed out, inflamed by the prospect of being parted from Lily for even a day. On reflection, however, he conceded that he would not have dreamt of marrying one of his own countrywomen without first approaching her family. 'Yes, you're right. That is how it should've been done—'

'By the time you return alone to your own home this night, you will have discovered one of life's unhappier truths,' Ersin contended. 'Nelispah cannot be fought. She'll be upset if you argue and distraught if you refuse her expectations and how can you risk that?'

Rauf frowned. '*Alone*…what are you talking about?'

'If you're not ready to admit that you are already married, you can hardly be seen to take Lily into your home. I understood that you had agreed to that extraordinary arrangement on the phone last night—'

'Rauf…' From across the room, his great-grandmother was already stretching out a gnarled hand in greeting.

Go home alone without his wife? Were they all out of

their minds to ask such an outrageous thing of him? That wasn't a pound of flesh, that was an entire body they were demanding!

'Until we celebrate your wedding, Lily can stay here with us as if we are her family too. That way there will be no gossip,' the old lady told him happily.

Faint colour accentuated the tough slant of Rauf's high cheekbones and his hands clenched. He encountered his mother's pleading look of appeal and he compressed his lips on a surge of such anger at the idea of being separated from Lily that for an instant he could not trust himself to speak.

'You can visit Lily all the time,' his grandmother, Manolya, suggested in her usual anxious, placating fashion.

'But Rauf cannot be alone with her…otherwise people will say she is fast and we are too free,' Nelispah warned.

'Lily is already my wife,' Rauf said drily.

'You will have her all your life…but this is the time of betrothal, courting and bridal visits.' Nelispah spoke as though the entire process were on a calendar written in stone and ignored his reference to the civil ceremony. 'You will not want it said that you valued your bride so little that you would not follow custom or convention.'

Rauf breathed in very deep. 'What was customary over seventy years ago is—'

'The forty days and the forty nights,' his great-grandmother slotted in, making him turn pale. 'But we do not live in a village and, although I think it is sad that weddings must now be rushed affairs with less honour, I know a week must suffice.'

Even relieved of the threat of the forty days and nights, Rauf swallowed hard. A week. A week; seven days without Lily. He was aghast. But he looked down into the old lady's trusting, hopeful dark eyes and he knew that he had brought the situation on himself and that he could not, must not, hurt her any more than he already had with a blunt refusal. He jerked his proud dark head in grim acknowledgement and agreement. Ninety-nine per cent of the anguished tension holding the rest of his relatives rigid vanished at that point.

'I must explain this to Lily…in private,' Rauf murmured flatly.

'Leave the door open…' Nelispah urged after frowning over that request.

Lily had absorbed the byplay of that curious little scene without the remotest understanding of what was happening. Rauf's mother had kept on talking to her while watching Rauf with a wary air of pronounced strain. But now everyone *but* Rauf seemed happy and relaxed. His lean, strong features were brooding and taut.

Extending a lean hand to Lily in silent invitation, he led her into the room next door. 'What's wrong?' Lily hissed in an urgent whisper.

Rauf growled something raw in Turkish under his breath and strode over to the tall windows, wide shoulders emanating wrathful tension. 'I've been stitched up by a ninety-two-year-old punishment professional!'

'Sorry?'

Rauf expelled his breath. 'Last night, I heard you talking to Brett on the phone—'

'You…*did*?' Lily exclaimed, trying to recall what she had said, belatedly grasping yet another unfortunate factor that might well have contributed to the angry distrust with which Rauf had reacted to the discovery that her name was on that bank account set up by the other man.

'While I was thinking about that…the matriarchs phoned me and I *may*…I really don't remember…have given Nelispah the impression that I was willing to go through with another more traditional wedding to soothe the feelings I had offended,' Rauf advanced. 'She is refusing to acknowledge the civil ceremony, which means that she expects us to behave as if we are still single.'

Lily frowned in bewilderment.

'Which entails you remaining here under this roof *without* me until we are married for a second time,' Rauf extended grittily.

'Oh…*oh*!' Lily gasped. 'But that's ten days away—'

'A week—'

'No, your mother was quite clear about the date.'

'Nelispah is behaving as though our marriage in the civil ceremony was an elopement…*ayip*…something shameful!' Rauf ground out.

'I don't think so. She's very accepting of me and I'd hate to cause her pain.'

Rauf explained that he was flying over to her home the following day to visit her family.

'Oh, no…Hilary hates you!' Lily exclaimed in dismay.

Rauf watched Lily pin an embarrassed hand to her parted lips as she appreciated what she had let drop and he squared his big shoulders, brilliant golden eyes shimmering.

'Because of the way you dumped me three years ago,' she added with a rueful grimace.

Every sin he had ever committed was now coming back to haunt him, Rauf reflected with a fatalistic feeling.

'What about the villas…and all that?' Lily prompted worriedly. 'Hilary and Dad need to be told.'

'Yes,' Rauf acknowledged. 'I'll take care of that—'

'I should phone her—'

'Yes, but only tell your sister that we've got married—'

'*But*—'

'I'll handle the bad stuff with tact. I'm family now too.'

His lean, gorgeous face serious, Rauf reached for her hands and drew her close. 'When I get back, I'll take you out on that tourist trail you were supposed to be following and nobody can argue about that. That's your duty to your sister, who sent you over here, and a business necessity.' A slumbrous smile of satisfaction slashed Rauf's handsome mouth as he came up with those indisputable facts, calculated to impress even his great-grandmother, who would be unable to even conceive that Lily might either travel round alone or fail to fulfil a family obligation.

'I'm still going to miss you,' Lily confided unevenly.

Rauf suppressed a groan. 'I should be back within forty-eight hours...but all of a sudden that seems a long way away...why *is* that?'

Lily wrapped her arms round his neck and pressed into connection with his lithe, powerful frame. In the very act of claiming her lush mouth with hungry heat, Rauf heard a slight cough sound from the hall and he yanked his dark head up again, eyes a blaze of smouldering gold. 'The second wedding can't come fast enough for me, *güzelim.*'

The next twenty-four hours were very busy for Lily. When she phoned her sister, Hilary was stunned to be told that Lily was already married to Rauf, but mollified by the discovery that there was a second, more formal wedding yet to come. 'Of course, we'll come over for it. With a little luck, Rauf will send his private jet to fetch us and we'll save on the fares,' Hilary teased with considerable amusement. 'In return, I will desist from calling him a rat and endeavour to like him.'

Lily got on like a house on fire with Rauf's relatives and she was warmed by their affectionate lack of reserve with her. A large ceremonial tea party was held that afternoon and every female acquaintance of the Kasabian family appeared to be on the guest list. Lily was the centre of an admiring and curious throng. When Nelispah Kasabian became tired, Lily accompanied the old lady into another room where she lay down on a couch to rest for a while.

As Lily emerged again a beautiful brunette, garbed in an elegant white trouser suit, intercepted her to introduce herself. 'I'm Kasmet. I've known Rauf almost all my life…'

Lily smiled.

'But I was very surprised to hear that he was getting married,' Kasmet continued, sultry dark eyes bright with scorn. 'After all, he's still in love with me!'

Lily blinked in bemusement. 'I beg your pardon?'

'Of course, Rauf would never admit that…even when we had an affair earlier this year. He's too stubborn and proud,' the other woman informed Lily, her ripe mouth setting into a thinned line. 'But I want you to know it. I want you to *know* that you're second-best. He fell for me when we were teenagers and he never got over me.'

Blue eyes wide with astonishment, Lily spoke her own first thought out loud without meaning to do so. 'You must be the girl he caught with one of his friends!'

Infuriated coins of scarlet bloomed over Kasmet's cheeks.

'I'm sorry…I didn't mean to say that,' Lily mumbled, shaken by the other woman's spite, but also rather embarrassed by her own rejoinder.

Unexpectedly, Kasmet loosed a bitter laugh. 'I had too much to drink and I was foolish. I didn't love my late husband but because I lost Rauf, I married him. Could you really imagine my preferring any other man to Rauf?'

After that revealing little speech, Lily was pale and, reluctant to listen to any further revelations from the aggressive brunette, she murmured, 'Please excuse me…'

The afternoon continued but, from that point on, Lily

was challenged to play the part of the happy bride-to-be. Her mind was in turmoil. Oh, yes, she knew Kasmet had been angry and resentful and keen to cause trouble and pain. She wasn't stupid, was she? But the problem was that Lily also knew Rauf and the darker side of his forceful character. No, not even if he had expected to love Kasmet to the end of his natural life would Rauf have forgiven her infidelity. For that reason, Kasmet's assurance that she had had a recent affair with Rauf had upset Lily the most. For why would Rauf have got involved again with a woman who had once betrayed him? The answer to that question could only be that Rauf must still have had strong feelings for Kasmet.

For the very first time ever, it occurred to Lily that there might actually be a very good reason why Rauf had only ever talked of 'caring' for herself: if all along he had loved another woman. A woman he wouldn't marry. Although he had had an affair with Kasmet, he had ended that relationship as well. He had succumbed to temptation and then fought temptation off again, which was exactly how Lily could picture him behaving: at war with himself from start to finish. Her own heart had sunk to the soles of her feet. Somehow she had contrived to come to terms with the idea that Rauf didn't love her, but the wounding suspicion that he might feel much more for another woman savaged her.

Fresh from his successful manoeuvres in England, and having stopped off in Paris to do some necessary shopping on the way home, Rauf watched the staff struggling to cart the vast bulk of the carved *düzen* up the steps of his family home. Lily would be surprised and pleased that he was getting into the spirit of the occasion. In eight days, fourteen hours and thirty seven minutes, Lily would be back where she belonged by his side, in his home and in his bed. While he waited, he would use that time to demonstrate what a wonderful husband he could be: romantic, tender, caring, considerate, sensitive, generous, patient, magnanimous and tolerant. Having mentally scored a little tick beside each and every one of those desirable qualities in the performance of which he was certain he could excel, Rauf made his entrance and was relieved to find Lily alone.

'Lily…' he breathed with satisfaction.

'Rauf…' Lily feasted her shadowed blue eyes on him for one painful moment and managed a lacklustre smile. In a lightweight dove-grey suit cut to fit his lithe, wide-shouldered masculine physique by a master tailor with designer style, Rauf looked utterly breathtaking: sleek, sexy, gorgeous. There he lounged, the ultimate fantasy fix of masculinity, his face slashed by a vibrant smile that was capable of melting the skin off her bones…*but* Lily blocked him out in self-defence and wished her rapid heartbeat had as much pride.

'Miss me?' Rauf demanded.

'We've been very busy here…' Lily compressed her soft mouth. After all, it had taken Rauf *two* days to return to Turkey while his father had flown back after less than twenty-four hours away. But then, just as she should have known, she told herself wretchedly, if her body was out of bounds Rauf had been in no great hurry to get back to her and that had hurt. But was it fair for her to judge him on that? After all, who had tossed and turned every night just thinking about *him*? Thinking blush-making stuff too, Lily reminded herself guiltily, recalling the depth of her own longing for him and striving not to cringe where she sat.

At that point a welcome diversion was created by the entry of a staggeringly large wooden trunk adorned with ornate carving.

'The *düzen*…my first gift to you.' Resisting a dangerous urge to ask what was the matter with her, reminding himself that his former lack of faith in her had undoubtedly made her think less of him, Rauf opened the trunk and removed a large box from the interior.

'What's this?' Lily asked weakly.

'The fabric for your wedding dress…it's an old custom for the bridegroom to provide it—'

'I thought you weren't into customs…' Determined not to be impressed, Lily lifted the lid on the box. An exquisite expanse of fine gold hand-embroidered white silk was revealed. 'Oh…it's out of this world!'

'Don't let me see it—' Rauf warned as she almost cast aside the lid in her excitement.

'I thought you chose it—'

Rauf dealt her a discomfited look that tugged at her heart no matter how hard she tried to resist. 'Don't mention it to the diehard traditionalists in the household, but I want it to be a surprise when I see you in your wedding gown. I just listed what I thought you might dislike and left the choosing to the designer. She's flying in this evening for a dress fitting.'

Lily replaced the lid on the box and studied him with dreamy eyes because she found that confession so sweet. It was no use. She couldn't be cool with him when she just loved him to death. So maybe he did have a slight secret yen for the svelte, sophisticated Kasmet but she was not about to make the crucial error of questioning him on that score. Of course, Rauf had had at least one significant relationship and if she pried into his past he would resent it and what would she gain? Well, he would tell her the truth if she asked, only sometimes the truth could hurt, she acknowledged ruefully.

'I picked everything else in the trunk,' Rauf assured her.

'Everything else…?' Lily got up to look down into the trunk in amazement. It was packed full of clothes.

'Your trousseau…' Rauf regarded her with vibrant amusement. 'But I had the lingerie conveyed up to your room in a separate delivery. I didn't want to embarrass you—'

'You bought me lingerie…?'

'And what a very erotic experience that was, *güzelim*.' The smouldering undertone Rauf utilised made her mouth run dry and her face burn.

The tap-tap of his great-grandmother's stick warned that they were about to have company. Nelispah Kasabian's delight at the sight of that giant trunk was touching to behold.

'Of course, I'm being shortchanged here,' Rauf murmured silkily to Lily under cover of the chatter that erupted between their companions.

'How?'

'You're supposed to respond with the equivalent of a bottom drawer you've been industriously sewing and collecting up since childhood,' Rauf shared mockingly. 'Full of useful items like saddlebags and saucepans and hand-stitched sheets.'

'I'm afraid you're getting the equivalent of the barefoot bride,' Lily confided, dying to ask him how he had got on with Hilary but reluctant to do so with an audience around.

Half an hour later, Rauf took Lily in his car to see the sumptuous Topkapi Palace, the former residence of the Ottoman sultans for over four hundred years, out at Seraglio Point.

'So what happened with my sister and why hasn't she phoned me?'

'She said that she would prefer to talk to you when she comes over for the wedding—'

'Stop holding out on me…was she horribly upset about the villas?'

'Shocked and extremely angry. However, your father has agreed that I can buy into Harris Travel in the guise of an equal partner,' Rauf divulged. 'Hilary said no initially but I can be very persuasive.'

'Yes, I know…' Studying his bold bronzed profile, picking up on the quiet note of satisfaction in his dark, deep drawl, she smiled. 'You've been incredibly kind—'

'Your family has had a rough ride and I wanted to help—'

'Do you always get what you want?'

'You were one of my very few failures.'

'And Kasmet?' The other woman's name just leapt off Lily's tongue before she could prevent it.

At the traffic lights, Rauf turned with a frown to shoot her a piercing dark glance of enquiry. 'Where did you meet her?'

Lily coloured. 'She was at the tea party your mother held—'

Rauf grimaced. 'My father still does business with her father but I'm surprised she had the nerve to attend. None of us like her—'

'According to her, you're *still* madly in love with her.'

Rauf dealt her a thunderstruck appraisal. 'Eleven years after I caught her in bed with someone else?' he demanded in disbelief.

'Then I gather you didn't have a recent affair with her.' Lily was amused.

Car horns shrilled behind them as Rauf's stunned scrutiny flared into outrage. 'Are you out of your mind? She told you *that*? Right,' he ground out, nosing the sleek sports car with aggressive intent into another lane. 'I'm going over to her home to settle this now—'

'No…no, please, let's not do that!' Lily exclaimed in lively dismay.

'If she wants to tell lies, she can pay the price of being called on them!'

'I wouldn't give her the satisfaction—'

'Of knowing that you believed every word?' Rauf slotted in. 'You're my wife and I won't be slandered, nor will I allow anyone to upset you—'

'I'll be much more upset if you make a big thing of this!' Lily warned. 'I just wondered…that's all, but now I can accept that Kasmet was simply being spiteful—'

'After I've spoken to her, she won't indulge that spite around you again,' Rauf swore, untouched by her efforts to cool him down.

Never had Lily been so relieved as when Rauf hit the bell on a smart townhouse some minutes later and nobody answered the door. Extravagantly handsome features still set with fierce determination, he swung back into the car.

'I can't wait to see the Topkapi Palace…' Lily murmured placatingly.

Rauf looked at her, beautiful eyes molten gold, and then he leant over her, closed one hand into the silky fall of her pale hair and kissed her with a drugging, possessive fervour that electrified her sensation-starved body. She tipped her head back, heart hammering, heat burning between her slender thighs, opening her mouth to his, trembling at the hungry thrust of his tongue into the tender interior.

With a driven groan, Rauf jerked back from her, dragged in a shuddering breath. 'You see…I lose it with you. I can't even keep my hands off you in public places!'

'So let's go somewhere private,' Lily heard herself whisper without even thinking about it.

'No...no sneaking around,' Rauf spelt out, shooting the powerful car into reverse without looking back at her.

Lily had flushed to the roots of her hair. 'We're married!'

'We've got a lifetime ahead,' Rauf asserted grittily, resisting temptation with all his might.

An hour later, in the shade of the garden pavilion in the fourth courtyard of the palace, Lily gazed at the spectacular view of the sea but her thoughts were far away. She was thinking of the immediacy with which Rauf had responded to her questions about Kasmet and comparing his blunt honesty with her own secrecy about Brett. Time and time again, she had utilised weak excuses to persuade herself that she need not tell Rauf the unpleasant truth about Brett's behaviour towards her, but in only telling half of the story she had not been fair to either herself or Rauf.

Drawing in a slow, strengthening breath of the hot, still air, Lily said in sudden decision. 'I have something I want to tell you...I want you to understand why I've always been scared of Brett.... No, *please* don't interrupt me!'

In open disconcertion, Rauf made a sudden movement towards her, his frowning dark golden gaze probing her pale, taut face.

In the uneasy silence, Lily jerked a slim shoulder. 'I suppose it's an irrational fear but, the trouble is, he got to me when I was too young to know how to handle a bully like him,' she confided heavily. 'That first time I saw Brett with another woman and told Dad, Brett realised that it was me who had seen him. He picked me up at school and acted like a madman because he wanted to frighten me. He shouted at me and threatened me and he said if I ever talked about him again, he would tell Hilary that I'd been...you know...er...trying to come on to him...'

As a revealing look of revulsion entered her stricken

gaze in remembrance Rauf bit out something savage in his own language and reached for her knotted hands to take them in his. His big, powerful frame was rigid and the pallor of deep shock and anger was visible round the harsh set of his firm mouth.

'Even now, I don't know whether or not Hilary would ever have accepted my word against Brett's. She was crazy about him and she thought he was very handsome and was always saying how other women flirted with him. So I kept quiet but that wasn't enough for Brett. He hated me and he liked to make me squirm,' Lily muttered through compressed lips. 'For three years until I was able to leave home to go to college, Brett tormented me.'

'*How?*' The demand left Rauf like a bullet and his hands closed taut over hers.

'When there was nobody else within hearing, he'd make sick comments and stuff…' Lily grimaced and had to steel herself to continue. 'About how my body was shaping up…and crack dirty jokes…he never laid a hand on me but I was very scared that, some day, he *would*.'

Rauf closed supportive arms round her slight, shivering figure and eased her close. He himself was literally shaking with rage. He knew that if he ever got within twenty feet of Gilman, he would want to kill him. He snatched in a great, shuddering lungful of fresh air in an effort to get a grip on himself. What a blind fool he had been not to put what he already knew together and come up with a more likely scenario than Lily having been in love with her sister's husband! Now he knew what his former accountant, Tecer Godian, had been warning him about: the older man had seen Lily's fear of her brother-in-law.

'I didn't tell Dad because I was afraid that Brett might carry out that threat he'd made and say that *I* had been trying to tempt *him*. How could I prove that he was lying when the truth would have wrecked Hilary's marriage? Who was going to even *want* to believe me? I couldn't cope with the situation—'

'Of course you couldn't...' Rauf breathed in a fierce undertone. 'You should have told me about all this three years ago.'

'I was afraid you might think that I'd encouraged him and, anyway, keeping it all a secret was too much of a habit by then,' Lily confessed jaggedly. 'It was because of Brett that I started to dress the way I do—I was trying not to attract his attention. It was only when I went to college that I realised how different I was from other girls. I was so nervous around the boys...I didn't even like being looked at because that reminded me of Brett and it made me feel unclean.'

'It's all right...all right,' Rauf muttered thickly, attacked by a raw mixture of guilt and even fiercer regret for his own lack of understanding.

'But I fell in love with you, so I tried harder with you,' Lily admitted painfully. 'After you...well, a good while after you, I went for counselling because I knew it wasn't normal to feel the way I did.'

For a long time, Rauf just held her close. When the sound of voices warned that they were about to be disturbed, Rauf took her to the restaurant. At a quiet table on the garden terrace, he asked her about the counselling sessions she had attended.

'Realising that I was letting Brett ruin my life was the start of my recovery,' Lily said with a wry grimace. 'All that awful secrecy in my family, the trapped feeling I used to have in our home when he was around, the feeling of helplessness...that was what made me the way I was. I let Brett turn me into a victim—'

'I didn't help...' Rauf closed a hand over hers, his dark-as-midnight eyes overbright with unashamed pain at what she had endured. 'All along I sensed your reserve with me and it made me uneasy and too quick to ascribe other motives to your behaviour. But I did nothing to encourage your trust, *güzelim*.'

Her throat thickened and she swallowed hard. It felt good that there were no more secrets between them. He had not doubted her either; no, he had not doubted her for even a moment. A winging sense of joyous relief filled her, natural colour warming her cheeks again, any lingering tension banished.

The days that followed in the run-up to their wedding were a hive of constant activity. Having given her a whistle-stop tour of the main sights of Istanbul, Rauf whisked Lily off to the sites that lay further afield. She made initially nervous inroads into her new wardrobe and discovered that, although the clothes Rauf had chosen for her were a feast of designer style, none could be deemed either revealing or daring, and she teased him about the reality that his great-grandmother admired most of the outfits too.

Midweek, Rauf brought her the evidence of Brett's attempt to involve her in the fake bank account he had set up at that Turkish bank in London. Rauf had obtained a copy of the signature purporting to have been hers and the handwriting did not even bear the slightest resemblance to her own.

'A clumsy forgery which would fool nobody,' Rauf pronounced with satisfaction. 'Gilman believes that he's very clever, but he falls down on all the finer details.'

'Yes, but what's going to happen about him?' Lily asked anxiously.

'I don't want you to let a single thought of him enter your head.' His lean, dark features full of purpose, his dark golden eyes rested with concern on her troubled expression. 'Trust me. He will be dealt with. Never again will he be in a position to hurt you or anyone else in your family.'

By the end of that week, cheerfully anticipating her own family's arrival for the wedding festivities, Lily hugged an entire series of happy memories to herself and myriad impressions of the rich Turkish culture.

Visiting the exotic Spice Bazaar in Istanbul where the heady aroma of countless spices mingled in the air had been interesting, but walking hand-in-hand with Rauf had been a quieter and more private pleasure. The fascination of wandering round the amazingly intact ruins of the ancient city of Ephesus had been eclipsed by the preparation with which Rauf had ensured that he could answer her every question as well as any guide and his touching pride and love of the history of his own country.

She had done the tourist trail for her sister: she had bathed in the warm pools on the blinding white travertine terraces at Pammukkale, wandered through an astonishing underground city once inhabited by early Christians in Cappadochia and, at Dalyan, sailed alone with Rauf along the sleepy river bounded on all sides by swaying thickets of reeds. They lunched from a hamper in the shade of a chestnut tree and she listened to him tell her about childhood picnics, attended by anything up to seventy members of his extended family and still a favoured way of entertaining.

'You like picnics too...' Rauf made that reminder in a teasing undertone as he banded both arms round her to tug her into closer connection with his long, powerful frame, sending a chain reaction of intense awareness travelling through her. 'Only a very obstinate male would have fought the inevitable as long as I did. But I must confess that it is three years since I chose the diamond ring you wear on your finger.'

'Sorry?' Blue eyes wide, Lily met his burnished golden gaze in pure shock. 'You bought me an engagement ring *then*?'

'Yes…I intended to ask you to marry me that last weekend I spent with you in England,' Rauf confessed ruefully. 'But your niece, Gemma, was ill when we arrived and your father was preoccupied with that contract. Even I could see that it wasn't the right time to stage a romantic proposal…I expected to fly back to see you the following week.'

'And instead you saw me with Brett at the hotel and assumed the worst.' Lily was overjoyed that, in spite of their imperfect relationship three years earlier, Rauf had wanted to marry her even then, but she was also hurt that they should still have parted in misunderstanding and lost each other.

'I was too proud to confront you with my suspicions. I will regret that for the rest of my life,' Rauf admitted in a roughened undertone, his hard-boned, devastatingly handsome features taut. 'But the conviction that you could never have felt for me what I felt for you because you loved someone else made the most sense to me then. I was devastated…*too* devastated to judge the facts with intelligence or even keep them in proportion. To save face, I said nothing.'

'Oh, Rauf…' Lily whispered unsteadily, her gaze clinging to his remorseful gaze. 'Do all Turkish men have such colourful imaginations?'

'We're a passionate people. But, between you and I, the greatest weakness was that too much had been left unsaid,' Rauf conceded half under his breath, rational thought receding as he met her beautiful eyes and struggled to concentrate.

Electric tension hummed between them in the stillness of the grassy glade.

'Left unsaid…' Lily echoed, mouth running dry, a languorous, wanton heat infiltrating her with the desire that he could awaken so easily.

Rauf bent his dark head and kissed her just once in a stormy surge of pent-up hunger that made her quiver with almost painful longing. As he jerked back from her, releasing his breath in a stark exhalation at the cost of that restraint, she was tempted to haul him greedily back to her.

'In a couple of days, we'll be together again, *güzelim*,' he framed unevenly, catching her hand in his, pressing his lips to the centre of her palm. 'I want that to be special.'

They flew back to Istanbul in the helicopter that afternoon. At the airport, Rauf received a call informing him of a dispute at one of his newspapers. With a long-suffering groan, he tucked her into the limousine that would take her back to his family home while he went into the office to deal with the threatened strike. 'I might not be able to make it back in time to take everyone out for dinner as I promised,' he warned her ruefully.

He did not make it back in time and, although the rest of his family went ahead on their own, Lily was feeling tired and, aware that her own relatives would be arriving the next day, she decided to have an early night instead. After a light meal, she was about to do exactly that when a maid entered to tell her that she had a visitor. Every evening over the preceding week Lily had sat with the matriarchs and received formal visits and gifts of gold jewellery from the older generation of guests who would be attending their wedding. On this occasion, shorn of the helpful support of Rauf's family, Lily could only hope that her unlucky last-minute visitor spoke a little English.

But when she walked into the airy drawing-room the welcoming smile on her lips fell away as her aghast gaze landed on the tall, lanky blond man posed by the fireplace.

Brett gave her an unpleasant smile. 'Didn't I tell you I'd see you soon?'

CHAPTER TEN

FOR possibly the longest moment of her existence, Lily was frozen to the spot.

She stared back at Brett with a choking sensation of fear in her throat and goose-flesh prickling the nape of her neck. Yet even as she looked, incredulous that he should have taken the risk of not only coming to Turkey, but also daring to visit her at the Kasabian home, she was noting the changes in him. Usually a very sharp dresser, he was wearing a crumpled suit, he needed a shave and his pale blue eyes were bloodshot. As he moved forward she got a whiff of the sour smell of alcohol and recognised the en-nervated edge of desperation he was striving to conceal.

'I know all the Kasabians are out tonight,' Brett told her in an effort to intimidate her. 'I watched them leave the house and I'm sure you'll want to keep this little courtesy call of mine to yourself.'

'And why would I want to do that?' Although Lily's own voice emerged faint in tone, she was already over-coming her old instinctive fear of him and seeing him with the eyes of a woman rather than a frightened teenager. The family might be out but the door onto the hall was still ajar and she knew that one of the staff would be hovering out there, waiting to receive the expected request for tea for her visitor.

'How could you think I would be dumb enough to credit that Rauf Kasabian had married you within a couple of days of your arrival here? Give me a break,' Brett mocked. 'The wedding of the year doesn't take place until the day

170

after tomorrow. I was able to read that in one of Kasabian's own newspapers. But the wedding of the year *won't* take place at all if I start shooting my mouth off...'

In spite of the knowledge that she could have nothing to fear from Brett and that she and Rauf were already married, a cold, chilled sensation infiltrated Lily's stomach, a hangover from the bad old days when Brett had seemed to second-guess her at every turn. She wanted to call the police but realised that she did not even know what phone number she needed to use, nor how she could contrive to leave Brett alone without making him suspicious.

'Won't it?' Lily lifted her chin and studied him with loathing. 'You can't hurt me any more.'

An unattractive flush of colour mottled Brett's sallow skin. 'Can't I? Let me share a secret with you. Kasabian's cash payments on that contract were never made and, sooner or later, the news that that money has gone missing will emerge and all hell is going to break loose at Harris Travel. But if you tell Rauf about that now, you'll be in big trouble too.'

'I don't think so,' Lily countered drily without turning a hair in receipt of what Brett had evidently hoped would be a bombshell.

Brett's full mouth twisted. 'Well, that just proves how stupid you are, because when I set up another bank account to syphon those payments off I put *your* name on that account too! If I go down, I'll take you down with me. I'll say we had an affair and that you were in on the theft every step of the way with me. So, you'd better keep quiet until you get that wedding ring on your finger—'

'Still the same old threats and they're sounding very tired,' Lily cut in with angry contempt. 'You're not dealing with a scared little teenager now and I know *you* have to be very scared to have risked coming over here—'

'Go upstairs, Lily…' Another achingly familiar male voice intervened from behind her. 'I'll deal with this.'

In the seconds that followed Rauf's quiet entrance, Brett succumbed to panic. Surging forward just as Lily spun round in surprise and relief to see Rauf, Brett gave Lily a violent shove out of his path in an effort to reach the door and Rauf went for him like a lion. But Rauf only managed to land one powerful punch on the other man before registering that Lily, who had been smashed up against the wall, had fallen. Rauf's rage that Gilman should have dared to approach his wife with threats again was overpowered by his fear that Lily might have been seriously hurt.

Dizzy and winded by that fall, Lily was gathered with anxious care into Rauf's arms and lifted over to the nearest couch. 'Are you all right?' he demanded rawly.

'Brett?' she gasped.

The slam of the front door answered that query and Rauf groaned out loud in frustration. 'I came back minutes after he arrived and I called the police immediately. I should've stayed out of the room until they arrived but I couldn't *stand* to hear him threatening you!'

'I'm just glad he's gone,' Lily confided unevenly.

Thinking that having Gilman arrested and charged just before their wedding might have cast something of a pall over the festivities, Rauf just held her close and wished he had contrived to get more than one healthy punch in.

'And I'm so grateful there wasn't a fight,' Lily added.

Again, Rauf said nothing, knowing that she would be dismayed by the admission that he felt seriously deprived of what had very probably been his one and only opportunity to pulverise the vicious little creep. He ushered Lily upstairs to her room and then went back down to deal with the police.

Lily's family arrived the following afternoon. Douglas Harris looked brighter than he had in months and her three nieces were bubbling over with excitement. After a slew of necessary introductions and socialising and talking to her father, who was full of praise for Rauf, Lily took Hilary into another room so that they could talk in private.

Her sister enveloped her straight into an unusually emotional hug before sighing. 'I didn't phone because I had too much to tell you. For starters, this week I heard that Brett and my erstwhile friend, Janice, had split up.'

'Oh…good,' Lily pronounced. 'That's justice.'

'Well, it may *well* be.' Hilary gave her a wry scrutiny. 'Apparently, Brett has done something dishonest with Janice's divorce settlement and the police are involved there too. There's a rumour that he's been gambling—'

'Gambling?'

'I suspect that explains what he did with all the cash he helped himself to from Harris Travel,' Hilary said with fierce resentment. 'But I can be grateful for two things… one, that Brett has been such a useless father that the girls won't ever miss what they've never had, and two, thank goodness, I wised up to what a louse I'd married years ago!'

Lily blinked at that blunt and surprising assurance. 'You… *did*?'

'Unfortunately, I hadn't the slightest idea that he couldn't be trusted with money,' Hilary conceded heavily. 'But just before Joy was born I realised that he was running round with other women. By then, though, Dad had gone and signed over the house and that and the girls made me feel that I had to try and keep our marriage together—'

'I can understand that, but if you didn't love Brett any more why did you always look so sad after the divorce whenever he was mentioned?' Lily prompted.

Her older sister winced. 'Put that down to the awful knowledge that I've wasted the last few years of my life. I just got on with being a mother and I turned a blind eye to Brett's affairs. If I had ever dreamt what was *really* going on under my own stupid nose, if I had known that, way before you even left school, Brett was threatening you...' she breathed painfully and slowly shook her head with bitter regret '...I'd have slaughtered Brett long ago!'

Thrown by that declaration, for Lily had still had no plans to tell her sister quite how low her ex-husband had sunk in the more distant past, Lily exclaimed, 'How did you find out?'

'Rauf brought me up to date and, no, don't you dare criticise him for interfering because I just know that you weren't *ever* going to tell me!' Hilary admitted ruefully. 'And after finding out about that, learning that my ex-husband is on the run from the Turkish police didn't phase me at all. If I knew where Brett was, I'd hand him over personally—'

'Are you serious?' Lily interrupted, for she had been wondering how on earth they would cope if Brett was caught before the wedding and had feared that her sister would be very distressed by any such development.

'I want him prosecuted and locked up too.' Hilary breathed in deep, her fine features rigid and flushed with anger. 'In fact, when Rauf told me about Brett having the neck to come here last night and try his old tricks on you, my blood just boiled!'

The sisters talked for over an hour and then Lily finally asked Hilary what she thought of Rauf.

'He just adores you. It shines out of him like a light,' Hilary quipped with sudden amusement. 'Why are you looking surprised? I mean, you've got to know that after he hauled you off to the altar so fast. I couldn't believe it!'

He adores you. Lily almost mentioned that Rauf had rushed into that civil ceremony primarily out of a wish to protect her reputation, but thought better of it because she could see that Hilary was charmed by the belief that she was on the sidelines of a true romance. Rauf was warm, tender, romantic and everything she had always known he could be, but he had yet to mention that word 'love' and Lily was already so happy that she was determined not to let that bother her.

At dawn the following morning, the pre-wedding preparations began. Lily was ushered out to the *hamam*, wrapped in a sturdy sarong and, surrounded by animated women, whisked through the entire invigorating process of being warmed, cooled down again by playful scoops of cool water tossed over her and then enveloped in loads of bubbles from head to toe and scrubbed by a lady built like a human tank with an abrasive mitt. It was fun and Lily giggled a lot. Finally rinsed clean while Hilary looked on in awe, Lily's hair was subjected to a camomile bath that left the strands as sleek and glossy as pure silk, and she was settled onto a couch where she was massaged with fragrant oil. Far from it being the over-vigorous process she had feared, it was very relaxing.

In the outer room, she was served with apple tea and her nails were manicured before an elaborate henna pattern was painted onto her right hand. 'To soothe Nelispah,' Rauf's mother whispered, explaining that the old lady had been a little disappointed to be told that Lily would not be entering the hotel ballroom, where the wedding would be celebrated, on the back of a white horse.

A couple of hours later, Lily pirouetted in front of a full-length mirror, hopelessly in love with her gorgeous wedding gown. The simple traditional design she had selected made the most of the exquisite fabric. An elaborate and beautiful gold necklace arrived from Rauf as a bride gift and Nelispah's bright gaze shone as much as Lily's at that evidence of custom being observed. Beneath her gown, Lily wore a blue satin garter that Hilary had given her as well as the raciest set of silk lingerie in her possession and when her nieces, Penny, Gemma and Joy, danced in to surprise her with their pretty bridesmaids' dresses she was delighted.

She left the Kasabian home on her proud father's arm to climb into an open carriage drawn by two white horses. But without a doubt the moment that was the highlight of her day was when she entered the opulent hotel and saw Rauf waiting for her. He just stared with such blatant appreciation that she blushed, her own gaze equally absorbed in taking in how drop-dead gorgeous her husband looked in a superb dark suit.

'You take my breath away, *güzelim*,' he confided huskily, dark golden eyes possessive as the wedding march was played and he led her into the ballroom with their families and all the guests trooping in behind them.

The ceremony over, they ate a meal that began with the official wedding soup and afterwards they cut the cake and offered it round to their relatives. Rauf claimed a kiss at that point that sent her heartbeat racing.

'I wasn't expecting that,' she confided breathlessly as he whirled her out onto the floor to begin the dancing.

'Perfectly acceptable at our wedding.' His brilliant smile warmed her like the bright clear Turkish sunlight. 'But don't be surprised when I disappear later. My family bring my bride to the very door of my home and then we get a month's break from the whole lot of them—'

'I *love* your family!' Lily protested.

'Tomorrow we set off on our honeymoon cruise round the coast on my yacht,' Rauf imparted with satisfaction. 'And if we get tired of that, we can go anywhere, do anything—'

'Or sneak back to Sonngul,' Lily whispered. 'It still feels like my favourite place in the world.'

Her own family were staying on for a week's vacation with Rauf's family and Lily parted from them with farewell hugs to be borne off in a limousine containing Nelispah and Manolya, for the bridegroom's mother was not allowed to play a part in delivering the bride to her future home.

Set down before yet another ancient and huge house where Rauf awaited her, Lily laughed as he swept her off her feet and carried her indoors. 'It's been a wonderful, wonderful day,' she told him happily.

'It's not quite finished yet.' Rauf set her down with pronounced care and guided her into a glorious light-filled bedroom that overlooked the very waters of the Bosphorus. 'Do you know that I have never said the words, "I love you" to any woman and even today I feel ashamed to offer you my love?'

'*Ashamed?*' Lily studied him in shaken disbelief.

'But my love is yours, for what it is worth, and it *always* has been,' Rauf proclaimed tautly, lodged by the French windows that opened out onto a deck festooned with tubs of beautiful flowers.

'Always has been…' Lily parrotted, mesmerised by the sight of Rauf struggling to find words that were so obviously difficult for him to speak, scarcely able to even think about what he was telling her.

'At nineteen, I was infatuated with Kasmet, but I never knew love until I met you. She only hurt my pride and gave me an excuse to say marriage wasn't for me,' Rauf murmured grimly. 'You know, I'm still very angry about her telling you those ridiculous lies this week.'

'Forget about that. She was just envious and wanting to spoil my happiness,' Lily said dismissively, far more interested in what he had admitted just a minute earlier.

'Three years ago, when we first met, I was a slick operator or, at least, I *thought* I was.' His wide, sensual mouth twisted with a derision directed at himself. 'I wanted you on my terms and you were worthy of much more, but success with too many other women had made me arrogant and selfish. My obstinate belief that I would never marry almost destroyed our relationship—'

'You still bought that diamond ring I wear back then,' Lily reminded him gently, her blue eyes soft with love.

Dark colour accentuated his fabulous cheekbones. 'I was still immature. The ring would have been given then with a certain amount of resentment that I could win you no other way,' he admitted heavily. 'That is nothing to be proud of either. But this time around, from the outset of our first meeting, I was even worse—'

'How?'

'I was just eaten by jealousy of Gilman. I thought you were only in Turkey because he had taken off with another woman. When I realised you were a virgin, I was shattered, but that bitter jealousy was so ingrained in me after three years that I just moved on to suspecting that, even though you hadn't had an affair with him, you *had* loved him. Those first couple of days we were together, I acted like a guy with only one not very reliable brain cell.'

'You were jealous of Brett—?'

'And then when I heard you on the phone to him, I suffered the tortures of feeling second-best all over again. I needed to hear nothing suspect in the conversation to torment myself even more.' Rauf groaned.

'Yet, in spite of all that, you *still* wanted to marry me and you knew that you loved me.' Lily worked out those facts for herself with immense satisfaction, for that was a level of love she had never dreamt a male with his fierce pride could feel for her. That was love in block capitals, a love big enough and generous enough to overcome every obstacle and his pride as well.

'Then I blew it again on our flight to Istanbul over your name being on that bank account and there was nothing more sobering than realising that I was losing you altogether.' Rauf swore and spread speaking hands expressively wide.

'I'm not so easy to lose,' Lily confided.

'My pride made me persuade myself three years ago that my love for you had died,' he confessed tautly. 'But I know now that you genuinely cared for me in those days and that I must have hurt you a great deal...'

'Yes...you hurt me terribly,' Lily told him honestly.

Rauf paled but reacted much as if he had expected to have that confirmed.

'One minute you were there and the next it was like you'd never existed and I started to believe that I'd just imagined that we'd ever shared anything worth holding onto,' Lily continued. 'I decided it could only have been a casual thing for you—'

'*Casual?*' Rauf loosed a bitter laugh of disagreement. 'It was six months before I could even catch sight of a blonde head in the street without secretly, crazily hoping it would somehow be you. I worked myself into the ground that entire year, because at least when I was working it took my mind off you for a while. I never believed in love like that until I was without you and the hardest thing for me to accept now is that I deserved to be miserable.'

Lily was over the moon to learn that Rauf had had such

a hard time getting by without her, but thought it tactful to conceal a delight that struck her as a little cruel. At the same time she was now quietly rejoicing in his staggering assurance that his love was hers and always had been. 'I wasn't exactly happy myself. Tell me, when did you decide that you were still in love with me?'

'I always knew it was there deep down inside me…lurking…' Rauf expelled a heavy sigh. 'But I didn't ever think about it after the first year we were apart. I just shut it out until I saw you again. I went haywire and made appallingly bad decisions—'

'Such as?' Lily probed in growing fascination as she tried to think of love as something that 'lurked' like a secret, dreadful threat.

'I told myself that I was taking revenge when I took you to Sonngul to stay with me but, in truth, I was only snatching at the first possible excuse to be with you again. I didn't know what I was doing…not *really* doing until it was too late. But I knew I loved you at the civil ceremony—'

'So why didn't you mention it…why wait until now?'

'I had treated you with dishonour and that shamed me. I had not valued you as I should have done. I had even less right to be talking about love. All I had done was cause you more distress and I regret that most of all.'

'But I brought a lot of that on myself,' Lily countered guiltily. 'I couldn't make myself tell you what I'd had to put up with from Brett—'

'I could see that you were hiding something from me. You're not a very good dissembler,' Rauf told her gently. 'Once I knew that there was a secret, my suspicions about the nature of your relationship with him refused to die. Yet the moment I heard the truth that was the end of them.'

Lily flushed. 'Honesty pays,' she muttered in discomfiture.

'But an atmosphere of suspicion and distrust does not encourage honesty.' Rauf studied her with marked strain in his gleaming gaze, lean, strong face clenched taut. 'All I want to ask you now is if some day you feel you could love me again?'

Lily screened her gaze, not wanting to let him off the hook too fast. 'Anything's possible.'

'I love you enough for both of us, *güzelim.*'

'I'm really beginning to believe that you do.' Lily crossed the room to where he stood so straight and tall and, meeting the loving intensity of his tawny eyes, she just couldn't keep him in suspense any more. 'But luckily for both of us, I wasn't any better at getting over you than you were at getting over me...I'm still very much in love with you.'

For several seconds, Rauf stared back at her in surprise and then, all of a sudden, he strode forward and just snatched her into his arms with an extreme lack of cool. He curved unsteady hands to frame her cheekbones. 'You're not just saying that to save face for me?' he probed tautly.

'No, I'm not that kind,' Lily declared with eyes brimming with amusement at that very Turkish suggestion. 'I just love you lots and lots and never met anyone who could make me feel as you could.'

'Must be a lot of real losers out there because I wasn't that impressive,' Rauf muttered, and then he claimed her mouth with all the passion of his volatile temperament.

Matters moved fast from that point. Curtains were hastily yanked shut, clothes fell away without ceremony and the bride and groom fell between the sheets of the marital bed to make up for ten nights of being kept apart.

'I've been up walking the floor every night this week…I just missed you so much!' Rauf confided raggedly.

In between frantic kisses, Lily hugged that sense of security to herself, revelled in his hungry tenderness, the sheer happiness that she saw in his eyes. There was a new dimension to their loving, a wonderful closeness and contentment in the aftermath.

Rauf told her about Talip Hajjar's visit to Sonngul and how complete his faith had been in her that evening when he had explained to the army police officer what she was doing in Turkey. Then he made her laugh out loud as he admitted that the sight of her name on that bank account with Brett's had, within minutes of his angry condemnation of her, put him in a literal panic on her behalf.

'I immediately lost all desire to press charges against Brett because I was afraid the police would not be able to prove your innocence,' Rauf stated in some embarrassment. 'About then, I realised that I would lie for you, break the law, do absolutely *anything* required to protect you and that shattered my view of myself as an honourable man.'

Lily looked up into the dark golden eyes resting on her with adoring intensity and kept quiet rather than tell him that, next to those words of love that she had convinced herself that she would never hear, that was the most touching admission she had ever heard. 'I *was* a bit disconcerted when you suddenly mentioned getting me out of the country as if I was a master criminal!' she confided with a helpless giggle.

'I hadn't yet even laid charges against Brett for those missing funds, so how *could* you have been at any risk? I was functioning on that single brain cell again,' Rauf groaned incredulously. 'I think I know why I never fell in love before…ESP must've warned me it was likely to be the most humbling and embarrassing experience of my life.'

As he smoothed down her tumbled hair and welded her to his lean, relaxed length Lily smiled with sunny contentment. 'But I'm your reward…and, let's face it, humility never used to be one of your more marked traits,' she teased with new confidence. 'I love you all the more for just being you.'

'Flaws and all?'

Lily nodded forgivingly.

His shimmering smile curved his handsome mouth and warmed her all the way down to her toes. 'You're the best thing that ever happened to me…I love you more than anything else in this world.'

Twenty months later, Lily settled her infant son, Themsi, into his canopied cot at Sonngul. Themsi was four months old. She hummed his favourite lullaby half under her breath until his big eyes slowly slid shut and the extravagant dark lashes he had inherited from his father drifted down onto his rounded little cheeks.

From the window of the nursery, she watched the sun go down in spring splendour over the beautiful gardens before she drew the curtains and walked back to check that her baby was as comfortable as he could be. Themsi was only just beginning to sleep in more than fits and snatches and she smiled at the memory of finding Rauf beating her to his first cry those initial broken nights, for nobody had fallen harder for Themsi at first glance than his father. Her son was a very much indulged baby. Nelispah Kasabian had wept over him in joy and her own daughter and granddaughter were equally enchanted with the new addition to the family.

'Four children?' Nelispah had whispered conspiratorially to Lily, her wise old eyes fixed with satisfaction to Rauf as he'd cradled his son with tender pride for a family photograph. 'He's good for at least six! He's all heart underneath the tough front.'

Yes, Lily had discovered that learning the Turkish language had paid definite dividends. Nelispah Kasabian knew Rauf back to front and inside out but would never have dreamt of revealing that fact to him.

Lily could barely believe that she had already been married for a year and eight months. The time had flown because she had never been happier. However, when Rauf and Lily had returned from their wonderful honeymoon they had been stunned to learn that Brett Gilman was dead. Soon after Brett had contrived to get himself back to England, he had been killed in a car accident. Apparently, he had been drunk, but mercifully no other car had been involved in the fatal crash. The files on Brett's criminal activities had been closed.

Hilary had been stunned when her ex-husband had been killed and the children had been very upset. At the same time, Lily's nieces had seen so little of their irresponsible father since the divorce that they had not been as badly affected as they might have been. Rauf had tried to persuade her sister to allow him to buy her a larger home, but her sister had said no. Hilary had been working hard to build up Harris Travel again and Serhan Mirosh, the quiet but very attractive forty-year-old investment consultant whom Rauf employed, had made increasingly frequent visits to offer his advice and guidance.

Rauf had given Lily a wicked grin of satisfaction one evening when he'd come home. 'Serhan has fallen in love with Hilary. He sees her as a damsel in distress and longs to take all her business burdens onto his own shoulders—'

'I don't believe you!' Lily laughed for Serhan had always struck her as a real sobersides for all his good looks.

Rauf's grin merely grew wider. 'He confessed this afternoon when he asked if I would have any objection to him taking your sister out to dinner. It might take him another month to work up the courage. He's very shy with women...why do you think he's still single?'

'I know Hilary likes working with him,' Lily conceded with a reflective frown. 'But she doesn't seem to have the slightest interest in meeting another man.'

'Serhan may be shy but he's also very determined when he sets his sights on something. If he's got anything to do with it, they'll be married within the year,' Rauf forecast with brazen confidence.

Lily had been overjoyed when Rauf's optimistic conviction had come true, although it had taken a little longer than a year for Serhan to get Hilary as far as the altar. His virtually proposing on the first date had been more of a hindrance than a help to his own cause. Just a month ago, however, Rauf and Lily had flown over to their wedding and had brought Penny, Gemma and Joy back home with them while the bridal couple had gone off on their honeymoon. Harris Travel had been sold and Hilary was planning to set up business again in Istanbul. Hilary had at last found the happiness she deserved and Lily was delighted that her sister and her daughters were now living nearby. Although pressed to take up residence with Serhan and Hilary in Turkey, Douglas Harris had decided to remain in England with his friends and all that was familiar and had moved into a comfortable flat in a retirement home.

Lily and Rauf came to Sonngul to unwind in peace and privacy whenever they could. Rauf strolled into their bedroom, his jacket slung over one broad shoulder, tie already loosened, and his dark golden eyes glittered with appreciation over the picture Lily made in her aqua-coloured nightdress. 'You look ravishing.'

'You're easily impressed,' Lily teased, but then if that was true she was a pushover on the same score: his lean, dark features and the lithe flow of his well-built physique set her heart jumping too.

'No, anything but. Every time I look at you, I know how lucky I am,' Rauf quipped as he went into the adjoining room, where Themsi always slept when they stayed at Sonngul, to have a look at his sleeping son. 'He's practically growing in front of our eyes,' he said fondly. 'He's going to be tall like me.'

Lily watched him from the doorway with amusement.

Rauf swung round. 'What's so funny?'

'I doubt that Themsi's had a growth spurt since you flew out of here this morning!'

Her tall, dark, handsome husband just closed his arms round her and lifted her right off her feet. 'He just might have had,' he told her stubbornly, and then he kissed her with passionate hunger, making her senses sing before conceding, 'but I suppose it's unlikely.'

Lying back on their bed, Lily reached up to tug him down to her again and smiled up into his clear golden eyes, loving every angle of his lean, strong face, rejoicing in their closeness and contentment.

'I hate being dragged away from you and Themsi when I'm here,' Rauf confided huskily. 'I'm going to set up a better office so that I can handle more on the spot.'

'Brilliant idea,' Lily told him.

A slashing smile curved his handsome mouth. 'I have my moments, *güzelim*.'

Lily gave him a mischievous look. 'Most days…why do you think I love you so much?'

He gazed down at her with amusement and love mingled in his possessive gaze. 'I adore you and you know it.'

And she *did* know that she was loved and, more than anything else, that security and confidence had added to her contentment. She found his mouth for herself and surrendered to the pleasure of their loving.

THE GREEK'S
VIRGIN BRIDE

by

Julia James

Julia James lives in England with her family. Mills & Boon were the first 'grown up' books she read as a teenager, alongside Georgette Heyer and Daphne du Maurier, and she's been reading them ever since. Julia adores the English and Celtic countryside, in all its seasons, and is fascinated by all things historical, from castles to cottages. She also has a special love for the Mediterranean – 'The most perfect landscape after England'! – and she considers both ideal settings for romance stories. In between writing she enjoys walking, gardening, needlework, baking extremely gooey cakes and trying to stay fit!

Don't miss Julia James' exciting new novel *Bought for the Greek's Bed*, out in June 2007 from Mills & Boon Modern Romance™

PROLOGUE

'YOU want me to do what?' Nikos Vassilis stared at the old man seated at the desk.

Yiorgos Coustakis looked back with a level gaze. At seventy-eight he was still a formidable figure of a man. His eyes were still as piercing as they had been when he was young. They were the eyes of a man who knew the price of everything.

Especially human souls.

'You heard me.' His voice was unemotional. 'Marry my granddaughter and you can go ahead with the merger.'

'Maybe,' replied the younger man slowly. 'I just didn't believe you.'

A twisted smile pulled at Yiorgos Coustakis's mouth. 'You should,' he advised. 'It's the only deal on the table. And a deal, after all,' he said, 'is what you've flown four thousand miles for, *ne*?'

His visitor kept his hard, handsome face expressionless. Revealing anything in front of Old Man Coustakis was a major error in any kind of negotiation with him. Certainly he did not reveal the exasperation he had felt when the head of the Coustakis empire had phoned him at three a.m. in his Manhattan apartment the night before last to tell him that if he wanted a deal he'd better be in Athens this morning to sign it.

If it had been any one else phoning him Nikos would have given him short shrift. He'd had Esme Vandersee with him in bed, and sleeping was not what they'd been doing. But Yiorgos Coustakis had attractions that even the spectacular Esme, queen of the catwalk, could not compete with.

The Coustakis empire was a prize worth forgoing any woman for.

But was it a prize worth marrying a woman for? Giving up

his freedom? For a woman he'd never met? Never laid eyes on?

Nikos shifted his gaze past the penetrating dark eyes and out through the plate-glass window. Athens lay below—crowded, polluted, unique. One of the most ancient cities of Europe, the cradle of western civilisation. Nikos knew it as a child knew its parent—he had been raised on its streets, toughened in its alleyways, tempered in its unforgiving crucible.

He'd clawed his way up off the streets, fighting tooth and nail, pushing poverty behind him deal by nerve-racking deal, until now, at thirty-four, it was as if he had never been that unwanted, fatherless boy running wild in the alleyways.

The journey had been long, and tough, but he had made it— and the fruits of his triumph were sweet indeed.

Now he stood poised on the edge of his greatest triumph— getting hold of the mighty Coustakis Industries.

'I was thinking,' he said, keeping his face blank, 'of a share-swap.'

He had it all planned. He would reverse Vassilis Inc into the far larger Coustakis empire, and take the lot in a cashless exchange of shares. Oh, Old Man Coustakis would need a lot of personal financial sweeteners, he knew that, but Nikos had that covered too. He knew the old man wanted out, that his health—deny it officially as he would—was not good. But he knew Yiorgos Coustakis would never cede control of his business without a top-dollar face-saving deal—he'd go out like a lion, with a final roar, not like an old wolf driven from the pack.

That didn't bother Nikos—when his time came to quit he'd drive a hard bargain too, just to keep his successor on his toes.

But what Coustakis had just thrown at him had winded him like a blow to the gut. Marry his granddaughter to get hold of the company? Nikos hadn't even known the old man *had* a granddaughter!

Inside, behind the mask that was the carefully schooled expression on his face, Nikos had to tip his hat to the old man.

He could still catch his rivals out—even a rival who was posing as a friendly merger partner.

'You can have the share-swap—on your wedding day.'

Yiorgos's reply was flat. Nikos kept his silence. Behind his composed appearance his mind was teeming. Racing.

'Well?' Yiorgos prompted him.

'I'll think about it,' returned Nikos. His voice was cool.

He turned to go.

'Walk out the door and the deal is off. Permanently.'

Nikos stopped. He rested his eyes on the man seated at the desk. He wasn't bluffing. Nikos knew that. Everyone knew Old Man Coustakis never bluffed.

'You sign now, or not at all.'

Nikos's slate-grey eyes—a legacy from his unknown father, as was his un-Greek height of well over six feet—met with Coustakis's black ones. For a long, timeless moment, they held. Then slowly, unflinchingly, Nikos Vassilis walked back to the desk, picked up the gold pen Yiorgos Coustakis silently handed him, and signed the document lying there.

Without a word, he set down the pen and walked out.

On his brief journey down to ground level in the plush executive lift in the Coustakis HQ, Nikos tried in vain to rein in his thoughts.

Exultation ran side by side with anger—exultation that his longed-for goal was now within his grasp, anger that he had been outmanoeuvred by the wiliest fox he knew.

He straightened his shoulders. Who cared if Coustakis had driven a bargain he hadn't even seen coming? No one could have. The man played his cards closer to his chest than anyone Nikos knew—himself included. And if he could suddenly produce a granddaughter out of thin air that no one had ever heard of till now, well, what did it matter to him, Nikos Vassilis, who was going to get what he'd wanted all his life—a safe, secure, glittering place at the very top of the greasy pole he'd been climbing all his life?

That the unknown granddaughter fated to be his wife was a

complete stranger was an irrelevance compared with taking over the Coustakis empire.

He knew what mattered in his life. What had always mattered.

And Old Man Coustakis—and his granddaughter—held the key to his dreams.

Nikos was not about to turn it down.

CHAPTER ONE

ANDREA could hear her mother coughing wheezily in the kitchen as she made breakfast. Her face tensed. It was getting worse, that cough. Kim had been asthmatic all her life, Andrea knew, but for the last eighteen months the bronchitis she'd got the winter before had never been shaken off, and her lungs were weaker than ever.

The doctor had been sympathetic but, apart from keeping Kim on her medication, all he'd advised was spending the winter in a warmer, drier climate. Andrea had smiled with grim politeness, and not bothered to tell him that he might as well have said she should take her mother to the moon. They barely had enough to cover their living expenses as it was, let alone to go gallivanting off abroad.

A clunk through the letterbox of the council flat she'd lived in all her life told Andrea that the post had arrived. She hurried off to get it before her mother could get to the door. The post only brought bills, and every bill brought more worries. Already her mother was fretting about how they would be able to pay for heating in the coming winter.

Andrea glanced at the post as she scooped it off the worn carpet by the front door. Two bills, some junk mail, and a thick cream-coloured envelope with her name typed on it. She frowned. Now what? An eviction order? A debt reminder? Something unpleasant from the council? Or the bank?

She ripped her thumbnail down the back and yanked open the paper inside, unfolding it. She caught a glimpse of some ornate heading, and a neatly typed paragraph—'Dear Ms Fraser....'

As she read, Andrea's body slowly froze. Twice she re-read the brief missive. Then, with a contortion of blind rage on her face, she screwed the letter into a ball and hurled it with all her force at the door. It bounced, and lay on the carpet.

Andrea had heard the phrase 'red-misting'—now she knew first-hand what it meant.

Bastard!

She felt her hands fist in anger at her side. Then, with a deep, controlling breath, she made herself open her palms, bend down, and pick up the letter. She must not let Kim find it.

All that day the contents of the letter, jammed into the bottom of her bag, burned at her, the terse paragraph it contained repeating itself over and over again in Andrea's head.

You are required to attend Mr Coustakis at the end of next week. Your airline ticket will be at Heathrow for you to collect on Friday morning. Consult the enclosed itinerary for your check-in time. You will be met at Athens airport. You should phone the number below to acknowledge receipt of this communication by five p.m. tomorrow.

It was simply signed 'For Mr Coustakis'.

Dark emotions flowed through Andrea. 'Mr Coustakis's.' Aka Yiorgos Coustakis. Founder and owner of Coustakis Industries, worth hundreds of millions of pounds. A man Andrea loathed with every atom of her being.

Her grandfather.

Not that Yiorgos Coustakis had ever acknowledged the relationship. Memory of another letter leapt in Andrea's mind. That one had been written directly to her mother. It had been brief, too, and to the point. It had informed Kim Fraser, in a single, damning sentence, that any further attempt to communicate with Mr Coustakis would result in legal action being taken against her. That had been ten years ago. Yiorgos Coustakis had made it damningly clear that his granddaughter simply didn't exist as far as he was concerned.

Now, out of the blue, she had been summoned to his presence.

Andrea's mouth tightened. Did he really think she would meekly pack her bags and check in for a flight to Athens next Friday? Darkness shadowed her eyes. Yiorgos Coustakis could drop dead before she showed up!

A second letter arrived the next day, again from the London office of Coustakis Industries. Its contents were even terser.

Dear Ms Fraser,
You failed to communicate your receipt of the letter dated two days ago. Please do so immediately.

Like the first letter, Andrea took it into work—Kim must definitely not see it. She had suffered far too much from the father of the man she had loved so desperately—so briefly. A sick feeling sloshed in Andrea's stomach. How could anyone have treated her gentle, sensitive mother so brutally? But Yiorgos Coustakis had—and had relished it.

Andrea typed a suitable reply, keeping it as barely civil as the letters she had received. She owed nothing to the sender. Not even civility. Nothing but hatred.

With reference to your recent correspondence, you should note that any further letters to me will continue to be ignored.

She printed it out and signed it with her bare name—hard and uncompromising.

Like the stock she came from.

Nikos Vassilis swirled the fine vintage wine consideringly in his glass.

'So, when will my bride arrive, Yiorgos?' he enquired of his host.

He was dining with his grandfather-in-law-to-be in the vast, over-decorated house on the outskirts of Athens that Yiorgos Coustakis considered suitable to his wealth and position.

'At the end of the week,' his host answered tersely.

He didn't look well, Nikos noted. His colour was high, and there was a pinched look around his mouth.

'And the wedding?'

His host gave a harsh laugh. 'So eager? You don't even know what she looks like!'

Nikos's mobile mouth curled cynically.

'Her looks, or lack of them, are not going to be a deal-breaker, Yiorgos,' he observed sardonically.

Yiorgos gave another laugh. Less harsh this time. Coarser.

'Bed her in the dark, if you must! I had to do that with her grandmother!'

A sliver of distaste filtered through Nikos. Though no one would dare say it to his face, the world knew that Yiorgos Coustakis had won his richly dowered, well-born wife by dint of getting the poor girl so besotted with him that she'd agreed to meet him in his apartment one afternoon. Yiorgos, as ambitious as he was ruthless, had made sure the information leaked to Marina's father, who had arrived in time to prevent Yiorgos having to undergo the ordeal of sex with a plain, drab dab of a girl in daylight, but not in time to save her reputation. 'Who will believe she left my apartment a virgin?' Yiorgos had challenged her father callously—and won his bride.

Nikos flicked his mind back to the present. Was he insane, going through with this? Marrying a woman he hadn't set eyes on just because she happened to have a quarter of Yiorgos Coustakis's DNA? Idly he found himself wondering if the girl felt the same way about marrying a complete stranger. Then he shrugged mentally—in the world of the very rich, dynastic marriages were commonplace. The Coustakis girl would have been reared from birth to know that she was destined to be a pawn in her grandfather's machinations. She would be pampered and doll-like, her primary skill that of spending money in huge amounts on clothes, jewellery and anything else she took a fancy to.

Well, Nick acknowledged silently, glancing around the opulent dining room, she would certainly have money to spare as

his wife! Once he'd taken over Coustakis Industries his income
would be ten times what it already was—she could squander
it on anything she wanted! Spending money would keep her
busy, and keep her happy.

He paused momentarily. With a wife in the background he
would obviously have to keep his personal life more low-
profile. He would not be one of those husbands, all too familiar
in the circles he now moved in, who thought nothing of flaunt-
ing their mistresses in front of their families. Nevertheless, he
had no intention of altering the very enjoyable private life he
indulged himself in, even if he would have to be more discreet
about it once he was married.

Oh, he was well aware that as a rich man he could have been
as old as Methuselah and as ugly as sin and beautiful women
would still have fawned on him. Wealth was the most powerful
aphrodisiac to those kind of women. Of course even when he'd
been dirt-poor women had always come easily to him—another
legacy from his philandering father, no doubt. One of Esme's
many predecessors had said to his face, as she lay exhausted
and sated beneath him, that if he ever ran out of money he
could make a fortune hiring himself out as a stud. Nikos had
laughed, his mouth widening wolfishly, and turned her over…

He shifted in his uncomfortably ornate chair. Thinking about
sex was not a good idea right now. His razor-sharp mind might
not have objected to kow-towing to Old Man Coustakis's sum-
mons that night, but his body was reminding him that it had
been deprived of its customary satiation. Even though he'd put
in extra time these last few days at the gym and on the squash
courts in the exclusive health club he belonged to, Nikos could
feel a familiar tightening that presaged sexual desire.

As soon as he decently could he'd take his leave tonight and
phone Xanthe Palloupis. She was an extremely complaisant
mistress—always welcoming, always responsive to his physical
needs. Even though it had been three months since he'd last
visited her—Esme Vandersee had replaced her over two
months ago—he knew she would greet him warmly at her discreetly located but very expensive apartment, confident that he

would tell her in the morning she could go to her favourite jeweller's and order something to remember his visit by.

Would he keep her on when he had married this unknown granddaughter of Yiorgos Coustakis? She had other lovers, he knew, and it did not trouble him. Esme, too, right this moment was doubtless consoling her wounded—and highly developed!—ego by letting another of her crowded court do the honours by her. As a top model she always had men slavering after her, but for all that Nikos knew perfectly well that he would only have to snap his fingers and she would come instantly to his heel—and other parts of his anatomy.

He shifted uncomfortably in his seat again. He definitely needed some energetic physical release before his wedding night! The Coustakis girl would be a virgin, of course, and bedding her would be more of a duty, not a pleasure, though he would be as careful with her as was possible. He'd never taken a virgin—he would have to make totally sure he was not sexually frustrated on his wedding night or she'd be the one to suffer from it, however plain she was.

Just how plain was she? Nikos wondered, his mind running on. He had a pretty shrewd idea that from the tinge of open malice in Yiorgos's expression when he'd made that coarse comment about bedding her in the dark she had no looks at all. The old man probably thought it amusing that a man who was never seen without a beautiful woman hanging on his arm should now be hog-tied to a female whose sole attraction was as the gateway to control and eventual ownership of Coustakis Industries.

Another thought flitted through his mind. Just who exactly was this unknown granddaughter of Yiorgos Coustakis? One of the main attractions of taking over Coustakis Industries was that Yiorgos had no offspring to fight him for control. His only son had been killed in a smash-up years ago. Marina Coustakis had had some kind of seizure, so the gossip went, and had become a permanent invalid—though not managing to die until a few years ago. That meant that Yiorgos had not been free to marry again and beget more heirs. But then, mused Nikos, if the son had indeed been married when he died, and the grand-daughter already born, maybe that hadn't mattered too much to Yiorgos. The son's widow had presumably married again and was out of the picture, apart from having dutifully reared the Coustakis granddaughter to be a docile, well-behaved, well-bred Greek wife.

Her docility would certainly make things easier for him, Nikos thought. Oh, he wouldn't flaunt his sex-life in her face, but obviously her mother would have taught her that husbands strayed, that it was in their nature, and that her role was to be a dutiful spouse, immaculate social hostess and attentive mother.

Nikos's hand stilled a moment as he raised his wine glass to his mouth. Yiorgos was retelling the drama of some coup he'd pulled off years ago, clearly relishing the memory of having beaten off a rival, bankrupting him in the process, and Nikos was only paying attention with a quarter of his mind. Three-quarters of it was considering what it would be like to be a father.

Because that, he knew, was what all this was about. Yiorgos was approaching the end of his life—he wanted to know his DNA would continue. He wanted an heir.

And Nikos? Strange feelings pricked at him. What did he know about fatherhood? His own father didn't even know he existed—he'd impregnated his mother and sailed with the tide at dawn. He could even be alive somewhere, Nikos knew. It meant nothing to him. His mother had scarcely mentioned him—she'd worked in a bar, when she'd worked at all, and her maternal instincts had not been well developed. Her son's existence hadn't been important to her, and when he'd left home as a teenager she'd hardly noticed. As he had slowly, painfully, begun to make money, she'd accepted his hand-outs without question, let alone interest, and hadn't lived to see him make real money. She'd been knocked down by a taxi twelve years ago, when he was twenty-two. Nikos had given her an expensive funeral.

He lifted the wine glass to his mouth and drank. It was a

rare, costly vintage, he knew—learning about wines and all the other fine things of life was information he'd gathered along the way. He relished all fine things, and once he ran Coustakis Industries the finest things in the world would be his for the taking. He would have taken his place not just amongst the wealthy, as he now was, but amongst the super-rich. And if Coustakis wanted him to impregnate his granddaughter and give him a great-grandson—well, he could do that.

Whatever she looked like.

Andrea stood by the front door of the flat, staring at the opened letter. It was not from Coustakis Industries. It was from one of London's most prestigious department stores, and informed her that enclosed was a gold store card with an immediate credit limit of five thousand pounds. It further stated her that all invoices incurred by her to that limit would be forwarded to the private office of Yiorgos Coustakis for payment. A second opened letter underlaid the one from the store. That one *was* from Coustakis Industries, and it instructed her to make use of the store card that would be sent under separate cover in order to provide herself with a suitable wardrobe for when she attended Mr Coustakis at the end of the following week. It finished with a reminder to phone the London office to confirm receipt of these instructions.

Andrea's dark eyes narrowed dangerously. What the hell was the old bastard playing at?

What did he want? What was going on? Her scalp prickled with unease. She didn't like this—she didn't like it at all!

Her brain was in turmoil. What would happen if she did what she wanted to do and cut the store card in half and sent it back to her grandfather with orders to stick it where it hurt? Would he get the message? Somehow she didn't think so.

Yiorgos Coustakis wanted something from her. He'd never acknowledged her existence before. But he was a rich man—very rich. And rich men had power. And they used it to get their own way.

Her face set. What could Yiorgos Coustakis do to them if

he wanted to? Kim had debts—Andrea hated to think of them, let alone the reason for those debts, but they were there, like a millstone round their necks. Both of them, mother and daughter, worked endlessly, repaying them little by little, and given another five years or so they finally would be clear. But that was a long way off.

And Kim's health was getting worse.

Anguish crushed Andrea's heart like a vice. Her mother had suffered so *much*—she'd had such a rotten life. A brief, tiny glimpse of happiness when she was twenty, a few golden weeks in her youth, and then it had been destroyed. Totally destroyed. And she'd spent the next twenty-four years of her life being the most devoted, caring, *loving* mother than anyone could ask for.

I just wish we could get out, Andrea thought for the millionth time. The high-rise block they lived in was overdue for repairs, though she could understand the council's reluctance to spend good money on doing up an estate when half its population would simply start to trash it the moment the paint was dry. The flats themselves had a list as long as your arm of repairs needed—the worst was that the damp in the kitchen and bathroom was dire, which did no good at all for Kim's asthma. The lift was usually broken, and anyway usually served as a late-night public convenience, not to mention a place for scoring drugs.

For a brief, fleeting second Andrea thought of the immense wealth of Yiorgos Coustakis.

Then put it behind her.

She would have nothing to do with such a man. *Nothing.*

Whatever he planned for her.

CHAPTER TWO

NIKOS pushed the sleeve of his suit jacket back and glanced at the slim gold watch circling his lean wrist. What had Old Man Coustakis called him here for? He'd been cooling his heels on the shaded terrace for over ten minutes—and ten minutes was a long time for a man as busy as Nikos Vassilis. He did not like waiting patiently—he was a man in a hurry. Always had been.

The manservant approached again, from the large double doors leading into the opulent drawing room beyond, and deferentially asked him if he would like another drink. Curtly, Nikos shook his head, and asked—again—when Mr Coustakis would be ready to see him. The manservant replied that he would enquire, and padded off silently.

Irritated, Nikos turned and stared out over the gardens spread below. They were highly ornate, clearly designed to impress, not to provide a pleasant place to stroll around. Nikos had a sudden vision of a small boy trying to play out there and finding nothing but expensive specimen plants, and fussy paths and over-planted borders. His mouth tightened unconsciously. If he were to become a father he would need a decent place to raise his family...

His mind sheered away. The reality of what he was about to do—marry Yiorgos Coustakis's plain, pampered granddaughter, a female he'd never met—was starting to hit him. Could he really go through with it? Even to get hold of Coustakis Industries?

He shook the doubts from his mind. Of course he would go through with it! Anyway, it wasn't as if he were signing his life away. Old Man Coustakis would not live for ever. In half a dozen years he would probably be dead, and then Nikos and the unknown granddaughter could come to some sort of civilised divorce, go their separate ways, and that would be that.

And what about your son? What will he think about your 'civilised divorce'?

He pushed that thought from his mind as well. Who knew? Maybe the granddaughter would turn out to be barren, as well as plain as sin.

A footfall behind him made him turn.

And freeze.

Nikos's eyes narrowed as he saw the unfamiliar woman step onto the wide sweeping terrace where he stood. The cloud of dark bronze hair rustled on her shoulders, making him take notice of her long, slender neck. Then, as if a brief glance were tribute enough for that particular feature, his eyes clamped back to her face.

Theos, but she was a stunner! Her skin was paler than a Greek's, but still tanned. She had a short, delicate nose, sculpted cheeks, and a wide, generous mouth. Her eyes were like rich chestnut, the lashes ridiculously long and smoky.

He felt his body kick with pleasure at looking at her. As of their own volition, his eyes wandered downwards again, past that slender neck framed by that glorious hair, down over full, swelling breasts, superbly moulded by the tight-fitting jacket she wore, nipping in to a deliciously spannable waist, and then ripening outwards to softly rounded hips, before descending down long, long legs.

He frowned. She was wearing trousers. The sight offended him. With legs that long she should be wearing a short, tight skirt that hugged those splendid thighs and clung lovingly to the lush, rounded bottom he felt sure a woman like that must have...

Who the hell was she?

His brain interrupted his body's visceral contemplation of the female's physical attributes. What was a woman this lush, this drop-dead gorgeous, this damn *sexy*, doing here in Yiorgos Coustakis's house?

The answer came like a blow to the gut. There was only one

reason a woman who looked like this would be swanning around Old Man Coustakis's private residence, and that was because she was a private guest. Very private.

All of Athens knew that Yiorgos Coustakis liked to keep a stable of women. He was renowned for it, even from long before his wife became an invalid.

And they'd always been young women—even as he'd got older.

Even now, apparently.

Distaste filled Nikos's mouth. OK, so maybe the old man was still up for it, even at his age, but the idea of the man of seventy-eight keeping a woman who couldn't be more than twenty-five, if that, as his mistress was repugnant in the extreme.

Andrea blinked, momentarily blinded by the bright light after the dim shade of the interior of the huge house she had been deposited at barely five minutes ago by the lush limo that had met her at the airport.

Then, as her vision cleared, she saw someone was already on the terrace. She took in an impression of height, and darkness. Black hair, a sleek, powerful-looking business suit, an immaculately knotted tie—and a face that made her stop dead.

The skin tone was Mediterranean; there was no doubt about that. But what struck her incongruously was the pair of piercing steel-grey eyes that blazed at her. She felt her stomach lurch, and blinked again. She went on staring, taking in, once she could drag her eyes away from those penetrating grey ones, a strong, straight nose, high cheekbones and a wide, firm mouth.

She shook her head slightly, as if to make sure the man she was staring at was really there.

Suddenly Andrea saw the man's expression change. Harden with disapproval. And something more than disapproval. Disdain. Something flared inside her—and it was nothing to do with the unmistakable frisson that had sizzled through her like a jolt of electricity in the face of the blatant appraisal this startlingly breath-catching man had just subjected her to. She would have been blind not to have registered the look of out-right sexual attraction in the man's face when he'd first set eyes on her a handful of seconds ago. She was used to that reaction in men. For the most part it was annoying more than anything, and over the years she had learnt to dress down, concealing the ripeness of her figure beneath loose, baggy clothes, confining her glowing hair into a subdued plait, and seldom bothering with make-up. Besides—a familiar shaft of bitterness stabbed at her—she knew all too well that any initial sexual attraction men showed in her would not last—not when they saw the rest of her...

She pulled her mind away, washing out bitterness with an even more familiar upsurge of raw, desperate gratitude—to her mother, to fate, to any providential power, to everyone who had helped her along her faltering way in the long, painful years until she had emerged to take her place as a functioning adult in the world. Considering what the alternatives might have been, she had no cause for bitterness—none at all.

And if she felt bitter about the man who was her father's father—well, that was not on her own behalf, only her mother's. For her mother's sake *only* she was here, now, standing on this terrace, over a thousand miles from home—being looked at disdainfully by a man she could not drag her eyes from.

It had been a hard decision to make. It had been her friends Tony and Linda who had helped her make it.

'But why is he *doing* this?' she'd asked them, for the doz-enth time. 'He's up to something and I don't know what—and that worries me!'

'Maybe he just wants to get to know you, Andy,' said Linda peaceably. 'Maybe he's old, and ill, and wants to make up for how he treated you.'

'Oh, so that's why I've been getting letters just about or-dering me to go and dance attendance on him! *And* not a dickey-bird about Mum, either! No, if he'd really wanted to make up he'd have written more politely—and to Mum, not me.'

'If you want my advice I think you should go out there,' said Linda's husband, Tony. 'Like Linda said, he *might* be after a reconciliation, but even if he isn't, suppose he wants to use you for his own nefarious ends in some way? That, you know, puts you in a strong position. Have you thought of that?'

Andrea frowned.

Tony went on. 'Look, if he does want you for something, then if he doesn't want you to refuse he's going to have to do something *you* want.'

'Like what?' Andrea snorted. 'He doesn't have a thing I want!'

'He's got money, Andy,' Tony said quietly. 'Shed-loads of it.'

Andrea's eyes narrowed to angry slits. 'He can choke on it for all I care! I don't want a penny from him!'

'But what about your mum, Andy?' said Tony, even more quietly.

Andrea stilled. Tony pressed on, leaning forward. 'What if he forked out enough for her to clear her debts—and move to Spain?'

Andrea's breath seemed tight in her chest. As tight as her mother's breath was, day in, day out. Instantly in her mind she heard her mother's dry, asthmatic cough, saw her pause by the sink, breathing slowly and painfully, her frail body hunched.

'I can't,' she answered faintly. 'I can't take that man's money!'

'Think it through,' urged Tony. 'You wouldn't be taking his money for yourself, but for your mum. He owes her—you've always said that and it's true! She's raised you single-handed with nothing from him except insults and abuse! He lives in the lap of luxury, worth hundreds of millions, and his grand-daughter lives in a council flat. Do it for her, Andy.'

And that, in the end, had been the decider. Though every fibre of her being wanted never, ever to have anything to do with the man who had treated her mother so callously, the moment Tony had said 'Spain' a vista had opened up in Andrea's mind so wonderful she knew she could not refuse. If she could just get her grandfather to buy her mother a small apartment somewhere it was warm and dry all year round…

It was for that very reason that Andrea was now standing on the terrace of her grandfather's palatial property in Athens.

She would get her mother the dues owed her.

She gave a smile as she looked again at the impressive man who stood before her. A small, tight, defiant—dismissive— smile. So, he knew who she was, did he, Mr Mega-Cool? He looked so sleek, screaming 'money' in his superbly tailored suit, with his immaculately cut dark hair, the gleam of gold at his wrist as he paused in the action of checking his watch— oh, he must be one of her grandfather's entourage. No doubt. One of his business associates, partners—whatever rich men called each other in their gilded world where the price of elec- tricity was an irrelevance and there was never green mould on the bathroom walls…

So much, she thought with self-mocking acknowledgement, for the shopping spree she'd been on with Linda and Tony in that ultra-posh London department store, courtesy of its gold store card! She'd thought the outrageously priced trouser suit she'd bought, shouting its designer label, would do the trick— fool anyone who saw her that the last thing she could possibly be was a common-as-muck London girl off a housing estate! And Linda had even done her hair and make-up that morning, before she'd set out for the airport, making her look svelte and expensive to go with the fantastic new outfit she'd travelled in. Obviously she need not have bothered!

The man looking at her so disdainfully out of those cold steel-grey eyes knew perfectly well what she was—who she was. Yiorgos Coustakis's cheap-and-nasty bastard granddaugh- ter!

Her chin went up. Well, what did she care? She had her own opinions of Yiorgos Coustakis—and they were not generous. So if this man standing here on her grandfather's mile-long terrace, looking down his strong, straight nose at her, his mouth tight with disdain, thought she wasn't fit for a palatial place like this, what was it to her? Zilch. Just as Yiorgos Coustakis was nothing to her—nothing except the price of some small, modest reparation to the woman he had treated like dirt…

Her eyes hardened. Nikos saw their expression change, saw the derisive smile, the insolent tilt of the woman's chin. Clearly the female was shameless about her trade! The distaste he felt about Old Man Coustakis keeping a mistress at his age filtered into distaste for the woman herself. It checked the stirring of his own body, busy responding the way nature liked it to do when in the presence of a sexually alluring female.

So when the woman strolled towards him, the smile on her face unable to compensate for the hardness in her eyes, he responded in kind.

Andrea saw the withdrawal in his eyes, and suddenly, like a cloud passing in front of the sun, she felt a chill emanate from him. Suddenly he wasn't just a breath-catchingly, heart-stoppingly handsome man, looking a million dollars, tall and lean—he was an icily formidable, hard-eyed, patrician-born captain of industry who looked on the rest of humanity as his inferior minions…

Well, tough! She tilted her head, almost coquettishly, letting her glorious hair riot over her shoulders. An intense desire to annoy him came over her.

'Hi,' she breathed huskily. 'We haven't met, have we? I'd remember, I know!' She let a gleam of appreciation enter her glowing eyes. That would annoy him even more; she instinctively knew.

She held her hand out. It was looking beautiful—Linda had given her a manicure the night before, smoothing the work-roughened skin and putting on nail extensions and a rich nail-varnish whose colour matched her hair.

Nikos ignored the hand. A revulsion against touching flesh that had caressed, for money, a rich old man, filled him. It didn't matter that half his body was registering renewed arousal at the sound of that breathy voice, the heady fragrance of her body as she approached him. He subdued it ruthlessly.

Besides, it had just registered with him that the woman was English. That would account for the auburn colouring.

Presumably, he found himself thinking, for a woman of her profession hair that colour would command a premium in lands where dark hair was the norm.

The man's rejection of her outstretched hand made Andrea falter. She let her hand fall to her side. But still, despite the shut-out, she refused to be intimidated. After all, if she failed at the first test—being sneered at by a complete stranger for being the bastard Coustakis granddaughter—then she would be doomed to fail in her mission. Intimidation was, she knew from the painfully extracted reminiscences of her mother's abrupt expulsion from Greece twenty-four years ago, the forte of the man who had summoned her here like a servant. She must not, above all, be intimidated by Yiorgos Coustakis as her mother had been. She must stand up to him—give him as good as she got. Tony's words echoed in her mind—if he had summoned her here, he wanted something. And that made her position powerful.

She had to remember that. *Must* remember that.

She was in enemy territory. Confidence was everything.

So now, in the face of the obvious disdain of this stunning stranger, she refused to be cowed. Instead, she gave that derisive little smile again, deliberately tossed her head and, shooting him a mocking glance, strolled right past him to take in the view over the grounds. She leant her palms on the stone balustrade, taking some of the weight off her legs. They were aching slightly, probably tension more than anything, because she'd been sitting down most of the day—first in the luxurious airline seat and then in the luxurious chauffeur-driven car. Still, she must do her exercises tonight—right after she'd phoned Tony, as they'd arranged.

Her mind raced, thinking about all the safety nets that she and Tony had planned out. The man behind her was totally forgotten. However good-looking he was—however scornful of the Coustakis bastard granddaughter—he was not important. What was important was going through, for the thousandth time, everything she and Tony had done to make sure that her grandfather could not outmanoeuvre her. Had they left any holes? Left anything uncovered?

Working on the premise that Yiorgos Coustakis was totally ruthless in getting what he wanted, she and Tony had planned elaborate measures to make sure that Andrea always had an escape route if she needed one. The first was to ensure that every evening of her stay in Greece she would phone Tony on the mobile he had lent her. If he did not hear from her by eleven p.m., he was to alert the British consul in Athens and tell them a British citizen was being forcibly held against her will. And if that did not do the trick—her mouth tightened— then Tony's second phone call would be to a popular British tabloid, spilling the whole story of how the granddaughter of one of the richest men in Europe came to be living on a council estate. Yiorgos Coustakis might be immune to bad publicity, but she wondered whether his shareholders would be as sanguine about the stink she could raise if she wanted…

And then, if her grandfather still didn't want to let her go, she had left her passport, together with seven hundred euros, plus her return ticket, in a secure locker at Athens airport—the key to which was in her make-up bag. She had also, not trusting her grandfather an inch, purchased a second, open-dated ticket to London while she was still at Heathrow, which she had not yet collected from the airline. She had paid for that one herself.

Andrea smiled grimly as she stared out over the ornate, fussily designed gardens. Though she hadn't been able to afford to buy the full-price ticket from her own meagre funds, she had come up with a brilliant idea for how to pay for it. The day that she and Tony and Linda had gone into the West End to buy her outfit, they had also visited the store's jewellery department. The balance from the five thousand pounds after buying the trouser suit and accessories had purchased a very nice pearl necklace—so nice that they had immediately taken it to another jewellery shop and sold it for cash. With the money they had bought the airline ticket, a wad of traveller's cheques, and split the rest into a combination of sterling, US dollars and euros. That, surely, she thought, her eyes quite unseeing of the view in front of her, should be enough to ensure that she could simply leave whenever she wanted.

Behind her, Nikos Vassilis had stiffened. The woman had simply walked past him as if he were no one! And that derisive little smile and mocking look of hers sent a shaft of anger through him! No woman did that to him! Certainly not one who stooped to earn her living in such a way. He stared after her, eyes narrowing.

Then a discreet cough a little way to his side caught his attention, as it was designed to do. The manservant was back, murmuring politely that Mr Coustakis would see him now, if he would care to come this way.

With a last, ireful glance at the woman now leaning care-lessly on the balustrade, totally ignoring him, her hair a glori-ous sunset cloud around her shoulders, Nikos stalked off into the house.

CHAPTER THREE

AN HOUR later, as she was shown into the dim, shaded room, Andrea straightened her shoulders, ready for battle. At first it seemed the room was empty. Then a voice startled her.

'Come here.'

The voice was harsh, speaking in English. Clearly issuing an order.

She walked forward. She seemed to be in a sort of library, judging from the shelves of books layering every wall. Her heels sounded loud on the parquet flooring. She could see, now, that a large desk was positioned at the far end of the room, and behind it a man was sitting.

It seemed to take a long time to reach him. One part of her brain realised why—it was a deliberate ploy to put anyone entering the room at a disadvantage to the man already sitting at the desk.

As she walked forward she glanced around her, quite deliberately letting her head crane around, taking in her surroundings, as if the man at the desk were of no interest to her. Her heels clicked loudly.

She reached the front of the desk, and only then did she deign to look at the man who had summoned her.

It was the eyes she noticed first. They were deepset, in sunken sockets. His whole face was craggy and wrinkled, very old, but the eyes were alight. They were dark, almost black in this dim light, but they scoured her face.

'So,' said Yiorgos Coustakis to his granddaughter, whom he had never set eyes on till now, 'you are that slut's brat.' He nodded. 'Well, no matter. You'll do. You'll have to.'

His eyes went on scouring her face. Inside, as the frail bud of hope that maybe Yiorgos Coustakis had softened his hard heart died a swift, instant death, Andrea fought to quell the upsurge of blind rage as she heard him refer to her mother in such a way. With a struggle, she won the battle. Losing her temper and storming out now would get her nowhere except back to London empty-handed. Instead, she opted for silence.

She went on standing there, being inspected from head to toe.

'Turn around.'

The order was harsh. She obeyed it.

'You walk perfectly well.'

The brief sentence was an accusation. Andrea said nothing.

'Have you a tongue in your head?' Yiorgos Coustakis demanded.

She went on looking at him.

Was a man's soul in his eyes, as the proverb said? she wondered. If so, then Yiorgos Coustakis's soul was in dire condition. The black eyes that rested on her were the most terrifying she had ever seen. They seemed to bore right into her—and, search as she would, she could see nothing in them to reassure her. Not a glimmer of kindness, of affection, even of humour, showed in them. A feeling of profound sadness filled her, and she realised that, despite all the evidence, something inside her had been hoping against hope that the man she had grown up hating and despising was not such a man after all.

But he was proving exactly the callous monster she had always thought him.

'Why did you bring me here?'

The question fell from her lips without her thinking. But instinctively she knew she had done the right thing in taking the battle—for this was a battle, no doubt about that now, none at all—to her grandfather.

He saw it, and the dark eyes darkened even more.

'Do not speak to me in that tone,' he snapped, throwing his head back.

Her chin lifted in response.

'I have come over a thousand miles at your bidding. I am entitled to know why.' Her voice was as steady as she could make it, though in her breast she could feel her heart beating wildly.

His laugh came harsh, scornful.

'You are entitled to nothing! *Nothing!* Oh, I know why you came! The moment you caught a glimpse of the kind of money you could spend if you came here you changed your tune! Why do you think I sent you that store card? I knew that would flush you out!' He leant forward, his once-powerful arms leaning on the surface of the polished mahogany desk. 'But understand this, and understand it well! You will be on the first plane back to London unless you do exactly, *exactly* what I want you to do! Understand me?'

His eyes flashed at her. She held his gaze, though it was like a heavy weight on her. So, she thought, Tony had been right—he *did* want something from her. But what? She needed to know. Only when she knew what the man sitting there, who by a vile accident of fate just happened to be her grandfather, wanted of her could she start to bargain for the money she wanted from him.

Play it cool, girl…play it cool…

She lifted an interrogative eyebrow.

'And what is it, *exactly*, that you want me to do?'

His brows snapped together at the sarcastic emphasis she gave to echo his.

'You'll find out—when I want you to.' He held up a hand, silencing her. 'I've had enough of you for now. You will go to your room and prepare yourself for dinner. We will have a guest. With your upbringing you obviously won't know how to comport yourself, so I shall tell you now that you had better change your attitude! In *this* country a woman knows how to behave—see that you do not shame me in my own house! Now, go!'

Andrea turned and left. The walk back to the door seemed much further than it had in the opposite direction. Her heart was pounding.

It went on pounding all the way back upstairs to her room. She shut the door and leant against it. So, that was her grandfather! That was the man whose son had had a brief, whirlwind romance with her mother, who had thrown her, pregnant and penniless, out of the country, and left her to bear and raise his grandchild in poverty, refusing to acknowledge her existence.

She owed such a man nothing. Nothing! Not duty, nor respect—and certainly not loyalty or affection.

What does he want of me?

The question went round and round, unanswered. Fretting at her.

In the end, to calm herself down and pass the time, she decided to make use of the opulent bathroom. Inside its lavish, overdone interior she could not but help revel in the luxury it offered.

The bath was vast, and it had, she discovered, sinking into its deep scented depths, whirling jets that massaged her body, easing the aching muscles in her tense legs. Blissfully, she gave herself to the wonderful sensation. Towering bubbles from the half a bottle of bath foam she'd emptied in veiled her whole body, from breasts to feet.

You walk perfectly well...

She heard the harsh accusation ring in her head again, and her mouth tightened.

When she emerged from the bathroom, entering her lavishly decorated bedroom suite, swathed in a floor-length towel, it was to see a maid at the open door of her closet, hanging up clothes. The girl turned, bobbing a brief curtsey, and hesitantly informed Andrea that she was here to help her dress.

'I don't need any help,' said Andrea tersely.

The girl looked subdued, and Andrea immediately regretted her tone of voice.

'Please,' she said temporisingly, 'it's quite unnecessary.'

She walked past the huge bed, covered in a heavy gold and white patterned bedspread, and across to the room-sized closet. Whatever Yiorgos Coustakis had imagined she'd bought with her gleaming gold store card, all she was going to appear for dinner wearing was a chainstore skirt and blouse. But suddenly she stopped dead.

The racks were full, weighed down with plastic-swathed clothes.

'What—?'

'Kyrios Coustakis ordered them to be purchased for you, *kyria*. They were delivered just now by a personal shopper. There are accessories and lingerie as well,' said the maid's softly accented voice behind her. 'Which dress would you like to wear tonight?'

'None of them,' said Andrea tightly. She reached for the hanger carrying her own humble skirt and blouse.

The maid looked aghast. 'But…but it is a formal dinner, tonight, *kyria*,' she stammered. 'Kyrios Coustakis would be very angry if you did not dress appropriately…'

Andrea looked at the maid. The expression on the girl's face made her pause. There was only one word for the expression, and it was fear.

She gave in. She could defy her grandfather's anger, but she was damned if he would get the chance to terrorise one of his own staff on her account.

'Very well. Choose something for me.'

She went and sat back on the bed while the girl leafed through the clothes hanging from the rail. After a few moments she emerged with two, deftly removing the protective wrapping from them and laying them carefully across the foot of the bed. Andrea inspected them. Both were clearly very expensive, and although it was the short but high-necked cocktail length one that she preferred for style, she nodded at the other one, a full-length gown.

'That one,' she said.

It was emerald-green, cut on the bias, with a soft, folding bodice and a long, slinky skirt. Andrea found her hand reaching out to touch the silky folds.

'It is very beautiful, *ne*?' said the maid, and sounded wistful as well as admiring.

'Very,' agreed Andrea. She glanced at the girl. 'I don't know your name,' she said.

'Zoe, *kyria*,' said the girl.

'Andrea,' she replied. 'And I don't believe in servants.'

Some twenty minutes later, staring at herself in the long mirror set into the door of the closet, Andrea was stunned.

She looked—fantastic! That was the only word for it. The dress was a miracle of the couturier's art, its soft folds contrasting with the rich vividness of its colour. True, the bodice, held up by tiny shoestring straps, was draped dangerously low over her full breasts, encased in a fragile, strapless bra, but she had to admit the effect was very…well, *effective*! It gave the dress the finishing touch to the 'wow' impact it made.

She had scooped her hair up into a knot on her head, with tendrils loosening around the nape of her neck and gracing her cheeks and forehead, and she'd redone her make-up to match the impact of the dress.

With a final look at her reflection, she turned and headed towards the door, where the manservant who had come to summon her stood waiting. Staff though he was, she could see the admiration in his eyes. For an instant, in her mind's eye, it was not one of the house staff who stood there, but the man she had encountered on the terrace that afternoon, looking at her with those powerful grey eyes, making her stomach give a little skip…

She bestowed a slight, polite smile on the manservant, and headed towards the curving marble staircase.

It was time to go into battle once more…

Nikos Vassilis stepped on the accelerator, changed gear and heard the powerful note of the engine of the Ferrari change pitch. He was not in a good mood. Twice in one day now he'd made the journey out of Athens at the behest of Yiorgos Coustakis. Tonight was not a good night to be dining with the old man. He'd planned a leisurely evening with Xanthe, whose petite, curvaceous body was, he had discovered, a pleasant alternative to Esme Vandersee's greyhound leanness. Xanthe was proving very attentive—she was clearly keen to take his mind off Esme Vandersee, and was now pulling out all the stops to renew Nikos's interest. Which meant, he mused, that she was coming up with some very interesting ideas indeed to do so…

A smile indented his mouth. Last night with Xanthe had been very enjoyable—she had seen to that. Ah, he thought pleasurably, there was nothing like a Greek woman for making a man feel good! Yes, Esme Vandersee might be eager for him, he was certainly a catch for her, but as an American she suffered that infernal affliction of thinking that a woman had a right to give a man a hard time if she chose! Usually, of course, any petulance that Esme displayed he disposed of very swiftly— she was as sexy as a cat and getting her horizontal soon improved her mood…

But even so, he mused, Xanthe understood what it was that a man wanted a woman to be. And she made it obvious that she was keen to be so very attentive to his every need….

His smile vanished. Well, he'd be kept waiting tonight before availing himself of Xanthe's rediscovered charms! Yiorgos Coustakis was obviously taking considerable pleasure in jerking his strings—just for the hell of it, it seemed. Their meeting that afternoon, ostensibly to discus the technicalities of reversing Vassilis Inc into Coustakis Industries, had hardly been urgent, and could have been left to their respective finance directors to sort out. But obviously Old Man Coustakis had relished getting Nikos Vassilis to come traipsing out of Athens to that overblown villa of his whenever he snapped his fingers.

Thinking about the afternoon meeting brought another image vividly to mind—that of Yiorgos Coustakis's flame-haired mistress.

Nikos's mouth tightened. The woman had been so blatant, and so unashamed of what she was doing at the Coustakis villa. Not to mention eyeing him up and trying her wiles out on him to boot!

Mind you, Nikos thought, had the woman not been tainted by her distasteful association with a man old enough to be her grandfather, then her approach to him might well have got a warmer welcome.

Considerably warmer, in fact…

An image of her dark auburn hair floating around that perfect face, the way her breasts had thrust against the material of her jacket, played in his memory. Oh, yes, she was worth remembering, all right! Her beauty was so flamboyant, so eye-catching, that almost—almost he had been tempted to overlook just for whose benefit it had been paraded that afternoon. Not for him—for a seventy-eight-year-old man.

He thrust her memory from him. However alluring the woman, she was beyond the pale so far as he was concerned.

He revved the engine again, enjoying the superb handling of the extortionately expensive car beneath his hands. Driving a high-performance car like this was like having sex with a high-performance woman…they were both so extraordinarily responsive to his touch…

His mind snapped away from the analogy. For the next few hours, until the ordeal of a tedious, overlong dinner with Yiorgos Coustakis was done with, he had better keep his libido under control.

Think of your bride, Nikos!

That sobered him all right. It was about time Old Man Coustakis brought the girl out from wherever he had her stashed. She would know all about her intended bridegroom by now, no doubt, and she and her mother were probably already waist-deep in wedding plans. Presumably the girl wanted a lavish society wedding. Well, he didn't care one way or the other, and, since the whole purpose of marrying her was to seal his acquisition of Coustakis Industries, the more high-profile the better! After all, he had nothing against the girl—let her have her extravagant wedding if she wanted. Once she was his wife it would be *her* who would have to fit herself around what *he* wanted—that was what Greek wives did. Oh, he would be generous, of course, and considerate to her position—he had no intention of making a bad husband—but he did not envisage changing his life a great deal on account of the Coustakis heiress.

Pity she was obviously so plain… The thought of having a

sexually desirable, docile and attentive wife had its attractions, now he came to think of it.

He braked the Ferrari in front of the security-guarded gates of the Coustakis villa, presented his credentials, and moved on down the drive at a speed greater than he would normally. He wanted this evening over and done with.

CHAPTER FOUR

NIKOS stood in the ornate salon, itching for dinner to be announced. His host seemed to be in no hurry. He was regaling his guest with a lengthy description of his latest toy—a one-hundred-and-fifty-foot yacht which he had just taken delivery of. It was, by all accounts, an opulent vessel, and Yiorgos was telling him in great detail about the splendour of the décor of its interior—and how much it had all cost. The telling seemed to be putting him in a good humour. His colour was high, but his eyes were snapping with satisfaction.

'And you, my friend,' he said, slapping Nikos on the back with a still powerful hand, 'will be the first to try her out! You will spend your honeymoon on it! What do you think of that, eh?'

Nikos smiled briefly. Again, a honeymoon spent on board Yiorgos Coustakis's new yacht would send just the message to the world he wanted.

'Good, good,' said his grandfather-in-law-to-be, and slapped him once more on the back. Then his head snapped round. Automatically Nikos followed his gaze. A servant had opened the double doors to the salon.

A figure stepped through.

It was the flame-haired temptress!

Nikos felt a kick to his gut that was as powerful as it was unwelcome.

What the hell was she doing here?

The woman had paused for a moment in the doorway—*making sure all eyes were on her*, Nikos thought—and now started to glide forward towards them. Her head was held high—that glorious dark auburn hair twisted up into a topknot that revealed the perfect bone structure of her stunning face.

As for the rest of her…

Nikos felt his breath catch again. The dress was simply breathtaking on her, revealing the lushness of her figure even more generously than the close-fitting jacket had that afternoon. Now, instead of only being able to imagine the rich creaminess of her skin, he could see acres of it displayed for him, from her swan-like neck down across the sculpted beauty of her shoulders, the graceful curve of her bare arms and, best of all, towards the swell of her ripe breasts…

He felt himself ache to caress them…

Like a chill breath on the back of his neck, he felt Yiorgos Coustakis watching him. Watching him lust after his mistress.

Disgust flooded through him. Whatever the hell the old man was playing at, bringing his mistress to dinner, taking pleasure in seeing his guest responding to her lavish charms, he would have none of it! His face hardened.

For Andrea, walking in through the doors and then freezing to a stupefied halt at seeing the very man she had been trying not to think about all evening standing there beside her grandfather, it was like *déjà-vu* all over again. Just as the first sight of her had brought instant sexual appreciation into the man's eyes, so, an instant later, that had been replaced by disdain— all over again.

And, just as she had on the terrace, she reacted instinctively. Her chin went up; her eyes glinted dangerously.

She was glad of her anger—it took her mind off the fact that her heart was racing like a rocket and that her eyes were glued to his face.

She stopped, resting her hand on the back of an antique sofa beside her. Her eyes met those of the stranger, defiant and glittering.

'Well,' said Yiorgos Coustakis to the man he had chosen to be his son-in-law, 'what do you think of her?'

What the hell do I say? thought Nikos savagely. He said the only thing he could.

'As ever, Yiorgos, you have impeccable taste. She is…outstanding.'

They were speaking Greek, Andrea registered. Well, of course they would be! Her eyes flew from one to another.

'You are to be envied,' Nikos went on, with gritted politeness, wondering what the hell to say to the old man about the woman he was warming his bed with. Disgust was filling his veins. He wanted out of here—fast.

Yiorgos Coustakis smiled.

'I give her to you,' he said. He made a gesture of presentation with his hand. The satisfaction in his voice was blatant.

Nikos froze. *What the hell was this? Was this supposed to be some kind of sweetener that the old man imagined he might want in order to bed his plain, sexless granddaughter?* If so, he had better extricate himself from the delusion.

'Your generosity is…overwhelming, Yiorgos,' he managed to get out. 'But I cannot accept.'

A look of deliberate astonishment lit Yiorgos Coustakis's face. 'How is this?' he demanded. 'I thought…' He paused infinitesimally, milking the pleasure he was getting from the situation to its utmost, watching this arrogant, ambitious pup squirm for one moment longer. 'That you *wanted* my granddaughter? That you were impatient to meet her…'

He gave a short laugh, his eyes snapping with malicious pleasure as he watched Nikos's face change expression as the truth dawned.

'She is my granddaughter, Nikos—what did you imagine, eh?' he asked softly.

Only Nikos's years of self-discipline enabled him to keep his expression steady. Inside, it felt as if the floor had given way beneath him.

'This is your granddaughter?' he heard himself say, as if seeking confirmation of the unbelievable.

Yiorgos laughed again, still highly pleased with the joke he had played on the younger man. He knew perfectly well what conclusions he had jumped to when, just as Yiorgos had planned, he had first set eyes on the girl that afternoon, sublimely unaware that the plain-faced fiancée he had been led to expect was no such thing at all.

He glanced across at the girl and beckoned imperiously.

'Come here,' he commanded in English.

Andrea walked forward. Her heart was pounding again. She could feel it thrilling in every vein. The man with the steel-grey eyes was looking at her full on, and she was all but knocked senseless by the way he was looking at her—either that or jolted by a million volts of electricity scorching through her.

If she'd thought he'd looked a knock-out that afternoon, in his hand-made business suit, the way he looked now, in his tuxedo, simply took her breath away! She swallowed. This was ridiculous! No man should have such an effect on her! She'd seen good-looking blokes before, been eyed up by them—even kissed some in her time—but never, *never* had any man made her feel like this.

Breathless, terrified—enthralled. *Excited!*

Beside the man, her grandfather ceased to exist. She took in a vague impression of a stockily built figure, shoulders bowing with age, and that craggy, heavy-featured face she had registered as he'd sat at his desk that afternoon.

But right now she had no eyes for him.

She was simply drinking in the man at his side—she wanted to stare and stare and stare.

'My granddaughter,' said Yiorgos.

Nikos hardly heard him. The entire focus of his attention was on the woman in front of him. *Theos*, but she was fantastic! Was she really the Coustakis girl? It couldn't be possible. Then, with a fraction of his brain that worked, he realised that the old man had set him up deliberately—leading him on to think that he was going to be shackled to a plain wife, when all along...

He smiled. Oh, what the hell—so the old man had set him up! He didn't care! Hell, he could even share the joke! A sense of relief had flooded through him, he realised, and something more—exultation.

Yes! That woman, that fantastic flame-haired temptress, was *not* out of bounds after all. In fact—his smile deepened—she was very, very within bounds…

Andrea saw the smile, brilliant, wolfish, and felt her stomach lurch. Oh, good grief, but he was something all right! She felt the breath squeeze from her body.

Nikos reached and took the girl's hand. He lifted it to his mouth. Andrea watched the dark head bend as if in slow motion. She still couldn't breathe, her lungs frozen as she felt the long, strong fingers take hers.

Then even more sensation laced through her. He was brushing her fingers with his lips. Lightly, oh, so lightly! But oh, oh, so devastatingly. A million nerve endings fired within her, like the *whoosh* of a rocket cascading stars down upon her head.

As he raised his head he smiled down at her.

'Nikos Vassilis,' he said, and looked right into her eyes.

His voice was low—the tone intimate.

She stared up at him, lips parted. She could say, or do, nothing.

'Andrea—'

The word breathed from her. She could hardly speak, she found.

'Andrea…' His voice echoed her name, deeper than her husky contralto. 'It is good to meet you.'

He let his eyes linger on her one last, endless moment, then, tucking her hand into the crook of his arm, he turned to his host.

'You're an old devil, Yiorgos,' he said with grating acknowledgement. 'But in this instance the joke was worth it.'

Andrea's eyes flew between them—the language was back to Greek. What was going on? Then, suddenly, Nikos turned back to her.

'Come, let me take you through to dinner.' His voice was warm, and the caress in it made her nerve-endings fire all over again. That and the over-powering closeness of him, her hand caught in his arm. She felt she ought to pull away from him—but for the life of her she could not.

As if in a dream she let herself be escorted from the room, across the vast entrance hall, and into a grandiose dining room.

With the utmost attentiveness this most devastating man, Nikos Vassilis—*Who is he?* she found herself wondering urgently—drew back her chair, waving away the manservant who came forward to perform the task, and settled her in her seat.

She wanted to glance up and smile her thanks politely, but she could not. Shyness suddenly overwhelmed her. This was like something out of a fairytale—she dressed like a princess, and he, oh, he like a dark prince!

Instead she mumbled a thank-you into her place-setting.

As he took his place opposite her—only one end of the long mahogany table was occupied, with Yiorgos taking the head and his granddaughter and her fiancé on either hand—Nikos felt a deep sense of well-being filling him.

He couldn't have asked for a more beautiful bride! Old Man Coustakis was doing him proud. Oh, he would never have been unkind, even to a plain wife, but having that flame-haired beauty at his side, in his bed, was going to make married life a whole, whole lot sweeter for him!

He glanced across at her. She was still staring at her place-setting as if it was the most interesting thing in the room, but she was aware of him all right. Every male instinct told him that. But if she were behaving as a well-brought-up young girl should—showing a proper shyness in the face of the man she was to marry—well, who was he to complain?

A memory of the way she had boldly walked up to him on the terrace, her voice husky as she sought to introduce herself, intruded, conflicting with the image of the meekly downturned head opposite him. A frown flickered in his eyes. Then it cleared. She must have seen the look he had given her then and been angered by it—and rightfully so! No gently reared female would care to be taken for such a one as he had first thought her. Well, now that misunderstanding was out of the way it would not trouble them again.

Another frown flickered in his eyes. The girl was English,

that was obvious—both by her colouring and her use of the language, quite unaccented.

As the manservant drew forward to start serving dinner Nikos glanced at his host.

'You did not tell me that your granddaughter was half-English, Yiorgos,' he opened. He spoke in Greek, and as he did he noticed Andrea's head lift, her eyes focus intently on him, concentrating.

Yiorgos leant back in his chair.

'A little surprise for you,' he answered. His eyes gleamed.

Nikos let his mouth twist. 'Another one,' he acknowledged. Then he turned his attention to Andrea.

'You live in England? With your English mother?' he asked politely, in Greek. That must be the reason she had addressed him in English this afternoon.

Andrea looked at him. She made as if to open her mouth, but her grandfather forestalled her.

'She does not speak Greek,' he said bluntly. He spoke in English.

Nikos's eyes snapped together. 'How is this?' he demanded, sticking with English.

'Let us say her mother had her own ideas about her upbringing,' said Yiorgos.

Andrea stared at her grandfather—just stared. Then, as if knowing exactly why she was staring, he caught her eye. Dark, intent. Warning.

His words echoed in her mind from the afternoon. *You will be on the first plane back to London unless you do exactly, exactly, what I want you to do!*

She felt her blood chill. Was going along with some fairy story he wanted to tell this guest of his about her upbringing part of that imprecation? What do I do? she thought wildly. Open my mouth and set the record straight right away?

And achieve what, precisely?

She knew the answer. Get herself thrown out of her grandfather's house and sent back to London without a penny for her mother. And she wouldn't go home empty-handed; she *wouldn't*! She would get Kim the money she deserved, what-ever it took. Even if it meant colluding with Yiorgos Coustakis's attempt to whitewash his behaviour.

So she buttoned her lip and stayed silent.

From across the table Nikos saw her expression, saw the mutinous gleam in those lustrous chestnut eyes. So, the girl had been brought up in England, by a mother who had her own ideas, had she? Ideas that included depriving the Coustakis heiress of her natural heritage—the language of her father, the household of her grandfather. What kind of mother had she been? he wondered. An image presented itself in his mind—one of those sharp-tongued, upper-class, arrogant Englishwomen, expensively dressed, enjoying a social round of polo and house-parties at one stately home after another. He frowned. Why had she married Andreas Coustakis in the first place? he wondered. Doubtless the marriage would not have lasted, even if Yiorgos's son had not been killed so young. He found himself wondering why Yiorgos had so uncharacteristi-cally let the widow take his granddaughter back to England with her, instead of keeping her in his household. Well, his generosity had been ill-paid! Now he had a granddaughter who could not even speak his own language!

I could teach her…

Another image swept into his mind. That of this flame-haired beauty lying in his arms as he taught her some of the more essential things that a Greek bride needed to be able to tell her husband—such as her desire for him…

He let his imagination dwell pleasantly on the prospect as they began to dine.

Through his long lashes, Nikos watched with amusement as Andrea began to eat appreciatively. Though he was pleased to see her take evident sensuous delight in fine food—Esme's gruelling diet had always irritated him, and Xanthe was picky about what she ate as well—he would have to keep an eye on his bride's appetite. At the moment she could get away with hearty eating—her figure was lush and queenly, and she carried no surplus pounds at all, he could tell—but if she continued to put food away like that for the next twenty years she would be fat by forty! A thought struck him. How old was she, exactly? When he'd first set eyes on her he'd taken her for twenty-five or so, but surely Yiorgos would not have kept her unmarried for so long? She must be younger. Probably her English mother and that sophisticated aristocratic society she doubtless enjoyed had served to make her appear more mature than she really was.

Yet another thought struck him, less pleasant. If she'd been brought up in England just how sure could he be that she was coming to him unsullied? English girls were notoriously free with their favours—every Greek male knew that, and most of them took advantage of it if they got the chance! Upper-class English girls were no longer pure as the driven snow—some of them started their sexual lives at a shamefully early age. Could she still be a virgin? He thought of asking Yiorgos outright, but knew what the answer would be—*Do you care enough to walk away from Coustakis Industries, my friend?*

And he knew what his own answer to that would be.

Virgin or no, he would marry Andrea Coustakis and get Coustakis Industries as her dowry.

Eating the delicious dinner—there seemed to be an endless array of courses—served to take Andrea's mind a fraction off the man opposite her. But only by a minute amount. Then, just as she was beginning to calm, he started talking to her.

'What part of England do you live in, Andrea?' he asked her civilly, clearly making conversation.

'London,' she replied, daring to glance across at him briefly.

'A favourite city of mine. Your life there must be pretty hectic, I guess?'

'Yes,' said, thinking of the two jobs she held down, working weekends as well as evenings, putting aside every penny she could to help pay off those debts hanging over her mother. Kim worked too, in the local late-night-opening supermarket—neither of them got much time off.

'So what are the best clubs in London at the moment, do

you think?' Nikos went on, naming a couple of fashionable hot-spots that Andrea vaguely recognised from glossy magazines.

'Clubbing really isn't my scene,' she answered. Not only did she get little free time to go out, but the kind of nightlife available in her part of London was not the kind to feature in glossy magazines. Anyway, dancing was out for her, and Kim had brought her up to appreciate classical music best.

'Oh,' replied Nikos, realising he felt pleased with her answer. Clubbing was strongly associated with sexual promiscuity, and he found himself reassured by her answer. 'What is your "scene", then, Andrea?'

She looked at him. Presumably he was just making polite conversation to his host's granddaughter.

'I like the theatre,' she said. It was true—the biggest treat she could give Kim, and herself, was to see the Royal Shakespeare Company, visit the National Theatre, or go to any of the great wealth of other theatres London had to offer. But tickets were expensive, so it was something they did not indulge themselves in often.

Nikos named a couple of spectacular musicals running in the West End currently—obviously he was no stranger to London, Andrea thought. She shook her head. Tickets for such extravaganzas were even more expensive than for ordinary theatre.

'I prefer Shakespeare,' she said.

She could tell, immediately, she had given the wrong answer. She glanced warily at her grandfather. His eyes had altered somehow, and she could sense his disapproval focussing on her. Now what? she wondered. Wasn't it OK for her to like Shakespeare, for heaven's sake?

She got her answer a moment later.

'No man likes a woman who is intellectually pretentious,' the old man said brusquely.

Andrea blinked. Liking Shakespeare was intellectually pretentious?

'Shakespeare wrote popular plays for mass audiences,' she pointed out mildly. 'There's nothing intellectually élite about his work, if it isn't treated as such. Of course there are huge depths to his writing, which can keep academics happy for years dissecting it, but the plays can be enjoyed on many levels. They're very accessible, especially in modern productions which make every effort to draw in those who, like you, are put off by the aura surrounding Shakespeare.'

Yiorgos set down his knife and fork. His eyes snapped with anger.

'Stop babbling like an imbecile, girl! Hold your tongue if you've nothing useful to say! No man likes a woman trying to show off!'

Astonishment was the emotion uppermost in Andrea's re-action. She simply couldn't believe that she was being criticised for defending her enjoyment of Shakespeare. Automatically, she found herself glancing across at Nikos Vassilis. Did he share her grandfather's antediluvian views on women and their 'intellectual pretensions'?

To her relief, as she met his eye she realised that there was a distinct gleam of conspiratorial humour in it.

'So,' said Nikos smoothly, coming to the girl's rescue after her grandfather's reprimand, 'what is your favourite Shakespeare play?' He ignored the glare coming from his host at his continuing with a line of conversation he disapproved of.

Andrea ignored it too, glad to find her grandfather's dinner guest was more liberal in his expectations of female interests.

'*Much Ado About Nothing,*' she replied promptly. 'Beatrice and Benedict are my favourite hero and heroine! I just love the verbal warfare between them—she always answers back to every jibe he puts on her, and never lets him put her down!'

The humour vanished from Nikos's eyes. A bride with a penchant for a heroine specialising in verbal warfare with her future husband was not his ideal. However stunning her auburn looks, he found himself wishing that the Coustakis heiress was all-Greek after all. A pure Greek bride would never dream of taking pleasure in answering her husband back!

Andrea saw his disapproval of her choice, and her mouth tightened. Nikos Vassilis might be a drop-dead smoothie, but scratch him and he was cut from the same metal as her grandfather, it seemed. Women were not there to be anything other than ornamental and docile.

She gave a mental shrug. Well, who cared what Nikos Vassilis thought women should be—let alone her grandfather? She wasn't here to win the approval of either.

She went back to eating her dinner. Across the table, Nikos was distracted from thinking further about the woman he had elected to marry by Yiorgos peremptorily asking his opinion on some aspect of global economic conditions. Clearly he had heard quite enough from his granddaughter. It was obviously time for her to revert to being ornamental and docile. And silent. Knowing nothing about global economic conditions, only a great deal about her straitened personal ones, Andrea tuned out.

Then, after the final course had been removed—and she felt as if she could never look another rich, luxurious dish in the face again—her grandfather abruptly pushed his chair back.

'We will take coffee in the salon, after I have checked the US markets,' he announced. He looked meaningfully at Nikos as he stood up. 'Join me in twenty minutes.'

He left the dining room. Nikos glanced after him, then back at Andrea.

'Even at his age he does not relinquish his mastery, not for a moment,' he said. He sounded, thought Andrea, almost approving.

'Surely he's got enough money,' she said tartly.

Nikos, who had got to his feet as the older man had risen, looked down at her.

'Easy to say that,' he observed evenly, 'when you have lived in luxury all your life.'

She stared at him. Again, astonishment was uppermost in her breast. Was this more of her grandfather's fairytale at work? She said nothing—Nikos Vassilis was the dinner guest of the man who was going to fund her mother's removal to Spain. Baring her family's unpleasant secrets to him was unnecessary.

He came around to her side of the table and held out his hand, a smile parting his lips. 'Come,' he said. 'We have been given twenty minutes to ourselves. Let us make the most of them.'

Thinking that the company of Nikos Vassilis was a good deal more bearable than that of her grandfather—even if he clearly didn't like her approving of Shakespeare's feisty heroine Beatrice!—Andrea went along with him. He escorted her, hand tucked into the crook of his arm again—a most disturbingly arousing sensation, she rediscovered—from the dining room, opening large French windows to emerge out on to the same terrace where she had first seen him that afternoon. After the brightness of the dining room the dim night outside made her blink until she got her night vision. She glanced up.

The night sky was ablaze with stars. Though it was early summer still, the air was much warmer than it would have been in England. She gave a little sigh of pleasure and walked forward, disengaging herself to place her hands on the balustrade and look out over the dim gardens.

All around in the darkness she could hear a soft chirruping noise.

'What's that?' she asked, puzzled.

'You would call them by their Spanish name, I think—cicadas,' said Nikos behind her. He had come up to her and was, she realised, standing very close to her. It made her feel wary, and something more, too, that made her heart beat faster. 'They are like grasshoppers, and live in bushes—they are the most characteristic sound of the Mediterranean at night.' He gave a frown. 'Surely you have heard them before?' he asked.

Whether or not she had been brought up in England, it was impossible to imagine that a girl from a background as wealthy as hers would not be well-travelled, especially in fashionable parts of the Mediterranean.

She shook her head, not really paying him much attention. Cicadas—so that was what they sounded like. She remembered how her mother, when Andrea was just a little girl, asking after the father she had never known, had sat on her bed and told her, her soft voice sad and happy at the same time, how she had walked along the sea's edge, so many years ago, hand in hand with the man she loved, heard the soft lapping of the Aegean, the murmurous sound of cicadas in the vegetation. Her heart squeezed—*Oh Mum, why did he have to die like that?*

'What are you thinking of?' Nikos asked in a low voice as his fingers drifted along the bare cusp of her shoulder.

That the touch of your fingers is like velvet electricity...

'Just someone I think about a lot,' she answered, trying to make her voice sound normal when every nerve in her body was focussed on the sensations of his skin touching hers.

Why is he touching me? He shouldn't! He's only just met me!

She wanted to move away, but she couldn't.

'A man?' There was the slightest edge in his voice, but she didn't hear it. She was only aware of the drift of his fingers on her bare shoulder.

'Yes,' she said dreamily.

His hand fell away.

'What is his name?' The question was a harsh demand. She turned, confused. Why was he angry? What on earth made him think he had any business being angry? Was it just because an unmarried Greek girl shouldn't think of men?

'Andreas,' she answered tightly. As she spoke she found herself noticing that anger, though it shouldn't, seemed to have sharpened his features into bold relief. He looked, though she shouldn't think it, even more gorgeous.

'Andreas? Andreas who?'

She lifted her chin. Whatever right this complete stranger seemed to think he had subjecting her to an inquisition, she answered him straight.

'Andreas Coustakis,' she bit out. 'My father.'

He was taken aback, she could see.

'Your father?' His voiced echoed hollowly. He nodded his head stiffly. 'My apologies.' He paused. 'You knew him?'

She shook her head. Her throat felt tight. He must have

walked on this very terrace, she suddenly thought. Known this house. Stormed from it the night he was killed…

'No. But my mother…tells me of him…'

Nikos heard the betraying husk in her voice. It struck a chord in him deeper than he had thought possible. He, too, had never known his father. Never even known who he was…

And his mother had never talked of him, except to say that he had been a sailor on shore leave. From a northern clime. Given his son's height, a Scandinavian, perhaps? She hadn't known. Hadn't cared.

Andrea's mother had cared. Cared enough to tell her daughter about the father she had never known.

A shaft of envy went through him.

'What does she tell you?' he heard himself asking.

Was it the soft Aegean night? Andrea wondered. The kind, concealing blanket of the dark that made her feel, suddenly, that she could tell this man anything—that he would understand?

'She tells me how much she loved him,' she answered, her eyes skimming out into the darkness of the gardens below, lit by the stars above. 'How he loved her, so dearly. How he called her his sweet dove—how he would lay the world at her feet…'

Her voice broke.

'And then he died.' The sob sounded deep in her throat. 'And the dream ended.'

Tears pricked in her eyes. Blinding her vision. Blinding her senses. So she did not feel his arms come around her, turning her into him, folding her head upon his chest so that the tears might come.

'Hush,' he murmured. 'Hush.'

For a long, timeless moment she let herself be held by this man, this complete stranger, who had shown her so unexpectedly the kindness of strangers.

'I'm sorry,' she mumbled. 'I think it's being here, in the house he lived in, and realising how real he once was.'

She pulled away from him, but he caught her elbows so she could not back away completely.

'Don't be ashamed to weep for him,' he said to her quietly. 'You honour him with your tears.'

She lifted her face to his. The tears gleamed on her lashes like diamonds beneath the starry heavens. Her soft mouth quivered.

He could not help himself. Could not have stopped himself if an earthquake had rumbled beneath his feet.

His mouth lowered to hers. Caught her sweetness, her ripeness. His hands slipped from her elbows, around her slender back, pulling her in towards him.

She gave a soft gasp, and it was enough. His tongue slipped between her parted lips, tasting the nectar within. He moved his mouth slowly, but, oh, so sensuously on hers, and he felt her tremble in his arms.

A rush of desire flooded through him. She was exactly how he wanted her to be. Her body ripe in his arms, her mouth tender beneath his.

He deepened his kiss, his hands as of their own volition sliding down her back to shape the rich roundness of her bottom.

Sensation whirled through Andrea. She felt as if she was melting against him, her body moulding to his, and her mouth—oh, her mouth was like a flower, dissolving in sweetness.

Warm shivers ran through her body. She couldn't think, couldn't focus on anything, anything at all, except the sensations flooding through her veins, liquid, honeyed, sweeping her away, drowning her in desire.

And then, with a rasp of reality, she surfaced, pulling away from him. She was shocked, trembling.

'No—' The denial breathed from her, eyes distended. Heart pounding.

What was she denying? she thought wildly. Denying his helping himself to her? Denying that a moment's brief human comfort had suddenly been transformed into a sensuousness so overwhelming she was reeling with it?

Or more? Denying—and her stomach clenched as she faced

up to what she was really denying—denying that never, ever in her whole life had she ever dreamt it was possible to feel such sensations...

He had not let her go, she realised. Although she had pulled away, he was holding her still, his hands in the small of her back. She was arching back, away from him, totally unaware of how the gesture thrust her breasts towards him, making him ache to bend his head and touch his mouth to their swollen fullness, aroused, all against her knowledge, to crested peaks.

'No—' she breathed again. Her hands came up to the corded strength of his arms and tried to dislodge them.

He felt the pressure on them and released her immediately, though it went against every primal instinct, which was to keep her close against him, closer still, press her warm, ripe body against his, moulding her to him, feeling every rich curve, every soft, delicious inch of her...

Theos, but he wanted her! Wanted her with an urgent aching that was nothing, he realised, nothing at all like the controlled, detached sexual desire that he felt for Esme, or Xanthe—or any other woman he had ever bedded, he realised with a shock.

Was it because this woman here, now, was to be his bride, his wife? Was it the primeval emotion of bonding, cleaving, that had released something in him he had never known existed?

Until now?

A rush of fierce possessiveness surged through him. It was like a revelation. He had never felt possessive about his women before—had always known that for them he was just one more male, just better-looking, richer—or both—than most of the men they took to their beds. Exclusivity, on either side, was not a word applied to the relationships he had enjoyed. He knew perfectly well that Esme Vandersee had a whole court she picked her lovers from, depending on her whim and their availability in her hectic globe-trotting life. And Xanthe—well, he was not the only man keeping her in the luxury she enjoyed so much. Of course she was skilful enough, tactful enough, never to let her lovers catch a glimpse of each other, but Nikos could have named a handful of wealthy Athenians who enjoyed her carefully disposed favours.

It didn't bother him.

Not like the thought of Andrea Coustakis thinking about another man…

The rush of possessiveness intensified. It was as alien as it was heady, and he gave himself to it totally.

Then, as the rush consumed him, he realised that he was going too fast—much too fast. Too fast for him—and certainly too fast for her.

His eyes focussed on hers.

She was standing, backed against the balustrade, still close enough for him to reach and pull her to him, but he did not. The expression in her eyes stopped him.

They were shocked, staring.

For a moment exultation speared him. She felt the same way he did! As if a revelation had suddenly made her see the world in a completely different way. Then, with a sobering recognition, he realised that her reaction to what had just happened was more complex than his.

More fearful.

'Andrea,' he said softly, 'don't be alarmed. I'm sorry—I'm rushing things too much.' A wry smile tugged at his mouth as she stared at him, half of her mind drinking in the male beauty of his face, the other still too shocked to take in anything at all. 'You must blame your beauty,' he told her. 'It is too lovely to resist.'

She shivered. He fancied her, and so, on the briefest acquaintance imaginable, he had pounced on her?

'Don't look at me like that,' he said ruefully. 'I will not touch you again until you want me to. But you must not blame me—' the tug of wry humour came again to his well-shaped mouth in a way that did strange things to her insides '—if I try very hard to make you want me to touch you again…'

He stepped back a pace, giving her more space.

'Come,' he said and his breath was more ragged than he

preferred, 'take my hand, if nothing else, and let us talk a while. We have, after all, much to talk about.'

He took her hand, and she let its cool strength curl around her fingers and draw her away from the balustrade. They began to head down towards the far end of the terrace at a leisurely pace. The night air fanned Andrea's heated face and gave her a moment's breathing space.

But her mind was racing as fast as her heart!

What was she doing out here on a starlit terrace with a man who took her breath away, who had casually kissed her as she had never been kissed in her life?

A man she didn't even know.

But who had promised to make her want him touch her again...

What was it he had said? she wondered. *'We have, after all, much to talk about.'*

Puzzlement suffused her. Was that some kind of Greek pick-up line? Or was he simply trying to take the pressure off her and make polite chit-chat again?

She looked up at him as they walked.

'Why have we got so much to talk about?' she asked. Her voice was still husky, even though she did not mean it to be. It was also puzzled.

He glanced down at her. His lashes were extraordinarily long, she found herself thinking irrelevantly. It made her completely miss what he said in answer.

Except for one word.

She stopped in her tracks.

'Say that again,' she said. Her breathing seemed to have stopped.

Nikos smiled down again at her, his eyes warm.

'I said, my sweet bride-to-be, that perhaps we should start by talking about our wedding.'

Andrea's breathing stopped totally.

CHAPTER FIVE

IT WAS as if, in front of his eyes, she had changed. Like some alien shape-shifting from a harmless creature into some terrifying monster.

She thrust her hand from him, backing away, freezing as she did so.

'Our *what*?'

'Our wedding,' he repeated. His voice was tighter now, automatically responding to the visible rejection her whole body was projecting.

She was staring at him as if he had grown another head.

'Our *wedding*?' She could hardly get the word out. Then, as terror seized her, she found her voice. Only a frail one. 'Oh, my God,' she breathed, as the only possible truth dawned, 'you're some kind of lunatic—'

She swirled around, catching at the narrow skirt of her dress, forcing her legs—weak, suddenly—to hurry back along the stone terrace towards the lights—the safety—of the open French windows at the other end.

He caught her wrist before she could even take a single frantic step.

'*What* did you call me?'

The circle of his strong fingers crushed her bones. She tugged to free herself, but to no avail.

'Let me go!' The fear was naked in her voice now, her eyes wide with panic.

His face darkened. 'What the hell is going on?' he demanded. 'I simply said we ought to discuss our wedding—I am quite prepared to give you as free a hand as possible, but I have to say,' he went on, still at a loss to account for the bizarre reaction he was getting from her, 'I would prefer to be married here in Greece.'

'*Married?*' She echoed the word with total incredulity.

'Yes, married. Andrea, why on earth are you behaving like this?' There was impatience in his voice, as well as bewilderment.

'Married to *you?*'

His mouth thinned. It was the way she said that, as if it was the most outrageous idea in the world. He glared down at her.

He let her hand go abruptly. She rubbed her wrist, and would have tried to bolt to the doors leading inside, but he was blocking her back against the stone balustrade.

'We need to talk,' he said abruptly.

Andrea shook her head violently. The only thing she needed to do was to get inside, away from this lunatic who had suddenly gone nuts and started talking about weddings and getting married...

'Answer me,' he commanded. 'Why did you let me kiss you just now if you did not believe that I would marry you?'

Her heart was plummeting around all over the place inside her. Panic was nipping at her, ready to explode again at any moment. Now it did.

'Oh my God, you are completely nuts!' She tried to push past him, but he was an immovable block.

Nikos, not moving an iota, gave a heavy, impatient sigh and tried hard to hold on to his patience. Why she was throwing this fit of hysterics was incomprehensible. Could it really be that she did not know about their marriage? How could that possibly be? Of course she knew! She *must* know! So why the hysterics now?

Did she not *want* to marry him?

The thought enraged him suddenly! How dared she lead him on as she had this evening, letting him taste the sweetness of her lips, inflaming his desire with the allure of her body, if she did not agree to their marriage? And why should she not agree? What, if you please, was so very wrong about the idea of being his wife?

Perhaps because you are the bastard son of a barmaid and an unknown sailor?

The poisonous root took hold and would not be shaken loose. His jaw tightened. If she had objected to their marriage on those grounds she had had time enough to make her opinions clear to her grandfather.

And was Yiorgos Coustakis the kind of man to listen to his granddaughter's objections about the social origins of her intended husband?

He thrust the thought from him. It was irrelevant. Right now he simply had to stop her throwing a full-scale fit of hysterics.

'Be still. You are not going anywhere until you have calmed down—'

His words were cut off by a sharp expletive as he registered pain in his shins. Then, as he was caught off-balance, Andrea thrust him back with all her strength and hurtled as fast as her evening dress would allow towards the open doors at the end of the terrace.

Pain forgotten, Nikos surged after her and intercepted her at the threshold to the dining room.

'Enough!' He was angry now. His hands closed over her shoulders and he gave her a brusque shake. 'Behave yourself! There is no need for such a ludicrous reaction to what I have said!'

As he spoke, it dawned on Nikos that that was what was angering him most of all—her instant and total rejection of the notion of marrying him! He found it intolerable! Here he was, having steeled himself for the past couple of weeks to doing the unthinkable—marrying at all, and to a complete stranger—and then finally, tonight, to have all his worries so deliciously and unexpectedly set aside by seeing just what a peach the Coustakis heiress actually was…and here she was having a fit of hysterics over it! As if the prospect of marrying Nikos Vassilis was the most repellent in the world!

Andrea arrowed her hands and forearms up between his and jerked them sideways with a violent movement to free herself.

Her heart was pounding now—panic, disbelief and above all hot, boiling anger was pouring through her.

She could not believe what she had just heard—couldn't *believe* it! It couldn't be true! It just couldn't!

Her face twisted. 'This is some kind of joke, yes? Talking about me marrying you! Some idiotic, warped idea of a joke, right?'

Nikos bristled. A joke, the idea of marrying him? A fatherless bastard raised on the streets of Athens? His face darkened. He looked scary suddenly, she realised.

'You are the Coustakis heiress,' he said coldly. 'I am the man who will take over the company when your grandfather retires. What else but we should marry?'

'The Coustakis heiress?' Andrea echoed in a strange voice. A laugh escaped her. High-pitched. Distorted. She took a deep, shuddering breath. 'Let me get this right. You, Mr Vassilis, want to marry me because I am Yiorgos Coustakis's granddaughter and you want to run his company for him—is that it?'

He assented with a brief, glancing nod of his dark head. 'That is so. I am glad you understand.'

Completely missing the ironic tone of his voice, she took another breath—a tight one this time. 'Well, sorry to disappoint you, chum, but it's no go. You'll have to find yourself another heiress to marry!'

She made to turn away. She felt in urgent need of escape, not just into the villa, but up to the sanctuary of her own room.

An arm barred her way in.

'You are offensive.'

The voice was soft, but it raised the hairs on the back of Andrea's neck.

She turned back slowly. Nikos Vassilis was very close. Far too close.

'*I* am offensive? Mr Vassilis, you are a guest in my grandfather's house and I suggest you start remembering your responsibilities in that role.' She spoke in as forbearing a manner as possible, which was extremely taxing in the circumstances.

'I make due allowance for the different customs in Greece, but if you imagine that kissing me on a terrace somehow converts instantly into a proposal of marriage you are living in the Middle Ages! You have *not*, I do assure you, compromised me into marrying you! So you can just forget all about black-mailing my grandfather into marrying me off to you just be-cause I was stupid enough to fall into your arms like a…like an *idiot*!'

Her anger was with herself as much as him. This was what came of letting herself be swept away by a drop-dead gorgeous stranger on a starlit terrace! He suddenly got ideas of catching himself a rich wife. A sudden, inexplicable stab of pain went through her as she realised that that was all the kiss had meant to him—it had been nothing to do with *her*, just a cheap way to entrap the girl he thought was Yiorgos Coustakis's heir!

The Coustakis heiress he had called her! Hysterical laughter threatened in her throat. God, it might almost be worth indulg-ing his insane pretensions just for the joy of seeing her grand-father's reaction when he demanded marriage to save the 'hon-our' of the offspring of a woman he'd called a slut to her face—and her daughter's!

'Blackmail?' The word ground out. Furious outrage seared in Nikos voice. To have his behaviour likened to that of Yiorgos Coustakis when he had forced his father-in-law's hand to get his daughter and her dowry was insupportable. 'How dare you make such an accusation!'

Andrea threw back her head. 'What else should I call it? Sliming around after me like a dog sniffing out a bone! Well, let me tell you something, Mr Vassilis—my grandfather will laugh in your face at the idea of your marrying me to get hold of Coustakis Industries!'

The scorn in her voice enraged him.

'You are mistaken.' His voice was icy. 'It was his idea in the first place.'

She stilled.

'Are you saying—' her voice was choked '—that my grandfather is in on this?' Her insides were hollowing out all over again. 'My *grandfather* wants me to marry you?'

'What else?' Could it really be that she did not know? That Old Man Coustakis had not bothered to tell his granddaughter what his plans were? Another of his 'little jokes', Nikos thought grimly to himself.

'Let me get this straight.' Andrea's voice was controlled. 'My grandfather wants *me* to marry *you*—'

'In exchange for my taking over Coustakis Industries when he retires, which will be shortly after our marriage. It is all agreed between us,' Nikos elucidated. He felt in no mood to spare the girl's feelings any more. Her reaction to the discovery of their betrothal was insult enough to warrant his spelling out the financial grounds of their marriage very, very clearly.

'How very convenient.' Her voice was flat. And still very, very controlled.

'Is it not?' agreed Nikos. The irony was back in his voice.

Disbelief washed over Andrea, wave after wave. Total disbelief at what she had heard. She felt quite faint with it. Then, deep, deep inside, she felt the waves break upon some hard, immovable bedrock.

'Excuse me—'

She moved past Nikos Vassilis. The man who had just told her that her grandfather—her dear, kind grandfather, who had ignored her existence all her life—had plans for her. Marriage plans.

Marriage!

She had thought Nikos Vassilis insane, and assumed he was just chancing it. But his assumptions were based on something much, much more solid than a soft, seductive kiss...

As she walked across the dining room she could feel the rage mounting. Misting over her eyes like a red miasma. She marched through the double doors into the wide, marble-floored hallway and strode across, flinging open the doors to the library.

At her entrance her grandfather looked up from the bank of

computer screens flickering on the console drawn up beside his mahogany desk.

'Out!'

The order was given imperiously. She ignored it. She surged forward.

'This man,' she burst out, gesturing wildly behind her to where Nikos had paused in the doorway, following her dramatic entrance, 'has announced that he will be marrying me! I want you to tell him *right now* that it's not going to happen!'

Her grandfather's face had hardened.

'You heard him correctly. Why else would I send for you? Now, leave—you are disturbing me.'

The sick hollowness caverned in Andrea's stomach.

'Are you completely out of your mind?' Her voice was hard—hard, and trembling with fury. 'Are you completely insane—to bring me here, spring this on me and think I'd go along with it? What the *hell* do you think you're playing at?'

Yiorgos Coustakis got to his feet. He was no taller than his granddaughter, but his bulk was considerable.

And suddenly very, very formidable.

Almost she faltered. Almost she quailed beneath the look of excoriation on his lined, powerful face. But rage carried her forward.

'You must be *mad* to think you can do this! You must be completely ma—'

Her denunciation was cut short. A look of blinding fury flashed across Yiorgos Coustakis's face.

'Be silent!' he snarled. 'You will not speak in such a fashion! Go to your room! I will deal with you in the morning!'

She stopped dead.

'Excuse me?' Her eyes were wide with disbelief. 'You think you can give me orders? I am not one of your hapless lackeys!'

'No, you are my granddaughter, and as such I demand obedience!'

Andrea's mouth fell open.

'Demand away,' she told him scornfully. 'Obedience isn't a word in my vocabulary.'

Behind her, Nikos's eyes narrowed. He was witnessing, he knew, something that very few people had ever seen—someone standing up to the vicious, domineering and totally ruthless head of Coustakis Industries.

For a brief, fleeting second Andrea could see by the expression in her grandfather's heavy hooded eyes that he had *never* been spoken to in such a fashion. Then, swiftly, his face hardened into implacable fury at her defiance of him.

'You will leave this room now or I will have you removed! Do you understand?'

He jabbed his finger at an intercom button on his desk and snarled something into the speaker in Greek. Then he turned his attention back to Andrea.

She was in front of the wide desk now, adrenaline running in every vein. She was simply too furious to be frightened. Besides, deep down in her consciousness she knew that if for a moment she gave in to her grandfather, let herself be cowed by him, it would all be over. He would have won and she would have been reduced to a terrified, intimidated wreck. Just the way he had terrified and intimated her mother. Well, he was not going to do the same to her! No way! It was essential, absolutely essential, that she outface him.

And she had every right to be angry—every right! The very idea that he had been discussing marriage…*marriage!*…at all, let alone behind her back like this, was so appalling she could hardly believe it to be true. It couldn't be true! It just couldn't!

'I'll go when I'm ready!' she bit at him. 'When you tell me that this lunatic you invited here is out of his mind!'

She had enraged her grandfather all over again.

'Silence! You will not shame me in my own home, you mannerless brat! And you will not speak of your betrothed husband like that!' The flat of his hand slammed on the surface of his desk to emphasise his anger.

Andrea's eyes widened with shock. 'You don't mean that,' she said. 'You don't seriously mean that. You can't! Tell me this is some kind of idiotic joke the two of you are playing!'

Yiorgos Coustakis's face was like stone.

'How dare you raise your voice to me? Why do you think you are here? You are betrothed to Nikos Vassilis and will marry him next week. Anything else is not your concern! That is an end to it! Now, go to your room!'

Faintness drummed at her. This was unreal. It had to be. It just had to be...

'You can't *possibly* have brought me here for such an outrageous idea,' she said. Her breathing was heavy, heart pounding in her chest. 'It's the most insane thing I've ever heard in my life! And *you* must be insane to think I'd go along with it!'

Somewhere, behind her, she could hear a sharp intake of breath. She didn't care. A whole lot of anger was coming out now—twenty-five years' worth of anger against the man who had behaved so unforgivably to her mother. She owed him nothing—nothing at all.

And as for this insane idea of his...

Her grandfather was standing up, coming out from behind his desk. His face was almost purple with anger.

The blow to the side of her head sent her reeling. She gasped with the pain and the shock, unable to believe that she had just been struck. Automatically she stepped back, almost tripping in her long tight skirt, raising her right forearm into a blocking gesture.

'Go to your room! This instant!' snarled Yiorgos Coustakis again. His eyes cut into her like knives.

Lowering her guard by merely a fraction, Andrea thrust her head forward. 'If you ever hit me again I'll send you flying, so help me! You're a vile, callous *bastard*, and you don't push me around, not *ever*, so get that through your head right now!'

'Get out of here!' A stream of vituperative Greek poured out of Yiorgos Coustakis's mouth.

She took a deep, shuddering breath. 'I'm going. Don't worry! But before I go,' she said, her jaw tight with controlled rage, 'you had better understand something! I am *not* some pawn, some patsy for your vile machinations! The very *idea* that you seriously thought you could marry me off like some *chattel* is so ludicrous I can't *believe* you even entertained it for a second! So go take a hike, Yiorgos Coustakis!'

She saw his hand lift again and threw her arm back up to block him just in time. The blow landed on her arm-bone, jarring it painfully, but it had shielded her face.

She screamed, in shock, rage, pain and horror, and then suddenly her left arm was being taken in a grip she could not shake off, her right arm forcibly lowered from its blocking position.

'Enough—'

Nikos's voice was harsh and imperative. It was directed at both of them.

Yiorgos's face was contorted, eyes alight with a viciousness that would have scared her had she not been so overwhelmed. Then his eyes shot past her, towards the door. Two men were standing there, deferentially awaiting further orders. Nikos's head swivelled around to look at them. Security guards.

'Get her out of here,' Yiorgos Coustakis instructed them curtly. His breathing was heavy, his colour dangerously high. The two men started towards Andrea.

'Stop.' Nikos's voice held the note of command and it stopped the men in their tracks.

Andrea twisted in Nikos's unshakeable grip, taking in the uniformed men. Her eyes had widened yet again, in even greater disbelief.

'This is not necessary, Yiorgos,' said Nikos tightly.

'Then *you* get her out,' growled his host. 'And you had best take a whip to her to control her! She needs a good beating!' He raised his hand again, as if he would start the process himself, and willingly.

'You *bastard*!' spat Andrea at her grandfather.

Nikos jerked her backwards, turning her around to get her out of the room.

She went. Getting away from that vile, ugly scene was suddenly the most urgent thing in the world. As she was frog-marched out she tried to shake herself free.

'Let me go! I'm getting out of here!'

As they entered the hallway, the two security guards stepping smartly aside to let them pass, Nikos released her.

'You little savage! What were you thinking of, behaving like that? Do you run so wild you can't have a civil discussion without yelling your head off?'

Her eyes flared.

'He hit me! He *hit* me and you defend him?'

Nikos, exasperated, gave a sharp intake of breath. 'No, of course I do not defend him, but—'

The two security staff walked by, heading back to their own quarters. Nikos waited till they were out of earshot. He knew the type. Utterly professional, utterly incurious. They would do the bidding of their employer, whatever orders they were given. Manhandling a young woman upstairs to her bedroom would have been a piece of cake for them.

A thought struck him and he called out after the men as they were about to disappear. Old Man Coustakis had looked fit to have a seizure—him dropping dead right now would be highly inconvenient.

'Send Kyrios Coustakis's valet to him—he may need attention.'

One of the men paused and nodded, then went off with his companion. Nikos glanced back at the woman he had agreed to marry for the sake of Coustakis Industries. His mouth tightened.

Andrea was holding the back of her hand to her reddened cheek. Her own colour was high, irrespective of the blow she had taken. *Theos*, she had obviously inherited the old man's temper, thought Nikos. What a termagant!

An immense sense of exasperation overcame him. What the hell was he doing here, stuck in the middle of a battle between Old Man Coustakis and his spitting she-wolf of a granddaughter? Why the hell couldn't the old man have sorted it out first with the girl, telling her about the husband he had chosen for her instead of letting him get caught in the cross-fire like this?

He needed a drink. A strong one. Perhaps that would calm the girl down as well.

She was still trembling with anger. His frown deepened. Her ear and cheek were still red where Yiorgos's hand had impacted.

He tilted her face into the light. 'Let me see.'

She brushed his arm aside, and jerked free. 'Don't touch me!' she spat.

She was still in complete meltdown, chest heaving, stomach churning, adrenaline going crazy inside her.

'You need a drink—it will calm you down.' He spoke grimly.

He took her elbow again, and this time Andrea let herself be led back into the drawing room. She collapsed down on a silk-upholstered sofa while Nikos went to raid the antique inlaid drinks cabinet. He returned with two generous measures of brandy.

'Drink,' he ordered, handing Andrea one of the glasses.

She took a sip, finding her hands were shaking. The fiery liquid seemed to steady her, and she took another sip. Across the room Nikos was standing, his expression closed and moody, one hand pushing back his tuxedo jacket, resting on the waistband of his trousers. Absently she noticed the way the white lawn shirt showed the darker shading of chest hair, the way the material stretched across toned pecs and abs.

She dragged her eyes away and rubbed again at her stinging cheek. She was in shock, as well as everything else, she knew.

I've got to get out of here, she thought wildly. She would leave, first thing in the morning, and head back to London. To home, to sanity.

It was the only thing to do.

She still couldn't take it in. Couldn't believe it.

'Is it true? Tell me?' She heard the question burst from her. Nikos frowned.

'That you and he have hatched some idea of me…me marrying…marrying you?' She could hardly get the words out.

'Yes.' Nikos's voice was terse. Dear God, what an unholy mess! 'I had thought,' he went on, openly sarcastic, 'that you had just obtained irrefutable corroboration from your grandfather?'

Her face hardened.

'That bastard!'

Nikos's expression iced. He had no love for Coustakis—he doubted if anyone in the world did, now that his poor besotted wife was dead!—and certainly he should not have hit her, but Andrea must be stupid indeed if she did not realise that her grandfather would not tolerate her shouting defiance at him, let alone in front of another male, and her selected husband to boot! Yiorgos Coustakis would never permit himself to lose face in front of the man he had accepted would run the empire he had amassed. Moreover, whatever his faults, Andrea should be mindful of the fact that it was Yirogos's money that kept her in her luxurious lifestyle, and that she owed him courtesy, if nothing else.

'You will not use such language.'

'Or what?' she spat. 'You'll take a whip to me like he told you to?'

Nikos swore. He wanted out, right now. He wanted to be miles from here, away from this madhouse! The thought of Xanthe Palloupis hovered tantalisingly in his mind. She would be soft, and warm, and soothing, and cosseting. She would sit him down and make him comfortable, and relaxed, and speak only when he wanted her to speak, and never say a word otherwise, would know instinctively, from long practice, what he wanted, what he did not want...

But he wasn't with Xanthe; he was listening to this red-headed hot-head spitting venom.

'You certainly need *something* to stop you behaving like a foul-mouthed spoilt brat!' he barked back at her.

She got to her feet. 'I suggest you leave, Mr Vassilis,' she said. 'And I also suggest, next time you get around to thinking of marrying someone, you have the courtesy to ask her first before announcing a done deal! However much you want to get your greedy hands on Coustakis Industries, I'm not available—especially not to some pretty-boy fortune-hunter like you!'

She slammed the brandy glass down on the sideboard, not caring that the liquid slopped on to the marquetry surface, spun on her heel and stormed out of the room, clattering up the marble staircase to get to her room as soon as she could.

Behind her, Nikos's face was rigid with fury. Ten seconds later he was out of the house and gunning his Ferrari down the driveway as if possessed by demons.

Andrea's fingers were trembling as she punched the buttons on the mobile phone Tony had leant her. Reaction had set in with a vengeance, and she felt as weak as a kitten.

The conversation was brief and to the point—if for no other reason than she did not want to run up Tony's phone bill more than she had to.

'Tony—it hasn't worked out. I'm going to have to come home. Tomorrow. Don't worry.' She swallowed, not daring to let herself start on what had happened. 'It's nothing drastic, but I'm just going to come home anyway. OK?' She paused fractionally. 'Look, if you don't hear from me from Athens airport tomorrow, go on yellow alert, will you? And if I don't show up at Heathrow—or, worse, don't phone tomorrow evening— go to red, OK? I've met my beloved grandfather and he's—' she swallowed '—running to type.'

After she'd hung up, desperately grateful not only to have heard Tony's familiar calming voice, but also just to have been reminded that a sane, reasonable world existed outside the confines of this palatial madhouse, Andrea realised her hands were still trembling.

How she managed to get any sleep at all that night she didn't know. She awoke late in the morning, with a jolt, woken by Zoe gently shaking her shoulder. Her grandfather, it seemed, wished to see her. Immediately.

Oh, does he? Well, as it happens, I want to see him as well! To order a car to take me to the airport!

He was in his bedchamber, Andrea discovered as, grim-faced, hastily dressed in a cheap blouse and cotton trousers of her own, she followed the maid along the corridor. With clammy hands she walked into the room.

Her grandfather was sitting up, propped on an array of pillows, ensconced in a huge tester bed that would not have looked out of place in Versailles. He did not look well, Andrea registered, and for the first time she realised that he was an old man not in the best of health.

I'll do this civilly, she thought. *I can manage that if I try.*

She approached the foot of the bed. Dark, hooded eyes bored into her. Yiorgos Coustakis might be confined to his bed, but the power he could wield had not lessened an iota.

'So,' he said heavily, 'you are worse than I ever feared. Insolent beyond belief! I should have taken you from your slut of a mother and raised you myself! You would have learned proper respect from the back of my hand!'

Every good intention vanished from Andrea's breast instantly. She felt the fury surge in her veins. But this time she would not lose control.

Instead she simply stood there, looking at the man who had fathered her father. It seemed unbelievable that they should be related in any way.

'Silent at last! A pity you could not have held that hellish tongue of yours last night, instead of showing yourself up so abominably in front of your husband!'

'Nikos Vassilis is not my husband, and he never will be,' replied Andrea. Her anger was like ice running in her blood.

Yiorgos Coustakis made a rasping sound in his throat.

'And you could whistle for him now! No man would touch you after witnessing your despicable display last night! But then—' his dark eyes filled with contempt '—without Coustakis Industries as your dowry you would be fit only to warm a man's bed for hard cash, like your whore of a mother!'

'This conversation,' said Andrea, her voice as tight as a drawn bowstring as she tamped down the fury that filled her as she heard this vile man speak so of her mother, 'is pointless.

I am leaving for London. Be so good as to order a car to take me to the airport.'

Yiorgos Coustakis's dark face suffused with colour.

'You are going nowhere! You will stay in your room until the morning of your wedding if you take that attitude with me! I will be master in my own house!' His fist slammed down on to the bedcovering. 'And if it takes something more than incarceration to bring you to heel, then so be it! A good beating will turn you docile!'

Andrea paled. A memory of those two expressionless security staff sprang into her mind. Fear stabbed at her. He saw it, and smiled. Her blood chilled as she saw him.

'Hah! Do you think I wouldn't? I thrashed your father with my belt often enough! He soon learnt obedience!' His face darkened. 'Until he met the whore who gave you birth! Then he defied me! I sent him packing! He would have got not a penny from me—if he hadn't smashed himself to pieces in his hurry to get back between the slut's legs!'

She felt the horror of it as if it had been yesterday. Her father, terrorised and abused by this foul man who had caused such misery, and then, just when happiness was at last within his reach, to have it all snatched from him—even his life.

'You vile, vile man…'she whispered. 'You're not fit to live.'

The dark, soulless eyes scorched through her. 'Get out, before I take my belt to you myself! I will not be defied by you— or anyone!'

'Oh, I'm going,' said Andrea. 'If I have to walk into Athens on foot, I'm going!'

His face contorted.

'You will not be allowed to step foot outside this house until Nikos Vassilis takes you off my hands!'

She shook her head. 'You are mistaken. I am leaving—today.'

'From inside a locked room? I think not!'

Andrea looked at him steadily. Now was the time to make things clear to him.

'That,' she said, her eyes like stones, 'would be unwise. You see, if I don't make a certain phone call every night, the British embassy in Athens will be alerted that I am being held against my will. You will not, I am sure, wish to be charged with imprisoning me! Let alone invite the feast the press will make of it!'

The effect of her words was visible. He spat something at her in Greek. She smiled scornfully.

His face contorted. 'And if I *make* you make that phone call?'

The threat was open—and quite plain to understand.

'Oh, that would be unwise too. You see—' she smiled unpleasantly, hiding the shudder that had gone through her at his words '—if that should happen then I might give the wrong code word during the conversation...'

As if a shutter had dropped, her grandfather's face suddenly became completely unreadable. There was nothing there—none of the fury and temper that had been blazing from him a moment ago.

'Tell me,' he said suddenly, 'if you please, just why is it that you are so averse to the prospect of marrying Nikos Vassilis?'

His change of tack took her aback. Then she rallied. 'Is that a serious question? It's too absurd to be worth asking!'

'Why? Is he not a fine man to look at? He would make a handsome husband, *ne*? His reputation with your sex, I understand—' his voice became sly '—is spectacular! Women flock to him, and not just because of his money!'

'Money?' Andrea caught at the word. 'He's a fortune-hunter! He admitted as much.'

Yiorgos Coustakis gave a harsh laugh. 'He seeks to net a greater fortune, that is all! Do you imagine I would entrust my empire to someone untried and untested? Nikos Vassilis has his own fortune—he will not waste mine by incompetence and mismanagement!'

She frowned, trying to take in this turnabout. Her grandfather went on. 'Vassilis Inc is capitalised at over five hundred million euros! He's been after a merger with Coustakis Industries for the last eighteen months—he's an ambitious man, and now, finally, I have decided to let him realise his ambitions.' His voice hardened. 'But I've driven the price higher—he has to marry you before I sign the deal.'

Andrea's brain was racing, trying to make sense of what she was hearing.

'Why?' she said bluntly. 'You've denied my existence for twenty-five years, ever since your goons forced my mother to the airport and shoved her on a plane back to England!'

Nothing showed in his face, not a trace of regret or shame, as she related the way Yiorgos Coustakis had disposed of the woman who had dared to tell him she was pregnant by his dead son.

'Why?' Yiorgos Coustakis echoed. 'Because you carry my blood. You and no one else. I have no choice but to use you, tainted though your blood is. When you marry Nikos Vassilis he will guard my fortune, and my blood will pass through you to your son. He will be my heir. I have had to wait two generations, but I shall have my heir!'

There was a fierceness of possession in his eyes that even his inscrutable expression could not disguise.

So, thought Andrea, as his words sank in, this is what it's all about. I am the vessel for his posterity. Revulsion filled her. Yiorgos Coustakis was nearing the end of his misbegotten life and he wanted the only immortality he could find.

She looked at him. He had everything money could buy, but as a human being he was worthless. He had no kindness in him, no compassion, no gentleness, no feeling for anyone except himself. He had treated his own son like a possession to be beaten into obedience, and her mother had been instantly condemned as a gold-digger trying to get at his precious money!

And now, twenty-five years later, she was standing in front of him, knowing that she was the only person in the world who could give him what he wanted. The final thing he wanted.

The memory of Tony's voice echoed in her mind. *Look, if*

he does want you for something, then if he doesn't want you to refuse he's going to have to do something you *want.*

And there *was* something she wanted. Something she had travelled over a thousand miles to get—the money for her mother that was not just her escape to the sun but her reparation as well. Justice. Finally.

Her grandfather's eyes were resting on her. Seeing her as a tool to be used. Nothing more. Her heart hardened. Well, tools had to be paid for.

Five minutes ago she had wanted nothing except to shake the dust of her grandfather's house from her feet. Now she wanted to get what she came for.

Money.

His shoulders relaxed into the pillow as he read her mind.

'So,' he said, 'tell me—what price do you set on opening your legs to Nikos Vassilis with a ring on your finger to keep you respectable?'

The sneer in his voice was irrelevant. So was the insult and the crudity. Everything about him was irrelevant—except the money he would pay her. Her heart was hard, like stone all the way through. Somewhere in the back of her mind a memory was flickering—the memory of being held in strong arms, her body on fire with soft, seductive flame…

She thrust it away. That kiss had been nothing to do with her. Nikos Vassilis had kissed her because she was the gateway to Coustakis Industries. No other reason. She just hadn't realised it at the time. Now that she did she must not read anything more into it. Nothing.

'Five hundred thousand pounds,' she announced crisply. 'Sterling. Paid into a bank account in London of my choosing, in my name—Andrea Fraser.'

She gave her mother's surname—her name—deliberately. She was no Coustakis. Never had been. Never would be.

His laugh was derisive. 'You set a high price on yourself for the daughter of a penniless slut!'

Nothing showed in her face. She would not allow it.

'You need me. So you'll pay for me. That's all.'

A flash of fury showed in his eyes. 'Do you think that as the wife of Nikos Vassilis you will live the life of a pauper? You will live in a luxury you can hardly dream of! You should be grateful, *grateful*—on your knees that I have plucked you out of your slum to live such a life as I am offering you!'

'Five hundred thousand.' Her voice was implacable. She needed that much to clear the last of Kim's debts, buy her a decent apartment in Spain, and have enough left over to invest safely for an income for her mother to live on, albeit modestly, for the rest of her life. 'Or I go back to London today.'

Dark eyes bored into hers. She could see the hatred in them. The loathing that this tool he wanted to use was daring to defy him. But defy him she would—she had something he wanted, and he would have to pay for it. Just as Tony had said.

But he would not go down easily.

'You get not a penny until you are married.'

She laughed scornfully. 'There will be no marriage,' she said as her eyes narrowed, 'unless I am paid.'

Even as she spoke her mind was splintering in two. What was she doing here? What was she thinking of, selling herself like this? She must be mad! Quite mad!

But then the other side of her mind slammed back. This was no time for scruples, no time for doubts! It was now or never—this was her one and only chance to get reparation for Kim. She would do whatever it took! And agreeing to marry a total stranger was what it was going to take.

A stranger who can melt your bones in a single embrace? Oh, be careful—be careful of what you are doing!

Compunction flashed at her. She was standing here, negotiating a price to marry Nikos Vassilis as if she were doing nothing more than haggling over a CD at a car-boot sale! How low was she stooping?

Then her heart hardened again. And hadn't Nikos Vassilis stood in front of Yiorgos Coustakis and negotiated a price to get hold of Coustakis Industries? A price that included marriage to a woman he'd never set eyes on? What kind of man did that?

No, she need feel no shame, no compunction. The man who had kissed her last night deserved no more regard than did her grandfather!

For one long, last moment she held her grandfather's eyes, refusing to back down. It was too important to even think of giving in. At last, after what seemed like an eternity of challenge, he suddenly snarled, 'On your wedding morning—and not till then! Now, get out!'

CHAPTER SIX

NIKOS sat in his boardroom, lounging back in his leather chair at the head of the table, listening to his directors droning on about the impact of the merger with Coustakis Industries. He wasn't listening. Wasn't paying the slightest attention. His heart was stormy.

What the hell kind of woman had he agreed to marry? A raging hell-cat! A spoilt brat of a pampered princess! An ill-mannered, ill-tempered, badly behaved harpy who threw tantrums and hysterics at the drop of a hat! A true Coustakis!

His jaw tightened. The last thing on earth he needed was a wife who took after Yiorgos Coustakis!

A splinter of grudging admiration stabbed him. The girl hadn't flinched from confronting Old Man Coustakis. She'd just stormed in there and laid in to him!

A smile almost curved his mouth at the recollection. *Theos*, but it had been a sight to see. Someone giving as good as they got from that vicious brute whose ugly reputation made most people walk on tiptoes around him, from house servants to business associates. Even he trod carefully around the old barracuda! At least until Coustakis Industries was his to run.

The smile turned to a frown. For all that, however, it was not behaviour to condone. Certainly not in the woman who would be Mrs Nikos Vassilis. It was unthinkable that his wife should behave like that—for whatever reason!

The frown deepened—but from a different cause this time. Had the girl truly not known of her grandfather's marriage plans for her? It was typical of Yiorgos Coustakis not to bother himself with trivial details such as telling his granddaughter what husband he had chosen for her. In which case, Nikos knew he had to acknowledge, the girl had a right to object to having been kept in the dark about such an important matter. True, her reaction had been wildly over the top, but in the first immediate shock of the news it was understandable that she should be affronted at her grandfather's typically high-handed behaviour in keeping her ignorant of her future.

An image flashed in his mind. Yiorgos Coustakis slashing his hand down across Andrea's cheek. Nikos straightened suddenly in his chair. Anger clenched at him. *Theos*, but the old man was a brute! Who cared if he was from a generation that thought nothing of beating children? Who cared if his granddaughter had provoked him by yelling like a harridan in front of the man he had chosen for her husband? No man ever hit a woman. Ever.

Revulsion filled him. Whilst he would never dream of raising his fist to a man of Yiorgos's age, the memory of him hitting his granddaughter burned.

I've got to get her out of there!

A surge of emotion swept through him—not anger with that brute of an old man. Something he had never felt about any woman before. A fierce, urgent burst of protectiveness.

Abruptly he lifted a hand, cutting off whatever his sales director was saying.

'Gentlemen, my apologies, but I must leave you. Please continue with the meeting.'

Ten minutes later he was in his Ferrari and nosing through the impossibly jammed streets of Athens. Heading out of town.

Andrea sat out on the terrace overlooking the ornate gardens that spread like an embroidered skirt around her grandfather's opulent villa. Her heart was heavy—but resolved. The final scene with her grandfather replayed itself over and over again in her head. Was she insane, even to contemplate going along with what he wanted? This wasn't just some kind of trivial business contract she had agreed to—this was *marriage*!

The enormity of what she committed herself to overwhelmed her, making it seem almost unreal. So much had happened so quickly! Less than two days ago she had been at home, in her own drab but familiar world. Now she was sitting on a sun-drenched terrace beneath a Mediterranean sun—about to marry a complete stranger!

Panic rose in her throat and she fought it down.

It's not a real marriage! It's just a wedding ceremony. That's all. The day after the wedding I'll be on a plane to London! My 'husband' will be glad to see the back of me!

And I'll have half a million pounds waiting for me in the bank!

She and Kim could be in Spain, house-hunting, in a month!

The warm sun poured down on her, bathing her legs stretched out in front of her. They had been aching since last night—wearing high heels was never a good idea—and the strain and tension of the past day and a half was telling. Gently she stretched and eased them, rubbing her hands lightly along her thighs in a careful massage.

The warmth did them good, she knew. Living in Spain would help. She would get work there, enough to keep Kim and herself, so that Kim could take life easy at last. Spain was full of Brits now; she was bound to be able to get some kind of job, even if she didn't speak Spanish yet.

I'll invite Tony and Linda for a holiday she thought happily. They'd been so good to her; it would be great to give some-thing back. She'd had to phone Tony from her room, just a short while ago, telling him she was staying after all. It had taken quite a lot to convince him she really meant it, that one of her grandfather's bully-boys hadn't been twisting her arm to say so!

Cold filled her. Her grandfather was unspeakable—her every worst fear about him was deserved! He really would have thought it perfectly acceptable to keep her a prisoner here and force her into marrying that man!

That man—

Memory leapt in her throat. It was here, on this terrace, that she had first laid eyes on him, not twenty-four hours ago. Here, beneath the beguiling stars, that he had slid her into his arms and kissed her...

I'm going to marry him…

A shaft of pure excitement sliced through her. She felt a quickening inside herself. That man, that drop-dead, fabulous-looking, breathtaking man, whose touch had set fire to her, melting her very being into him, Nikos Vassilis, was going to be her husband…

Reality hit like a cold douche. Of course he wasn't going to be her husband! Not for more than a day! All he was to her was her passport to Spain with her mother, nothing more!

And all I am to him is his passport to my grandfather's money!

Her lips pressed together. What kind of man was he that would even think of marrying a woman he'd never laid eyes on just to get hold of an even bigger fortune than he yet had? That he wasn't even a fortune-hunter somehow made it worse! Being poor herself, she knew how tempting it must be to think that you could claw your way out of poverty the easy way. But if Nikos Vassilis was already rich, had already made his pile, then why did he want even more? If his company really was worth five hundred million euros then a fraction of what he already possessed would have kept her and Kim in luxury by their standards!

Well, it was none of her business. She didn't care about Nikos Vassilis. He was using her to get what he wanted—and she was simply returning the favour! And she wasn't even cheating him. Even after she'd been packed off home he'd still have got what he wanted—Coustakis Industries—courtesy of his brand-new and totally unwanted wife! He'd be perfectly happy if the bride didn't stick around like glue! A grim smile played about her mouth. In fact, the only person who would end up with a bad bargain would be her beloved grandfather! He'd have handed over his company to Nikos Vassilis, along with his despised granddaughter, but he'd be waiting a long time for his precious heir!

The throaty roar of a high-powered car approaching the house along the long drive that was hidden from the front gardens interrupted her bitter reveries. She tensed. It did not sound like the purr of the huge limousine her grandfather had taken his leave in some half-hour ago—heading, she assumed for his office in Athens. This was a much more aggressive engine indeed—and it didn't take a genius to guess whose it was.

Some few minutes later her assumption was confirmed. Nikos Vassilis strode out on to the terrace. He came to where she was sitting.

Andrea felt her body tense. Something leapt inside her. He was looking spectacular again. A pale grey immaculately cut business suit, gleaming white shirt, grey silk tie, made him look taller and more svelte than ever. His expression was unreadable, made more so by the dark glasses covering his eyes, and as she looked at his face she felt her stomach hollow out.

Oh, dear God, he's just gorgeous! she felt herself thinking.

He sat himself down opposite her, stretching out his long legs, his feet almost touching hers. Automatically she drew her legs back, the sudden movement causing a jolt of mild pain to go through them.

He caught the expression on her face and frowned slightly. 'Are you all right?'

The rich timbre of his voice, so seductively accented, made her feel weak. She nodded briefly to answer his query, unable to speak.

'How is your cheek?'

The frown had deepened, and before she could stop him he had reached across the table and touched the side of her face with his fingers. They felt cool, but where they made a thousand sensations quiver through her. He tilted her head slightly, so that he could see where he touched.

There was a bruise, definitely, even if only faintly visible. She had made no attempt to cover it with make-up, though she had let her hair fall loose, so that it covered her right ear which was still red from having caught the main thrust of her grandfather's blow.

'Fine,' she said quickly, brushing his hand aside. She did not want his concern—the last words she had flung at him had been an atrocious insult, and his evident concern for her now put her off kilter. So did the echoing resonance of his light velvet touch just now…

The soft-footed approach of a servant carrying a tray of coffee for two was a welcome interruption. It gave Andrea precious moments to collect herself.

Nikos lifted off his dark glasses and slid them into his breast pocket. Andrea wished he hadn't. Although it was disturbing to address a man whose eyes she could not see, it was far, far worse to have those keen slate-grey eyes visible to her.

The eyes searched her face.

'You are upset still,' he said quietly. 'Last night was very distressing for you. I apologise—it should not have happened that way.' He paused, feeling carefully for his words. 'Your grandfather is a…difficult…man, Andrea, as you must surely already appreciate from all your years of knowing him. He is used to commanding others, to giving orders—and to getting his own way by the swiftest means possible. However brutal.' There was a frown in his eyes. 'Hitting you was insupportable. But—'.he held up a hand to ward off what her reply must be '—understandable. That is not to excuse him, Andrea—merely to point out that there was no way he was going to be outfaced by his own granddaughter in front of me, and that he comes from a generation which did not believe in sparing the rod.'

Andrea stilled. She thought of her father, brought up here, a vulnerable boy, bullied by his father from the day he was born—thrashed into obedience…

The only bright hope of his life had been Kim, the girl he'd met on a beach and fallen in love with on the spot, their young romance an idyll out of *Romeo and Juliet*. And just as doomed.

I'm not just doing this for you, Mum—I'm doing it for my father too. Looking after you the way he was never able to…

Nikos Vassilis was talking again. She forced herself to listen.

'You must believe me when I tell you that last night I naturally assumed you knew of your grandfather's marriage plans for you—and agreed to them.'

She reached forward to the coffee pot—filter coffee, she noticed gratefully, not the treacly Greek brew—and started to pour them both a cup.

'But I do agree to them,' she announced. 'I've had a talk with my grandfather this morning and it's all settled, Mr Vassilis. You can continue with your merger plans.'

Her voice was remarkably calm, she thought. But then that was the way to play it—cool, calm and collected. This was not a real marriage they were talking about; it was part of a business contract that would benefit them both. She must remember that and not think about anything else.

Certainly not about the way the sensual line of his mouth contrasted with the tough, cleanly defined edge of his jaw, or the way his dark silky hair made her long to reach her fingers to it...

She pushed the cup towards him.

'Milk and sugar?' she asked politely.

He shook his head briefly, a frown creasing between his eyes.

'Did he bully you again?' he demanded openly.

Her eyes widened in surprise.

'Certainly not,' she answered, economising on the truth to cut to the chase. 'We struck an excellent deal that I'm perfectly satisfied with.'

She poured milk into her coffee and took a reflective sip.

'Deal?' There was an edge in Nikos's voice that Andrea would have had to have been deaf not to hear. 'What deal?'

She smiled. It was an artificial smile, but for all that she could not stop a curl of satisfaction indenting her mouth. Satisfaction that at last, after a quarter of a century, her mother would get reparation from Yiorgos Coustakis. Devastated, heartbroken and pregnant, Kim had asked nothing from Andreas's father, had wanted only to offer him and Andreas's mother the comfort of knowing that, although their son had died so tragically, a grandchild had been conceived. She had not asked for money—she had offered comfort and consolation.

But Yiorgos Coustakis had treated her like a gold-digging whore...

'Finally, Mr Vassilis, I get money of my own.'

'Money?' There was a chill in his voice now that raised the hairs on her neck, but she kept the tight, artificial smile pasted to her lips.

'Yes, money, Mr Vassilis. You know—the crisp folding stuff, the bright shiny stuff, the silent, electronic stuff that wings its way into bank accounts and makes the world go round.'

Her eyes were bright and hard.

'Explain.'

That was an order, just as if Nikos Vassilis had been speaking to one of his underlings. And if he owned a company worth five hundred million euros, Andrea reminded herself deliberately, that meant he had one hell of a lot of underlings!

'Explain? Well, it's an extremely simple contract, Mr Vassilis. Just between me and my grandfather—it will have no impact on your own contract with him, I promise. My grandfather undertakes to make a certain amount of money over to me upon my marriage to you.' She smiled again, bright and hard. 'Unlike you, I prefer Coustakis cash, not shares.'

Nikos's face had frozen.

'He is *paying* you to marry me?'

Andrea could have laughed. Laughed right in his handsome face. He was angry! He actually had the nerve to be angry! God, what a hypocrite! But she couldn't laugh. Her throat felt very tight suddenly, as if there was a cord around her neck. Choking at her. All she could do was give a careless, acknowledging nod and take another mouthful of coffee.

She set her cup down with a click.

'Just as he is paying *you*,' she pointed out, 'to marry *me*.'

'That is different! Completely different!'

Refutation was in every syllable. Andrea busied herself topping up her coffee. She felt very calm now. Extremely calm.

'I don't see why. You would hardly hitch yourself to an unknown woman if there weren't something in it for you, would you? I just happen to come with enough Coustakis shares to make it worth your while.' She replaced the coffee

pot and looked straight across the table at the man she was
going to marry. For half a million pounds.

'Mr Vassilis, let us be completely up-front about this. You
did me the courtesy last night—' she did not trouble to hide
the sarcasm in her voice '—of pointing out that our marriage
was predicated upon your taking control of Coustakis
Industries. You can't do that without a majority shareholding.
Even I, with my tiny business brain, know that!'

Nikos looked at her. His grey eyes were like cold slate. 'I
am *buying* Coustakis shares! Not in cash, but in paper—exchanging them for Vassilis shares at a hefty premium, I assure
you! Your grandfather will do very well out of the deal! I'm
undertaking a reverse takeover, whereby the much smaller
Vassilis Inc can acquire the much larger Coustakis holding with
a minimum of debt purchase or rights issues to fund it.'

She waved her hand impatiently. 'Spare me the technicalities! The salient point, so far as I am concerned, is that my
grandfather will not agree to the merger—reverse take-over,
acquisition, whatever you call it—unless you marry me. That
means you're marrying me to get Coustakis Industries. Owning
the majority of Coustakis shares will make you even richer than
you are—i.e. you're being *paid* to marry me. End of story.'

Tony would be proud of my cool, clear logic, she thought
defiantly.

Every good resolution that Nikos had entertained since
brooding on Andrea Coustakis in his boardroom vanished.
Every last shred of sympathy. Sympathy for her being kept in
ignorance by Old Man Coustakis, sympathy for her having a
brute like him for a grandfather—all went totally. He had come
to make his peace with her, to start over again, begin his wooing of her as a man should woo his bride...

That hysterical harpy he had seen last night would never
come back—there would be no need for her. Instead only the
soft, yielding, sensual woman he had held in his arms so tantalisingly would be the bride he took for his wife.

But what did he find now? A woman sitting and talking

about marriage and money in the same breath. A woman with a mind like a cash-box.

Conscience pricked at him, but he pushed it away. No, of course he would not have dreamt of marrying an unknown woman without the chance to take over Coustakis Industries! But dynastic marriages of convenience were commonplace in the world of the very rich—that did not mean they had to be sordid. And since setting eyes on Andrea Coustakis he had known straight away that marriage to her would be anything but a marriage of convenience—it would be a marriage of mutual pleasure...

Andrea sat across the table and studied him dispassionately. He was offended. Offended by her frankness. She no longer wanted to laugh. Nor did her throat feel tight any more. Instead, a sort of dull, hard, unemotional carapace had descended on her, covering every inch of her.

As he looked back at her Nikos felt his gaze hardening. *Theos*, but she was a cool piece. Coustakis blood ran in her veins, no doubt about that!

Revulsion shimmered through him. The woman he had held trembling in his arms last night seemed a thousand miles away, as if she had never been. This was the true Andrea Coustakis now. Like her grandfather—knowing the price of everything, the value of nothing.

And she knew her own price, that was for sure. He smiled grimly. Well, he knew her price too. And he would treat her accordingly.

He got to his feet.

'Well—' his voice was abrupt '—since we now both know where we stand, we can begin.'

She looked up at him, uncertain suddenly.

'Begin what?'

He flashed a smile. It had no humour in it.

'Our official betrothal.'

He reached down and took her hand, drawing her to her feet.

'And, though you might wish to seal such an event with a chequebook, I prefer a more traditional method—'

She had a fraction of a second to read his intent. It was utterly inadequate to allow her to react in time and pull away.

His kiss was deep and sensuous. Slow and possessive.

Very, very possessive.

His mouth moved over hers, lazily, exploringly, tastingly…

Making absolutely free with her.

She felt her stomach plummet to the floor, felt adrenaline flood through her veins, felt weakness debilitate her totally.

Felt her hand lift of its own accord and curl around his neck, splaying its fingers into his silky hair. Felt herself moan softly, helplessly, as he played with her mouth.

He let her go, casually unwinding her hand and letting it drop nervelessly to her side. Then he took her chin in his fingers and tilted it up. Her mouth was bee-stung, lips red and swollen. Aroused.

Her eyes were lustrous, wide and staring at him, her lashes thick and lush.

'You are an acquisition, Andrea Coustakis, that I shall very much enjoy making,' he said softly, gazing down at her with gleaming possession in his eyes. His voice dropped, making her heart stop. 'I look forward, very much to our personal merger…'

His meaning made perfectly clear, he stroked her cheek and stood back. Then he glanced at his watch.

'Come—we shall lunch, and show the world that Vassilis Inc has plans for Coustakis Industries.'

He tucked her hand into his arm and led her off.

Andrea went with him helplessly. She hadn't a bone left in her body to resist.

The restaurant was plush and crowded. It was clearly excruciatingly expensive. Andrea didn't have to glance at the menu prices to know that.

As they'd walked in, she stiff and wary, concealing her nervousness at being in such a place, she'd felt every eye upon her. A covert glance around showed her that just about everyone here was male—the place was awash with suits. Very expensive suits. This was a place, she knew immediately, where the most successful businessmen in Athens took their lunch and cut their deals, made their contacts and their money.

The maître d' who advanced upon them at their entrance knew her escort, that was obvious. His manner was oh-so-attentive, oh-so-deferential. Though the place looked packed, he did not seem in the least dismayed by the prospect of having to find a table for his latest arrivals.

Nikos knew he'd sort something. For a start he was too curious about the female at his side not to want to find out more. Athens was a city that liked to gossip, and Nikos had made sure that it liked to gossip about him. Having a reputation as a connoisseur of fine women did him no harm at all in the business world. Men envied him—envied his success, his ability to have a beautiful woman on his arm, envied the fact that, unlike most of them, he did not need his money to keep them there—he could do it on his looks alone.

'Kyrios Vassilis,' smiled the greeter. 'How delightful to have you as our guest today. And your lovely companion, of course…'

His voice trailed away expectantly.

With an acknowledging half-smile, Nikos accommodated him.

'Thespiris Coustakis,' he obliged.

The man's face was a picture. Nikos almost laughed. Then, revealing nothing but the excited gleam in his eyes, the man immediately bowed to Andrea and murmured, in breathless tones, how greatly honoured he was to have her grace his establishment.

'No fuss, if you please,' said Nikos, and began to head for the bar area. 'We'll have a drink until our table is ready.' He caught the man's eye and made his message clear. 'Something as private as you can manage.'

'Of course.' The man bowed again, eyes gleaming even more, and clicked his fingers imperiously for a pair of minions, who were there immediately and then despatched variously at his bidding. Then, bowing yet again, he ostentatiously ushered Nikos and Andrea towards the bar.

'This way, if you please, Thespiris Coustakis,' he said, in a voice that was intentionally louder than before. Andrea could see a couple of men seated nearby, also waiting for their table, look up sharply, subjecting her to penetrating stares. Then one of them promptly got up and moved across to one of the tables in the dining area, bending low to speak into the man's ear. The man looked up abruptly and followed his line of gaze towards Nikos Vassilis and his companion.

As she took her seat—a huge, soft leather chair into which she sank almost completely—she said through clenched teeth, 'What the hell is this circus? Have I got two heads or something?'

Nikos gave a brief laugh, his teeth gleaming wolfishly.

'Oh, the show has begun, Andrea, *agape mou*. The show has most very definitely begun.'

It was not the most comfortable meal Andrea had eaten in her life, but it was certainly the most expensive. Not even dinner last night could match lunch today. For a start they were drinking vintage Krug champagne. Andrea did not even want to think what that must have cost. Then there were black truffles, caviar, exotic seafood she couldn't even identify served in a delicate sauce with exquisitely presented vegetables. As well as the champagne Nikos ordered wine as well, and by the reverence with which it was served—from displaying the label for his approval and the sommelier tasting some in his little silver cup, to Nikos's final approving nod as he sampled first the bouquet and then the wine itself—she could see it must be as expensive as the champagne, if not more so.

She wished desperately, as she ate her way through a lunch that it would have taken her six months to pay for herself, that she could enjoy it more. It seemed dreadful to have such expensive food in front of her and yet feel as if she had to force down every mouthful. Tension knotted in her stomach like rope.

It wasn't just that she could see she was being looked over by every person in the restaurant, from the humblest waiter to the richest patron, it was that she was lunching, in public, with Nikos Vassilis.

Who was making it very, very clear just who he was keeping company.

The Coustakis heiress.

It clearly, she thought, her lips tight, gave him one hell of a kick!

He said as much at one point. Leaning closer, as though to whisper some intimacy to her, he murmured, 'They are all agog, Andrea *mou*—your name has gone round like wildfire and they are desperate to know who you are! Strange as it seems, no one in Athens knew Yiorgos Coustakis had a grand-daughter—you have been kept as a card up his sleeve! And now—' satisfaction—the satisfaction of a hunger sated, a long hunger born many years ago in the streets of the city—gleamed in his slate eyes '—they can see exactly how the old man has decided to play you! There isn't a man here who does not realise the significance of your being here with me!'

'Is it public knowledge yet that you will be taking over Coustakis Industries?' Andrea asked. She kept her voice cool and businesslike, though it was an effort to do so. Since he had kissed her with such confident possession, sealing their bargain, it had been an effort to do anything except drown her memory of the recalled sensation of his lips tasting her mouth...

He took a mouthful of wine, clearly savouring it, then set down the glass.

'There have been rumours—there are always rumours. After all, Yiorgos is getting older—something must happen to the company. Up till now no one realised he had any heir at all— let alone a hide-away heiress! But now—well, I think they will draw their own conclusions, do you not, *agape mou*?'

'Don't use endearments to me!' she responded sharply. She didn't like the sound of the liquid syllables in his low, intimate voice.

He raised a mocking eyebrow. 'My dear Andrea, we are to

be married. We must, as I have just told you, put on an appropriate show. And, speaking of marriage, what are your wedding plans? I tell you frankly I would hope above all that they are speedy. But other than that you can have free rein. I assume your mother will fly out for it?'

Andrea's face froze. 'No,' she said shortly.

Kim mustn't even know about the wedding. Andrea would have to get Tony to say she was just staying on here for a few weeks, that was all. The last thing she wanted was Kim finding out just what she was planning to do!

'She dislikes your grandfather so much?' There was an edge in Nikos's voice as he remembered Yiorgos saying that Andrea's mother had had very different views on upbringing from him. Well, given Yiorgos's demonstration of grandfatherly chastisement last night, he could hardly be surprised.

'I don't want to talk about it,' said Andrea tightly.

Nikos's eyes narrowed, studying her closed face. There was something wrong here, he thought suddenly. Her eyes were a little too bright, her soft mouth almost trembling beneath the hardened line of her lips. The memory of her standing on the terrace, talking about her father and her mother's memory of him, came back to him. He cursed himself for an insensitive fool.

'I'm sorry,' he said suddenly. 'Of course she would find it distressing to revisit the place where she was so happy with your father.'

'Yes,' said Andrea, swallowing, 'that's it.'

'Then perhaps a private wedding would be best, *ne*?'

'Definitely,' she agreed. 'And as speedily as it can be arranged.'

She reached for her wine glass. She had drunk more than she had meant to, but her nerves, beneath the unemotional carapace that had descended on her, were shaky, she realised. As she moved forward his hand stayed her wrist, closing around it loosely.

'You are so eager to be my wife, Andrea?'

His voice had lowered again, taking on that intimate timbre

that made her go shivery. Her eyes flew to his. In her wrist, as his thumb rubbed casually along the delicate skin over her veins, a pulse throbbed.

'I meant,' she said, as brusquely as she could, 'that you must be keen to get the merger underway as soon as possible.'

She drew her hand away and picked up her wine glass, drinking deeply.

For a moment Nikos hovered between indignation and amusement. Amusement won out. Mocking amusement. She was responsive to him—he had proved that twice already—and he knew perfectly well that he would dissolve any last resistance to him. Knowing now that she was only interested in marrying him for money, he would take particular pleasure in revealing to her just how sexually vulnerable to him he could make her—when he chose. She would leave their marriage bed in no doubt whatsoever that he could turn her into a willing, purring sexual partner, eager to do in bed whatever he wanted her to...

He frowned. A moment ago he had been feeling sorry for her—mourning, with her mother, her lost father. The girl with the cash-box mentality had been completely absent then.

Now she was back with a vengeance.

'As eager to get on with your merger as I am to get my grandfather to release my capital,' she announced crisply.

The phrase sounded good in her ears. Made it sound the sort of thing that heiresses said—the sort of thing that went down well, with approving nods, in places like this. People were still looking at her, she knew. Word had gone round—the Coustakis heiress was in town.

And she was lunching with Nikos Vassilis.

Marriages or corporate mergers—they were all the same thing to people like these.

There was a sour taste in her throat, despite the wine.

CHAPTER SEVEN

LUNCH seemed endless, and it was well into the afternoon before Andrea could finally escape. And even then she could not escape Nikos.

He had phoned his office on his mobile, cancelling all his appointments. That alone, he knew, would accelerate the rumours. Nikos Vassilis never cancelled appointments—he was assiduous in his pursuit of business and profit.

He smiled down at his bride-to-be, an intimate smile that Andrea knew was for the benefit of the remaining diners, as they took their leave from the restaurant. 'I thought that you might like to go shopping. I'm sure you will wish for a spectacular trousseau!'

'I've got all the clothes I need,' she replied sharply. She didn't want any more clothes—the closets in her room at her grandfather's house were groaning. Today, having made the momentous decision to marry Nikos Vassilis, she had changed into one of the outfits Zoe had shown her—a pair of beautifully cut taupe trousers and a shaped appliquéd top. There were more than enough remaining to see her through to her wedding day.

He gave a disbelieving laugh. 'No woman has all the clothes she needs,' he commented dryly.

'I'm not interested in clothes,' she said carelessly.

He laughed again. 'Then you are unique amongst your sex! Besides...' his voice took on a caressing note '...even if you are not interested in clothes, Andrea, they most definitely are interested in you...'

His eyes worked over her torso, blatantly taking in how the jersey material of her top stretched across her full breasts, outlining their generous swell.

Unconsciously she tugged at the hem of her top, as if that would instantly conceal her figure.

'You only reveal yourself more to me,' he said softly, his breath warm on her throat. Fleetingly he ran the back of his hand down her cheek, making her breath catch. 'I would like to choose some clothes for you, Andrea—please allow me that privilege.'

'I told you I had enough!' She pulled away from him, wishing her heart-rate had not suddenly started to race at his touch.

'Something special,' he went on, as if she hadn't spoken, 'for our wedding night.'

She stilled. Then, with a curious twist to her lips, she nodded.

'If you insist.'

He smiled with satisfaction. 'Oh, but I do, *pethi mou*, I do.'

He took her to an exclusive lingerie boutique in the chic Kolonaki shopping area of Athens. It was the kind of place, Andrea thought, where if you asked for a cotton bra and panties they would throw you out! It was also the kind of place, she realised, the moment the attentive assistant started to fawn all over her escort, where Nikos Vassilis was clearly an extremely valued customer indeed.

And it didn't take a genius for Andrea to guess just what kind of woman he bought lingerie here for!

Oh, the assistant was polite enough to her, that was for sure, but it was obvious that she regarded her actual customer as Nikos Vassilis. Andrea knew she had been labelled a passing floozy with a single glance! She let the woman take her measurements and whisk out one gauzy confection after another, but declined the offer to try anything on.

She wouldn't be wearing any of it anyway. Her wedding night would be short—and very far from sweet.

Well satisfied with his purchases, Nikos was all set to keep going.

'Come,' he said persuasively, 'we are surrounded by designer shops—take your pick!'

'No, thanks,' she returned indifferently. 'I keep telling you I've got enough.'

'Then do me one favour, *ne*?' He caught her arm. 'Let me buy you a single skirt, now, to change into. You have worn trousers two days running. I far prefer women to wear skirts.'

'How surprising,' she said with a wry smile. 'Unfortunately for you, I don't wear skirts.'

He frowned. 'What do you mean, you don't wear skirts?'

'Exactly that,' she replied.

'You wore an evening dress last night!'

'That was long,' she said briefly. She wanted to change the subject—fast.

Enlightenment dawned on him—and relief. For a moment he had feared that she was the type of female who made some kind of nonsensical stand about insisting on wearing trousers on principle. Nikos saw no sense in such an attitude. He was no chauvinist—Vassilis Inc was unusual, he knew, in taking a proactive stance on hiring and promoting women—but he saw no reason why a woman should think she became demeaned as a sex object just for wearing a skirt!

Now he realised this was not Andrea's attitude.

'I'm sure your legs are beautiful,' he reassured her. 'They are long and elegant and shapely—I can see that even now.'

She glanced up at him. The curious twist was on her mouth again.

'Can you? You must have X-ray vision.'

He smiled indulgently. 'Even if they are not your best point, *agape mou*, I can make allowances.'

The twist to her mouth deepened, but she said nothing.

'So,' he said, 'let us buy you a skirt—and I will set your fears at rest.'

Her face went blank.

'I've done enough shopping for today. I'm bored.'

His eyebrow rose. He knew of no woman who was bored by shopping—especially when it was his money they were spending. Esme, naturally, was obsessed by clothes and her own appearance—it was her profession, after all. And Xanthe adored being taken by him to her favourite jewellers' shops. She was like a magpie for jewellery, and decked herself in glitter whenever she could. For her, Nikos knew with a cynical tightening of his jaw, it was an insurance policy for her old age, when she could no longer hold her rich lovers to her side.

Perhaps Andrea, born to expectations of vast wealth from birth, saw things in a different light.

'Well, I would hate you to be bored, so how can I amuse you?'

Andrea didn't like the note in his voice, hinting at meanings she would rather ignore. Didn't like it at all. She started walking along the pavement.

'I want to go sightseeing,' she said suddenly. After all, she would never come to Athens again. She might as well go sightseeing now, while she could.

A pang hit her, hard and painful. This was her father's city. He had been raised here. His blood sang in her veins. She was as Greek as she was English—and this was the first time in her life she was setting foot on Greek soil. And the last.

Sadness swept through her—sadness and bitterness.

'Sightseeing?' Nikos queried. 'But you will have seen all the sights a hundred times!'

She stared at him. 'I've never been to Athens before—never been to Greece before.'

Nikos looked at her, disapproval in his expression. It was one thing for Andrea's English mother to be worried about her father-in-law's views on disciplining children, or unwilling to revisit her dead husband's country herself, quite another to forbid her daughter to visit at all. It was bad enough Andrea did not speak Greek, let alone that she had never been here! He'd assumed that although Yiorgos Coustakis had not paraded his granddaughter to the world, she had, of course, been out here for holidays and so forth

'Then it is high time,' he said decisively, 'that I show you Athens.'

And he did. They spent the afternoon doing what all first-time tourists in the city did—climbing the Acropolis to pay homage to the glory of the first flowering of Western civilisation, the Parthenon.

Andrea was enthralled, refusing to acknowledge the wave of desolation that swept over her at the thought that soon, all too soon, she would never see Nikos again.

It didn't matter how much her eyes were drawn to him; it didn't matter how much she revelled in drinking in, as secretly as she could, the bounty that was this paean to manhood at her side. All of this, heady and intoxicating as she increasingly found his company, was nothing more than a temporary interlude in her life. Nikos Vassilis, though he could send a shiver of electricity through her with a single glance, the barest brush of his sleeve on her arm, was nothing more than a temporary interlude.

It was a phrase Andrea forced herself to remember day after day as, for the next two weeks, Nikos Vassilis made it very clear to the rest of the world that he had snapped up the Coustakis heiress as his forthcoming bride and that his sights were set, very firmly, on Coustakis Industries.

Andrea wished she could get used to him squiring her around—lunching in fashionable restaurants, dining in fashionable nightspots, always at her side, attentive, possessive, ramming home to all who saw them, time after time, that he was the favoured choice of Yiorgos Coustakis for the rich prize of Coustakis Industries—but she could not. Every time he picked her up in his gleaming, purring, powerful Ferrari she felt a kick go through her like an electric shock.

She did her best to hide it. Did her best to maintain the stony façade that she knew, instinctively, annoyed him.

Almost as much as it amused him.

'My English ice-maiden,' he said to her softly one evening, as she deliberately turned her face away from his greeting so that his lips could only brush her cheek, 'how I will enjoy melting you.'

She might think she was only marrying him to extract her

capital from the covetous claws of Old Man Coustakis—but he would prove otherwise.

And take great relish in it!

'You're mussing my hair, Nikos,' she replied snappily.

'It will get a lot more mussed than that soon,' he replied, eyes gleaming with mocking amusement—and promise. 'Tonight,' he went on, 'we shall go dancing.' He leant forward. 'I long to hold you in my arms again, Andrea *mou*.'

She backed away, almost tripping.

'I don't dance,' she said abruptly.

He laughed. The sound of it made her feel irritated. Among other things she didn't want to put a name to.

With every passing day her feet were getting colder and colder. She would wake in the middle of the night and the sheer disbelief of what she was doing would wash over and over her. Only one thought kept her going—money. Money at last. She had to hold out—hold out until the money was in the bank.

Then she could cut and run—and run and run…

From demons she refused to give a name to.

'I wasn't suggesting we go hot-clubbing till dawn,' he assured her. 'Since it isn't your scene anyway, I recall, I was thinking of something a little more….sophisticated. I think you will enjoy it. I know I will…'

She compressed her mouth. 'I said I don't dance. I mean it.'

He smiled lazily down at her, his mockery at her refusal glittering in his eyes like gold glinting in a sheet of slate, 'I can see I shall have to persuade you otherwise.'

He let the tips of his fingers brush lightly along her arm, amused at the way she jerked away again. He knew just how to handle her now, baiting her with her own responsiveness to him. She didn't like being that responsive, she was fighting against it, but it would be a losing battle, he knew.

And the victory would be his.

A sweet victory—reduced to abject pleading for his lovemaking this woman who made it totally, shamelessly clear that the only reason she was marrying him was to gain control of the capital her grandfather held for her. That would be a victory he would savour to the full.

As for Andrea, all she could do was put her mask in place and try and get through the evening.

Despite her protestations Nikos took her out later that night, and though it was not some packed and heaving strobe-lit club, there was no way she was going to let him lead her out onto the small, intimate floor in the rooftop restaurant he took her to.

'I said I don't dance and I meant it!' she repeated.

'Try,' he said. There was a glint in his eye, and it was not entirely predatory. There was determination in it as well.

Andrea gave in.

He led her out—she as stiff as a board—onto the dance floor. A love song was playing, and though with one part of her mind she was grateful, with the rest of it she felt her terror only increased, for reasons which had nothing to do with her habitual refusal to dance.

Nikos slid his arms around her, resting on the curve of her hips at either side. They burned through the thin fabric of her long peacock-blue dress with a warmth that made the pulse in her neck beat faster. She stood immobile. Her legs began to ache with the tension.

'Put your arms around my neck, *pethi mou.*'

The warmth of his breath on her ear made her shiver. He was too close. Much, much too close. The long, lean line of his body pressed against her, hip to hip, thigh to thigh.

Don't think! Don't feel! she adjured herself desperately.

Gingerly, very gingerly, she lifted her arms and placed one palm on either shoulder.

He was in evening dress, and the dark fabric felt smooth and rich to the touch. Beneath the jacket she could feel the hardness of his shoulders. She tensed even more.

'Relax,' he murmured, and with the slightest of pressures on her hip started to move her around with him.

For a brief moment she went with him, her right foot moving

jerkily in the direction he was urging her. Her legs were like wood, unbending.

'Relax,' he said again.

She moved her left leg, catching up with him, and they repeated the movement—him smoothly, she with a jerkiness that she could not control. Her spine was beginning to hurt with the effort.

She lasted another ten seconds, her face rigid, willing herself to keep going. Then, with a little cry, she stumbled away from him.

'I can't! I can't do this!'

She broke across the little dance floor, desperate to sit down, and collapsed back on her chair. Nikos was there in an instant beside her.

'What the hell was that about?' he demanded.

She could hear the annoyance in his voice. Only the annoyance.

'I told you, I don't dance!' she bit at him.

'Don't? Or won't?' he asked thinly, and sat down himself. He seized at the neck of the champagne bottle nestling in its ice bucket and refilled his glass. Hers was almost untouched.

'When we are married,' he said, setting down his glass with a snap, 'I shall give you lessons.'

'You do that,' she replied, and took a gulp of her champagne.

Nikos Vassilis would never teach her to dance.

Or anything else.

Surreptitiously, under the table, she slowly rubbed at her thighs. The ache went right through to her bones. And beyond.

Andrea clenched the phone to her ear.

'You're sure? You're absolutely sure?'

'Yes, Miss Fraser, completely sure. The sum of five hundred thousand pounds has been credited to your account.'

'And it can't be removed without my permission?' Her question was sharp.

'Certainly not!' The voice of the bank official, a thousand miles away in London, sounded deeply shocked as he replied.

It was the morning of Andrea's wedding.

The happiest day of my life! The day I finally, finally wave a wand over Mum and start our new lives!

As she terminated the call, with repeated assurances from her bank that the money deposited in her account first thing that day was totally and irrevocably hers to dispose of as she would, deep, deep relief flooded through her. She had done it! She had got what she had come for—the promise of freedom from poverty, from ill-health, from the grind and drab penury her mother had put up with for twenty-five years.

Now all she had to do was endure the next twenty-four hours and she would be on her way home.

I can do it! I've done it so far and I can do this last thing!

'*Kyria*, may I start to dress you, please?' Zoe's voice sounded anxiously from the doorway. 'Kyrios Coustakis would like you to go downstairs as soon as possible.'

Andrea nodded, and the lengthy process of dressing Yiorgos Coustakis's illegitimate granddaughter for her wedding to the man who would run his company and give him the heir he craved got underway.

Andrea felt the relief drain out of her, replaced by a tightness that started to wind around her lungs like biting cord. As she sat in front of the looking glass, Zoe skilfully pinning up her hair, she stared at her reflection. Her eyes seemed too big, her skin too pale. She clenched her hands together in her lap. The reality of what she was about to do hit her, over and over again, like repeated blows.

For all that it was a small, private wedding, it seemed to go on for ever, Andrea thought bleakly. She stood beside her bridegroom, unsmiling, her throat so tight she could hardly say the words that bound her to the tall, straight figure at her side. Sickness churned in her stomach.

She was marrying him! She was actually marrying Nikos Vassilis. Here. Now. Right now. Faintness drummed at her.

Her legs and spine ached with the tension wiring her whole body taut.

There was a ring on her finger. She could see it glinting in the sunlight.

It doesn't mean anything! This time tomorrow he'll have packed me off back to London and wished me good riddance. He'll have what he wanted—my grandfather's company. He'll be glad to see the back of me. He never wanted me in the first place.

And he doesn't even intend to be faithful…

Her lips compressed. Three nights ago her grandfather had summoned her again. Nikos had returned her from yet another night out, this time a concert, where the combination of Dvorak and Rachmaninov, plus the thrill of hearing one of the world's greatest soloists give the Dvorak cello concerto, had conspired to weaken her façade. As they left the concert hall she had turned impulsively to Nikos.

'That was wonderful! Thank you!'

Her eyes were shining, her face radiant.

Nikos paused and looked down at her. 'I'm glad to have given you pleasure.'

For once there was no double meaning in his words, no sensual glint in his eyes. For a moment they just looked at each other. Andrea's ears rang with the echo of the tumultuous finale of the Rachmaninov symphony. Her heart was almost as tumultuous.

Her eyes entwined with his and something flowed between them. She could not tell what it was, but it was something that made her want the moment to last for ever.

She was almost regretful that in fact she never was going to be his wife in anything but briefest name.

It was a regret that had been destroyed in the two-minute conversation with her grandfather on her return to his villa.

'There are things to make clear to you,' he began in his harsh, condemning voice, as she stood unspeaking in front of him to receive her lecture. 'From the moment you become Nikos Vassilis's wife you will behave as a Greek wife should.

He will teach you the obedience you so sorely lack!' His soul-less eyes rested on her like a basilisk, 'You will understand that you will gain no privileges from your connection with me. Nor should you imagine that you will gain any privileges from the fact that you are handsome enough for your husband to find you, for the moment, sexually desirable.'

He saw the expression on her face and gave a short laugh. 'I said "for the moment" and that is what I meant! Understand this, girl—' his eyes bored into hers '—in Greece a man who is a husband is still a man. And his wife must know her place. Which is to be *silent*! Nikos Vassilis has two mistresses cur-rently—an American model, a tramp who sleeps with any man who passes, and a woman of Athens who is a professional whore. He will discard neither for your sake.' His voice dropped menacingly. 'If I hear any whining from you, any screeching tantrums because of this, you will regret it! Do you understand?'

She understood all right and she felt revulsion shimmer through her.

Be grateful you're not marrying him for real!

But marrying him she was—if she wanted money for Kim then she must go through this farce of a wedding ceremony.

Not one mistress but two! Her mouth twisted. My, my, what a busy lad Nikos Vassilis was! And still intended to be, so it seemed! Well, that might be the way Greek males saw the world, but she would be having none of it!

The pop of a champagne bottle made her jump, exacerbating her jittery nerves. One of the servants was pouring out foaming liquid into tall glasses. Andrea sipped at hers and looked around her.

All this money, all this wealth, all this opulence and luxury, she thought. I've been drowning in it for two weeks, nearly three.

I want to go home!

The thought caught at her, making her want to cry out with it. She wanted to go home, back to Kim, back to the poky, damp flat that Nikos Vassilis would be appalled to know she had grown up in! He thought he was marrying the Coustakis heiress. What a joke! What a ludicrous, ridiculous joke!

Well, the joke would be on him before the night was out.

But she didn't feel like laughing.

Andrea sat in the Louis Quinze armchair, her eyes shut. The champagne had been drunk, she had endured the painfully polite congratulations of the household staff, and now she was waiting for her brand-new husband to emerge out of the library, where her grandfather was finally allowing him to sign the merger contracts. A bevy of men in suits had arrived on the doorstep an hour ago, all with aides and briefcases, and disappeared into the inner sanctum of Yiorgos Coustakis to conduct the real business of the day.

Her legs ached. Carefully she rubbed them through the material of her trousers. Zoe had helped her change out of the long ivory satin gown she had worn for the ceremony, and now she was back in the clothes she had arrived in. Although the staff had emptied just about the whole of the closet into half a dozen suitcases to see her through her honeymoon, Andrea had insisted on her own small case—the one she had brought with her—being handed to her personally. She had packed it the night before, with all her own clothes and the make-up bag containing the key to the airport locker holding her money and passport, right after phoning Tony and telling him that she was coming home in forty-eight hours, and asking him, as always, to give her love to Kim. She hadn't spoken to her mother since arriving here. Hadn't been able to bring herself to. She knew Kim would understand, would make do with having her love passed on every day by Tony.

The ormolu clock on the gilded mantelpiece ticked quietly. The room was silent. The only sound in it was Andrea's heavy heartbeat.

Let me just get through tonight, and then I can be gone!

There was the click of a door opening across the marbled hall, and the sound of voices. She opened her eyes. She could hear the besuited visitors taking their leave, their business done.

Time for Nikos to move on to the next item on his agenda—taking his bride on honeymoon, thought Andrea viciously. Being angry seemed like a good idea right now.

Safer.

She heard Nikos's voice in the hallway, and her grandfather answering shortly. Then footsteps as her grandfather trod heavily back to his own affairs. It must have been a good day's work for him, Andrea thought, selling his company and his bastard granddaughter at the same time.

Something flickered in the corner of her eye, and she twisted her head. It was just a drape, fluttering in the breeze from the open window. The day was warm, the sun inviting. Something caught at her heart, an echo from very long ago, from long before she was born.

Out of nowhere a memory came. A memory of something that had never happened but that she had so often, as a child, wished so ardently were real, and not a mere hopeless longing. The memory of her father, kind and smiling, calling her his princess, her mother his queen, crowning them both with happiness...

But it had never happened. Never. Instead he had died before she was born.

It shouldn't have been like this!

The silent cry came from deep inside her.

But it *is* like this, and there's nothing more I can do about it than I have already done.

'Are you ready?'

Nikos's voice was harsh, cutting through her sombre thoughts. He sounded tense.

She got to her feet.

'Yes,' she answered, and walked towards him where he stood in the doorway.

They took their places in the back of her grandfather's vast limousine, Andrea sinking back so far into the seat that she felt she would disappear. Nikos threw himself into the other corner. The car moved forward smoothly.

They did not talk, and Andrea was glad. She had nothing to

say to this man now. After tomorrow morning she would never see him again. He was a passing stranger, nothing more.

'Would you like a drink?'

She blinked. Nikos was pulling out a concealed drinks compartment, revealing an array of crystal decanters. She shook her head. He lifted one of the decanters and poured a measure of its contents into a glass. Andrea could smell whisky. He knocked it back in one shot, then replaced the glass and slid shut the cabinet.

'How are you feeling?'

The abrupt question took her by surprise. She shrugged.

'OK,' she said indifferently.

He made a sound in his throat that sounded to her ears like an impatient sigh, and then, with a swift movement, he loosened the tie at his throat and undid his collar. Andrea couldn't help looking across at him.

Immediately she wished she hadn't. She didn't know what it was about loosened ties and opened shirt collars, but the kick to her guts was immediate. Nikos ran a hand roughly through his hair, ruffling its satin smoothness. Another kick went straight through her guts.

To her relief, he wasn't paying her any attention, simply staring moodily out through the smoked glass window. Then, abruptly, he spoke.

'*Theos*, but I'm glad that's over!'

The kick in Andrea's guts vanished instantly. He was glad it was over. Fine. So was she. Very glad. Very glad indeed. Couldn't have been gladder. Her lips pressed together.

She looked away, staring out of her own window, and heard Nikos shift in his seat.

'Don't sulk, Andrea,' he told her tersely. 'You enjoyed that ordeal as little as I did! But it's over now. Thank God!' Then, on an even terser note, he said, 'Did you get your money?'

There was condemnation in his voice. Andrea thought of the merger contracts, signed not half an hour ago. Making Nikos Vassilis one of the richest men in Europe.

'Of course,' she answered.

'You won't need it,' said the man she had married. 'I will give you everything you want.'

She didn't reply.

He gave another, heavier sigh.

'Andrea, this is a time for plain speaking. We are married. And there is absolutely no reason to suppose things will not work out between us! Your grandfather is out of the picture now. He does not concern us. It is up to us to make this marriage work, and I believe it can—very successfully. If we both just make an effort to make it work! I am prepared to do so—and I ask that you are too. As soon as our honeymoon is over we shall fly to England to meet your mother, and mend bridges there. However much she disapproved of your grandfather, I hope she will think more kindly of me.'

She'll never lay eyes on you, thought Andrea, never even know you exist.

Nikos was talking still.

'For now you must put your mind to where we shall live. For the moment I propose my apartment in Athens, but I would prefer, I admit, a more permanent property. We can have a house in London, of course, for when you want to be with your English relatives, and I suggest we buy a villa on one of the islands as well, where we can relax in private.'

'Fine,' said Andrea. The issue was academic; it didn't matter what she said.

Tonight, she thought, over dinner, or perhaps, better still, in the hotel suite, where I don't have to worry about waiters hovering or other diners looking us over, I can tell him the truth about me. That will put an end to this farce.

Nikos gave up. He had done his best to be civil, but enough was enough. He felt rough. He had been working like crazy ever since Old Man Coustakis had dangled the prospect of a takeover in front of him. Mergers and acquisitions didn't happen overnight—the planning and preparation involved was immense. On top of that he still had to keep Vassilis Inc rolling along, even while he was gearing it up to ingest the much larger Coustakis Industries. It had not, he thought grimly, been the best time to have to go off wooing a bride! Nevertheless he had found the time to squire Andrea around, knowing that being seen prominently in public with her was all part of convincing the Athens business community—and beyond—of the reality of his intentions towards Coustakis Industries.

But for all the evenings spent taking Andrea out he was still no closer to seeing anything more of her than the closed, controlled surface she presented to him. There was certainly a deal of English blood in her, all right, he thought, exasperated. All that cool, calm, collected front she insisted on—polite, but distant. The only time he'd seen any trace of enthusiasm in her had been the other evening at the concert—then her eyes had shone like glossy chestnuts in autumn, and a vitality had filled her usually deadpan expression, catching at him. For a moment, he recalled, as he had looked down at her something had moved in her eyes....

But that had been the only moment. Maybe he had just imagined it anyway. Certainly the only way he was guaranteed to get a reaction from her was by reminding her, as he took such satisfaction in doing, of just how fragile that English sang-froid of hers really was! Of how a single touch could set her thrumming with sexual awareness of him. *That* was the only currency she responded to! However much she tried to suppress her responsiveness to him.

He looked across at her. She was still staring out of the window, ignoring him. Well, let her! It gave him the opportunity to look her over. Catalogue, in his discerning mind, all her sensual charms—from the generous fullness of her mouth to the richness of her breasts, the long line of her legs...

He felt himself relax for the first time that day. It was done. Today had set the seal on his long, long ascent from the rough streets of Athens to the pinnacle of his achievements.

And he knew exactly how to celebrate.

He closed his eyes and gave himself to the pleasure of contemplating just how good it would be to have the woman beside him beneath him.

*   *   *

'Where the hell are we?'

Andrea's voice was sharp.

'Piraeus,' replied Nikos. 'The port of Athens.'

'The *what*?'

'The port of Athens,' Nikos repeated. 'Where we embark.'

'Embark?'

Nikos looked across at her. Now what was she making a fuss about?

Andrea gazed wildly out of the window. She had been paying no attention to their journey from her grandfather's villa, deliberately diverting her mind from what she had just done by thinking about what would be involved in moving Kim out to Spain as soon as possible. But instead of drawing up outside some five-star hotel in the middle of Athens, whence she could easily take a taxi to the airport the following morning, the car had stopped on what she could now see was a quayside, alongside what seemed to be a huge, gleaming vessel.

The chauffeur opened her door and stood back to let her get out. Stiffly, aware that her legs had suddenly started to ache again with unexpected tension, Andrea climbed out and looked around her.

There was a vessel moored at the quayside all right. Absolutely huge. Vast. Stretching like a gleaming monster from bow to stern. A wide gangplank faced her.

'Come,' said Nikos.

He took her arm.

'I'm not going aboard that! What the hell is it?'

His mouth tightened. Hadn't Yiorgos even bothered to tell his granddaughter about his latest spending spree?

'It's your grandfather's new toy,' he told her. 'He's lent it to us for our honeymoon.'

Andrea stared. 'I thought we were going to spend the night in Athens. At a hotel.'

'What for?' countered Nikos. 'We might as well set sail as soon as possible.'

'I'm not going on that thing!'

Her face was set. Aware, as she was blissfully not, of the

highly interested if superficially indifferent attention not only of the chauffeur but of the crewmen at the foot of the gangplank, Nikos impelled her forward. He was not about to have his brand-new bride balk him.

She stumbled slightly, and with a sudden gesture Nikos swept her up into his arms. She gave a small shriek, but Nikos only gave a victor's laugh.

'I'm carrying you over the threshold.' He grinned down at her, as much for the sake of his audience as himself, and plunged up the gangplank.

Short of screaming blue murder, Andrea had no option but to let herself be carried aboard the monstrous vessel. She was too terrified to struggle in case they both landed in the murky water lapping beneath the gangplank.

Nikos set her down on the deck and said something in Greek to the man standing there. Hurriedly she smoothed down her jacket and tried to regain her composure. Then Nikos was introducing her.

'This is Captain Petrachos, Andrea *mou*,' he said smoothly.

Andrea took in a smartly dressed middle-aged man in an immaculate white naval uniform, with a lot of rings around his cuffs and gold epaulettes, sporting a trim, nautical beard.

'Welcome aboard, Kyria Vassilis. I hope you have a very enjoyable voyage.'

'Thank you,' she murmured in a strangled voice. It wouldn't be an enjoyable voyage, she thought wildly, it would be a very short one!

'If you're both ready, I'll get her underway.'

'Thank you,' said Nikos. He held out a hand to Andrea. 'Come, let us explore.'

His fingers closed around hers, tighter than was strictly necessary. Meekly, Andrea went off with him. She was rearranging her thoughts as quickly as possible. OK, so she had assumed— rashly so, it seemed!—that they would spend the first night of their honeymoon at some luxury hotel in the middle of Athens. Instead they were launching out on this floating private liner! Well, she thought grimly, so what? Her ludicrous marriage could come to a speedy and ignominious end here as well as anywhere else! They'd be docked right back here again before tomorrow morning.

Despite her best intentions to remain indifferent to her oh-so-temporary accommodation, Andrea found her eyes widening automatically as Nikos conducted her around the boat.

It was opulent beyond belief! Everywhere she looked there was rare wood panelling, silk, velvet and leather upholstery, gold and silver fittings, cashmere, suede and skins on floors and walls, inlays and gilding all around. A fortune must have been paid to fit out the interior, let alone the cost of the massive yacht itself, thought Andrea.

As they were shown round by an oh-so-attentive chief steward, Andrea felt increasingly oppressed. What had Nikos called it? Her grandfather's latest toy…

On the upper deck, she watched the mainland of Greece slip away behind them as the yacht nosed out towards the open sea. Meanwhile Nikos watched the wind billow through Andrea's exquisite hair. Her face was set. Clearly she was still in a mood.

Nikos's expression hardened. Just how spoilt was this woman? he thought. Here she was, aboard a yacht that was the last word in extravagance, and she still wasn't happy! He thought back to the days of his childhood, so long ago, when he had been a no-hope street kid. No pampered upbringing for him! He had got here, to the deck of a luxury yacht, as head of one of Europe's largest companies, Coustakis Industries, by his own efforts.

And now he was married to Yiorgos Coustakis's grand-daughter.

Well, he had better make the most of it…

CHAPTER EIGHT

CHAMPAGNE beaded in Andrea's glass, fizzing gently. She took another sip. Across the table from her, Nikos did likewise. They were in the dining room—a vast expanse dominated by a huge ebony table, lavishly set with crystal and gold. A suffocating smell of lilies permeated the atmosphere, emanating from the banks of bouquets all around the room. Above their heads a vast chandelier shed its light upon them. Four uniformed stewards stood in a line to one side, ready to do the slightest thing that the honeymoon couple required of them. Deep below the steady thrum of the vessel's motor was the only indication that they were actually on board a boat—the windows were obliterated by vast swathes of black velvet, tasselled in gold, reflecting the gold and black patterning in the deep, soft carpet under Andrea's feet.

She picked at her food. It had probably cost a fortune, just like everything else around her.

'You would prefer something else?' Nikos broke the oppressive silence.

'No, thank you. I'm simply not hungry.' Andrea's voice sounded more clipped than she intended, but civility was hard to project right now. Her whole body felt as if it had been tied into an excruciatingly tight knot.

You've got to tell him! End this farce right now! Then you can go to bed—alone!—and the yacht can start heading back to port.

She wished she had managed to talk to Nikos earlier. She should have stopped him leaving her alone on the deck, when he, with nothing more than a brief, 'There are a few matters I must attend to—excuse me,' disappeared into the interior. But he had not reappeared until a short while ago. In the meantime a stewardess had politely enquired when she would like dinner served, and when she would like to change for it. Helplessly, Andrea had gone along with her, telling her to refer to Mr Vassilis re the timing of dinner.

My, what a good little Greek wife I sound! she had thought. *Deferring to my husband right from the start!*

Husband—the word echoed in her brain.

I'm in shock, she thought, as her fork lifted mechanically to her mouth. I never really believed this would happen. I blanked it out, focussed only on the money for Kim. But it's real; it happened. I married Nikos Vassilis today and he's sitting opposite me, and I *still* haven't told him that this is going to be the shortest marriage in history!

So tell him now!

I should send away the crew, she thought—get rid of them all. Then simply open my mouth and tell him I'm leaving in the morning.

Instead, she found her mind wandering off. What on earth did all those stewards think? she wondered. A pair of newly-weds eating in stony silence? Did they think anything? Did they care? Were they even human? Their faces were totally expressionless. She had a sudden vision of them being androids, like something out of science fiction, and had to suppress a hysterical laugh. Quickly she snapped her mind onto something else.

Like who on earth had been in charge of the interior design of this place? They should be taken out and shot, she thought viciously. To spend such money for such atrocious results seemed like a criminal offence. The décor was hideous, just hideous!

Nikos looked across at her. Her eyes were working around the room disdainfully. Was she picking out flaws, signs of cheapness? he wondered sourly. He glanced down at her plate. She had stopped eating.

With sudden decision Nikos pushed his plate away from him. He was in no mood to eat. No mood to go on sitting here, with a row of statues like a silent Greek chorus witnessing his bride display her feelings about marrying him.

He got to his feet. Andrea started, and looked up at him.

'Come.'

He held out a hand to her. His mouth was a thin line.

She hesitated a fraction. There was something about him that unnerved her, but at the same time she, too, felt an overpowering urge to get out of this oppressive room. And after all she needed to speak privately with him, so she might as well go with him.

As he headed towards the door one of the stewards was there before him, attentively opening it. Andrea hurried after Nikos in the same tight green evening dress she'd worn her first night in Greece as he strode along the wide, thickly carpeted corridor. He flung open a door at the end and held it for her.

She went inside.

It was their bedroom.

Mahogany panelled the room from floor to ceiling, and in the middle a gigantic bed, swathed in gold silk, held centre stage. Ornate gold light fittings marched around the room. She dragged her eyes away.

Do it—do it now!

'I've got something to tell you.'

Andrea's voice sounded high-pitched and clipped.

'How remarkable. My silent bride deigns to speak.'

His sarcasm cut at her. She lifted her chin.

'You might as well know,' she said, 'I'm going back to England tomorrow. I'm filing for divorce.'

Nikos stared at her, completely stilled. The grey of his eyes was like cold, hard slate. Andrea felt her hands clench at her sides. Her legs had started to ache, sensing the tension in the rest of her body.

'You are mistaken.'

The brief, bald sentence was quietly spoken, but the nape of Andrea's neck crawled.

'I'm not staying with you!' The pitch of her voice had risen.

'And may I be permitted to ask—' the icy softness cut slivers of flesh from her '—what has led you to make this...unexpected announcement?'

Somehow she managed to stand her ground.

'I should have thought it was obvious! Your sole purpose in marrying me was to clear the way to get hold of my grandfather's company. Now you've done that you don't need to stay married to me for a second longer!'

'An interesting analysis, but fatally flawed,' he returned.

'Why?' she demanded.

'Because,' said Nikos in that same soft voice which now, instead of cutting slivers from her, had somehow, she did not know how, started to send shivers of a quite different nature quivering down her arms, 'you happen to possess charms beyond your possession of Yiorgos Coustakis's DNA. Charms,' he went on—and now the shivers spread from her arms across her breasts, her flanks, 'that I fully intend to enjoy.'

He took a step towards her, the expression in his eyes making it totally, absolutely clear just what charms he had in mind.

She jerked backwards.

'Stay away!'

He stopped again. 'Don't give me orders, *pethi mou*. You'll find I don't respond well to them!'

The edge in his voice, steel beneath the velvet, was a warning.

It was also a trip point.

'If you're after sex go and phone for one of your mistresses!' she flung at him.

He stopped dead.

'My what?'

'You heard me—your mistresses! You're running two that the whole world knows about and God knows how many more besides! Go and phone for one of them if you're feeling horny. But don't damn well come near me!'

His eyes were like splinters.

'And just how, may I ask, did you come by this information?'

'Oh, I got a full briefing from my grandfather! It was part

of his pre-wedding lecture to me not to kick up a fuss about you still having sex with other women. An obedient Greek wife—' she let the sarcasm flow into her voice '—doesn't make a scene over such trifles as her husband's mistresses!'

Comprehension flooded Nikos's expression, masked by anger. Not at Andrea, but at her wretched grandfather. So that was why the girl had done nothing but sulk all day! Thanks, Yiorgos, for another big favour you've done me! Screwing up my marriage before I even get started on it!

'Right,' he began, 'we'll get a few things clear, I think. Firstly, yes, of course I have had liaisons with other women— I was free to do so and I did! But—' he held up his hand '—I have not set eyes on another woman since the day I met you.'

His assurance left Andrea less than impressed.

'So you just dumped them, did you? Charming!'

Nikos shut his eyes briefly, then opened them. 'My relationships with both women are—were—what you might call "open",' he said. 'Xanthe Palloupis has several other rich lovers who help keep her in the style she fully intends to hold on to for as long as her looks last, and Esme Vandersee—'

'Esme Vandersee? The supermodel?' Andrea's voice cut in incredulously. 'She's one of the world's most beautiful women!'

There was a note in her voice that Nikos did not miss, and it sent a shaft of satisfaction through him which, right now, he badly needed. It had been something between dismay and jealousy.

'She is also,' he said, 'quite happy to reward a large assortment of her chosen admirers with a hands-on tour of her spectacular body. I'm confident she found it extremely easy to replace me,' he finished dryly.

But Andrea didn't want to hear about Esme Vandersee and her spectacular body. In fact if the supermodel had suddenly beamed aboard right in front of her she would have got a dusty reception from her lover's bride. Extremely dusty.

She quelled the stab of pure possessiveness that darted through her at the thought of Esme Vandersee or Xanthe

Whatever-her-name-was making moves on Nikos Vassilis. It was utterly inappropriate.

And totally irrelevant.

Why am I discussing Nikos's mistresses? she thought. They've got nothing to do with why I'm going home tomorrow!

'So,' Nikos continued smoothly, 'now I understand the reason for your ill-temper all day, Andrea *mou*—'

'I'm still leaving tomorrow morning! And it's got nothing to do with any of the women you put out for! I have absolutely no intention of staying married to you!'

The glitter was back in Nikos's eyes.

'And what objection, may I ask again, are you going to put forward now?'

Her eyes flicked to the opulence all around them. Kim's entire flat would just about fit into the space of this single stateroom! *Tell him the truth about yourself now—he'll send you packing the moment he hears!*

'For heaven's sake, how could I possibly even *think* of being married to you? We come from totally different worlds—'

She broke off. Something was in his face that made her feel frightened suddenly.

Different world? Oh, yes, different worlds indeed. A fatherless street boy and a pampered heiress...

'Nevertheless...' the softness was back in his voice, and it was slicing at her flesh again '...you are my wife, Andrea Vassilis, and if you understand nothing about what it means to be Greek, understand this—no husband lets his bride make a laughing stock of him by walking out on him straight after their wedding! And never, ever—' his eyes slid over her face, her body '—before their wedding night...'

He came towards her. She could not move. Slate eyes fixed her where she was. Slate eyes with only one purpose in them.

The fear dissolved. For a brief moment desire flooded through her, powerful and irresistible. She crushed it aside. There was no place for it. There could not be. There must not be. In its place came a flat, dull resolve. So it was going to be like this, was it? Very well, so be it. She'd see it through to the bitter end—and be on a plane home tomorrow.

She stood there motionless. In her mind she searched for the impenetrable mask she had donned every time she was in his company. It was time to wear it again.

He stopped in front of her. She was very still. Like a statue. He reached a hand towards her. The back of his fingers brushed her cheek, trailing down over the column of her neck, turning to close over the cusp of her shoulder, bared except for the narrow straps of her dress.

'The last time you wore this you melted into my arms like honey on a warm spoon.'

The thumb of his other hand came up to ease along the trembling line of her lips.

She stiffened, clutching the carapace to her.

She was holding out on him. Denying her response to him. He smiled. This and this alone was the way to communicate with the woman who today had been joined in matrimony to him. And when, eventually, she lay beneath him, and throbbed in his embrace, then—oh, then—let her think of the 'different worlds' they came from. Let her think of the 'release of capital' she'd gained today. Let her think of walking out of their brand-new marriage. Let her think of anything she liked—if she could.

But all she would be capable of thinking about, he knew, with every fibre of his being, would be him and him alone.

He let his hands fall to his sides. She was resisting him—she would do so no longer. Swiftly he crossed to the banks of wardrobes lining the side of the room, throwing open one door after another until he found what he was looking for. Then, grasping delicate folds, he tossed it at her.

'Go and change!'

He nodded towards the *en suite* bathroom. Andrea looked at the garment he had thrown her. She knew what it was—the negligee he had bought her in the shop that had treated her like a rich man's floozy.

She turned and walked into the bathroom. Well, in a few minutes now she would be a rich man's unwanted wife.

The knowledge stabbed at her. It hurt—it hurt more than she had ever dreamt it could. Knowing what was coming. Knowing that she was to be Nikos Vassilis's oh-so-unwanted wife.

But it was inevitable. Had been from the moment he had looked across her grandfather's terrace at her and she had seen the flare of sexual interest in his eyes—felt it set light in her an answering flame.

Time to douse the fires.

Permanently.

She hugged the carapace to her more tightly than ever.

As the bathroom door clicked behind her Nikos got busy. Ringing for a steward, he had the scarcely touched bottle of champagne brought to him, and let the man turn down the bed. Then, retiring to the matching *en suite* bathroom he prepared himself. He had already shaved before dinner, and now it was a matter of moments to strip off and don a bathrobe.

He was already aroused. His celibacy of the last few weeks was obviously being felt—protestingly—by his body. He found himself thinking back to when he'd first thought through the implications of marrying Yiorgos Coustakis's unknown grand-daughter. He had worried about her lack of looks, her virginity, the fact that he would have to steel himself to get through his wedding night while making it as physically painless as possible for his dutiful bride.

His mouth twisted. Well, that was one word he didn't have to apply to Andrea! Dutiful she was not!

Would you want her to be? came the immediate ironic question, and the answer was immediate. No way! What he wanted her to be was…passionate, ardent, melting, molten, sensual, arousing, scorching, purring…

The litany went on inside his head, each word an image that burned with increasing fire in his guts. *Theos*, he wanted her! Wanted her as he wanted no other woman!

As an academic exercise he tried to make himself remember

what Xanthe looked like, Esme—but he could not do it. There was only one face, one body that he could see.

Andrea's.

My wife.

Possession surged through him. He was about to make her his in very truth, physically merging their bodies into one.

Desire kicked at him again, more urgent than ever.

With a tug he opened a shallow drawer in the vanity unit and drew out a handful of the small silvery packets that nestled within. He gave a wolfish grin. Oh, he'd get through the lot of them tonight, he thought.

He felt his body tighten. Sexual anticipation flooded him.

He strode out of the bathroom.

She was there, waiting for him. His breath caught.

Beautiful! His body jerked in salute of the image she made.

She stood in the centre of the room like a flame-haired queen. Her glorious locks were loose, tumbling down over her shoulders. The white, almost transparent silk of her negligee outlined her body, her full breasts thrust forward, straining against the taut material.

Desire kicked in him, hard and insistent.

'You're so beautiful—'

His voice was husky.

Andrea heard it, heard the note of raw desire in it. Her breath caught, and a shot of pure adrenaline surged through her. Then the words he had uttered penetrated, and the rush died, draining away like dirty oil from the sump of a wrecked car.

You're so beautiful...

Her mouth made a tight twist, and her eyes took on a strange brightness.

'Am I? Am I beautiful?'

Her voice was as strange as the twist to her mouth, the brightness of her eyes. She spoke to him, spoke to the man who stood waiting for her, stripped and ready for action.

A man who made her feel weak all over, inside and out, who made her heart clench and her breath catch just with looking at him.

But now it was him looking at her. She let him look. Wanted him to look.

That was the only way she could play this now—nothing else had worked. This must. It could not fail.

She went on speaking in that low, strange voice.

'This is what you want, isn't it, Nikos? A beautiful woman in your bed. Am I beautiful enough, Nikos? Am I?'

Her hands slid around the nape of her neck, lifting up her hair. She moved her head so that the glorious tumble flamed like fire. Then her hands slid down to the bodice of her negligee, fingers sliding beneath the delicate expensive material. She slipped it back, baring her shoulders, her hands grazing her breasts.

And all the time her eyes held his, never letting them go for a second.

'Am I beautiful, Nikos? Your beautiful bride?'

He couldn't answer her. His breath was frozen in his throat, though in his veins the blood roared.

She smiled. A fey, taunting smile.

Inside her head, behind the mask of her face, she was filled with flat, cold desolation. She was being cruel, she knew, but it was the only way. The only way.

She moved towards the bed, gliding softly, and lay down upon it, one hand loosely gathering the half-discarded material of her negligee to her breasts, the other smoothing the silk along the line of her legs.

'Am I your beautiful bride, Nikos? Beautiful enough for your bed?'

He came towards her. Purpose, desire, arousal—all in his eyes, his face—his ready, hungry body.

He could not resist her! Not for a second longer! Tumult consumed him. Who was this woman? One moment a cold, sulking ice-maiden, denouncing him for his sexual appetites, icily demanding a divorce before the ink was dry on the marriage certificate, sneering at him for his lowly origins. And now—now she was lying here, eternal Eve, displaying her body for him, lush and beautiful, oh, so beautiful, tempting him, arousing him—inviting him.

He looked down at her, caught in a pool of light, her body on show for him, veiled only by the sheerest of fabrics.

'Show me your body, Andrea—'

It was a rasp, a husk—a command, a plea.

There was a brightness in her eyes, a strangeness to her lips. He did not see it, saw only the soft outline of her limbs, her breasts, her belly...

'Show me...'

Her hand moved on her thigh, sliding the silk away, letting it slither from her thighs to the bedclothes on either side.

She looked at him. There was no expression in her eyes. None at all.

There was silence. A silence so profound Nikos knew he could hear his own heart beating.

Oh, dear God, dear God...

He stared down, the twisted, pitted surface of her legs scarring into his retinas as deeply as the scars that gouged and knotted her limbs from hip to ankle, runnelling through her wasted muscles, winding around her legs like some hideous net.

Horror drowned through him. She saw it in his face, his eyes. The brightness in her own eyes burned like acid. The tightness in her throat was like a drawn wire. Then deliberately, jerkily, she covered her legs again and stood up.

He stood aside to let her get to her feet. She yanked the negligee back into place over her shoulders, tugging at the belt to make it tighter—hugging her carapace into place. She must not lose it now. She must not.

'The comedy is ended,' she announced. Her voice was flat. 'I'll sleep in another room tonight. If you could be so good as to ensure we dock back at Piraeus tomorrow, I'll make my own way to the airport.'

She turned to go.

He caught her arm.

She looked down to where his fingers closed around her flesh.

'Let me go, Nikos. There's no need to say anything. Not a thing. I'm—sorry—it came to this. I thought it wouldn't be necessary. That you would accept the dissolution of our ridiculous marriage without any need to get this far., But in the end—' her voice tightened yet another unbearable notch '—it seemed the quickest way to convince you. Now, please let me go. I'll get my things and find another room…cabin…whatever they're called on a boat like this.'

He let her go, but only to slide his hand past her wrist and take her hand.

It was strange, thought Andrea, with the part of her mind where her act did not seem to work. The feel of his fingers wrapping hers was making her feel very strange. Very strange indeed.

He sat down on the edge of the bed, drawing her down beside him. His hand did not let go of hers.

'What happened, Andrea?' he asked.

There was something in his voice that made her eyes blink. The acid was burning them and she couldn't see properly. Something was misting her vision.

'What happened?' he asked again. His voice was very quiet.

She stared down at the carpet. There was a gold swirling in the pattern. It shifted in and out of focus. It seemed very important that it stay in focus. She stared at it again.

After a while, she spoke.

'It was a car crash, when I was fifteen. The older brother of one of my classmates was driving. He was driving us home— we'd been to the movies. I—I don't remember much. We swerved suddenly—a tyre burst, apparently—glass on the road, a broken bottle or something—and hit a wall. I was in the passenger seat. I was knocked out. I got trapped. The firemen had to cut me out. My legs were all smashed up. In hospital…in hospital…the doctors wanted…wanted…' Her voice was dry. 'They wanted to amputate—they said they were so smashed up they couldn't save them.'

She didn't hear the indrawn breath from the man sitting beside her. Nor did she feel the sudden tightening of his grip on her hand.

She went on staring at the carpet.

'My mother wouldn't let them. She said they had to save them. Had to. So—so they did. It…it took a long time. I was in hospital for months. Everything got pinned together somehow, and then, eventually, I was allowed into a wheelchair. They said I'd never walk. So much had gone. But Mum said I was going to walk. She said I had to. Had to. So…so I learned to walk again. I got sent to a special place where they help you learn to use your body again. It took a long time. Then they sent me for more operations, and that set me back, but Mum said it didn't matter, because I was going to walk again. I had to. And I did.'

The pattern in the carpet was going out of focus again. She swallowed.

'The only thing is, I can't do things like…like dance, and so on. It…it hurts. And I get frightened I'll damage them somehow. And though I can swim—it was part of my physio and still is, because the water helps to take the weight off my legs as I exercise them—I do it very early in the morning, when no one can…no one can see me.'

She blinked. 'I'm very lucky. Incredibly lucky. I learnt that in hospital, and in the physio place. There were others much worse off than me. Now the only thing wrong with me is that I have to be careful and not overdo things. And never marrying—' Her voice shook, but she steeled it to be still, and carried on. 'Never marrying won't be so bad. I've accepted that. I know no man can want me, not when they know, not when they've seen—'

Her voice broke.

Quietly, Nikos slid his hand out of hers. Then, just as quietly, he slipped to his knees on the floor at her feet. The dark of his head gleamed like black satin. He put his hands on her thighs. Beneath the flawless silk of the negligee he could feel the surface of her legs, uneven and knotted. Slowly he pushed the material aside.

She tried to stop him, tried to jerk her legs away from him, but his hands pressed on the sides of her thighs. His head bowed.

Slowly, infinitely slowly, Nikos let his hands move with absolute gentleness over the scarred, runnelled tissue of her legs, across the twisted muscles of her thighs, down over the knife-cut knees, along the warped, lumpen line of her calves, to circle her ankles. Then slowly, infinitely slowly, with the same absolute gentleness, he moved his hands back up, to rest once more on the sides of her thighs.

Then he lowered his mouth to her legs and kissed them— each thigh, each knee.

She sat still, so utterly still. All that moved within her body was her heart. She could not breathe; she could not think. Could not understand.

How can he touch them? How can he not be revolted? Disgusted?

A cruel memory surfaced in her thoughts. His name had been Dave, and he'd had a reputation with the girls. He'd made a play for her the moment he'd set eyes on her, and her refusal to go out with him had only made him more determined. She'd been twenty-two, and by then she had known just how ugly her legs were going to be all her life. She'd been chary of men. But Dave had gone on at her and on at her, and he was good-looking, with winning ways, and she couldn't help but fancy him, and in the end she'd given in to temptation and gone out with him. She'd wanted so much to be normal again—have boyfriends, discover sex. Fall in love. They'd dated quite a while, and he hadn't seemed to mind that she couldn't go clubbing, and she'd even, after a few weeks, told him about her accident. He hadn't seemed to mind.

Until the night she'd finally decided that twenty-two was no age to be a virgin still, and Dave had wanted her, so very, very much...

She could remember the look on his face as if it was yesterday. The strangled noise in his throat as she took her jeans off in his flat, the undisguised expletive that exploded from him. The word he'd called her.

Freak.

Crippled freak.

It's what I am. What every man will think me...

'Nikos—'

She caught his head with her hands. His hair was like black silk to her touch.

'Nikos—don't, please—'

He raised his mouth, lifting his face to her.

'Hush, *agape mou*, hush.' His voice was low.

He slipped his forearms underneath her thighs, and with the lightest exertion swung her legs round and on to the bed, following them himself to lie beside her. He leaned over her as she lay there, eyes wide and confused.

'Nikos—' Her voice was faint

He laid a finger over her mouth.

'This is not a time for talking,' he told her.

Then slowly, sensually, he began to make love to her.

It was like walking along the blade of a knife. Every move, every gesture, every touch was crucial. Control beaded in every nerve.

This is for her, not for you—

Carefully, incredibly carefully, Nikos kissed her. His mouth was light, as light as swansdown, his lips feathering hers, his tongue flickering at the corners of her mouth until it opened to him, and then slowly, delicately, he explored within.

Her eyes had shut. He hadn't noticed when, but it didn't matter. He knew she could not help it. Knew that the only way she could accept what was happening to her was by closing herself to everything but sensation—pure, blissful sensation.

And it was the same for him. He too knew that he must focus only and absolutely on what was happening now. Not just because of the utter physical control he had to impose on himself, but because somewhere, deep down inside, emotions were running so deep he could not name them. All but one.

Anger. Anger at a universe where such things happened. Anger at himself for being such a boor, a fool. Anger, most of all, at the men who had looked at her and let her feel that she was repulsive to them...

His mouth glided down the smooth, flawless column of her throat, seeking the hollow at its base where her pulse throbbed. With the skill of all his years he parted her robe, shaping delicately, sensuously, the sweet richness of her breasts. His mouth moved to their reddened tips and his tongue flickered over the hardening peaks.

Her heard her gasp, low in her throat, felt her head roll back as she savoured the sensations he aroused in her.

His body surged, and he quelled it urgently. He wanted—*Theos* how he wanted—to take her swollen nipple into his mouth, to suck and take his fill, move his body over hers at once, fill her with his, and feed and sate his appetite on her.

This is for her, not you—

With extreme control he held back, focussing only on her response, compressing her ripe breasts together so that his tongue could move from one peak to the other, endlessly keeping both in straining engorgement while little moans pulsed in her throat.

He felt her fingers come around his shoulders, beneath the towelling of his robe, pushing it back, sliding it from him, seeking the broad swathe of his shoulderblade to press into the smooth, flawless flesh of his back. He eased the robe from him to let her access him, never for a moment lifting his mouth away from her, only letting it drift down, over the swell of her breast, to lave the suddenly tautened plane of her belly.

And soon beyond.

As his fingers began to thread, tantalisingly, oh, so tantalisingly, in the tight curls that nested above the vee of her legs, Andrea thought she could stand no more. The sensation overload of her whole body was so intense, so exquisite she could not bear it.

But she could not escape it. It was like being sucked into a dark, breathless whirlpool, circling with infinite slowness, infinite power. She knew she ought to open her eyes, but she could not. Knew she ought to stop this, now, right now, push away those hands, that mouth…

But she could not. She was drowning in sensation, lost to all reason. There was nothing, nothing in the universe except what she was feeling now—as if her whole body were one whole, sweet mesh of soft, liquid pleasure that suffused every cell, every fibre of her being.

A pleasure that was growing with a mute, remorseless crescendo, spreading out in one sweet wave after another, quivering down all her nerves, washing through and through her as the slow, dark whirlpool took her with it.

His mouth was where his fingertips had been, and now his fingertips had moved on, brushing down the tender flesh on either side of the tightly curling nest of hair, seeking the parting of her legs.

Almost she tensed. Almost she thrust him back—away. Almost the knowledge of her disfigurement triumphed. But then, with a breathless sigh of pleasure, she felt her thighs loosen, fall open.

The whorls of pleasure intensified. She was weightless, floating in some sea of bliss that took everything away but the flickering of his tongue, the soft easing of his fingertip through folds made satin with a dew that his touch drew out of her.

The sensation was all there was.

Nothing had felt like this. Nothing in all her life. She had not known such sensation could exist.

A long, sweet moan escaped her. Her head rolled back, shoulders almost lifting from the bedclothes. The flickering intensified, the stroking fingertip easing her lips apart, exposing new, sweet feminine flesh to his skilled, exquisite touch.

Her hands clenched in the bedcover and she moaned again. Sensation broke over her again, wave after wave. And yet, with an instinct she did not know existed, she knew she was not yet sated. These were just the shallows of sensation.

She felt her hips lift and strain towards him, seeking more—more.

He answered her supplication. His fingertip drew back, gliding delicately in the flooding dew, circling slowly, rhythmically, like the vortex of a whirlpool, at the entrance to her body. Her fingers clenched again into the heavy folds of the bedspread, and her hips called to him again.

His tongue hovered minutely, and then, as the most drowning sensation yet broke through her, its very tip touched at the part that had swollen, all unbeknownst to her, past the protective furrow which had sheltered it.

Her breath caught, lips parting. What she had felt till now had been an echo, a shadow. Now, *now* was the true flame to her body lit. It burned beneath his touch, like a sweet, intense fire, making her whole body molten, focussing her entire being, as through a burning lens, on that single point of heat. It grew, and grew. She did not know how, or why—could feel nothing now, not the closeness of his body, nor the ministrations of his fingertip circling steadily, steadily, as her body opened to him, nor even the controlled, oh, so controlled accuracy of the flickering of his tongue, just there, just *there*, until the heat there, just *there*, was all there was, all there could ever be.

She was molten, molten, the warmth welling from the only centre of her body that could exist now, until it ascended through every vein, higher, ever higher, as the whirlpool sucked at her and sucked, and she could hear, from far, far way, a long, slow, rising cry that came from somewhere so deep inside she had never known its existence, reaching out, reaching out to exhale through her lifted, opening mouth…

Heat flooded through her, a huge, overwhelming sheet of flame that simply raced to encompass her whole body. It flooded again and again—a surge of flame, lifting her body, arching her spine, her neck, a surge of pleasure so intense, so absolute, it filled her with incredulity and awe that her body could feel so much…so much.

And go on feeling. It came, wave after wave, one more blissful than the next, and the cry from the heart of her being went on, and on, and on...

She could feel the internal muscles of her body rippling inside her, feel the blood surging, feel the pulsing of every fold, the rush of moisture releasing.

Time lost all meaning as she gave herself, consumed, to the molten overflow flooding and flooding again through her. And still it came. Until, singing its ecstasy, her ecstasy, her body began, finally to ebb, exhausted, sated, the vast, encompassing whirlpool slowly, slowly stilling...

Arms were holding her. There was the alien scent of maleness, the strong hardness of masculine muscles, the brush of body hair against the new softness of her breasts. She was folded into it. Folded against him.

Slowly reality came back to her, and she realised what had happened.

Andrea lay in his arms as motionless as a rag doll. Her entire body was limp. He was not surprised. When she had peaked it had been like an endless outpouring of her whole body, the flush of ecstasy suffusing the paleness of her skin, her eyes fluttering beneath her long, long lashes, her breath exhaling in a long, slow susurration of bliss.

And now she lay in the sheltering circle of his arms.

Nikos held her quietly, not moving, not stirring, knowing his own body was at peace as well.

And more than his body.

He had done the right thing, he knew. Followed his unconscious instinct—knowing, somehow, that he must take her on a journey she needed to make. A journey that must be an exorcism of all her fears, a healing of the wounds that had been laid upon her.

He felt the inert length of her legs beside him and coldness iced through him. He heard her words again—*The doctors wanted to amputate...*

Inside his head he heard his answering cry of negation of such a fate.

'*Andrea mou…*' He did not know if he said the words aloud or not. But they echoed in him all the same.

His eyes were heavy. At his side, in the cradle of his arms, he felt her body slacken imperceptibly, saw her face slide into repose, her breath shallowing into sleep. He felt its call, his eyelids too heavy to hold apart, and as his own breathing slowed his muscles relaxed, like hers, into the sweet embrace of sleep as well.

CHAPTER NINE

THERE was sunlight in the room, bright and pouring, flooding in from the wide-set windows. Andrea stirred, surfacing unwillingly from sleep. There was some reason she didn't want to wake up, but she didn't want to think about what that might be.

But wake she must. Someone was shaking her shoulder. Not roughly, but insistently.

'Andrea, *mou*, we are wasting a glorious day! Come, breakfast awaits.'

Nikos's voice was a mix of chiding and encouraging, his tone deliberately light. It would be the best way to play it, he knew. For the moment at least. She didn't want to move, didn't want to acknowledge his existence, but she must—this was not something she could run away from or deny any longer. He would not hurry her, he would be as gentle as she needed, but her denial must end. He desired her and she desired him—and the trifle of her scarred legs must not get in the way of her acceptance of that inalienable truth.

He dropped a kiss on her exposed cheek.

'What do you say in English? Lazybones?' He stood up. 'There is a pot of tea for you here to wake you up—the chef poured all his genius into making you the perfect English "cuppa"—you must not offend him by rejecting it! He will sulk for days and we shall starve! So, drink your tea like a good girl, and come and join me on deck in fifteen minutes.' He stooped briefly, to brush her cheek very softly with his fingers. 'It will be all right, Andrea—trust me.'

Then he was gone.

She needed every one of those fifteen minutes he had allowed her. As she showered and dressed a single thought

132

drummed through her brain—*Don't think about it! Just don't think about it!*

But the moment she emerged onto the sunlit deck, where a breakfast table was set up, and laid eyes on Nikos sitting there it was all for nothing. Memory, in total, absolute detail, came flooding back to her.

He could see it in her face, her eyes, and acted immediately. He got up and came across to her swiftly, taking her hands.

'Come—breakfast,' he said. 'What would you like to have?' He swept an arm to indicate a sideboard groaning with enough food to feed an army, with everything on it from fresh fruit to devilled kidneys.

Grateful, as he had intended, for the banality of choosing something to eat, she let him help her to lightly scrambled eggs, toast, and a plate of highly scented freshly cut pineapple. She felt surprisingly hungry.

If I don't think about it, it never happened… she told herself, sitting herself down at the table.

There were no crew in sight, and she was grateful for that too. Whether it was Nikos being tactful she didn't know, but she simply couldn't have borne to have that mute chorus in attendance.

Instead, she looked about her. The deck they were seated on faced the stern, and all Andrea could see all around was a glorious expanse of sparkling blue water. The sight lifted her spirits of its own accord. A tiny breeze whisked around her cheeks, fanning the tendrils of her hair. It was a bright, fresh, brand-new day.

From nowhere, absolutely nowhere, a sense of wellbeing filled her. It was illogical, impossible, but it was there. She felt her spirits lighten. Who could be otherwise on a morning like this?

She set to, demolishing her breakfast swiftly. She'd only picked at her food over that excruciating dinner last night, and now she was making up for it. There was something so incredibly comforting about scrambled eggs on toast…

Nikos said nothing, just busied himself leafing through a

newspaper as he worked steadily through a surprisingly hearty breakfast. As they ate, with him paying her no more attention than from time to time checking if she would like more tea, more toast, more butter, little by little she found herself capable of lifting her eyes from her food, and instead of sliding them immediately to the sparkling horizon let them pass, in focus, over the man sitting opposite her.

Don't think about it! she reminded herself, and to her surprise the technique seemed to work.

Maybe it was because Nikos seemed so totally relaxed. He sat there, a man at peace with the world, eating his breakfast beneath an Aegean sky. Maybe too, Andrea realised, it was because for the first time she was seeing him in informal clothes. Instead of the habitual business suit or evening dress this morning he was wearing a beautifully cut but informally tailored short-sleeved, open-necked fawn-coloured shirt and tan-coloured chinos.

He still looked devastating, of course, but the air of command was absent—or, if not absent, definitely off-duty.

As he swallowed the last of his coffee, folded up his newspaper and glanced towards her some twenty minutes later she realised she was just sitting there, her own breakfast finished, content to feel the warm sun on her face, the air ruffling her hair occasionally, and watch the stern flag flap in the breeze.

It dawned on her that they were not moving.

'Where are we?' she asked, puzzled. 'Why have we stopped?'

'We are on the approach to Heraklion. If you wish, we can make landfall.'

'Heraklion?' queried Andrea. 'Isn't that on Crete?'

'Yes. The island is visible from the aft. Shall we go and look?'

There didn't seem to be a particularly good reason not to, and Andrea found herself standing up as Nikos moved to draw back her chair. She walked beside him along the side of the vessel, and as they drew clear onto the foredeck she could see the long east-west land mass of Greece's largest island lying to the south of them. Mountains rose in the interior, almost all along the spine of the island, and Nikos pointed to the town of Heraklion on the coast in front of them.

'Knossos is only a few kilometres inland. Would you like to go and visit the Minotaur?' he asked genially.

The prospect tugged at her. Then, sinkingly, she realised she must ask for the yacht to put about and return to Piraeus. She had a plane to catch.

As if reading her thoughts, Nikos touched her arm lightly. Though it was only the briefest gesture, she felt her skin tingle.

'Stay a little, Andrea *mou*. What harm will it do, after all?'

His voice was light, but there was a cajoling beneath the lightness. 'Today we could just play tourists. It's been a strain, these last weeks—let us relax a little, *ne*?'

She tried to answer, but couldn't. If she answered him she would have to open that door that she had banged tightly shut this morning as she got out of bed. And she couldn't face that.

The alternative was to go on along this path she was on now. It would be temptingly easy to do so.

She had never seen Knossos, and was unlikely ever to get the opportunity to do so again. Just as she had wanted to see Athens while she was there, now she wanted to see the famous site of the very first civilisation Europe could boast, the Minoans, whose vast, labyrinthine Bronze Age palace at Knossos made the Parthenon look modern.

And see it she did, joining the throng of tourists who poured over the massive remains of the excavated and partially restored site, amazed at the sheer size of a palace first built over four thousand years ago and destroyed so cataclysmically. She was both fascinated and awestruck—and saddened. The exquisite murals, even if restored, caught at a world where militarism and armaments seemed quite absent—a world where nature and fertility were more valued than war and conquest.

'They did not need military might—all the Minoan palace sites lack ramparts,' Nikos reminded her when she found herself remarking on it. 'Theirs was a maritime trading empire, a thalassocracy, linking Egypt, the Levant, Asia Minor and Greece. And, of course, the legend of the annual tribute of seven youths and seven maidens to feed to the Minotaur, so central to the story of the gallant Theseus, more likely represents the tribute the ancient mainland Greeks, the Myceneans, were required to pay the Minoans. It was more likely commercial rivalry that brought down the Minoan empire, not the death of a monster!'

'And the earthquakes and tidal waves,' added Andrea. 'How terrible it must have been!' She shuddered, remembering a television programme she had once watched which had recreated, with computer simulation, the terrifying volcanic explosion of the island of Thera, modern Santorini, which had blasted the atmosphere with dark, choking, poisonous dust and sent a wall of water hurtling south to crash devastatingly upon the low, defenceless Cretan shore.

She looked around her. All about had once been walls and rooms, stairs and chambers, courtyards and gardens, storerooms and towers, bustling with people carrying on their ordinary, everyday lives. All gone now. All silenced.

They were once as alive as you are now. Felt the warmth of the same sun upon their faces, felt the same earth beneath their feet as you do now.

As if he could read her thoughts on her face, she heard Nikos say quietly at her side, 'We must live while we can, Andrea. We have no other choice except to make the most of what is given to us. Our minds, our hearts—our bodies and our passions.'

For a moment, the briefest moment, she met his eyes and read what was in them. Then, his message sent, he lightened his expression.

'Are you hungry? Let us eat.'

They lunched, at Andrea's instigation, at a small tourist restaurant close to the palace of Knossos, which, though clearly catering for the masses, appealed to her with its vine-dappled terrace set back, overlooking the road. It was pretty, and quite unpretentious, and they both ate a typical tourist salad of feta cheese and tomatoes drizzled in olive oil, followed by the ultimate Greek tourist dish of lamb kebabs.

If Nikos was taken aback by her choice, he hid it. Maybe after a lifetime of eating only in the most expensive restaurants it was amusing for her to eat such humble fare and mingle with ordinary folk whose grandfathers were not multimillionaires.

She looked quite natural in such a place, he suddenly realised. Her hair was drawn back into a simple plait, and if he did not know better he'd have said that her clothes—jeans and a simple white T-shirt—could easily have come out of a chainstore. She must be favouring a designer who charged a fortune to achieve that very effect.

Nor did she balk in the slightest at the taste of the robust but rough Domestica wine she drank. To Nikos it brought back memories from his early years, before his palate had become exposed only to the finest vintages. He wondered when it was that he had last drunk such table wine as now filled his glass.

Too long. The words echoed inside his head, and he put them aside with a frown.

'Where would you like to go this afternoon?' he asked, to change his thoughts. 'Shall we drive to a beach and sun ourselves?'

Immediately he cursed himself. In his head he heard her low words, filled with quiet, unemotional anguish, saying how she only swam very early in the morning, when no one could see her legs...

'Or perhaps you would like to see Heraklion?' he hurried on. 'Or we could drive further into the interior, perhaps? There is Mount Ida to see, where the god Zeus is said to have been born, in a cavern there.'

'I'd like that,' Andrea replied. 'I...I'm not sure I'm up to much more walking, I'm afraid. I'm rather feeling it in my legs after tramping around Knossos. Not that I'd have missed it for the world!' she added, lest she sound whining.

'I'll phone for the car,' said Nikos, and got out his mobile phone to summon the large, chauffeur-driven hire car that had brought them here from the yacht and which was now parked in the palace car park.

'Nikos—' She stayed his hand and he stopped, surprised. 'I—I don't suppose,' she found herself saying wistfully, 'it would be possible—if not today, then perhaps tomorrow—if we are still here, of course,' she burbled, feeling awkward suddenly, 'to have a car like that one there to drive around in, would it?'

She pointed down to where one of the legion of open-sided four-by-fours, favoured by tourists as hire cars, was making its way along the road.

'They look such fun,' she said.

They *were* fun, she discovered shortly. For the first time it dawned on her that being the wife of a rich man—however fraudulently, to her mind, and certainly however temporarily— had its compensations. A swift phone conversation with the chauffeur and the luxury limo had been traded for a self-drive bouncing Jeep.

She had to hang on tight, especially as they started to climb into the central Cretan mountains. The hairpin bends were tight, and got tighter, but as they did the views got more and more stupendous. The mildness of the lowland air crispened into a clarity that cleansed the lungs.

'This is wonderful! Thank you!'

They had stopped at a viewpoint and were looking down over the island, towards the sea beyond. Forested slopes spread out like skirts around them.

'I am glad you are enjoying yourself, *agape mou.*'

He smiled down at her. Again, as in the aftermath of the concert, there was nothing in Nikos's reply except open appreciation of her gratitude for showing her Crete.

She smiled back up at him, her eyes warm, and in that moment she saw his expression change, as if her smile had done something to him.

Hurriedly she looked away, saying the first thing that came into her head.

'For a Greek island, Crete is very forested,' she observed.

'It was not always so,' he answered, accepting her gambit. He must go slowly—oh, so slowly—with this wounded deer, lest she flee him and wound herself even more in the process. 'When the Venetians ruled Crete, and then the Turks, much of the forest was cut down for timber for ships. In those days public enemy number one for trees were mountain goats, who ate the saplings before they could mature. So a decree went out offering a bounty for every dead goat brought down from the mountains.' His voice became very dry. 'It is perhaps predictable to relate that an active goat-breeding programme was soon well underway amongst the impoverished but financially astute mountain-dwelling peasants...'

She laughed, as he had intended.

'The best-laid plans of bureaucrats,' she commented, equally dryly.

He slipped his hand into hers, making the movement very casual. 'Indeed. Come—back on the road again. Finding a café would be very welcome, *ne*?'

They stopped for coffee at a little *cafeneion* perched precariously, so it seemed to Andrea, over the side of a precipitous slope. The view, however, more than made up for it. They sat in silence, absorbing the peace and serenity around them, but it was a silence a world away from the silence at dinner the night before, Andrea found herself thinking. Then it had all been strain and horribleness. Now—now it was...companionable.

The thought was odd. Almost unbelievable.

As she sat there, sipping her western filter coffee while Nikos drank the undrinkable treacly brew of the native, she decided she did not want to think about it.

She just wanted to enjoy the moment. For now, it was enough.

It was early evening by the time they got back to the coast. They did not arrive back at Heraklion, but further west, at Rethimnon.

'Just in time for us to make our *volta*,' said Nikos.

'Volta?'

'In the early evening, after work and before dinner, we take our stroll around the town—to see and be seen,' explained Nikos.

With the westering sun turning the azure sea to turquoise, and yellowing the limestone buildings around the pretty Venetian harbour of the town, it was a pleasant thing to do, discovered Andrea. They strolled around the quayside. And if at some point Nikos slipped his arm around Andrea's shoulders, to shield her from a group of lively tourists heading in the opposite direction, she found, when he did not remove it, that she did not mind. Indeed, the opposite was true. The warmth of his casual embrace was comforting. And when, as they took their places at a table set out on the quayside to have a drink, he let go of her, she felt, she realised, strangely bereft.

Nikos took a beer, Andrea a tall glass of fruit juice, and they watched the world go by. It was very easy, very relaxed. They talked about Crete—its long struggle for independence, its ordeals under Nazi occupation, and its modern Renaissance as a tourist destination. Neutral subjects. Safe subjects.

'Do you know the island well?' she asked.

He shook his head. 'I'm afraid my visits have mostly been brief, and in respect of business. I've seen more of Crete today than ever before.' He paused, then said with deliberate casualness, 'Shall we stay a few days longer?'

She stilled. 'I—I...'

He covered her hand with his. 'You do not need to decide now, Andrea *mou*. Let us take things as they come, *ne*?'

There was meaning in his words, but she could not challenge him. Instead she looked out over the gilded water, streaming with the setting sun.

'Shouldn't we start heading back to Heraklion? Won't they be wondering where we are?'

He gave a laugh. 'Captain Petrachos sailed the yacht along the coast—he's anchored off the shore now. We'll take a launch back to it whenever we want. There's no hurry.'

'Oh,' said Andrea. Once again she realised how very, very

easy being a holidaymaker was if you had a luxury yacht trailing around after you.

'Shall we dine ashore?' enquired Nikos, calling for another beer.

'Can we?'

He laughed again. 'Andrea, this is our hon—' He caught himself, and amended his words. 'Our holiday—we can do anything we like!'

Andrea looked around. Everywhere were open-fronted restaurants, tables spilling out onto the quayside and the pavements, happy holidaymakers enjoying their escape from humdrum lives. It was livening up now, and she could hear the throb of bazouki music emanating from the bars.

'Let's eat here!' she enthused. She could not face returning to that opulent monstrosity of a yacht, whose garish luxury appalled her so. Besides, she felt safe here, amongst so many people....

And Nikos was being so *nice*...

She sipped her orange juice, nibbling moist, succulent olives out of the dish placed in front of them, staring out over the harbour. Carefully, tremulously, she opened her mind and let herself face up to what had happened.

Nikos had made love to her. He had taken her naked body and brought it to ecstasy. Initiated her into the realm of sensual experience. Changed her from an unknowing, virginal maiden into a woman who knew the power of the senses. The overwhelming, irresistible power that took away all reason, all logic, and swept her away, to let her do things, experience things that she had never, ever thought to experience.

It happened. It was real. I let it happen.

She could have stopped him—*should* have stopped him—but she hadn't. She hadn't found the strength to stop him.

Even though she knew exactly why he had done what he had.

She said the words to herself, spelling them out. Letting there be no mistake about it. Refusing to deceive herself.

He made love to me. Last night Nikos made love to me because he felt sorry for me.

That was the truth of it.

It tore at her, pulling her in two. Part of her was filled with mortification that this most perfect paean to masculine perfection should have had to force himself to make love to her scarred, disfigured body. But part of her was filled with wonder—wonder that a man who had married her for no other reason than to get her grandfather's business empire should have had the compassion, the kindness, to feel sorry for her…

Emotions stirred in her heart, welling up, but she knew they were dangerous. Very dangerous.

Nikos Vassilis, who had married the splendid Coustakis heiress, not the humble, ordinary Andrea Fraser, would have no use for such emotions—and neither must she.

It was late before they returned to the yacht. They had eaten in one of the harbourside restaurants, filled with chattering, cheerful tourists. It had been fun, and had distracted Andrea from her deeper thoughts. But now, as the motor launch creamed its way across the dark sea towards the string of lights that edged the massive bulk of her grandfather's latest toy, those thoughts surfaced.

Nikos could tell. As he helped her up the lowered steps to gain the safety of the deck he knew, by the way she immediately pulled her hand free of his, that she was filled with nervous self-consciousness.

Keep playing it easy, he adjured himself.

Dismissing the crewman with a smile, he turned to Andrea. 'Come, let us watch the night.'

He led her up to the uppermost deck, towards the stern. They would not be overlooked there. The bridge crew were out of sight, and he had given orders that the rest of the staff could stand down.

Glad for a reprieve from having to go to bed, and not having the faintest idea what on earth Nikos was going to do about sleeping arrangements now, Andrea followed him. It was, she had to admit, a glorious sight. The twinkling line of lights along the Cretan coast echoed the blaze of stars in the celestial oceans above their heads.

They stood side by side, leaning on the railings, trying to identify constellations.

'I only know the Plough and Orion in winter,' admitted Andrea. 'London isn't very good for star-gazing.'

'We should sleep in a goat hut on the top of Mount Ida to have the clearest view on the island!' teased Nikos, and she smiled.

'Crete was wonderful,' she said wistfully. 'Thank you for taking me there today.'

Lightly, very lightly, he slipped his hand underneath the plait of her hair at the back of her neck.

'As I said, *pethi mou*, we can spend as long as we like here. Shall we do that?'

His fingers were brushing her nape. Very lightly.

It set every nerve in her body quivering.

Danger!

You've got to stop this—now!

'Nikos—'

'Hmm?' His fingertips were playing with loose strands of hair. She felt ripples of sensation down her spine.

'Nikos—'

She paused again, trying to concentrate, trying to focus on what she had to tell him. *Must* tell him. Right now.

'I—I have to talk to you!' The words came out in a rush.

It did not stop his fingers gentling at the tender skin beneath her ear, nor did it stop the shivers of pleasure vibrating in her.

'What about?' he asked idly. His other hand had come around her spine to rest on her hip. It felt large, and heavy, and warm. And dangerous.

Still he went on feathering the loosening tendrils of her hair, brushing the velvet of her skin.

She forced herself to concentrate.

'About…about…what happened.'

'When?' asked Nikos, in that same lazy tone, as his thumb moved to brush along the line of her jaw.

'Last…last night….'

'Ahh,' breathed Nikos. 'That.'

'Yes! That!' echoed Andrea. It was supposed to come out forcefully, but as his thumb grazed the cleft of her chin it only came out as a sigh.

'This?' queried Nikos. His fingertips still stroked her cheek lightly, oh, so lightly, but now his thumb pressed lightly, oh, so lightly, on her full lower lip.

'No!'

'Ahh. Then *this*, perhaps…'

His hand smoothed over her hip languorously, shaping its feminine contour with lazy ease.

She felt her muscles clench spasmodically, unable to control them. She could feel how close he was behind her now, his body almost encircling hers. How had he got so close suddenly?

She had no time to think of an answer.

'Oh,' he murmured, 'then it must be *this, ne*?'

His thumb pressed on her lower lip and slid into the moistness within, gliding along the tender inner surface.

Sensation shimmered at his velvet touch, vibrating through her like a siren call she could not resist—could not.

She moaned, and softly bit the fleshy pad, drawing it into her mouth to do so.

She could not help herself. She simply could not help herself.

She heard herself moan again, a little whimper in her throat, and now his hand was cupping her jaw, and his thumbpad was grazing the edge of her teeth.

She bit again, laving it with her tongue longingly, helplessly.

He turned her in his arms and kissed her properly.

She yielded without a word, her eyelids fluttering shut as she gave herself to the bliss of having Nikos kiss her.

It was a deep, sensual kiss. A kiss filled with all the hunger he had suppressed. A kiss for himself as well as her.

His arms slid around her, holding her tight against him, his hand spearing her hair, holding her head steady for him as he plundered the sweetness of her mouth, tongues mating and writhing.

Hunger flooded through her. Her body leapt in recognition of what was happening. This was no seduction. It was rediscovery. Glorious, potent rediscovery. Her hands wound around his neck, holding him to her, unable to let go—not while the hunger that suddenly seared within her was feeding on him, mouth to mouth, shaping and touching, wanting and needing...

Needing so much more... Wanting so much more...

Wanting everything. Wanting possession.

His possession. Nikos Vassilis. Only his.

Now—oh, right now...now...

Reality douched through her. She yanked away from him, breathless, horrified.

'Nikos! No!'

Her rejection was a gasp of disbelief that she had actually got to this point. She twisted free, backing away.

'No?' The tone was quizzically ironic. She did not see the control he had to use to maintain so light a voice.

'No,' she said again, more firmly now, swallowing, trying to still the frantic beating of her racing heart. Trying to find reason, logic, hard sense. 'You don't have to do this. I...I said we had to talk about...about last night, and we do—but it's just to say I understand. I know why you...why you did what you did. I accept that. You felt sorry for me. You felt sorry for me because you saw me as an object of pity. But it's OK—' she held her hand up '—it's OK. I understand.' She swallowed again. 'You don't have to feel you must give a repeat performance. I understand.'

As she spoke Nikos had leant back against the rails, resting his elbows on the guard rail.

'I'm glad you understand,' he said lightly. 'It was certainly the worst night of my life, I can tell you!'

He looked at her, watching her face change as she took in

what he had just said. There was a stricken look on it, but he ignored it.

'Yes,' he said again, 'certainly the worst night of my life.'

Andrea could feel her nails digging into her palms. Did he have to be so brutal about it? Did he have to ram home just how repugnant he had found the ordeal of making love to a freak? Her throat had tightened, wire pulling on it. Agonising. He was talking again. She could hardly bear to hear what he was saying. But the words penetrated all the same.

'I've never done what I had to do last night,' he told her. 'It was excruciating.'

The expression on her face was devastated, but he ploughed on. 'And I never, ever want to go through it again. I tell you—' he eyed her straight, and said what he had to say '—having to hold myself back like that was absolute agony. I was aching for you—totally bloody *aching* for you.' A long, shuddering sigh escaped him. '*Theos*, you've no idea what it was like, Andrea *mou*—having your fantastic, gorgeous body stripped naked and pulsing for me and not being able to possess you totally. God, it was hell—sheer hell!' He shook his head. 'Never again, I promise you—never again!'

He straightened suddenly, and rested his hand on either shoulder. 'But you needed your space, and I knew I owed you that. So…' He looked down at her, starlight in his eyes. 'Last night was your night, Andrea *mou*. But tonight—oh, tonight—' his voice had changed, husky suddenly '—tonight is *mine…*'

He pulled her into him, jerking her, and closed his mouth over hers. Then, with a rough, urgent motion, he swept her up into his arms and strode off with her, to make her his wife.

It was, she realised some eternity later, the rawness of his hunger, the voracity of his appetite that convinced her. As he tumbled her down upon their vast bed, coming down beside her and pinioning her hands either side of her head as he lowered his mouth to hers again to feed and feed upon her, she felt rush up from the depths of her being such a gladness, such a glory, she was breathless with it.

His mouth ravished hers, allowing her no quarter, no defence, and he overpowered her effortlessly, easily. She was a willing traitor, oh, so willing! His body arched over hers and her hands ran over the smoothness of his shirt, fumbling with buttons as, overcome with a desperate urge she had never felt before, never known existed, she longed frantically to feel his skin, his flesh, his muscle and sinew beneath her seeking hands.

He helped her—shucking off his shirt, peeling off her T-shirt while he did so, slipping the clasp on the back of her bra in one unseen skilful movement. Her breasts spilled free and she heard his throat rasp with pleasure at the sight before he buried his face in their ripeness, his questing mouth homing in on what he sought.

She gasped with pleasure as he suckled her, thrusting her breasts up, bearing down upon the bed with her hips, her shoulders. He fed voraciously, licking and sucking until her nipples were as solid as steel, radiating fiery points of pleasure fiercely through her body. Her hands roamed over the smooth steel of his back, glorying in the power of his perfect musculature, revelling in the feel of his body over hers.

He swept on, mouth racing down the flat, taut plane of her belly, tongue whirling within the secret of her navel even as he was urgently undoing the fastening of her jeans, sliding her zip open and then in the same movement sliding his hand inside. She gasped and roiled as a thousand fires lit where he touched.

Her heart was racing, thundering. There was no light in the room and she could not see its garish, tasteless opulence. She could feel only the satin of the bedclothes beneath her naked back, her naked bottom and thighs, for her jeans were gone and her panties too were tossed aside. Now Nikos was moving over her, and she realised that somehow, somehow, he was as naked as she.

She gloried in the feel of him, revelled in it, racing her hands all over his body. Flesh to flesh, skin to skin, mouth to mouth, hip to hip. She felt him straining at her, felt his engorged length against the softness of her belly, and the realisation, searing through her, sent a shockwave of exultation through her. He wanted her! Nikos wanted her! She knew it—knew it absolutely. Men could not fake it. Their desire, their lust, surged in their bodies, signalling the urgency of their passions.

Like an outgrown cloak her fears fell away from her, cast aside in the revelation, and in their place, released like a tiger from its cage, she was filled suddenly, desperately, with a longing so intense, a hunger so searing that her hand slid from gripping his shoulder as his mouth consumed hers down between their bodies to grasp him.

She wanted to feel him, strong and potent in her hand, his surging masculinity inflaming her with a hunger that only he could fulfil. She clasped him greedily, feeling the strength of him.

She heard him gasp with pleasure, sending a power-pulse of desire through her. She wanted to please him, wanted to give him pleasure now, right now, just as he was filling her with feelings, sensations that stormed within her, roiled and rocked her. She wanted him—wanted him to pierce and fill and stretch her, flood her with his seed, his very being.

'Nikos!' Her voice was a cry, a plea, an exultation.

He reared over her. '*Theos*, but I must have you!' His voice was a rasp of hunger, intensity. His hand caressed her belly, her thighs, then parted her legs for him. She guided him to her, heart pounding, blood surging in her veins, her body afire. She was flooding for him, her body straining to his, hips twisting and lifting to him, reaching for him, and then she felt, with a thrill that went through her whole body, that he was poised above her, ready to thrust and pierce her to the very core, her very heart.

'I must have you—'

The words grated from him and he took each of her hands, lifting and placing them each side of her head, pinioning them with his, holding her body still for him, spread for him, hips lifting to receive him.

She could feel the urgency of his need for her. Power surged through her. The power of her sex, flowering in a glorious, heady welling of sensation that fused her body to her mind, fused her aroused, throbbing flesh to the incandescence lighting her whole being.

She raised her mouth to his and bit softly, deliberately at his.

'Then take me,' she answered. 'Take me.'

He waited no longer. With slow descent he lowered his body into hers.

His control, his purpose was absolute. Her dew-drenched readied body parted for him, accepting him within her as a needed, hungered-for presence. She stretched around him, and as pain fluttered briefly, fleetingly, it was swept away by the drowning tide of exultation that consumed her as he made her his.

He filled her absolutely, and she gasped with the realisation that their bodies had fused, become one, pulsing, beating to the same single heartbeat that throbbed between them, sex to sex, thigh to thigh, palm to palm, pressing and joining.

Her mouth opened in a wondrous, wordless cry, neck arching back, hips lifting higher to meld their flesh together.

He was reared over her, fused within her, and she gloried in it. Around his manhood's strength her muscles clenched, holding him tightly, dearly, and the pressure of his body in hers thickened him in answer to her. It was all she needed. Like a long, slow wave her body detonated around his, sending a tidal pulse through all her flesh.

She buckled around him, every muscle straining, and the detonation came again, surging out like a shockwave.

She cried out, gasping, spine arching like a bow.

It was liquid pressure, liquid pleasure, so intense, so absolute that it shocked her even as it convulsed her. It flooded through her, reaching through every vein, every overloaded nerve-fibre, rushing out to fill her fingertips, her toes, flushing her body with its tide.

And behind it surged another tide, and yet another, and with one, wondering, stunned part of her mind she realised her body was resonating with another's. Nikos was gasping, surging, pulsing into her, and she was drawing him in, the tide convulsing her sucking him into her, possessing him utterly.

She heard him gasp, cry out in triumph, and the triumph was hers too, and his, and theirs, and still their bodies surged to the tidal wave carrying them on its endless bounty.

Her fingers clutched his, squeezing so tightly she could feel the slick between their joined palms seal them unbreakably, just as their bodies were joined—unbreakably.

Slowly, oh, so slowly, the tidal pulse began to ebb, draining deep away, back into the core, the heart of her body, where it had come from. Slowly, oh, so slowly, he lowered himself to her, to rest his exhausted, sated weight upon her, crush the slackening tissues of her breasts.

They were both panting, breathless with exertion, hearts thundering in their chests. His body covered hers, slick with sweat. Her hands slid free and came around his back, wrapping him to her. She could feel, against her own, his heartbeat slamming, then slowly, slowly, as the torpor of inertia took them over, it began to ease and lessen.

How long they lay like that, their bodies fast entwined, motionless with satiation and exhaustion, she did not know, could not tell. Time had no meaning any more. She had discovered eternity.

After a while, a long, endless while, he stirred. The sweat had dried on his back, and where her arms did not enfold him his skin was cold.

Heavily, he lifted his head from her shoulder.

She felt the movement of muscles in his back and instinctively tightened her grip around him.

He gave a laugh. A low, brief laugh.

'No, I, too, do not wish to move, Andrea *mou*, but yet we must.'

He managed to lever himself up to his elbows, making her slacken her grip on him so that only her hands could touch either side his spine.

'Come—I must tend to you.'

Carefully, he eased from her.

She felt bereft, empty, desolate. He slipped away from her in the dark and she heard him cross the carpeted floor. Then a door opened, and a light flooded briefly, before closing to dimness. She shut her eyes. Her heart was in tumult. But she could not think, could not reason. Could only lie and let the dimness close her round.

Exhaustion claimed her.

His footsteps crossing towards the bed roused her from the slumber she had sunk into. As she surfaced she could hear, she realised, the sound of water running. Before she realised what he was intending he scooped his hands underneath her and folded her up into his arms.

'I don't want you to feel sore, *pethi mou*,' he murmured, and took her through into the bathroom, lowering her gently into the swirling water in the huge, circular bath, foaming high with bubbles.

It was bliss of a different kind. She gave a sigh, and gave herself up to the warmth, pausing only to reach and twist her hair into a precarious self-fastened knot on top of her head. She closed her eyes and let the water swirl around her.

There seemed to be fine jets of water shushing out at her from all around, and she realised the huge bath must be some kind of Jacuzzi. As the tumult in her heart subsided, washed away by the warm, relaxing water, she felt for the first time the physical effects of what had happened to her. She eased her thighs, letting the water swirl gently, soothingly, around her ravished body.

'Are you in pain?'

Nikos's voice was concerned. She opened her eyes. He had not put on the central light in the bathroom, only the light above the mirror, so the brightness was mellow, not glaring. He had put on a bathrobe and was looking down at her, his hands plunged into its pockets.

She could not quite meet his eyes. Not yet.

'No, not pain, but…I feel…exercised.'

She caught his eye then, and suddenly there was an answering gleam in his.

'Oh, yes,' he answered softly. 'As do I, I assure you…'

He held her gaze, and the knowledge in his eyes flooded her. For a moment the mutual acknowledgement of what had happened flowed between them.

'Nikos, I—' she began—because she had to say *something*, she must.

He shook his head, silencing her. 'No. Say nothing. We will take this slowly, Andrea *mou*. As slowly as we need. Now—' he held up a hand '—I shall leave you in privacy a while. Relax and recover. Don't move until I come and get you.'

He left her in peace, the silence broken only by the occasional popping of a bubble. She felt—*fulfilled*, she realised, and a quiet wonder went through her to lie like a fine, rare sheen over her heart.

The warmth and the water, the silence and the solitude eased her, lapping her spent body. With a light tap to the door Nikos returned after a little while and helped her out of the bath, enveloping her in a huge fleecy bathtowel. She was almost asleep, and he could see that all she would do now was rest for the remainder of the night.

He gave a private rueful smile. He could have kept going all night, but for now he must let her set the pace. She had entered a new kingdom—he must give her time to take possession of it, to know its ways and passions.

So he simply lifted her off her feet, carrying her back to the bed like a swaddled baby, and set her down between smooth satin sheets, gently drawing the towel off her. The satin felt cold to her skin, and when he returned from the bathroom a moment later, and turned off the night, she welcomed the warmth of his encircling embrace.

'Nikos,' she breathed, as his arms wrapped around her from behind and her spine warmed itself against his hair-roughened chest.

'Hush,' he said. 'Go to sleep.'

He soothed his hand over her rough thigh and for a moment

she went rigid in his arms, and then, with a little sigh, she relaxed again.

Slowly, soothingly, he smoothed the scarred and runnelled skin, as if it were lustrous marble.

CHAPTER TEN

His hand was still covering her thigh when she awoke. Sunlight pressed against the heavy drapes, dimly illuminating the oppressively decorated bedroom. She felt the bed swaying slightly, she thought, and remembered that this was no ground-based dwelling, but that they were afloat upon the bosom of the sea.

When she stirred, Nikos did too. And as he moved she realised, with a little gasp, that as she lay spoon-like, back against him, his body was taking notice of the fact.

He felt it too, the moment he surfaced into consciousness. The same sense of ruefulness he had felt last night filled him. Whatever his leap of appetite right now, he must not risk hurting her.

Besides, he thought encouragingly, abstinence now would bring its own rewards later.

So he stretched backwards and away from her, languorously extending his limbs before lithely jack-knifing and getting out of bed.

'This morning,' he announced, 'we shall have breakfast in bed. And then more sightseeing!'

He certainly needed something, Nikos thought, throwing on his bathrobe before striding to the phone to order breakfast, to divert him from what he really wanted to do right now.

Sightseeing would do as well as anything.

In fact, he acknowledged later, it had its own compensations. It was another glorious day, fresh and sweet in the early summer. Setting off in the four-by-four, Nikos at the wheel, they merged into the general throng of holidaymakers.

They headed for Samaria and the famous gorge. Andrea had

154

read about it in the guidebook Nikos had bought for her before they left Rethimnon.

'I know I can't walk it,' she said, 'but at least I can see it.'

Nikos took her as close as he could, driving deep into the heart of the White Mountains of western Crete. They drank coffee on the terrace of the little *cafeneion* near the start of the walk, the Xiloskala, wooden stairs that led into the gorge. Above them towered the bare, bleak heights of the Gingalos peak, skirted by rock and scree.

'Tomorrow we'll sail round to the mouth of the gorge, Agia Roumeli, and cruise along the southern coast,' said Nikos. 'In fact—' he glanced at his watch '—we have time to drive down to Sougia today, if you wish.'

Andrea nodded, happy to go anywhere with him. 'What does *agia* mean?' she asked. 'There are so many places called "Agia" something or other.'

Nikos laughed. 'Saint—a female saint. Male saints are *agios*.' He looked at her a moment. 'You must learn the language of your forefathers, Andrea *mou*. Now that you are to live here.'

She was silent. Emotions racketed around inside her. Nikos was opening doors she must keep shut.

'What about *mou*?' she asked. She did not want to think about what he had said. 'You keep saying, "Andrea *mou*".'

'*Mine*,' he said softly. The grey eyes held hers. 'My Andrea.'

She looked away, her face troubled.

She felt the brush of his fingers on her hand.

'I have made you mine, have I not, Andrea *mou*?' he murmured.

Colour stole into her cheeks, feeding the tumult in her heart. *I can't think about this! I can't think about anything!*

She swallowed. 'Where are we heading next?' she said brightly. 'I'm starting to get hungry!'

His fingers closed around hers, his thumb lazily smoothing her skin. 'So am I, *agape mou*, so am I...'

But it was a hunger he was to be prevented from sating for many hours to come. Even so, he consented to be her holiday companion, her fellow-explorer, willingly enough. She was a different person, it seemed to him, here on Crete. The reserved, composed, controlled Englishwoman who was such hard work to entertain, whom he had got used to squiring around Athens, had transformed into a vibrant, open personality who was a delight to be with. Was it just because the appalling tensions of the last weeks had finally resolved themselves? Or was it because he had made her his own?

For she was his own now; he knew that. No other man would ever touch her. She was his wife. Already he cherished her. A surge not just of possession but of protectiveness speared through him whenever he looked at her. No man would hurt her again, for she would need no other man now. Only him.

The future looked bright. Brighter than ever he had dared hope.

All that panic-generated talk she had spouted at him on their wedding night about leaving him in the morning was nothing. It had been her fears speaking; that was all. And those fears he had shown to be nothing more than phantasms haunting her. - He had exorcised her ghosts, he knew, and from now on their path was clear and thornless.

This rushed arranged marriage would work out for them— he was sure of that now. Together they would move on through the years ahead.

Well-being filled him, and the future was bright with promise.

At his side, as they zig-zagged down the winding road through the lovely Agia Irini gorge towards the southern coast, Andrea could not stop herself from looking at him.

Her breath caught every time she did so. It was everything about him—everything! From the satin sheen of his dark hair, the impossible glamour of his sunglasses, the firm, sensual line of his mouth, the vee of his open collar, the flexible strength of his hands curving around the wheel of the car, the tanned sinews of his bare forearms—all, all made her want to drink him in, feast her eyes on him more and more.

And yet while her senses feasted her emotions swirled within her. His words at the *cafeneion*, about learning Greek, had filled her with dismay.

How could she live here, in Greece? How could she be truly married to Nikos Vassilis?

It was unthinkable!

And yet, and yet...

Too much pulled at her. Too many emotions.

I can't think about it! I just can't!

She knew she would have to, eventually. Knew that the future was looming over her like a dark, overpowering wall. But for now she would turn her back on it.

She had a few days' grace, she knew. The quick staccato phone call she had made to Tony from the bedroom, before they had set off for Knossos yesterday, had simply communicated an unforeseen change of plan. He had been worried, she could tell, for all she had said was that she was fine, but would not be coming home quite yet; she would let him know when.

'I'm not at my grandfather's house,' she had reassured him rapidly. 'I'm...I'm...somewhere else...with someone else.'

Tony had been alarmed, despite her use of the code word they had agreed.

'Where else?' he demanded.

'I'm on my grandfather's yacht,' she had admitted. 'But he's not here. I'm OK, truly. I have to go; someone's coming! Give my love to Mum. I'll be home soon—promise.'

But would she be home soon? She stared out of the windscreen, out over the alien landscape of Crete.

What am I doing? What am I doing?

She had no answer. She was adrift on a new ocean, carried by an unstoppable tide.

At her side, Nikos slipped his left hand from the wheel and took her hand, sensing her troubled frame of mind.

'All will be well, Andrea *mou*. Trust me.'

For now there was nothing else for her to do.

For now it was enough.

*   *   *

They had lunch in the little town of Sougia, at a tourist taverna overlooking the shingle beach.

'It is a pity you are not up to walking,' remarked Nikos. 'There is, so I have just been told, a very popular walk to a place called Ancient Lissos—it is a Roman site, small, but very pretty. Perhaps we can land there from the yacht, another day. You cannot get there by road, I understand.'

'Is it a long walk?' Andrea asked.

'About an hour, the waiter told me, but it could be rough, and I don't want to risk it.'

'I'm sorry to be such a drag on you,' Andrea said quietly.

He took her hand. 'You are not a drag. You have done your best against great odds. I cannot begin to think what you must have gone through.'

His kindness nearly undid her. She felt tears misting her eyes. He saw them, and patted her hand encouragingly.

'No, do not cry, Andrea. As you said to me yourself, there are others so much worse off!' His gentling smile took any reproof from the words. 'And think too how much worse it would have been, what you went through, had you not been cushioned by your grandfather's wealth. I know that money cannot buy health, but it can buy comfort, and freedom from financial stress, in ways you cannot, perhaps, imagine. Your mother could afford the best treatment for you, the best doctors, the best care—it is something to be grateful for, *ne*?'

Cold drenched through Andrea. Cushioned by her grandfather's wealth? She saw again, vivid in her mind, the letter from his office, replying, finally, to the desperate pleadings of her mother after Kim had sent Yiorgos Coustakis all the medical reports on his granddaughter, detailing all the injuries she had suffered, recommending operations and physiotherapy that were so extensive, so expensive, that only private health care could provide for the years it would take to complete the treatment. The reports had been returned, accompanied by a terse letter to the effect that they were obviously gross exaggerations, and it was clearly nothing more than a ploy by a mercenary gold-digger to extort money from a man she had no claim on whatsoever.

And then Andrea chilled even more at the recollection of the final letter that had come, not from her grandfather, but from his lawyers, informing Kim that any further attempt at communicating with Yiorgos Coustakis would result in legal action.

Nikos watched her face shadowing. He had not meant to be harsh, but it was true, what he had said. Like so many born to wealth, Andrea seemed to take it all for granted. Oh, she was polite to servants, waiters and so on, but she never seemed to appreciate just how privileged her upbringing had been. In fact, he mused, she seemed to take more pleasure in something like a simple meal at a cheap taverna than in the lavish delicacies of a five-star restaurant...

If she'd had to work for her money, as he had done, she might appreciate the finer things of life more, he thought.

And do you appreciate anything else any more? Or will only the finest do for you now?

The quizzing voice sounded unwelcome in his mind, and he put it aside. He deserved his wealth—he had worked day and night to get where he was now. And Coustakis Industries was his rightful prize.

And the Coustakis heiress....

His mood lightened, and he lifted her imprisoned hand to his lips, grazing it lightly.

'I long for tonight, my sweet, passionate Andrea. I long for it—and you.'

Colour stained her cheekbones as she read the message in his eyes, and he sat back, well pleased.

Right now life was good. Very good.

And the night was even better. All the rest of the day Andrea found her awareness of Nikos mounting and mounting—during the drive back to the north of the island, during dinner eaten by the harbour in Chania, this time, not Rethimnon, and the drive back across the isthmus of the Akritori peninsula to the deep water of Souda Bay, where the yacht was moored. That night she hardly noticed the garish décor of the staterooms, hardly noticed the polite greetings of the crew, only noticed the way Nikos's eyes looked at her, wanting her, wanting her.

Desire swept through her, and the moment they gained the privacy of their bedroom she turned to him, and he to her. That night their coming together was even more incendiary—she knew now, so well, just what passion and desire, unleashed, could bring, and she revelled in it.

She felt wild and wanton, desirable and daring.

'I do believe,' Nikos murmured to her, his eyes glinting wickedly as she climbed astride him at his urging, eager to find more and more ways of showing her desire for him and sating her own, 'that you are making up for lost time.'

He slid his hands helpfully under her smooth, round bottom, lifting her up and positioning her exactly where he wanted her to be. Then he relaxed back.

'Take me.' The eyes glinted even more wickedly, making her feel weak with desire. 'I'm yours…'

She looked down at him, her red hair streaming like a banner down her naked back.

And slowly, tasting every moment of the experience, she came down on him. Possessing him.

It was the first of numberless possessions, each giving and taking as much as the other, their appetites feeding on each other, inflaming each other, sating each other, long into the following day. They did not go ashore that morning, letting Captain Petrachos take the yacht westwards, to round the island into the Libyan Sea and nose along the southern coast. Though the day was warm, and fine, Andrea and Nikos found a strange reluctance to take the fresh air.

'We should get up,' murmured Andrea, nestled against Nikos's hard-muscled chest.

'It's our honeymoon, Andrea *mou*. There is no hurry. We have all the time in the world.' He began to nuzzle at her tender earlobe, and she felt—extraordinary though it was, considering how short a time ago they had come together this latest time— her body beginning to respond to his caressing. 'On the other hand,' he considered, 'perhaps we should get up. Of course...' his teeth nipped gently, arousingly at her lobe '...we would need to have a bath first...'

Making love in a Jacuzzi was, Andrea discovered, a breathtaking experience, and one that lasted a long, long time. It was after noon before they finally emerged on to the deck, to take a long, leisurely lunch under an awning as the mountainous coastline of southern Crete slipped slowly past them. After lunch the launch was lowered, and Nikos took her first, as he had promised, to the tiny cove of Ancient Lissos, to explore the remains of the *asklepieion*—healing centre—and then sailing onwards, past the pretty whitewashed village of Loutro, along the piratical Sfakiot coastline until they made landfall at a beach marked on the map as 'Sweetwater Beach'.

'What a strange name,' said Andrea, and marvelled when she was shown the reason. Tiny freshwater springs pearled from beneath the pebbles. Andrea scooped some of the water to her lips.

'It *is* fresh!' she exclaimed in wonder.

It was such a beautiful afternoon, and the beach—unreachable by road—so relatively uncrowded, that they stayed to enjoy it. As Andrea started to relax, Nikos produced a swimsuit from amongst the towels.

'No one will look at your legs, Andrea,' he told her. 'They will all be too busy looking at your glorious figure.' He leant and kissed her softly. 'You are so beautiful. Your legs do not matter. Not to me. You must know that by now—you must!' He smiled cajolingly. 'Do it for me, my beautiful bride.'

How can I refuse? she thought. How can I refuse him anything?

Handing her a vast towelling changing tent, he helped her slip on the plain black one-piece he had acquired for her. As she stepped free she felt overcome with self-consciousness, but after a while she realised it was true—the others on the beach, scattered as they were, were not looking at her.

'Come,' said Nikos. 'That sea looks too tempting!'

He was stripping off before she could reply, baring everything down to a pair of trunks under his trousers, and then he was taking her hand and leading her into the clear water.

This early in the year the water had a bite to it that made her gasp, but Nikos only laughed. He drew her in relentlessly, and then, letting go, dived into the turquoise water, surfacing to shake a shower of diamonds from his head.

'Come on! You'll thank me!'

And she did. When they finally emerged, some fifteen minutes later, she felt glorious, reborn. He swathed a towel around her and sat her down, pausing only to run a towel over his back before joining her.

He grinned at her. She grinned back. The water on his long eyelashes caught the sun, his damp, towel-dried hair made her ache to touch it, and the expression in his eyes as he looked at her made her weak.

All that marred her pleasure was the prospect of having to go back on board her grandfather's yacht. It oppressed her more and more. Not just because of the tasteless extravagance of its opulent décor, but because it reminded her, as she did not want to be reminded, of just why she had come to Greece at all.

And she did not want to think of that.

'Nikos?' She sat up, looking at him questioningly. 'Do we have to stay on the yacht?'

'You don't want to?' He sounded surprised. He didn't know a woman who wouldn't have adored to luxuriate on board such a floating palace!

But then Andrea, he was beginning to realise, was like no woman he had ever known...

For so many reasons.

She shook her head.

'Can't we stay here, on Crete?'

He smiled indulgently. 'Of course. I will phone the yacht and book a suitable hotel. Or would you prefer a private villa?'

'Can't we just take our chances? Wander around, stay where we want? There are rooms to let everywhere, and we've passed many little hotels in the Jeep.'

He looked at her. 'You'd like that?'

'Oh, yes! They look such fun. I've never done anything like that—'

Her voice was full of longing. How ironic, thought Nikos, that for someone raised in luxury, the commonplace was exotic!

He smiled lazily at her. 'Your wish, my most lovely bride, is my command!'

For five, wonderful, unforgettable days Andrea toured the island with Nikos. For five searing, incandescent nights she flamed with passion in his arms. All cares were left behind. This was a special time, she thought—all she would have. She must make the most of it. Make the most of Nikos.

She knew, with a terrible clenching of her heart, that it would be all she would have of him. The realisation struck like a cold knife at her.

She heard his words at Knossos echo in her heart—*'We must live while we can, Andrea. We have no other choice except to make the most of what is given to us. Our minds, our hearts— our bodies and our passions.'*

And she *would* make the most of it—draw every bead of happiness, every pulse of pleasure and desire, every moment of calm, quiet bliss.

And make it last her all her life.

But I want it to last for ever!

That was impossible, she knew. This time with Nikos was nothing more than a brief, magical sliver of time. It shimmered with radiance, but it could not last.

Reality had to return, and she must accept that. Not willingly, but with a heavy, heavy heart. She knew, more than any, just how brief a portion of happiness life could hold. Her mother was testament to that. And yet she knew, for she had asked her once, that her mother would never have forgone the brief, fleeting bliss she had had with the man she loved, however long the empty years since then.

And I will be the same...

As they drove into Souda on their last evening on Crete, the setting sun turning the sea to gold, and saw the yacht moored there, Andrea's spirits became heavy. Her happiness was coming to an end and would never come again.

She looked across at Nikos, etching every line of his face into her memory.

I love him, she thought. I love him.

As the words formed in her mind she knew them for a truth she could never deny. Never abandon.

And never tell.

Andrea paced the deck of the yacht as it headed steadily, remorselessly, north in the starlight towards Piraeus. To the east the sky was beginning to lighten. It must be near dawn, she thought. Inside, Nikos lay asleep, exhausted by passion.

Our last time together, she thought in anguish.

She had slipped noiselessly away, needing—oh, needing solitude to think. To agonise.

This wasn't supposed to happen! This was never in the plan! I never meant to fall in love with him!

She stared blindly out over the sea, feeling the deck swell with the waves beneath the hull. The hull of a luxury Greek yacht.

This wasn't real—none of it was real! It was nothing more than a dream, a chimera. Reality was at home, in that drab council flat where she had lived all her life, bowed down by the debts that hung around Kim's neck—the money she had borrowed at ruinous interest, unsecured as it had to be, since they owned nothing of value, to pay for the private treatment Andrea had needed to make her walk again.

That's what I came to Greece for—to free her from that burden at last. To set her free from the cage and let her have some happiness in life at last, some comfort and ease.

And there was nothing stopping her—the money her grandfather had paid her to marry Nikos Vassilis was in her bank account. All she had to do was go home and spend it.

Leaving Nikos behind.

You'll never see him again! Never make love with him! Never hold him in your arms!

A cold wind gusted over her, and she shivered in the fine silk negligee.

So what? So what if you've fallen in love with Nikos Vassilis? He doesn't love you. He married you to get your grandfather's company. And if he seduced you, took you to his bed, made you his wife in deed as well as name, well, that is what a Greek husband would do with his bride—even one with crippled legs! Oh, he's been kind to you! Released you from your fears and made a woman of you! But he doesn't love you—and he doesn't want your love.

That was not in his plan. Don't think it was.

She hugged the negligee to her, but it could not keep out the cold that was seeping into her heart.

And how thrilled do you think he'll be when he discovers, as he must, that you are no more the precious Coustakis heiress than the Queen of Sheba? That you're nothing but the spurned, unwanted, bastard granddaughter of Yiorgos Coustakis, who's used you because he's got no one else to use to make a final stab at his own posterity! Do you think a man as rich as Nikos Vassilis wants a wife from a council flat?

She didn't even have to answer.

Desolation washed through her. Cold and empty.

At breakfast, taken indoors this time, as they made their way through the busy shipping lanes approaching Piraeus, Nikos, too, was not in the best of moods. The week away from Athens had made him forget the pressures that would await him on his return. Tonight, and for the foreseeable future, he would be burning the midnight oil with a vengeance, as the process of merging Vassilis Inc and Coustakis Industries got underway. Already, before breakfast, he had been on the phone to his secretary, his directors, setting wheels in motion. But for the first time in his life he had no appetite for work.

Only for Andrea...

He felt his body stir, and crushed it ruthlessly. It would be at least late tonight before he was free to enjoy his passionate bride again. His jaw tightened. He would have to explain to her that their time together would be at a premium now. At least until he had completed his takeover of her grandfather's company.

Did she realise that already? She was not looking happy, he thought, studying her across the table. In fact, she looked different altogether. She had lost the casual, easygoing look she had had for the last week. Now she looked stiff, and tense, picking at her food.

'I'm sorry we couldn't have stayed away longer,' he said. 'But doing an M&A takes a lot of work.'

Andrea looked at him. He was wearing a business suit again, and it made him look formal. Distant. The man she had spent the most blissful week of her life with had vanished. In his place was the man who had married her to get hold of Coustakis Industries. And for no other reason.

She must remember that.

'I'm sure it does,' she said impersonally.

Nikos's mouth tightened. She was ready enough to accept the lavish lifestyle her family wealth afforded—but balked at how it had been earned in the first place.

'A corporate merger is not a trivial thing to accomplish, Andrea…'

He paused suddenly. There was a bleakness in her eyes he could not account for.

No, she thought, a corporate merger was not a trivial thing at all—it was something you could marry a stranger for!

And then make love to her until she fell in love with you—hopelessly, helplessly!

But he hadn't asked her to fall in love with him, she thought. He had asked for nothing more than a passionate companion for a week—a pleasant, relaxing interlude before resuming his real life. Making money.

Well, I made money out of it too, she thought defiantly. And now I'm going home to spend it. It's what I came for, and it's what I'm going home with.

Falling for Nikos was an aberration, a mistake. I'll go home and forget all about him.

I have to!

A steward came into the room and walked up to Nikos, saying something to him in Greek. Nikos nodded curtly, and the man hurried off.

Nikos got to his feet. He looked so tall, Andrea thought. And so devastating. Just the way he'd looked the first time she'd set eyes on him. It seemed a lifetime ago, not just a few short weeks.

Weeks that had changed her life for ever.

'Excuse me—but I have to take a phone call.' He sounded remote. Preoccupied.

She nodded. There seemed to be an immovable lump in her throat suddenly.

'Of course.'

Later, she stood on deck beside him, watching the yacht slide into its moorings. Then, later still, she sat beside him in the chauffeured limo driving them back to Athens. There was a third passenger, a young man introduced as Nikos's PA, and the moment the doors were closed the PA extracted a sheaf of papers and documents. In a moment he and Nikos were deep in business talk. Andrea looked out of the window.

She felt bleak, and sick, cold all the way through.

I'm leaving him, she thought. *I'm leaving him right now…*

The car made its slow way into Athens's business quarter, and as it finally pulled up outside Vassilis Inc she felt even bleaker, and sicker.

Nikos turned to her briefly.

'Yannis will drive you to the apartment. You must make yourself at home. I am sorry not to be able to accompany you myself, but something has come up—hence Demetrios's reception committee. I am sorry, but I could not avoid it. I will escape from the office as quickly as I can and we will have the evening together. Until then—'

He bent forward to kiss her.

She could not bear it. She jerked her head sideways, conscious, if nothing else, of the PA's presence. Nikos's kiss landed on her cold cheek.

Can you feel your heart break? thought Andrea, as Nikos climbed out of the car after his PA. Because mine broke, I know, just then.

She shut her eyes, leaning back into the seat. The car moved off.

Tears misted over her eyes.

After a while, she realised she would have to give the driver new instructions. He seemed surprised when she asked him to drive her to the airport, but did it dutifully enough.

On the way there she wrote a note. Every word drew blood from her heart.

> *Dear Nikos*
>
> *I am going back to England. We have both got what we wanted out of this marriage. You got Coustakis Industries. I got my money. Thank you for our time together in Crete— you were a wonderful first lover. I'm sure you'll make a huge success of running Coustakis Industries. Please ask your lawyers to sort out our divorce as soon as possible. Thank you.*
>
> *Andrea.*

It was all she could manage. And it cost her more than she could bear to pay.

She left it with the chauffeur to deliver it to Nikos.

CHAPTER ELEVEN

'WHAT do you think, Mum? Down on the coast or further up in the hills? Where do you want to live?'

Andrea's voice was bright and relentlessly cheerful, just as it had been since she had arrived back two weeks ago, bursting with the wonderful, glorious news that her grandfather, so she had told her mother, had given them enough money to settle their debts and allow them to move to Spain.

But, for all her determined high spirits, Andrea could see her mother was worried about her. Oh, she had been bowled over by the fantastic news about the money, which had settled their debts with a single cheque, and she had commented on how well Andrea looked with her sun-bronzed skin and burnished hair, and how she was walking, it seemed, with much greater confidence and assurance, but even so Andrea could sense Kim's concern.

She didn't want her mother worrying. Not about anything— least of all her. So she chattered away brightly as she prepared their evening meal, talking about Spain and the imminent prospect of living there. She was desperate to move as soon as possible. Perhaps, in Spain, starting her new life, she could start to forget Nikos...

Nikos—

Pain clenched at her heart. No—she mustn't think, mustn't remember. It was gone, over, finished. She was starting a new life now—that was the only important thing to think about. That and making Kim happy. She mustn't, *mustn't* let Kim suspect anything...

She mustn't see your heart is broken...

She smiled determinedly at Kim.

'It's going to be all right, Mum. Everything's going to be just wonderful from now on! Just wonderful!'

Kim smiled and took her daughter's hand. 'You are the best daughter a mother could have—always know that, my darling girl,' she said softly, her eyes searching her daughter's face.

'I love you so much,' Andrea choked, realising it had been worth everything just to know that she could at last repay her mother for her years of devotion. What did a broken heart matter?

The sudden imperative knocking on the front door made them both start.

Kim immediately looked nervous, and Andrea pugnacious.

'Ignore it, Mum. They'll try somewhere else.'

Increasingly wild and aggressive kids often did the rounds at this time of day, the early evening, knocking on doors to see if they could cadge money from anyone inside.

Thank God we're getting out of here, thought Andrea feelingly.

They would be in Malaga in forty-eight hours—not for good, just for a fortnight's flat-hunting—and Andrea could hardly wait. Searching for an apartment would occupy her mind. Stop her thinking, remembering…aching…

The knocking came again, even more imperative.

'Right,' said Andrea, 'I've had enough of this.'

She marched out of the kitchen and to the front door, ready to confront them, but the dark outline showing behind the strengthened frosted glass panel revealed a tall, masculine frame.

The demanding knocking came again, and Andrea heard the futile buzz of the broken doorbell being sounded. Like so much else on the estate, it was still waiting for the council to mend it.

As she yanked the door open to find steel-grey eyes blazing down at her, her heart stopped.

Nikos Vassilis stepped inside, forcing her to stumble backwards on numb, frozen legs.

'Don't *ever*,' he said in a voice that made her spine chill, 'walk out on me again.'

Shock drenched through Andrea, wave after cold wave. But beneath the disbelieving horror another emotion had seared like flame through her.

'How—how...?' she floundered.

'How did I track you down? With great difficulty, I assure you!' His voice grated the words. He glanced around disparagingly at the shabby, narrow hallway, its smell of damp quite perceptible. 'And with such a bolt-hole as this I am not surprised it took the investigators so long to find you! What is this dump?' His mouth twisted disdainfully at the evident poverty of her surroundings.

'This *dump*,' said a quiet voice from the kitchen doorway, 'is my home, Mr—?'

Andrea whirled. Kim was standing there, her expression wary and questioning.

'Vassilis,' supplied Nikos curtly. 'Nikos Vassilis. I have come for Andrea.'

'I'm not going with you!' Andrea cried out. She couldn't believe what was happening—couldn't believe it was really Nikos standing there, his svelte, expensive presence shrieking money, looking as out of place in the hallway of a tower block council flat as if he were an alien from another planet.

'What's going on?' asked Kim anxiously, coming forward.

'Nothing! Nothing at all,' Andrea replied instantly. 'Mr Vassilis,' she gritted, 'has made a mistake! He's leaving right now! Without me!'

'Wrong.' Nikos's voice was deadly. His eyes narrowed. 'Get your things—and make sure your passport is among them!'

'I'm not going anywhere!'

'You are going,' he ground out, 'back to Athens! You were somewhat premature in your departure, I must point out. You might have got the money you wanted from your grandfather—your main interest, was it not—?' his voice was scathing '—but your precipitate departure has made him feel...cheated.

He wants you back in Athens to fulfil your…obligations. Otherwise,' he spelt out, 'he will not proceed with the merger!'

It was her turn for her face to harden.

'Oh, well, we mustn't get in the way of the precious merger, must we?' she flared. 'That was, after all, *your* main interest, was it not?' Deliberately she echoed his words, confronting him with the truth of why he had ever looked twice at her!

It did not hit its mark.

'There were other…interests…as I recall… Ones that I fully intend to resume when you return to Athens to fulfil your…obligations. *Ne?*' His voice trailed off, but his eyes washed over her. Weakness flooded through her—and memory—hot, humid memory.

He saw it in her eyes, and smiled. A blighting smile that had no humour in it. 'You see, I too, Andrea *mou*, feel cheated by your precipitate and so *unexpected* departure.'

She heard the anger in his voice—suppressed, restrained, but savage beneath the words. There was something more than anger in it too, she realised. Something raw, and painful.

Then he had snapped his gaze past her, the tight, controlled mask back on his face, and rested it where Kim was hovering, a puzzled, anxious look on her face.

'I need to speak to Andrea. Privately. If you would be so kind—?'

'I've got nothing to say to you!' Andrea flashed back at him.

Steel eyes, flecked with gold, rested on her. 'But I,' he said with a softness that raised the hairs at the nape of her neck, 'have a great deal to say to you, Andrea *mou*.'

She felt faint, hearing him say her name, that had once been an endearment, now edged with scorn. Behind her, Kim stepped forward and closed her hand protectively around Andrea's arm.

'Mr Vassilis, if my daughter does not wish to speak to you—'

The rest of her words were cut off by a rasp sounding in Nikos's throat. Shock etched across his face, and his eyes flashed back to Andrea.

'This woman is your *mother*?' Disbelief was in every word.

It was Kim who answered. 'Yes, I am Andrea's mother, Mr Vassilis. And perhaps…' she took a faltering breath '…you would explain what is going on?'

Nikos's eyes were scanning from face to face, his eyes narrowed, comparing the two women. Andrea knew what he would see—she and Kim did not look much alike. Kim was slighter in build, and her hair was fair, greying now at the temples, her faded eyes blue. All that she had got from her mother was her bone structure and her fine skin. Her red hair had come from Kim's grandmother, she knew, and her chestnut eyes were a legacy from her father.

But whatever he saw must have convinced him. 'Mrs Coustakis—' he began. His voice sounded shaken, but determined none the less.

Kim shook her head. 'I'm Kim Fraser, Mr Vassilis. Andreas and I never married.'

Her words were quietly spoken, and not ashamed. She had, her daughter knew, nothing—*nothing*—to be ashamed of.

Shock etched across Nikos's face again. It stabbed at Andrea. Telling her everything she needed to know. Bitter, bitter though that knowledge was.

'You see—' she twisted the words out of her mouth '—I'm not the woman you thought I was! Look around you!' Her arm swept the narrow hallway. 'Do I look like an heiress? Living here?'

Her words were a bitter, defiant challenge.

'This isn't possible.' Nikos's voice was flat. His denial total.

She gave a mocking, angry laugh. She had known, always known, that he would be horrified to discover her humble origins—to discover she did not come from his rich, sophisticated world. After all, what would a man as rich as Nikos Vassilis want with a wife from a council flat?

He moved suddenly, a hand flattening on the door beside him that led into the living room, pushing it open. He walked in. The room was clean and tidy, but the carpet was cheap and

worn, the chairs and sofa-bed where Andrea slept shabby and
frayed.

'You live here?'

His voice was still flat. Andrea followed him in.

'Yes. All my life.'

'Why?'

The word exploded from him. Andrea gave a high, short
laugh.

'Why? Because it's all Mum could afford, that's why! She
lived on benefits until I was old enough to start school, and the
council housed us here—she was lucky to get it, a flat of her
own, a single, teenaged mother as she was! When I started
school she got a part-time job, but it's hard work to put aside
enough money to try and buy a place of your own when you've
a child to bring up single-handed.'

'Single-handed? When your grandfather is Yiorgos
Coustakis?' His voice was a sneer.

Her eyes flashed. 'Yiorgos Coustakis—' she ground out her
grandfather's name with contempt '—told my mother she had
no claim on my father's estate. She's brought me up on her
own—totally.'

As she spoke, his lips compressed. He scanned the room
again, taking in every last detail. His gaze hardened.

'Are you telling me,' he demanded, and his face was set,
tight as a bow, 'that your grandfather does not support you?'

'That's right,' she said evenly. 'I told you—I'm not a
Coustakis at all.'

Kim's voice intervened, sounding confused and distressed.

'Andrea, what about the money? You told me Yiorgos had
given you all that money of his own free will! If you extorted
it from in any way then you must give it back! You *must*!'

'No!' she cried, appalled. 'No! The money's yours, it's *yours*
totally—to buy you an apartment in Spain, to pay your debts,
to—'

'Debts?' Nikos pounced on the word. His face was still
carved from stone.

'Yes,' said Kim, turning to him. 'I'm afraid, Mr Vassilis, I owe rather a lot of money. You see, when she was younger, Andrea had a very bad road accident. The therapy needed to enable her to walk again was only available privately, so I had to borrow money to pay for it. We're still paying it back— Andrea helps all she can. She has two jobs, and every penny she can spare goes towards it!'

Nikos looked numb, then he recovered.

'You never asked Yiorgos Coustakis to help you?' The question grated from him.

A harsh laugh escaped Andrea. 'Oh, Mum asked, all right! She went down on her knees to ask him to help her! She sent him all the doctors' reports on me—every last one of them! She begged him to help for the sake of his son—she promised she would repay the money as soon as she could.'

'And?' Nikos's voice was chill.

'He refused. He said she was trying to get money out of him by false pretences! His lawyers wrote telling Mum that if she tried to contact him again for any reason they'd take legal action against her for harassment.' She took a steadying breath, and went on. 'That's why I won't give the money back to him! Whatever Mum says! I've cleared her debts and I'm going to buy her a flat in Spain. There'll be enough change from the five hundred thousand pounds to invest safely for her and give her an income to live on, and a pension, and all that stuff, and—'

Nikos's face had stilled again. 'Five hundred thousand pounds?' His voice was hollow. 'Are you telling me that's what Yiorgos Coustakis paid out to you?'

She lifted her chin defiantly. 'I know it's a huge amount, but it's what I needed to get Mum sorted and settled.'

'Five hundred thousand,' he echoed. 'Half a million pounds.' His eyes blazed again suddenly. 'Do you have any *idea* how much your grandfather is worth?' He took a step forward and his hands closed around her forearms. He was close, much too close to her. 'Half a million is a pittance to him! A *pittance!*'

She jerked away.

'I don't care what he's worth! I don't care anything about

him! He treated Mum like dirt and I loathe him for it! I don't want more of his filthy money—I just wanted enough to get Mum out of here to somewhere safe and warm, with enough to live on without worrying the whole time! She's got asthma, and the damp in the flat makes her really ill…'

Her voice trailed off. He was not listening. He was staring around him, taking in every shabby detail.

That's right, thought Andrea viciously, pain stabbing at her as he looked round so disdainfully at the place she lived in. *Take a good look! This is where I come from! This is my home! Now you will despise me for it!*

Now, into the silence, Kim spoke.

'Mr Vassilis, I can see this has been an unwelcome shock to you, and I am sorry for that. But…' She hesitated, then went on. 'I would be grateful if you would please explain what the purpose of your being here is—'

His eyes flicked to her. 'My purpose? My purpose, Ms…Fraser—' he said her maiden name as if it pained him '—has just changed.'

Andrea's throat tightened. *I'll just bet it's changed! You came here to take me home with you and now you probably can't wait to get out of here as fast as you can…*

His attention suddenly swivelled to her. Her breath caught. His eyes were like slate, his face closed and shuttered.

And yet it was the face of the man she loved. Loved so much, so unbearably much!

I never thought I'd see him again! Thought I'd live the rest of my life without him! But he's here, now—

A vice crushed her heart.

Yes, and he's just about to walk out—for ever now he knows the truth about you.

A shaft of self-accusation hit her.

I should have been honest—right from the start. I deceived him—no wonder he is angry!

She took a deep, shuddering breath.

'Look, Nikos—I'm sorry. Truly. I didn't realise that my coming home would jeopardise your merger!'

A grim expression crossed his face. 'There is no merger. Nor will there be.'

No—how could there be? thought Andrea bleakly. Nikos Vassilis had thought he was marrying the Coustakis heiress— not the unacknowledged bastard of a woman Yiorgos Coustakis thought a gold-digging slut! Nikos had thought he was getting a wife who came from his world—not a girl who'd been born and bred in a decaying council flat.

'I should have told you,' she said heavily.

His eyes rested on her like unbearable weights. 'Yes, you should have told me, Andrea. You *should* have told me.'

'I'm sorry,' she said again. It seemed the only thing she could say.

'Are you?' There was something very strange in his voice. 'So am I.'

Well, of course he was. Andrea knew. Of course he wished he'd known from the start just how *tainted* she was! As if it wasn't bad enough to discover she was crippled—she was common as well…

Nikos's eyes had slid past her, lingering briefly on the tense, anxious figure of her mother, and then out, out through the window.

He wants to get out of here, Andrea thought. Get back to his own world. Where she had no place. Nor ever could have.

Through the window Nikos saw the other tower blocks of the estate and, far below, the world beneath. The sun was setting, starting to turn everything to gold. He stared down. All the kingdoms of the world spread before him.

He thought of the journey he had made—the long, hard journey from the streets of Athens—with only one focus, only one goal. Making money. More and more of it. Acquiring Coustakis Industries would have been the pinnacle of his achievement.

And he was a young man still. Who knew what kingdoms he could buy and sell before his time was up? Who knew what souls he could buy and sell with all his riches?

A face stole into his mind's eye. An old man's face, whose eyes knew well the price of a man's soul.

What is mine worth? thought Nikos. And the answer came clear. Clarion-clear.

Too much for Yiorgos Coustakis to pay.

He stepped away from the window and looked back at the two women in the shabby room. The kingdoms of the earth disappeared from view.

His hand slipped inside his jacket, taking out his mobile. He punched in a number. His voice, when he spoke, was curt. 'This is Nikos Vassilis. I have a message for Yiorgos Coustakis. Tell him I am standing in front of Kim Fraser and her daughter in their home—the merger is off.'

Then he disconnected.

As he slipped the phone back in his pocket his eyes met Andrea's.

She reeled.

The blaze of emotion in them was like a flash-flame.

'I will make him pay,' he said softly. 'If it takes me the rest of my life I will make him pay for what he has done to you.'

Andrea stared. His mouth twisted at her expression and he forged on. 'I knew the man was ruthless—all the world knew that! But that he would stoop so low... *Christos*, he has behaved like an animal!'

She couldn't speak—couldn't do anything but stare at him, disbelieving.

Nikos's eyes raced around the room again. 'To make you live like *this*,' he grated. 'To turn his back on his own flesh and blood—to leave you to struggle on your own all these years. Not even—' His voice hardened like the edge of a knife. 'Not even to lift a finger when his own granddaughter faced a lifetime in a wheelchair...' He shut his eyes. 'Dear God in heaven, what kind of scum is he?'

His eyes snapped open. They glinted like steel. He reached for his phone again. 'Well,' he said grimly, 'the world will soon know.'

Before Andrea's very eyes she saw him speak in English

again. 'Demetrios? Prepare a press-release. The Coustakis merger is off. Yes, you heard me. And I shall be making my reasons for pulling out very, very clear. The stink will reach heaven, I assure you! I'll phone again in an hour, when you've had time to contact the board.'

He snapped the phone off again.

'Mr Vassilis.' Kim spoke, her voice agitated and perturbed. 'Please—I don't understand any of this! What is happening?'

'What is happening...' Nikos's voice softened as he saw how disturbed Kim was '...is that I have decided not to take over Coustakis Industries. I refuse, absolutely—' his voice hardened again '—to have anything to do with a man who could behave in such a way to you and your daughter! I refuse, absolutely,' he finished, 'to do business of any kind with him!'

'But—but...' stammered Andrea. 'But the merger means so *much* to you—'

A hand slashed through the air. 'No. Only one thing means anything to me, Andrea.' His voice changed. 'Only one thing.'

He took a step towards her. She wanted to step back, but she couldn't. She was rooted to the spot.

'Don't you know what it is, Andrea *mou*?' His voice had softened. 'Surely you must know?' His hand reached out to touch the flaming aureole of her hair. Her breath caught. 'Surely?'

He looked down at her, his eyes flecked with gold. 'When you left me it was as if you had stabbed me to the quick. To the heart. I bled, Andrea *mou*. I bled.'

His fingers brushed her cheek, and she felt faint. 'Come back to me, *pethi mou*, come back to me—'

Her throat was tight, but she tore the words out. 'What for? If there's to be no merger then you don't have the slightest need of me!'

He smiled. Her heart turned over.

'Need? Oh, my Andrea, I need you to breathe. Without you I cannot live. Do you not know that?'

His hand cupped her cheek. 'I need you to light my way, to walk at my side all my life. I need you to be with me, every day and night.' His other hand closed around her other cheek, cupping her face, lifting it to his.

It was odd, Andrea thought. His face had gone out of focus; the flecks of gold in his eyes were misting. Something must be in her eyes—some mote of dust.

'But—' she swallowed '—but I don't see why you need me...'

He smiled, and it filled a gaping hole in her heart.

'Didn't I show you every night, every day we spent together? Didn't you show me?'

'Show you what?' she breathed. Her eyes were brimming now; she could not stop it.

He lowered his head and kissed her softly.

'That we were falling in love, Andrea *mou*.'

'Love?' It was a whisper, a breath.

'Oh, yes. Love—quite definitely love.' There was no doubt in his voice. None at all. 'There can be no other word for it. How else could the wound you dealt me when you left me have been so mortal to me? How else—' a finger lifted to her lashes and let the tears beading there spill onto him '—could these tears be making diamonds of your eyes?'

'But you don't love me—you can't—you don't have to! It was only because of the merger that you married me—'

The gasp from Kim went unheard.

'Our marriage, my sweet, most beloved Andrea, is the only good thing to come of that cursed merger! I always meant to make you a good husband, even when I thought ours was to be nothing more than a mutually beneficial arranged marriage. Once I would have been content with that. But on Crete—ah, then it became much, much more! And when I discovered you had left me, oh, I realised just how much more! The pain of losing you was agony—and I knew then that something had happened to me that I did not ever dream of. I had fallen in love with you—fathoms deep.' He looked down at her tenderly, possessively—lovingly.

'You can't love me...' Her voice was a whisper, a thread. 'We come from such different worlds. Look—'

She gestured helplessly with her hand at the shabby apartment.

He followed her gesture with his eyes, knowing now why she had said the same words to him on the night of their wedding. To think he had thought it was because she had been born to a wealth he'd had to fight all his life to acquire!

'When you return to Athens with me,' he said in a low voice—and there was a strangeness in it Andrea had never heard, 'I will show you were I was born—where I lived until I crawled from the gutter as a young man. A man, Andrea, who never knew his father, whose mother did not care whether he lived or died. A man, Andrea, who vowed—*vowed* he would make something of his life! I was determined to achieve the success and recognition I craved!'

He took a deep, shuddering breath, and Andrea stared at him, wordless, as suddenly—totally—she saw the man Nikos really was—not the gilded scion of a wealthy patrimony, but someone with the guts, the determination, the courage, to make something of himself out of the nothing he had been born with.

'But I have learnt...' his voice had softened, taken on a sense of wonder '...that true riches are not in gold and silver. True riches...' his eyes melted her, and she felt her heart turn over '...are here—inside us. I envy you so much, Andrea.' His eyes glanced across to where Kim stood staring, bemused and wondering. 'To have had the love of your mother—and I envy even more—' his voice, she thought, almost cracked '—your love for her. And so I ask you—beg you—' as he spoke her throat tightened to an unbearable tightness '—to accept my love for you—and to give me yours.'

He paused, looking down at her, gathering her hands against his heart.

'Come back to me, Andrea, and be the wife of my heart, for I love you more than I can bear.'

The tears were spilling down her cheeks now.

'Yes!' she uttered as he kissed her tears away, and then his mouth closed over hers, and what was the gentle, soft touch of homage became a salutation to the future they would have to-gether.

He released her, and turned to face Kim. Andrea could see the tears shining in her mother's eyes.

'Have we your blessing?' Nikos asked her quietly.

For a moment her mother could not speak. And then, with a broken cry, she answered.

'Oh, yes! Oh, *yes*!'

EPILOGUE

'IF IT is a boy, then Andreas. If a girl, then Kim.'

Andrea smiled. 'Kim isn't very Greek.'

Her husband brushed this unimportant objection inside. His hand moved over the rounded contour of her belly.

'He kicked!' Nikos's voice was full of wonder—and astonishment.

'Or she,' pointed out Andrea. Her hand closed over Nikos's. She leant her head back against his shoulder, her gaze stretching out over the azure Aegean that spread all around them, feeling the familiar swell of the sea beneath the hull. 'How can I be so happy?' she asked.

With his free hand Nikos stroked her hair.

'Because you deserve it,' he said.

Andrea reached up to kiss him. 'And you do too.'

It seemed to her still such a miracle—to be so happy together. Since that magical, miraculous evening, when Nikos had come to claim her heart for his own, her life had turned upside down all over again. And she rejoiced in it totally!

Nikos had whisked them both off to Greece, sweeping Kim with them as well, and settled them in a hired villa on a private island.

'I don't want you exposed to what will happen now,' he had told Andrea. 'It will be very ugly.'

Then he had gone to Athens, to face Yiorgos Coustakis. His denouncement had been merciless—and so had the press coverage that had ensued. The scandal of the way one of the richest men in Greece had behaved to his own granddaughter had shocked the nation. That, and the cancellation of the expected merger with Vassilis Inc, had caused a steep plunge in the Coustakis share price, had precipitated the normally cowed board of Coustakis Industries into drastic action. Yiorgos had been deposed as chairman, forced to retire, a social pariah.

The seizure that had killed him a month later had moved few to pity a man who had had no pity in him for anyone else, no kindness in his hard, selfish heart.

His entire fortune had passed to his despised granddaughter, for in his rage at his new son-in-law he had destroyed the will that had left his wealth to his future great-grandson, and Andrea had become, by default, the Coustakis heiress after all.

It was a troubling inheritance.

'Nikos—are you sure, very sure, about what you want me to do?' Her voice was anxious as she stood in the circle of his arms, looking out over the shining Aegean sea.

He turned her round to face him.

'Completely sure.' His answer came unhesitatingly. 'The Andreas Coustakis Foundation will be a fine and fitting monument to your father—and your mother is in agreement as well. After all,' he went on, 'all three of us know what it is to be poor, Andrea *mou*. The foundation will give a chance to so many children blighted by their families' poverty.'

Her eyes were still troubled. 'But we could keep the Coustakis shares, and you could run the company as you always intended...'

He shook his head decisively. 'No. We have more than enough money, Andrea—we will never be poor. To me, Yiorgos's wealth is tainted. His neglect of you proves it. Let it be put to good use now.' His mouth twisted. 'Perhaps if we use his wealth to some good end, people might have something pleasant to remember him by.'

'He was so vile to Mum, so needlessly cruel and offensive, and yet...' her voice sounded strained '...it was a miserable end for him—collapsing and dying alone, with not a soul to care about him.'

'But then, he did not care for anyone except himself,' Nikos answered soberly. 'You and your mother were not the only ones he injured—there were many victims of Yiorgos Coustakis. When the newspapers ran the story of his shameful treatment of you and your mother other stories came out too, showing his brutality, his ruthlessness, his absolute disregard for anyone else.'

He took her hand. 'And now the Coustakis fortune is yours. Let it do some good for others, for a change—as Yiorgos Coustakis never did. Come,' he said, starting to stroll down the deck with her, 'we might as well make the most of our farewell cruise on this floating monument to execrable interior yacht design!'

Andrea laughed. 'I'm sure some billionaire somewhere will love it—and that hideously gilded house he lived in as well! The sale of both will boost the coffers of the foundation handsomely!'

'Indeed. However,' Nikos mused, 'I think perhaps we ought to see if we can persuade Captain Petrachos not to leave us— I'm sure we can find some way of tempting him to stay. He was saying over dinner last night that he would be happy to help with the seamanship aspects of the youth training programme for the foundation.'

Andrea exchanged glances with him. 'Funnily enough,' she commented dryly, 'that was the very thing Mum said she was keenest on helping to set up. A striking coincidence, wouldn't you say?' Her voice changed. 'Oh, I do so hope that something might come of them being together! I always dreamed of Mum meeting someone else—I know she was so in love with my father, but if she could find companionship, at least, it would be so wonderful for her!'

Nikos smiled. 'Let us wish them well—for we have happiness and enough to spare, *ne*, Andrea *mou*?'

She wound her arm around him.

'I do love you, Nikos,' she said, 'so very much.'

He stopped, and turned her in his arms, and kissed her.

'And I love you, Andrea *mou*. Through all the years we have.'

The future, as bright and golden as the sun pouring over the Aegean sea, beckoned to them, and they walked towards it together.

THE ITALIAN PRINCE'S PROPOSAL

by

Susan Stephens

Dear Reader,

A visit to the endlessly photogenic provinces of Umbria and Tuscany in Italy prompted me to write this book about Alessandro, Crown Prince of Ferara. The fabulous architecture, the history, the traditions, together with the innate and well-justified pride of its people, demanded a response.

And, although a city of Ferrara already exists, my own conjuring up of the principality of Ferara was prompted by my first sighting of Orvieto – a city that truly seems suspended in the clouds…

I hope you enjoy Emily and Alessandro's story.

Best wishes,

Susan Stephens

For Steve, my hero.

CHAPTER ONE

CROWN PRINCE ALESSANDRO BUSSONI OF FERARA narrowed amber eyes in lazy speculation as he continued to stare at the brightly lit stage. 'She'd do.'

'I beg your pardon, sir?'

There was no emotion in the question. The man sitting next to the Prince on the top table at the lavish Midsummer ball wore the carefully controlled expression of a career diplomat, and had a voice to match. Thin and lugubrious, with sun-starved features, it would have been impossible for Marco Romagnoli to provide a sharper contrast to his employer, and Crown Prince Alessandro's blistering good looks were supported by one of the brightest minds in Europe, as well as all the presence and easy charm that was his by right of birth.

'I said she'd do,' the Prince repeated impatiently, turning a compelling gaze on his aide-de-camp. 'You've paraded every woman of marriageable age before me, Marco, and failed to tempt me once. I like the look of this girl—'

And it was a lot more than just her stunning appearance, Alessandro acknowledged silently as his glance went back to the stage. The girl possessed an incredible energy not dissimilar to his own—an energy that seemed to leap out from the gaudily dressed performance area and thump him straight in the chest.

All he had to offer her was a cold-blooded business deal, but… His sensuous mouth curved in a thoughtful smile. In this instance mixing business with pleasure might not be such a bad thing.

'Are you serious, Your Royal Highness?' Marco

5

Romagnoli murmured, taking care not to alert their fellow diners.

'Would I joke about so serious a matter as my future wife? Alessandro demanded in a fierce whisper. 'She looks like fun.'

'Fun, sir?' Marco Romagnoli leaned forward to follow his employer's eyeline. 'You are talking about the singer with the band?'

'You find something wrong with that?' the Prince demanded, swivelling round to level a challenging gaze on his aide's face.

'No, sir,' Marco returned in a monotone, knowing the Prince would brook no prejudice based on flimsy face-value evidence. 'But if I may ask an impertinent question…?'

'Ask away,' Alessandro encouraged, his firm mouth showing the first hint of amusement as he guessed the way Marco's mind was working.

'She'd do for what, exactly, sir…? Only she's rather—'

'Luscious? Bold? Striking? In your face? What?' the Prince prompted adjusting his long legs as if the enforced inactivity was starting to irk him.

'All of those,' Marco suggested uncomfortably, his glance flashing back to the stage, where Emily Weston was well into her third number and clearly had the affluent, well-oiled crowd eating out of her hand. 'I can see that a young lady like that holds a certain attraction for—' Marco Romagnoli eased his fingers under a starched white collar that seemed to be on the point of choking him.

'Go on. Don't stop now,' Prince Alessandro encouraged, reining in his amusement.

Taking a few moments to rethink his approach, the usually unflappable courtier replied carefully, 'Well, sir, I can see she's a beauty, and undoubtedly perfect for certain activities. But you surely can't be thinking—'

'You mean I should bed her, not wed her?' Alessandro suggested dryly, as he looked back to where Emily had the microphone clutched between both hands for a slow number, looking as if she was about to devour it.

'I couldn't have put it better myself, sir. In my opinion such an ill-judged match would only create more problems than it would solve.'

'I disagree,' the Crown Prince of Ferara countered, 'and nothing you can say will persuade me that the girls you have paraded before me would fill the role any better—or vacate it without causing problems.'

He paused, and took another long look at the stage. 'As it is not my intention to break any hearts, Marco, this is the perfect solution. I want a straightforward business deal and a short-term bride—'

'Short-term, sir?'

Alessandro turned to answer the disquiet so clearly painted across the other man's face.

'I know,' he said, leaning closer to ensure they were not overheard. 'You're thinking of all the other implications such an arrangement would entail—I would expect nothing less of you, my old friend.'

The Prince's companion grew ever more troubled. Even if he could have shed the role of cautious professional advisor, Marco Romagnoli had known Alessandro from the day of his birth, and was considered an honorary member of the royal family.

'I wouldn't wish to see anyone take advantage of you, sir,' he said now, with concern.

'I shall take good care to ensure that none of the parties involved in my plan is taken advantage of,' Alessandro assured him. 'Thanks to our country's archaic legislation I can think of no other way to solve the problem of succession. If my father is to have his wish and retire I must marry immediately. It's obvious to me that this young woman has spirit. When I put my proposition to her I think she will have an instant grasp of the advantages that such a match can bring to both of us.'

'Yes, sir,' Marco agreed reluctantly, flinching visibly as Emily launched into a raunchy upbeat number.

'I have seen enough, Marco,' the Prince said, reclaiming his aide's attention. 'And I like what I see. Please advise the young lady that Alessandro Bussoni wishes to talk with her after the performance tonight. No titles,' he warned. 'And if she asks, just say I have a proposition to put to her. And don't forget to ask her name,' he added as, without another word, Marco Romagnoli rose to his feet.

After the show, Emily Weston, the singer with the band, was having a tense debate over the phone with her twin sister Miranda.

'Well, how *do* you deal with them?' she demanded, shouldering the receiver to scoop up another huge blob of cleansing cream from her twin's industrial-sized pot.

'Who do you mean?' Miranda snuffled between ear-splitting sneezes.

'Stage Door Johnnies—'

Miranda's summer cold symptoms dissolved into laughter. 'Stage Door Whosies?'

'Don't pretend you don't know what I'm talking about,' Emily insisted, flashing another concerned glance towards the dressing room door.

'I didn't think there was such a thing as Stage Door Johnnies nowadays,' Miranda said doubtfully.

'Well, I can assure you there is,' Emily insisted. 'What else would you call uninvited gentleman callers who won't take no for an answer?'

'Depends on who's doing the calling, I suppose,' Miranda conceded, blasting out another sneeze. 'Why don't you just take a look at him first, before you decide?'

'No way! That's never been part of our agreement.'

'But if he looks like Herman Munster you can send him packing...and if he's a babe, pass him on to me. He'd never know the difference. If Mum and Dad can't tell us apart, what chance does this man stand? What have you got to lose?'

'Look, I'll have to go,' Emily said as another rap, far more insistent than the last, bounced off the walls around her head. 'I told his messenger I couldn't see anyone I didn't know immediately after a show—pleading artistic temperament. He still hasn't taken the hint.'

'He sent someone round first?' Miranda cut in, her voice taut with excitement. 'He sounds interesting. He might be a VIP.'

'I doubt it,' Emily said as she peered into the mirror to peel off her false eyelashes. 'Though when I said I wouldn't see him I thought his representative muttered something about Prince being disappointed—'

'Emily, you dope,' Miranda exclaimed through another bout of sneezing. 'Prince Records is the recording company my band's been hoping to sign with. And you've just turned away their scout.'

'Can't I get one of the boys to see him?' Emily suggested hopefully. After all, there were five male members in Miranda's band.

'Are you kidding?' Miranda exclaimed. 'First of all they'll be in the pub by now…and secondly, do you seriously think I'd trust them to discuss business without my being there?'

Remembering the dreamy idealism of Miranda's fellow musicians, Emily could only respond in the negative. 'It might have helped if you had warned me this might happen,' she protested reasonably. 'Have to go,' she finished in a rush, wiping her hands on the towel across her lap as another flurry of raps hit the door. 'Whoever this is, he's not about to give up.'

Cutting the connection, Emily grabbed a handful of tissues as she shot up from her seat in front of the brilliantly lit mirror. Then, scooting behind a conveniently placed screen, she called out, 'Come in.'

This was the craziest thing she had ever done, Emily thought nervously as she swiped off the last of her make-up and stuffed the used tissues into the pocket of her robe. She tensed as the door swung open.

'Hello? Miss Weston? Miss Weston, are you there?'

She had heard male voices likened to anything from gravel to bitter chocolate, but this one slammed straight into her senses. Italian, she guessed, and with just the hint of a sexy mid-Atlantic drawl. She pictured him scanning the cluttered space, hunting for her hiding place, and felt her whole being responding to some imperative and extremely erotic wake-up call.

'Make yourself comfortable,' she sang out, relieved she was hidden away. 'I'm getting changed.'

'Thank you, Miss Weston,' the voice replied evenly. 'Please don't hurry on my account.'

Just the authority in the man's voice made the hairs stand on the back of her neck. And there was a stillness about it that made her think of a jungle cat, lithe, impossibly strong—and deadly.

It was in her nature to confront threats, not hide from them. So why was she skulking behind a screen? Emily asked herself impatiently. Could it be that the force of this man's personality had taken possession of what, in Miranda's absence, was her territory?

'Can I help you?' she said, struggling to see through a tiny crack in the woodwork.

'I certainly hope so.'

There was supreme confidence and not a little amusement in the response, as well as the type of worldliness that had Emily mentally rocking back on her heels. It was almost as if the man had caught her out doing something wrong—as if she had no right to be looking at him.

Drawing a few steadying breaths, she tried again. But all she could see through the crack in the screen was the broad sweep of shoulders clad in a black dinner jacket and a cream silk evening scarf slung casually around the neck of an impressively tall individual. A man whose luxuriant, dark wavy hair was immaculately groomed and glossy…the type of hair that made you want to run your fingers through it and then move on to caress— She pulled herself up short, closing her eyes to gather her senses…senses that were reacting in an extraordinary manner to nothing more than a man's voice, Emily reminded herself. She spent her working life objective and detached…yet now, when it really mattered—when Miranda's recording contract was at stake—she was allowing herself to be sideswiped off-beam by a few simple words. 'I'm sorry, Mr…er—'

'Bussoni,' he supplied evenly.

'Mr Bussoni,' Emily said, her assurance growing behind the protection of the screen. 'I'm afraid I didn't give the gentleman who works for you a very warm welcome—'

'Really? He said nothing of it to me.'

She was beginning to get a very clear picture of the man now. The image of a hunter sprang to mind…someone who was waiting and listening, using all his senses to evaluate his quarry. 'I understand you'd like to discuss the possibility of signing the band?' she said carefully.

There was another long pause, during which Emily formed the impression that the man was scanning all her neatly arranged possessions, gathering evidence about her and soaking up information—drawing conclusions. And from his position in front of the mirror he could do all of that—and still keep a watch on her hiding place.

Taking over last minute from Miranda meant she had been forced to come straight from work. There had been no time to find out about the event, let alone who might be in the audience. She had certainly not anticipated the need to be on her guard—to hide everything away. 'You are from Prince Records?' she prompted in a businesslike tone, hoping to bounce the man into some sort of admission.

'Do you think you could possibly come out here and discuss this in person?'

It was a reasonable enough suggestion. But Miranda was never seen without full war paint, and after liberal applications of cold cream Emily's own face had returned to its customary naked state. If she hoped to impersonate her twin an appearance right now was out of the question.

'I know this must sound rude, after you've taken the trouble to come backstage, but I'm rather tired this evening. Do you think we could talk tomorrow?' she said, knowing Miranda should have recovered and taken her rightful place by then.

'Tomorrow afternoon, at three?'

Emily's hearing was acutely tuned to his every move. He was already turning to go, she realised. Suddenly she couldn't even remember what she had on the following day, let alone specifically at three o'clock in the afternoon. The only thing she was capable of registering—apart from an over-active heartbeat—was that the recording contract for Miranda's band was vital.

'OK. That's fine,' she heard herself agreeing. 'But not here.'

'Anywhere you say.'

Possibilities flooded Emily's mind. She dismissed each one in turn...until the very last. 'Could you come out to North London?' Her mother and father had insisted that if Miranda's cold had not improved by tomorrow she should be brought home to recuperate. Emily knew she could rely on her parents to fill in any awkward gaps...smooth over the cracks when she changed places with her twin.

'I don't see why not.'

'That's if you're still interested?'

Interested? Alessandro thought, curbing his smile just in case Miss Weston decided to suddenly burst out from her hiding place. If he had been fascinated before, now he was positively gripped.

He ran one supple, sun-bronzed finger down the slim leather-bound diary he so longed to open, and traced the length of the expensive fountain pen lying next to it before toying with a pair of cufflinks bearing some sort of crest.

The handbag on the seat had quality written all over it, rather than some flashy logo. And the smart black suit teamed with a crisp white double-cuffed shirt hanging on a gown rail was Armani, if he wasn't mistaken.

His gaze swept the threadbare carpet that might once have been red to where a pair of slinky high-heeled court shoes stood next to a dark blue felt sack, ornamented with a thick tassel. Alongside that, a pull-along airline case—

'Mr Bussoni?'

His gaze switched back to the screen.

'Mr Bussoni, are you still interested?'

There was just a hint of anxiety in the voice now, Alessandro noted with satisfaction. This contract obviously meant a great deal to her. He cast a look at the discarded stage costume... Something jarred. No, he realised. Everything jarred.

'Only on one condition,' he said, adopting a stern tone as he assumed the mantle of time-starved recording executive.

'And that is?' Emily said cagily.

'That you come to supper with me after our meeting.' Alessandro was surprised when a curl of excitement wrapped around his chest as he waited for her answer. 'You may have questions for me, and there's sure to be a lot we have to discuss,' he said truthfully, satisfied that he had kept every trace of irony out of his voice.

Emily let the silence hang for a while. Miranda would definitely have to be better by then, she thought crossing her fingers reflexively. 'That's fine,' she confirmed evenly. 'I'll let the rest of the band members know—'

'No,' the voice flashed back assertively. 'It only needs one person to take in what I have to say...and I have chosen you, Miss Weston. Now, are you still interested in progressing with this matter, or not?'

'Of course I'm interested,' Emily confirmed, suddenly eager to be free of a presence that was becoming more disconcerting by the minute.

'That's settled, then. I'll write my number down for you. Perhaps you'll be good enough to get in touch first thing…leave the address for our meeting with my secretary?'

'Of course.' She felt rather than heard him prepare to leave.

'Until tomorrow, Miss Weston.'

'Until tomorrow, Mr Bussoni.'

Emily held her breath and tried to soak up information as the door opened, then shut again silently. The man might have three humps and a tail, for all she could tell, but her body insisted on behaving as if some lusty Roman gladiator had just strolled out of the room after booking her for sex the next day.

After he'd left it took her a good few minutes to recover her equilibrium. And when she moved out from behind the screen everything seemed shabbier than she remembered it, and emptier somehow, as if some indefinable force had left the room, leaving it all the poorer for the loss.

By early afternoon the next day, Emily had cancelled all her appointments for the rest of the week and was ready to take her sister back to their parents' house.

Drawing up outside the front door on the short gravel drive, she switched off the engine and tried for the umpteenth time to coax her twin into facing reality.

'This man is different to anyone I've ever encountered before. It would be a real mistake to underestimate him, Miranda.'

'He made quite an impression on you, didn't he?' Miranda replied, slanting a glance at her twin.

'I didn't even see him properly,' Emily replied defensively. 'And don't change the subject. It's you we're talking about, not me.'

After assuming a low-profile role in an orchestra for a number of years, Miranda had attracted the attention of a leading Japanese violin teacher. In order to fund the lessons Emily's twin had started a band—a band that in the beginning had taken up only the occasional weekend; a band that was now taking up more and more of her time…

'I only need this recording contract for a year or so,' she said now, as if trying to convince herself that the scheme would work. 'Just long enough for me to launch my career as a solo violinist.'

Emily frowned. She wanted to help, but only when she was confident Miranda understood what she was letting herself in for. 'Are you sure Prince Records understands that? They would have grounds to sue if you let them down.'

'They won't have any trouble finding someone to replace me; the boys are great—'

'I'm still not happy,' Emily admitted frankly. 'I just can't see what you'll gain going down this route.'

'Money?' Miranda said hopefully.

Emily shook her head as she reasoned it through aloud. 'You're not going to be able to honour a recording contract drawn up by a man like Mr Bussoni and put in the practice hours necessary to study the violin with a top-flight teacher like Professor Iwamoto.'

'It won't be for long,' Miranda insisted stubbornly, unfolding her long limbs to have a noisy stretch. 'I'll cope.'

Before Emily had a chance to argue Miranda was out of the smart black coupé and heading up the path.

'Don't be silly,' Emily said, catching up with her sister at the front door. 'The more successful the band, the less likely it is that this crazy idea of yours will work. I know the money would be great, but—' The expression on her twin's face made Emily stop to give her a hug. 'I know you're still pining over that violin we saw in Heidelberg.'

'That was just a stupid dream—'

'Well, I don't know much about violins,' Emily admitted, 'but I do know what a sweet sound you produced on that lovely old instrument.'

'Something like that would cost a king's ransom anyway,' Miranda sighed despondently. 'And it's sure to have been sold by now.'

Emily made a vague sound to register sympathy while she was busy calculating how much money she could raise if she sold her central London apartment to the landlord who already owned most of the smart riverside block, and then rented it back from him. Miranda need never know. It was a desperate solution, but anything was preferable to seeing her sister's opportunity lost. 'If I can help you, I will,' she promised.

With a gust of frustration, Miranda hit the doorbell. 'You do enough for everyone already. You won't even let me pay rent—'

'If I didn't have you around, who else would keep the fridge stocked up with eye masks?' Emily demanded wryly.

Their banter was interrupted when the door swung open. 'Girls—'

Then another idea popped into Emily's head. 'I've got some investments—'

'No!' Miranda said, shaking her head vehemently. 'Absolutely not.'

'You're not arguing,' their mother said wearily, giving them both a reproving look.

'Heated discussion, Mum,' Emily said as she shut the door behind them. 'Where's Dad?'

'In his study, of course.'

Of course. Emily stole a moment to inhale deeply, taking in the aroma of a freshly baked cake coming from the kitchen, along with the gurgle of boiling water ready for tea.

'You look tired,' her mother said softly, touching her arm. 'And as for you, Miranda—' Her voice sharpened as if her maternal engines had revved to a new pitch. 'What you need is a good dose of my linctus, and a hot cup of tea—'

'Did I hear the magic words?'

'Dad!' the girls cried in unison.

After giving them both a bear hug, Mr Weston linked arms with his daughters and followed their mother into the kitchen.

'It will be easy for you, Emily,' her mother asserted confidently, after Miranda had outlined her plan to secure the recording contract. 'You're not emotionally involved like Miranda. And you'll run rings around this record company man when it comes to securing the best terms for Miranda.'

Emily was surprised by her reaction to this vote of confidence. It was unnerving to discover that her mother's assessment of the situation could be so far off the mark. Intuition told her that running rings around Alessandro Bussoni was out of the question. But her main worry was the strange way her heart behaved just at the thought of him joining them in the tiny house. The man behind the voice would fill every inch of it with presence alone, never mind the unsettling possibility that she might brush up against him—

'Are you sure you're all right with this, Emily...? Emily?'

Finally the concern in her father's voice penetrated Emily's dream-state, and her eyes cleared as she hurried to reassure him. 'Of course, Dad. Leave it to me,' she insisted brightly, 'I can handle Signor Bussoni—'

'Italian!' her mother exclaimed, showing double the interest as she unconsciously checked out her neat halo of curls. 'How exciting. And when did you say he was arriving?'

'Right now, by the looks of it,' Emily's father said as he peered through the window.

CHAPTER TWO

'OH, NO!' Miranda gasped, looking to her sister for guidance.

'Stay upstairs until he's gone,' Emily suggested briskly. 'I'll come and get you when the coast's clear. Mum. Dad. Act normal.'

'Yes, dear,' her mother said breathlessly, exchanging an excited glance with her father.

Don't look so worried,' Emily called after Miranda. 'I promise not to turn anything down without your approval.'

Exchanging quick smiles, the girls were just on the point of parting at the foot of the stairs when they stopped, looked at each other, and then swooped to the hall window.

Standing well back from the glass, Emily ran a finger cautiously down the edge of the net curtain.

'Oh, boy,' she murmured, watching the tall, darkly clad figure unfold his impressive frame from the heavily shaded interior of a sleek black car.

'You said Herman Munster,' Miranda breathed accusingly.

'I said he might have been Herman Munster for all I could see of him,' Emily corrected tensely.

'Looks like you were both wrong in this instance,' their father commented dryly.

Alessandro felt a frisson of anticipation as he double-checked the address his private secretary had passed on to him that morning.

He wasn't used to waiting, and eighteen hours was far too long in this case.

But then he wasn't used to speaking to someone hiding

behind a screen either, or accepting anyone's terms but his own—which was how he now found himself getting out of a rented Mercedes outside a perfectly ordinary semi-detached house in North London.

He smiled a little in amused acceptance. He couldn't recall a single instance of being turned down by a woman, let alone agreeing to a time of her choosing for an audience as begrudging as this one. His sharp gaze took in the small rectangular lawn, freshly mowed, and then moved on to the splash of vivid colour provided by a pot of petunias to one side of the narrow front door. For someone who moved between palaces, embassies or the presidential suite in some luxury hotel when he was really slumming it, this chance to sample suburbia was a novelty… No. A welcome change, he decided as he swiped off his dark glasses.

Behind a snowy drift of net, the Weston family watched Alessandro Bussoni's progress towards the house in awe-struck silence.

'He's absolutely gorgeous,' Miranda murmured. Their distracted mother barely managed a weak gasp of, 'Oh, my!'

'Go, before he sees you,' Emily suggested urgently, having already turned her back on the window.

'But your make-up,' Miranda said, hopping from foot to foot, torn between going and staying.

Emily's hand shot automatically to her face. 'What about it?'

'You're not wearing any,' Miranda exclaimed with concern.

'Can't be helped. He'll still think I'm you. Why shouldn't he? Anyway, you're not wearing any make-up,' Emily pointed out.

'Only because I'm sick.'

'Well, there's no time for me to do anything about it now,' Emily said firmly. 'I'll be fine. Don't worry about me.'

'Sure?' Miranda asked hopefully.

'Sure,' Emily said briskly, hoping no one had noticed that her hand was shaking as it hovered over the doorknob.

'I'm going to change,' Miranda shouted, on her way up the stairs. 'Then I'm taking over from you.'

'No!' But even as Emily's gaze raked the empty landing to call her sister back she knew it was too late. Sucking in a deep, steadying breath, she seized the doorknob tightly and began to turn...

'You go and wait in the lounge, pet.'

'Dad—'

'Go and compose yourself,' Mr Weston urged gently, refusing to let go of her arm until Emily allowed him to steer her away from the door. 'You look like you could do with a few minutes. I'll keep him busy until you're ready.'

'You're an angel,' Emily whispered, reaching up on tiptoe to give her father an affectionate peck on the cheek. But a moment alone was all it took her to realise that she couldn't go ahead with the charade after all, and she rushed upstairs to find her sister.

The twins waited motionless, hardly daring to breathe as they stood just inside the door to Miranda's bedroom. It felt as if the conversation downstairs had been going on for ever while their father satisfied himself as to their visitor's identity and then invited him into the house, but at his signal they started down the stairs.

Emily was dressed in her customary relaxing-at-home-uniform of blue jeans and a simple grey marl tee shirt. Her well-buffed toenails, devoid of nail varnish, were shown off in a pair of flat brown leather sandals, while her long black hair was held up loosely on top of her head with a tortoiseshell clip.

In complete contrast, Miranda had somehow found enough time to coat the area around her large green eyes with copious amounts of silver glitter, add blusher to her cheeks and staggeringly high platform shoes to her seem-ingly endless legs.

Surely there could be no mistake, Emily thought, giving her twin the final once-over before they reached the sitting room door. Signor Bussoni would immediately presume it was Miranda he had seen on stage. 'Relax,' she whispered, taking hold of her twin's wrist. 'It'll be all right.'

'Then why are you shaking?' Miranda remarked percep-tively.

'Girls? What's keeping you? You've got a visitor.'

'We're coming now, Dad,' Emily called back, hoping she sounded more confident than she felt. She had no idea what she was up against, and had nothing to go on but that disconcerting voice. For all she knew it might be Herman Munster hiding behind that impressive physique and those super-sleek clothes.

'Come on, love. What's the hold-up?' Popping his head round the door, her father drew her into the room. 'Your mother will have tea ready in about fifteen minutes,' he said. 'You two know each other,' he added, with an ex-pectant smile.

Emily felt as if her powers of reason had vanished. Her mind's eye wasn't simply unreliable, it was positively de-fective, she decided, gazing up into a man's face that was almost agonising in its perfection. Thick ebony-black hair, cut slightly longer than was customary in England, was swept back and still tousled from the wind. Conscious he would think her rude, she forced her gaze away, only to discover lips that were almost indecently well formed and the most expressive dark gold gaze she had ever encoun-tered.

Restating his name with a slight bow, Alessandro viewed the two sisters standing one behind the other. 'Miss Weston,' he murmured.

Lurching forward in response to Emily's none too subtle prompting, Miranda extended her hand politely. 'Delighted to see you, Signor Bussoni,' she said, letting out an audible sigh when Alessandro raised her hand to his lips.

'And I you,' he said in a voice as warm as the sunlight that had tinted his skin to bronze. 'But, forgive me, it is the other Miss Weston I have come to see.'

'The other Miss Weston?' Miranda squeaked, looking helplessly behind her to where Emily was standing rigid, wishing the ground would swallow her up.

'Indeed,' Alessandro said in a voice laced with humour. 'You did invite me, Miss Weston,' he said, looking straight at Emily.

Shock rendered both sisters speechless, and for a moment no one moved or spoke. If their own parents couldn't tell them apart, how could Signor Bussoni? Emily wondered tensely. She breathed a sigh of relief as her mother breezed into the room.

'Ah, Signor Bussoni, what a pleasure it is to have you in our midst.'

'The pleasure is all mine, I assure you,' Alessandro said, inclining his head towards the older woman in an elegant show of respect.

'I see you've met my girls.' Looking from Emily to Miranda, she clearly couldn't contain herself another moment. 'Have you heard Miranda play yet?' she said expectantly. 'The violin,' she prompted, when Alessandro stared at her blankly. 'Her interpretation of the Brahms ''Violin Concerto'' is second to none, you know. She won a competition with that piece.'

Emily's face flared hot as she realised that her mother was completely oblivious to the tension building around her.

'The violin?' Alessandro's face betrayed nothing but polite enquiry, but beneath the surface his mind was working overtime. Had he been hoist by his own petard? His plan had seemed audacious enough, but this family appeared intent on embroiling him in something even more ambitious. He glanced again at the girl her mother had called Miranda. Her provocative clothing and extravagantly made up face marked her out as a showgirl…but apparently she was a classical violinist. And then his gaze switched to the fresh-faced beauty he had come to see…the angel with the faintly flushed cheeks and the incredible jade-green eyes who masqueraded as a showgirl by night… To say the contrast intrigued him was putting it mildly. But what the hell was he getting himself into? Taking another look at Emily, he found he could not look away. He would have carried right on staring, too, had it not been for her sister's protestation providing him with a distraction.

'Oh, Mother, really,' Miranda said now, looking at Emily to back her up. 'Signor Bussoni doesn't want to hear about all that—Emily, say something.'

Emily, Alessandro mused, running the name over and over in his mind and loving its undulating form, its perfect proportions, its old English charm… Emily, Emily— Her mother fractured his musings with terrier-like determination.

'Emily won't stop me telling Signor Ferara all about your wonderful talent, Miranda. If no one speaks of it, how will you ever play that violin you so loved in Heidelberg?'

'Mother, please,' Emily cut in gently. 'I imagine Signor Bussoni's time is very precious. He's come here to talk about recording contracts for Miranda's band. I'm sure there will be other occasions when he can hear her play the violin.'

'Oh…' Mrs Weston hesitated, looking from one to the other in frustration.

'That would give me the greatest pleasure,' Alessandro agreed. 'But it was you I heard singing last night,' he stated confidently, turning to Emily, his bold gaze drenching her in the sort of heat she had only read about in novels.

'Emily took over for me because I caught a cold and lost

my voice,' Miranda confessed self-consciously. 'As a rule, no one can tell us apart.'

'I see,' Alessandro said, nodding thoughtfully as he studied Emily's face. He would have known her anywhere…even if there had been five more identical sisters lined up for his perusal.

Emily tried hard to meet his stare, but he disturbed her equilibrium in a profound and unsettling way.

'Singing is just a hobby for me,' she started to explain. 'You would have signed up the band right away if Miranda had been onstage—'

'Possibly,' Alessandro murmured, confining himself to that single word while his eyes spoke volumes about his doubt. He couldn't have cared less if Emily had a voice like a corncrake…and beauty was in the millimetre, he realised, as he filled his eyes, his mind and his soul with the face and form of a woman he desired like no other. Emily Weston was everything he wanted…everything he needed to set his plan in motion. No, much more than that, he realised, and only managed to drag his gaze away from her when the telephone shrilled and everyone but he made a beeline for the door.

'Let me,' Emily's father insisted calmly, easing his way through the scrum.

'Won't you sit down, Signor Bussoni?' Mrs Weston said awkwardly. 'Miranda, go and fetch the tea tray.'

'Do you mind if I—?' Swaying a little, Miranda stopped mid-sentence and passed a hand over her forehead.

'You've still got a fever. You really should go to bed,' Emily observed, taking hold of her twin's arm. 'You'll never get better if you don't rest. I'll see her upstairs,' she said, turning to her mother. 'If you'll excuse me for a moment, Signor Ferara?' she added to Alessandro. 'I'll come down and serve the tea,' she promised, ushering her sister out of the door. 'Just as soon as I see Miranda settled.'

'That won't be necessary.'

Alessandro's voice stopped Emily dead in her tracks.

'You're not going—' she said quickly…far too quickly, she realised immediately, noting the spark of interest in his eyes. Her heart thundered as he shot her an amused, quizzical look. 'Well, we haven't discussed the contract yet,' she said, attempting to make light of her eagerness for him to stay.

'Emily,' Miranda murmured weakly, 'I really think I should…'

'Of course,' Emily said, welcoming the distraction as she looped an arm around her sister's waist. 'Let's get you to bed.'

'Can I help?' Alessandro offered.

'That won't be necessary,' Emily said, urging her sister forward.

'Emily's right, Signor Bussoni,' Miranda murmured faintly. 'I'll feel better after a short rest. My sister has my full confidence. I am quite content for you to put your proposition to her.'

Alessandro answered with a brief dip of his head. 'I feel equally confident that your sister will find my proposal irresistible, Miss Weston.'

'I'm very grateful to you, Signor Bussoni,' Miranda replied as she stood for a moment, framed by the door, her carefully made-up face illuminated by an oblique shaft of late-afternoon sunlight.

Beautiful, Alessandro thought dispassionately, and if you stripped away the paint and glitter almost a carbon copy of her sister. But there was no attraction there. None at all. Not for him, at least.

'You will sort it out for me, won't you, Emily?' Miranda said anxiously as they left the room together.

'When have I ever let you down?' Emily teased gently as they started up the stairs.

'Never,' Miranda said softly, turning to give her sister a kiss.

Emily came back into the room to find Alessandro comfortably ensconced on the chintz-covered sofa, with her mother beside him chatting animatedly. But the moment she arrived his focus switched abruptly.

'Do you handle all your sister's business affairs?'

Emily prided herself on her ability to recognise exceptional adversaries on sight. And she was facing one right now, she warned herself. 'Not all,' she said carefully. She saw his eyes warm with amusement and knew he had her measure, too.

'Just contracts?' he pressed.

Emily's heart gave a wild little flutter, like a bird trapped in an enclosed space.

'We're not here to talk about me, Signor Bussoni—'

'Alessandro, please,' he said, embellishing the instruction with a small shrug intended to disarm, Emily guessed, as she watched her mother's eyes round in approval at what she clearly imagined was an enchanting display of Latin charm. But her mother had missed the shrewd calculation going on behind that stunning dark gold gaze, Emily thought, feeling her own body respond to the unmistakable masculine challenge.

'I'm sure you're very busy, Signor Bussoni,' she said, struggling to sound matter-of-fact with a heart that insisted on performing cartwheels in her chest. 'And it's the contract for Miranda's band you've come to discuss after all.'

'Correct,' he agreed.

His voice streamed over Emily's senses like melted fudge. How could a voice affect you like that? she wondered. Surely the cosy little room with its neatly papered walls had never housed such a dangerous sound as Alessandro Bussoni's deep, sexy drawl.

'It seems you and I have rather a lot to discuss, Miss Weston,' he said, reclaiming her attention. 'Far more, I must confess, than I had at first envisaged. I'll send my car for you at eight this evening.'

As he stood the room shrank around him.

'But surely you will stay for tea, Signor Bussoni—?'

'No—' Emily almost shouted at her mother. 'I'm sorry,' she said, instantly contrite. 'But Signor Bussoni must have other appointments—' was that a note of desperation creeping into her voice? She made a conscious effort to lower the pitch before adding, 'It's enough that he's making time to discuss Miranda's future tonight, Mother.'

He inclined his head to show his appreciation of her consideration.

'Until this evening, Miss Weston.'

'Signor Bussoni,' Emily returned with matching formality.

'Alessandro,' he prompted softly.

Emily felt her gaze drawn to dark, knowing eyes that seemed to reach behind her own and uncover the very core of her being. She felt deliciously ravished by them and immediately on guard, all in one and the same confusing moment.

A thrill ran through her as he lifted her hand and raised it to his lips. The contact was brief, but it was enough for her logical brain to be set adrift and her veins to run with sweet sensation. Then her father returned from his telephone call and she was able to take refuge behind the bustle of departure, easing into the background as Alessandro strode back down the path to his car.

Was he psychic? Emily wondered, as the unmistakable figure emerged from the grand entrance and came down the hotel steps at the precise moment the limousine she was arriving in swept to a halt outside.

Nothing would have surprised her about Alessandro Bussoni, Emily realised as he beat both the doorman and the chauffeur he had sent to collect her to the car door. As it swung open her mouth dried, and her body felt as if it was contracting in on itself in a last-ditch attempt to conceal anything remotely capricious in her appearance, though she had taken the precaution of wearing an understated navy blue suit with a demure knee-length skirt.

'Welcome, Miss Weston,' he said, reaching into the limousine to help her out.

Or to stop her escaping? Emily thought in a moment of sheer panic when his fingers closed over her hand.

'Please. Call me Emily,' she managed pleasantly enough, while her thought processes stalled.

Precaution, my foot! She should have worn a full protective body suit...with ski gloves, she reasoned maniacally, as a flash of heat shot up her arm. What was she thinking? The first rule of business was to keep everything cordial but formal. And here she was, unbending already as if she was on a date! Gathering herself quickly, she removed her hand from his clasp at the first opportunity.

'I must apologise for not coming to pick you up in person, Miss Weston,' Alessandro said, standing back to allow her to precede him through the swing doors.

Emily made some small dismissive sound in reply, and was glad of the distraction provided by a doorman in a top hat who insisted on ushering her into the hotel. But she was so busy trying to keep a respectable distance from her host she almost missed his next statement.

'I wanted to come myself, but there were some matters of State I was forced to attend to: matters that demanded my immediate attention—'

'Matters of State?' Emily repeated curiously. But it was hard to concentrate on what he was saying when they were attracting so much interest.

When the first flashbulb flared she glanced round, imagining some celebrity was in view. But then she realised that the cameras were pointing their way, and a small posse of photographers seemed to be following them across the lobby.

She smiled uncertainly as she tried to keep up with

Alessandro's brisk strides. 'It must be a quiet night for them,' she suggested wryly.

'What? Oh, the photographers,' he said, seeming to notice their presence for the first time. 'I'm sorry. You get so used to them you hardly know they're around.'

Having seen a pack of photographers waiting around on the night of the charity event, snapping away at anything and everything, even the spectacularly ornate heels on one woman's shoes, Emily took it for granted that hotels of this calibre attracted the attention of the world's media as a matter of course.

'I suppose they have to do something while they're waiting for the main event to arrive.'

'Main event?' Alessandro quizzed as he broke step to look at her.

'You know…personalities, showbiz people, that sort of thing.'

He pressed his lips together and he gave her an ironic smile, his dark eyes sparkling with amusement. 'I guess you're right. I'd never thought of that. It must get pretty boring for them…all the hanging around.'

But it wasn't just the photographers, Emily thought. She couldn't help noticing all the other people staring as Alessandro ushered her across the vast, brilliantly lit reception area.

Hardly surprising, she decided, shooting a covert glance at her companion. He was off the scale in the gorgeous male stakes. His dark suit was so uncomplicated, so beautifully cut, it could only have come from one of the very best tailors…yet somehow the precision tailoring only served to point up his rampant masculinity. His crisp, cotton shirt, in a shade of ice blue, was a perfect foil for his bronzed skin, and somehow managed to make eyes that were already incredible all the brighter, all the keener—

She looked away, knowing she would have to pull herself together if the evening was to fulfil its purpose as a business rather than a social occasion. 'Matters of State?' she repeated firmly, determined not to let him off the hook.

She was rewarded with a low, sexy laugh that revealed nothing except for the fact that she was fooling herself if she imagined that she would be able to overlook the power of his charm for one single moment.

At a small, private lift, tucked away out of sight from the main lobby, she watched as he keyed in a series of numbers. Heavy doors slid silently open and then sealed them inside a plush, mirrored interior. There was even a small upholstered seat in the corner should you require it, Emily noted with interest, and apart from the emergency intercom a telephone for those urgent calls between floors. The only users of this exclusive space would be pretty exclusive themselves, she deduced with a thoughtful stare at her companion.

'You didn't answer my question yet,' she prompted.

'I've taken the liberty of ordering a light supper to be delivered to us later.'

He might have said it pleasantly enough, but the effect was offset by a flinty stare that suggested that he alone would direct the course of their conversation.

Alessandro knew he was in for a rocky ride the moment he saw the defensive shields go up in Emily's eyes. And no wonder she thought him harsh. He was struggling to reclaim control of a situation that was slipping away from him as fast and as comprehensively as sand through a sieve. Logically, all he had to do was bring her to the point where she would sign the contract drawn up by his lawyers, but she had turned everything on its head, this woman he felt such a crazy compulsion to woo.

'Rather than go out to eat I thought it better that we devote ourselves entirely to the matter in hand,' he said, hoping to placate her. The last thing he wanted was to explain what this was about in a lift!

'You said something about matters of State earlier,' Emily pressed doggedly, 'and, if you remember, I asked—'

Words had always been the most effective weapon in her armoury, but where Alessandro Bussoni Ferara was concerned they seemed utterly ineffectual. Emily was starting to seethe with exasperation.

'So, what's this?'

In the split second between her lunge to grab his wrist and Alessandro's reaction to it Emily knew she had made her biggest mistake. What on earth was she doing, assaulting a strange man in a lift, snatching hold of him, grabbing on tight to the gold signet ring on his little finger? And why was he allowing her to hang on to him, even though he was twice her size and could have moved away from her in an instant? Worse still, the flesh beneath her sensitive fingertips felt warm and smooth and supple— She blinked, and recovered herself fast, removing her hand self-consciously from his fist where it had somehow become entangled.

'It's my family crest,' he volunteered evenly. 'Does that satisfy your curiosity?'

No! Not nearly! 'Your crest?' she said curiously.

His whip-fast retaliation left Emily with no time to hide the cufflinks on her own white tailored shirtsleeves.

'Shall we start with your explanation for these?' he countered smoothly, bringing her wrist up.

The sheer power in his grip was impossible to resist. But Emily found she didn't want to, and incredibly, was softening. 'That's my—'

'Yes?' he pressed remorselessly.

'My cufflinks are engraved with the crest of my Inn of Court,' she admitted, averting her face.

'Ah,' he murmured, as if pleased to hear his suspicions confirmed. 'Barrister?'

Emily nodded tensely. 'And you?'

Now it all made sense, Alessandro realised—the tasselled sack to hold her robes and wig, the pull-along airline case to transport her briefs, along with all the other papers she would have to carry around…the severe cut of the restrained outfit she wore to court beneath her gown hanging up in her dressing room at the hotel while she sang that night, the only nod to feminine sexuality displayed in the power heels of her plain black court shoes—

'This is our floor,' he said as the lift slowed.

Another evasion! Controlling herself with difficulty, Emily hunted for something…anything…to derail her mounting irritation—unfortunately, the first thing she hit upon was how well the light, floral perfume she had chosen to wear mingled with Alessandro's much warmer scent of sandalwood and spice, and that didn't help at all! As the lift doors opened she sprang to attention, noticing that he stood well back to let her pass. Now she registered disappointment. Disappointment that he didn't yank her straight back inside the intimate lift space, close the doors and make it stop somewhere between floors…for a very long time indeed.

'Emily? Did you hear me?'

Refocusing fast, she saw that he had already opened the arched mahogany double doors to his suite and was beckoning her inside.

'I'm sorry—'

'I said,' he repeated, 'would you care for a glass of champagne?'

'Oh, no, thank you. Orange juice will be fine until we conclude our business.'

'And then champagne?'

'I didn't say that, Signor Bussoni—'

'Alessandro.'

'Alessandro,' Emily conceded. 'And when our business is concluded I will be leaving.'

'Whatever you like,' he agreed evenly. 'I've no wish to tangle with lawyers in my free time.'

The throwaway line ran a second bolt of disappointment through her. She would have to be under anaesthetic not to register the fact that Alessandro Bussoni was a hugely desirable male. It was time to tighten the bolts on her chastity belt, Emily told herself firmly, if she had a hope in hell of being ready for what promised to be a tough round of business negotiations.

And she would deal with the lazy appraisal he was giving her now how, exactly?

She only realised how tense she had become when Alessandro turned away to pour them both a glass of freshly squeezed orange juice and each of her muscles unclenched in turn. Keep it cool, Emily warned herself silently. Cool and impersonal. It's only business after all...

CHAPTER THREE

LEAVING her handbag on the pale, grey-veined surface of a marble-topped console table, Emily dragged in a deep, steadying breath as she took in her surroundings.

The hotel room was decorated in English country house style, but at its most extreme, its most sumptuous: a symphony of silks, cashmere, damask and print. And Alessandro's accommodation wasn't just larger than the usual suite, it was positively palatial. In fact, Emily guessed the whole of her parents' house would fit comfortably into the elegant drawing room where they were now holding their conversation—a room that at a rough estimate she judged to be around forty feet in length.

'Not very cosy, is it?'

His voice startled her, even though it was pitched at little more than a murmur.

'Sorry?' she said, turning around.

'This room,' Alessandro said, holding her gaze as he carried the juice over to her.

'It's very—'

'Yes?' he said, noticing how studiously she avoided touching his hand as he passed her the crystal glass.

'Well…' Emily chose her words carefully. She didn't want to cause offence—maybe he loved this style. 'It tries very hard—'

'—to condense all the flavours of your country into a single room in order to impress the well-heeled tourist?' he supplied, looking at her with amusement over the top of his glass.

'Well, yes,' Emily said, discovering that a smile had edged on to her own lips. 'How did you guess? That's my

35

opinion exactly.' Nerves were making her facial muscles capricious, unpredictable…and somehow she found herself smiling up at him again.

'Let's hold our meeting somewhere more…snug,' Alessandro suggested. 'Don't look so alarmed,' he said, shooting her a wolfish grin that failed entirely if it was meant to reassure her. Thrusting a thumb through the belt-loop of his black trousers, he slouched comfortably on one hip to put his glass down on the table. 'My bedroom can hardly be described as snug—it's almost as large as this room. Fortunately there are two bedrooms, and I've had the smaller of the two turned into an office for the duration of my stay.'

'I see,' Emily said, watching him extract some documents from the folder on the table and wondering why all she could register was how tanned, and very capable his hands were—

'Daydreaming again, Emily?'

'I beg your pardon?'

'And I beg you to pay attention when I ask you if you would care to join me in my office—so that our meeting can begin.'

His tone was amused—tolerant. And her expression must have been blank and dreamy, Emily realised, hurriedly adopting an alert look.

'Shall I lead the way?'

Retrieving her handbag, Emily hurried after him, but as he opened the door to the next room, and stopped beside it to let her pass, she juddered to a halt. The remaining space inside the doorframe was small…too small.

The difference in size between them seemed huge, suddenly, though it was his aura of confident masculinity that was his most alluring feature, Emily thought as she skirted past him. 'Very impressive,' she managed huskily, pretending interest in all the high-tech gizmos assembled for his use in the skilfully converted bedroom.

'Why don't you sit over there?' he suggested, pointing towards a leather button-backed seat to one side of a huge mahogany desk.

Perching primly on the edge, Emily watched in fascination as Alessandro sat or rather sprawled on his own chair with all the innate elegance of a lean and hungry tiger.

'Would you care to open the discussion?' he invited.

Folding her hands neatly in her lap, Emily attempted to sweep her mind clear of anything but the facts. 'Well, as you know, I'm here to secure the best possible deal for my sister's band—'

'For your sister, primarily?'

'Well, yes, of course, but—'

'Miranda needs the money a recording contract will bring her in order to buy a rather special violin and to complete her training, is that correct?'

'That's putting it rather crudely.'

'How else would you put it, Emily? What I want to know is, what's in it for me?'

'Surely that was self-evident when you saw the band perform. They're excellent—'

'Without you?' he cut in abruptly. 'How do I know what they'll be like? What if I said I'd sign the band if you remained as lead singer?'

'I'm afraid my obligations at work would not permit—'

'Ah, yes,' he cut in smoothly. 'I'll come to that later. But for now let's consider your proposal regarding the recording contract for your sister. How does she intend to fulfil both her commitment to the record company and to her tutor at the music conservatoire?'

'I'm here to ensure that whatever contract she signs allows her to do both—for the first year at least.'

'And then she will drop the band?' Alessandro suggested shrewdly.

'She will fulfil all her contractual obligations,' Emily stated firmly. 'I can assure you of that.'

'As well as put in the necessary practice hours to become a top-class international soloist? Somehow I doubt it,' he said, embroidering the comment with a slanting, sceptical look.

'You clearly have no experience of what it's like to strive to achieve something so far out of reach,' Emily said, over-ruling her cautious professional persona in defence of her sister, 'that most people would give up before they had even started.'

'Perhaps you're right—'

'Many artistes are forced to take other jobs to pay their way through college,' she continued passionately, barely registering Alessandro's silent nod of agreement.

'Not just musicians or artistes—'

But Emily was too far down the road either to notice his comment or to hold back. 'You're making assumptions that have no grounds in fact,' she flung at him accusingly.

'And you're not even listening to me,' Alessandro replied evenly, 'so how do you know what I think?'

'You've already decided she can't handle both commitments,' Emily said, realising she hadn't felt this unsteady since delivering her first seminar as a rookie law student. 'Right now, Miranda's not feeling well. But as soon as she's feeling better I know she'll do everything she says she will.'

'You say—'

'Yes, I say,' Emily said heatedly. 'I know my sister better than you…better than anyone—' She broke off, suddenly aware that all the professional expertise in the world was of no use to her while her emotions were engaged to this extent.

'I'm sure you're right,' Alessandro agreed quietly, showing no sign of following her down the same turbulent path. 'But why on earth choose a band as a way of making money? Why not find it some other way?'

Emily made an impatient gesture as she shook her head

at him. 'Because she's a musician, Alessandro. That's what she does.'

'A cabaret singer?'

'What's wrong with that?'

As he shrugged, Emily guessed every stereotypical piece of nonsense that had ever been conceived around nightclub singers was swirling through his brain.

'Miranda makes an honest living,' she said defensively. 'Would you rather she gave it up…gave up all her ambitions…just to satisfy the prejudice of misguided individuals?'

Alessandro confined himself to a lengthy stare of good-humoured tolerance, and then held up his hands when a knock came at the door just as Emily was getting into her stride. 'Excuse me, Emily. I won't be a moment.'

As Alessandro left her Emily felt a warning prickle start behind her eyes. No one had ever made her lose her temper like this before…not once. She hadn't ever come close. Plunging her hand into her handbag, she dug around for some tissues, then rammed them away out of sight again when he came back.

'Come on, Emily,' he said, staying by the door. 'Supper's arrived.'

'I think I'd better go.' She resorted to hiding her face in a hastily contrived search for the door keys in her handbag.

'After supper,' Alessandro insisted as he held out his hand to her.

Was she meant to take it? Emily wondered as she stared up at him in surprise.

'Come,' he repeated patiently.

It was tempting. Maybe supper would give her a chance to relax, regroup, gather what remained of her scattered wits. She was here for Miranda, wasn't she? And the job she had come to do wasn't nearly finished. Eating was harmless…civilised. Lots of deals were cut over power breakfasts and business lunches; she'd done it herself on numerous occasions.

Romantic suppers?

Muffling the tiny voice of reason in her head, Emily convinced herself that the meal was nothing more than a brief interlude, a welcome break that would give her the chance to get her professional head screwed on ready for the discussions to come. But when she walked back into the first room she saw that a great deal more than a light snack awaited her.

'When you said supper, I imagined...' Her voice tailed off as she surveyed the incredible feast that had been laid out for them along the whole length of a highly polished mahogany table.

'Aren't you hungry?' Alessandro demanded, cruising along the table, grazing as he went. 'I know I am.'

She tried not to notice the way he seemed to be making love with his mouth to a chocolate-tipped strawberry.

'You can eat what you want when you want,' he said, sucking off the last scrap of chocolate with relish. 'And we can keep on talking while you do,' he added, his curving half-smile reaching right through her armour-plated reserve to stroke each erotic zone in turn. 'Would you like me to make a few suggestions?'

Withdrawing the plundered stalk from between his strong white teeth, he deposited it neatly on a side-plate.

Emily forced her mouth shut, but kept right on staring at him.

'Food?' Alessandro offered with an innocent shrug as he cocked his head to one side to look at her.

'That's fine, I can manage,' Emily said, almost snatching one of the white porcelain plates from his hands.

'Shrimp, *signorina*?'

'Don't you ever take no for an answer?'

The look he gave her sent a flame of awareness licking through every inch of her body.

'Relax, Emily. I deliver what I promise—just a light snack, in this instance.'

'I'm perfectly relaxed, thank you,' Emily retorted, concentrating on making her selection from the platters of delicious-looking salads...a selection she was making with unaccustomed clumsiness, thanks to the route her thoughts were taking.

Was it her fault that those beautifully sculpted lips provided a rather different example of a tasty snack...or that stubble-darkened jaw? Not to mention the expanse of hard chest she supposed must reside beneath his superior-quality jacket and shirt—and, talking of superior quality, what about the muscle-banded stomach concealed beneath that slim black leather belt? Distractedly, she spilled half a bowl of coleslaw on top of the mountain of food she seemed to have absent-mindedly collected on her plate.

'I don't think the pudding will fit,' Alessandro pointed out, removing a serving spoon holding a heaped portion of sherry trifle from her hand.

'Of c-course not,' Emily stammered, while the erotic mind games kept right on playing—ignoring her most strenuous efforts to put all thoughts of whipped cream and tanned torsos out of bounds.

When later she found herself drawn towards a tower of honey-coloured choux balls drizzled with chocolate, he asked, 'Do you like chocolate, Emily?'

'I love it. Why?' she said suspiciously.

Alessandro shrugged as he piled some profiteroles onto a plate, adding some extra chocolate sauce and pouring cream for her. 'We have a chocolate festival in Ferara every year; free chocolate is handed out all over the city. We even have a chocolate museum—you should make time to see it.' As he handed her the plate his amused golden gaze scanned her face. 'What do you say?'

'Thank you.' Was she accepting an invitation to consume a plate of delectable pudding, or something rather more?

'Imagine this, Emily—a thousand kilos of delicious chocolate sculpted into a work of art before your very eyes; artists coming from all over Europe to compete for a prize for the best design—'

He turned to pour them both a steaming cup of strong dark coffee from an elegant silver pot.

'Clean sheets are placed underneath each block so that the onlookers can help themselves to slivers as they watch—' He stopped, and stared straight into her eyes, his expressive mouth tugging up in a grin. 'Well?'

Emily's pulse-rate doubled. 'No cream, no sugar,' she blurted, certain he intended to provoke her—a chocolate festival, for goodness' sake!'

Murmuring her thanks as he pressed the coffee cup into her hand, she glanced up, only to encounter a dangerous gaze alive with laughter. She was right to be wary, she realised, looking away fast.

But thankfully this was his final sally, and he allowed her to finish her meal in peace. When they returned to his luxurious bedroom-turned-office, he kept the lights soothing and low as he slipped a CD into the music centre.

Emily smiled. Brahms, she realised, surprised he had remembered her mother mentioning Miranda's competition piece.

He poured champagne and brought two crystal flutes across before settling himself down on the opposite sofa.

'Better?' he murmured, watching her drink. 'Do you mind if I take my jacket off?' he added, loosening a couple more buttons at the neck of his shirt.

'Not at all,' Emily said, forgetting her pledge to keep champagne celebrations until later as she watched him ease up from the chair to slip off a jacket lined with crimson silk. Freeing a pair of heavy gold cufflinks from his shirt, he dropped them onto the table and rolled up his sleeves to reveal powerful forearms shaded with dark hair. There couldn't have been a more striking contrast to the type of pasty-faced executive she was accustomed to dealing with.

'So, Emily,' he challenged, eyes glinting as he caught her staring at him. 'Do you still think I'm one of those misguided individuals you referred to?'

For his opinion of cabaret singers, yes; where everything else was concerned—

'I take it from your expression that you do.'

His smile had vanished.

'Let's get one thing straight between us before we go any further. I don't give a damn what people do, as long as they're not hurting anyone else in the process. But I do care about motives—what makes people tick. What makes you tick, Emily?'

Racing to put her brain back in gear, the best she could manage was a few mangled sounds.

'Barrister by day,' he went on smoothly, 'moonlighting as a cabaret singer by night. There's no harm in that, if you can cope with the workload. And it's even more to your credit that you were moonlighting to help your sister out of a fix. What is not to your credit, however, is the fact that you intended to deceive me. Why was that, Emily?'

'I admit things got out of hand—'

The lame remark was rewarded by a cynical stare.

'You really thought you could pull this off?' he demanded incredulously. 'What kind of a fool did you take me for?'

Emily's face burned scarlet as she struggled with an apology. 'I didn't know you—I'm really sorry. I didn't think—'

Alessandro held up his hands, silencing her. 'As it happens, you're not the only one who hasn't been entirely straightforward.'

'Meaning?'

'Let's consider this plan of yours first.'

'My plan?' It was clear he was on a mission to tease out

her motives whilst taking care not to reveal any of his own, Emily realised.

'Amongst your misconceptions is the notion that your sister's crazy scheme is actually going to work.'

'Will you help her or not?'

'Without my co-operation your sister will never play the instrument she has set her heart upon.'

'What do you mean?' Emily said anxiously, finding it impossible to sit down a moment longer.

Stretching his arms out across the back of the sofa, Alessandro tipped his head to look at her. 'Why don't you sit down again, Emily?' he suggested calmly. 'You do want to help your sister, don't you? You do want her to be able to play that violin she saw in the instrument maker's shop near the castle in Heidelberg?'

Emily could feel the blood draining out of her face as she stared at him. 'How do you know about that?' she said in a whisper.

'I make it my business to know everything relevant to a case before I enter into any negotiation,' he said steadily. 'I never leave anything to chance.'

Emily's professional pride might have suffered a direct hit, but the only thing that mattered was Miranda's future… But what was Alessandro Bussoni really after? Why had he gone to so much trouble? And how did he come to have such a hold over a German violin maker?

'The violin in Heidelberg—' she began, but her voice faltered as she remembered Miranda playing the beautiful old instrument. 'What did you mean when you said that my sister might never get to play it?'

'Without my co-operation,' Alessandro reminded her, his expression masked in shade.

'I don't understand.'

'Sit down again, Emily. Please.'

'I think you owe me an explanation first.'

'The particular instrument you refer to is a museum piece

almost beyond price. It was being displayed by one of to-day's most celebrated instrument makers—'

'*Was* being displayed?' Emily asked. 'Why are you talking about it in the past tense?'

'Because it's no longer there,' he said evenly.

'You mean it's gone back to the museum?' Relief and regret merged in the question.

'Not exactly.'

'What, then?' Her look demanded he answer her fully this time.

But Alessandro still said nothing, and just stared at some point over her left shoulder.

Slowly Emily turned around, her eyes widening when she saw what he was looking at. A beautifully upholstered taupe suede viewing seat was angled to face a large entertainment system. Nestled in the corner of the unusual triangular-shaped seat rested a violin, propped up between two cream silk cushions. 'Should it be out of its case?' she mumbled foolishly, sinking down on the sofa again.

'I imagine that's the only way it's ever going to be played,' Alessandro said, levelling a long, steady gaze at her.

Emily's heart was thundering so fast she could hardly breathe. She had to turn round to take another look, just to make sure she wasn't dreaming—to prove to herself that she really was in the same room as the violin Miranda had played in Heidelberg.

'But you told me it was a museum piece—beyond price,' she said, not caring that her battered emotions were now plainly on show. 'I don't understand.'

'Everything has its price Emily,' Alessandro said with a small shrug as he regarded her coolly.

He was waiting. For what? For her to say something? But how could she when her brain had stalled with shock and her whole body was quivering from some force beyond her control? To make matters worse, Emily couldn't rid herself of the idea that she too was a prize exhibit—and with a rather large price tag dangling over her nose.

'You bought it?' she managed finally.

'I bought it,' Alessandro confirmed.

'But why on earth—?'

'As a bargaining counter.'

'A bargaining counter?' Emily spluttered incredulously. 'What are you talking about?'

'Will you allow me to explain?'

Emily clenched and unclenched her hands. She didn't like the look on his face one bit. 'I think you better had,' she agreed stiffly, feeling as if she was clinging to Miranda's dream by just her fingertips now.

'It would be far better for your sister if she had enough money to continue her studies without the distraction of working with the band.'

'Well, of course,' Emily agreed. 'But—'

Alessandro's imperious gesture cut her off. 'Let me finish, please. It would be better still if she could have the use of that violin behind you—'

'Is this before or after she wins the Lottery?' Emily demanded, rattled by his composure.

'What if I told you that I am prepared to give the violin to your sister…on permanent loan?'

A thundering silence took hold of the space between them—until Alessandro's voice sliced through it like a blade. 'Well, Emily, what do you say?'

'What would she have to do for that?' Emily demanded suspiciously.

'Your sister? Nothing at all.' Alessandro's mouth firmed as he waited for Emily's thought processes to crest the shock he had just given her and get back up to speed.

Emily's eyes clouded with apprehension as her brain cells jostled back into some semblance of order. 'What would *I* have to do?'

A smile slowly curled around Alessandro's lips, then

died again. She was so bright…so vulnerable. It was as if he had spied some rare flower, moments too late to prevent his foot crushing the life out of it.

Standing up, he crossed the room. He needed time to think…but there was none. Opening a door, he reached inside the small cloakroom where he had been keeping the flowers. He had ordered the extravagant bouquet to seal their bargain. As he grabbed hold of them he realised that his hand was shaking. He paused a beat to consider what he should do. He could ram them in the wastebin, where they belonged, or he could keep on with the charade…

Turning to face Emily, he held out the huge exotic floral arrangement. There was real hope in his eyes, and a sudden tenderness to his hard mouth.

'I'm sorry, Emily, I meant to give these to you earlier.' She looked so wary, and Alessandro knew he was the cause. What had started out as a straightforward business transaction had developed into something so much more. If Emily Weston accepted his proposal he would be the luckiest man in Ferara… No—the world, he thought, trying to second-guess her reaction.

'For what?' Emily said, glad to have the opportunity to bury her face deep out of sight amongst the vivid blooms as he handed them to her. 'I've never seen such a fabulous display,' she admitted, forced to pull her face out again when they began to tickle her nose.

'For agreeing to become my wife,' Alessandro said softly.

For a full ten seconds neither of them seemed to breathe, and then Emily whispered tensely, 'Are you mad?'

Alessandro's rational self gave a wry smile, and told him she might be right. But thirty generations of accumulated pride in Ferara insisted that no woman in her right mind would refuse the opportunity to become princess of that land.

'Not as far as I am aware,' he said coolly.

'I think you must be.'

'I said I had a proposition for you. I made no secret of it.'

'Yes, a recording contract…for my sister—from Prince Records,' Emily said, thrusting the bouquet away from her as if she felt that by accepting it she was in some way endorsing Alessandro's plunge into the realms of fantasy.

'I have no connection whatever with any company called Prince Records,' he said, brushing some imagined lint from the lapel of his jacket.

'What?'

'You assumed I was a recording executive,' he elaborated. 'I allowed you to go on believing that…while it suited me.'

'I see,' Emily said, finding it difficult to breathe. 'And now?'

'The deception is no longer necessary,' Alessandro admitted. 'Because I have something you want and you have something I want. It's time to cut a deal.'

Emily felt as if her veins had been infused with ice. She might be twenty-eight and unmarried, but when her prince came along she wanted more than a business deal to seal their union…she wanted love, passion, tenderness and a lifetime's commitment—not a charter of convenience to close a cold and cynical deal. 'So, who the hell are you?' she demanded furiously.

'Crown Prince Alessandro Bussoni di Ferara,' he said. 'I know it's rather a mouthful—Emily?'

Snapping her mouth shut again, Emily whacked the bouquet into his arms. 'Take your damn flowers back! My sister might be in a vulnerable position right now, but let me assure you, Alessandro, I'm not.'

'Your sister put herself in this position—'

'How dare you judge her?' Emily flared, springing to her feet to glare up at him. 'You don't have the remotest idea how hard she works!'

Alessandro felt as if he had been struck by a thunderbolt, and it had nothing to do with the fact that no one—absolutely no one—had ever addressed him in this furious manner in all his life before.

Just seeing Emily now, her eyes blazing and her hair flung back, her face alive with passion, intelligence and a truckload of determination, he felt a desperate urge to direct that passion into something that would give them both a lot more pleasure than arguing about her sister.

Was he falling in love? Could it be possible? Or was he already in love? Alessandro forced a lid on the well of joy that threatened to erupt and call him a liar for wearing such a set and stony expression in response to her outburst, when all he wanted to do was to drag her into his arms and kiss the breath out of her body. Had the thunderbolt struck the first moment he saw her, commanding that gaudily decorated stage...putting the harsh spotlights to shame with her luminous beauty—a beauty that had refused to stay hidden even under what had seemed to him at the time to be half a bucket of greasepaint?

'If you'll excuse me, I'll go and call my car for you,' he said steadily, revealing nothing of his thoughts. 'I can see you're upset right now. We will discuss this tomorrow, when you are feeling calmer—'

'Don't waste your time!' Emily snapped defensively.

'With your permission,' Alessandro said, swooping to retrieve the discarded bouquet from the floor by her feet, 'I'll have these couriered to your mother.'

'Do what the hell you want with them!'

But as she calmed down in the limousine taking her safely home through the damply glittering streets, Emily was forced to accept that without financial assistance Miranda would never achieve her full potential. A grant might be found to cover her lessons with the Japanese violin professor, but no one was going to stump up the funds necessary to buy her a violin of real quality.

But how could marriage to a stranger provide the answer? She gave her head an angry shake, then began to frown as she turned Alessandro's preposterous suggestion over in her mind. With the right controls in place it might be possible…it would certainly secure Miranda's future.

The ball was in Alessandro's court. If he was serious he wouldn't be put off by her first refusal; he would be back in touch with a firm proposition very soon… *Very soon.* How long was that? Emily wondered, feeling a thrill of anticipation race through her.

CHAPTER FOUR

EMILY'S family sat in a closely knit group on the sofa in front of her, their faces frozen with disbelief.

'And so we'll all board Alessandro's private jet and fly out to Ferara for the wedding,' Emily finished calmly.

Her mother recovered first. Glancing at the vivid floral display that took up most of the front window, she turned back again to Emily, her face tense with suppressed excitement. 'Are you quite sure about this?'

'Quite sure, Mother.'

'No,' Miranda said decisively. 'I can't let you do this for me.'

But as Miranda cradled the precious violin in her arms it appeared to Emily as if the wonderful old instrument had finally come home.

'Believe me, you can,' she said firmly, turning next to her father. 'Dad? Don't you have anything you'd like to say?'

Her father made a sound of exasperation as he wiped a blunt-fingered hand across his forehead. 'I've never understood this romance business. I just knew your mother was right for me and asked her to marry me. She accepted and that was it.'

'You can't mean you approve of this, Dad?' Miranda burst out, distracted from her minute inspection of the violin. 'Just because it worked for you and Mum doesn't mean it's right for Emily. She doesn't even know this Alessandro Bussoni—'

'Well, I only got to know your father in the first year,' their mother pointed out. 'And Alessandro's a prince.'

As Miranda groaned and rolled her eyes heavenwards, her father made his excuses.

'I have work to finish if we're all going off on this jaunt next week.'

'A jaunt?' Miranda exclaimed, watching him hurry out of the room. 'Doesn't Dad know how serious this is?'

'Alessandro has given me a cast-iron contract,' Emily said calmly. 'I've read it through carefully and even had it double-checked in Chambers.'

'And you're sure that Miranda's fees will be paid in full?'

Miranda flashed a look of dismay at her mother. 'Mother, really!'

Emily put a restraining hand on her sister's arm. 'Fees, as well as a grant, Mother, plus an indefinite loan of the violin.'

'And the only way Alessandro's elderly father can abdicate is if Alessandro marries you?'

'That's right, Mother. You see, we need each other.'

In spite of her bold assurances, Emily wondered if she really was quite sane. She could recall every nuance of Alessandro's telephone call—the call that had come through almost the moment she'd walked into her apartment after their meeting. He had signed off the deal with a generosity beyond anything she could have anticipated. At least, those were the tactics he had employed to make her change her mind, she amended silently. Tactics. She rolled the cold little word around her mind, wishing there could have been more—wishing she could have detected even the slightest tinge of warmth or enthusiasm in Alessandro's voice when he'd upped his offer to ensure her agreement. But it had been just a list of commitments he was prepared to make in exchange for her hand in marriage. He might have been reading from a list—perhaps he had been, Emily thought, trying to concentrate on what her sister was saying.

'And all you have to do is marry some stranger,' Miranda exclaimed contemptuously.

'Don't be like that,' Emily said softly.

Miranda made a sound of disgust. 'Well, I think you've all gone completely mad.'

Emily might have agreed, even smiled to hear the word she had so recently flung at Alessandro echoed by her sister, but noticing how Miranda held the violin a little closer while she spoke only firmed her resolve. 'This marriage lasts just long enough to allow Alessandro's father to abdicate in his favour and Miranda to complete her studies with Professor Iwamoto. That's it. Then it's over. So don't any of you start building castles in the air—'

'Castles,' her mother breathed, clapping her hands together as she gazed blissfully forward into the future. 'Who'd have thought it?'

'I'll make it work. I have to,' Emily said, when she was alone in her bedroom with Miranda later that day. 'I've got nothing to lose—'

'You've got everything to lose!' Miranda argued passionately. 'You might fall in love with Alessandro, and then what?'

'I'm twenty-eight and have managed to avoid any serious romantic entanglements so far.'

'Only because you're a workaholic and no one remotely like Alessandro has ever crossed your path before,' Miranda exclaimed impatiently. 'What are you going to do if you fall in love with him? He's one gorgeous-looking man—'

'Which makes it all the easier to keep the relationship on a professional level,' Emily cut in, seizing on the potential for disappointment. 'He's bound to be spoiled, selfish, inconsiderate and self-obsessed. Just the type of man I have always found so easy to resist.'

'And what if you get pregnant?' Miranda persisted.

'Absolutely no chance of that.'

'Now you do have to be kidding. You'll never be able to resist him. And Alessandro looks like one fertile guy—'

'It's never going to happen without sex.'

'What?' Miranda stared blankly at her.

'I've had it written into the contract,' Emily said, congratulating herself on her foresight. 'It seemed like a sensible precaution. And it saves any embarrassment for either party.'

'"It saves any embarrassment for either party",' Miranda mimicked, trying not to laugh. 'Get real! You'll never know what you're missing.'

'Exactly,' Emily confirmed. 'And I intend to go back to work when all this is over, so I don't need any distractions.'

'Alessandro isn't a distraction; he's a lifetime's obsession,' Miranda pointed out dreamily.

'Maybe,' Emily conceded. 'But he'll want out of this contract as much as I will do. Don't go making Mother's mistake and reading more into it than there is. This is a straightforward business deal that suits both of us. It's a merger, not a marriage.'

'Then I'm sorry for you,' Miranda said softly. 'For Alessandro, too. And it makes me feel so guilty—'

'Don't,' Emily said fiercely, clutching her sister's arm. 'Don't use that word. You have to support me, Miranda. It's too late to back out now. I've already arranged to take a career break. Just think—I'll be able to pay off my mortgage with Alessandro's divorce settlement, so you're helping me to achieve my dream, too.'

'In that case, I guess we're in this together,' Miranda said, pulling a resigned face.

'Just like always,' Emily admitted, forcing a bright note into her voice as she tried not to care that her marriage to Alessandro was doomed before it even began.

'Like for ever,' Miranda agreed, on the same note as her

twin. But her face was full of concern as she looked beyond Emily's determined front and saw the truth hovering behind her sister's eyes.

It was a beautiful summer's evening of the type rarely seen in England. The milky blue sky was deepening steadily to indigo, and it was still warm enough to sit out on the hotel balcony in comfort. The uniqueness of the weather was perfectly in accord with the mood of the occasion, Emily mused as she watched Alessandro come back to her with two slender crystal flutes of champagne. The business of signing the contract was over, and now it was time to celebrate a most unusual deal.

A little shiver ran through her as she took the glass. Marriage to a man like Alessandro would have been an intoxicating prospect whatever his condition in life... If there had only been the smallest flicker of romance—but there was none.

'To us,' he murmured, breaking into her thoughts with the most inappropriate toast she could imagine.

'To our mutual satisfaction,' Emily amended, only to find herself qualifying that pledge when she saw the look on his face. 'With the outcome of our agreement,' she clarified.

'Ah, yes, our agreement,' Alessandro repeated with a faint smile. 'It may not have been spelled out to you exactly, but you will be entitled to keep the title of Principessa if you so wish... Emily?'

'That's really not important—'

'Not important?'

She could see she had offended him. 'Look, I'm sorry. I—'

His dismissive gesture cut her off. Turning his back, he stared out across the rapidly darkening cityscape. 'Once we are married the title is yours for life, whether or not you choose to use it.'

'I will have done nothing to earn that right,' Emily protested edgily.

'Don't be so sure,' Alessandro countered, spearing her with a glance. 'There are bound to be difficulties before you settle into the role.'

'Please don't worry about me, Alessandro. I'm quite capable of looking after myself.'

Emily was convinced that she was right, but she hadn't reckoned with the speed with which Alessandro would put the plan into operation. By the end of the week even travel arrangements had been finalised. Emily and her family would fly to Ferara in Alessandro's private jet while he remained in London to conclude his business dealings there.

As the day of departure drew closer, the speed of change in Emily's life began gathering pace at a rate she couldn't control. It felt as if the carefully crafted existence she had built for herself was being steadily unpicked, stitch by intricate stitch. The first warning sign was when a young couple arrived unannounced to take her measurements and speak in reverent terms of Brussels lace and Shantung silk, Swiss embroidery and pearls. At that point Emily realised that if she didn't put her foot down she would have little to say even about the style of her own wedding dress. As if to confirm her suspicions, just a couple of days later clothes began arriving at her apartment—without anything being ordered as far as she was aware—as well as boxes of shoes by the trunkload.

Feeling presumptuous, almost as if she was attempting to contact someone she hardly knew, she picked up the telephone to call Alessandro at his London office.

She was so surprised when his secretary put her straight through that for a few moments she could hardly think straight.

'I know it's a bit crude,' he admitted, covering for her

sudden shyness with his easy manner. 'But time has been condensed for us, Emily, and I wanted you to feel comfortable—'

'Comfortable?' Emily heard herself exclaim. 'With clothes labelled "Breakfast, lunch, dinner: al fresco; breakfast, lunch, dinner: formal"! And that's only two of the categories. There must be at least a dozen more—'

'You don't like them?' Alessandro said, sounding genuinely concerned.

'I'm sorry. I don't mean to sound ungrateful.'

'Should we meet and discuss it, do you think?'

'Yes.' She should have pretended to think about his offer for a moment or two, she realised.

'Shall I come for you now?' There was a note of amusement in his voice.

'That would be nice,' she managed huskily.

Alessandro took her to lunch at one of the city's most exclusive restaurants. Somewhere so discreet that even a prince and his beautiful young companion could pass a comfortable hour or two consuming delicious food in a private booth well away from prying eyes.

Laying down her napkin after the most light *millefeuille* of plump strawberries, bursting with juice, sweetened with icing sugar and whipped cream, Emily wondered how she was going to refuse Alessandro's fabulous gifts without offending him.

'Is something troubling you?' he pressed, signalling to the waiter that he was ready to sign the bill. 'You surely can't still be worrying about those clothes?'

'I don't know what to think about them,' Emily admitted frankly, hiding her confusion behind the guise of practicality. 'There are just so many outfits—it would take me the best part of a year just to try them all on.'

'So leave it for now,' he suggested casually. 'Grab a few things you like, and I'll have the rest delivered to the palace. You can take your time over them in Ferara. I just thought as we were in London it was too good an opportunity to miss.'

'You're very kind…too kind,' Emily said impulsively. Her heart was hammering painfully in her chest, while Alessandro's gaze warmed her face, demanding that she look at him.

'I just want you to be happy,' he murmured.

A muscle flexed in his jaw, as if he was struggling with the situation almost as much as she was. 'For the duration of the contract,' Emily said, as if trying to set things straight in both their minds.

Inclining his head towards her, Alessandro gave a brief nod of agreement. 'Talking of which—' Reaching inside the breast pocket of his lightweight jacket, he brought something out, then seemed to think better of it and put it back again.

'Are you ready to go?' he said, standing up. 'I thought we might take a stroll around the park before I take you back.'

As they left the restaurant Emily was aware that the same men who had followed them discreetly from her apartment were just a few footsteps behind them now.

'Don't worry,' Alessandro said, linking her arm through his, seeing her turn. 'They're the good guys.'

'Your bodyguards?'

'Yours, too, now that you are to be my wife,' he reminded her.

The thought that she was to be Alessandro's wife excited her, in spite of everything, but the thought that she would never go anywhere again without bodyguards was the flipside of the coin. She needed Alessandro to guide her through this confusing new world, Emily realised. There were so many things she had to ask him…

'Would you like to come back to my place for coffee?'

The few seconds before he replied felt like hours. So long, in fact, that Emily began to feel foolish—as if she had made some clumsy approach to a man she'd only just met.

'Better not,' he replied with a quick smile.

'Don't worry—I just thought—'

Alessandro could have kicked himself. Emily's invitation had been irresistible—almost. But if they went back to her apartment there could only be one outcome and, to his continued surprise, Emily Weston had awoken a whole gamut of masculine instincts within him—prime amongst which, at this moment, was his desire to protect her. To protect her, to woo her, and then make her his wife. And he had already accepted that the timing of that last part of his plan might not coincide exactly with their wedding day.

'There's still time for that walk in the park.'

They were sheltering from rain beneath a bandstand when he said, 'You'd better have this.'

'What is it?' Emily said curiously, watching as again he dipped his hand inside the breast pocket of his jacket. She frowned when she saw the ring he was holding out to her.

'It would cause quite a stir in Ferara if you weren't seen wearing this particular piece of jewellery,' Alessandro explained, as coolly as if it was a laptop that came with the job.

Of course there would be a ring...she should have known. And it was a very beautiful ring. But shouldn't an engagement ring be given with love...and with tenderness?

'Don't you like it?'

It really mattered to him, Emily realised, taking in the fact that the ring was obviously very old and must have been worn by Alessandro's ancestors for generations—possibly even by his late mother.

'If you prefer you could just wear it on public occasions.'

'I love it,' she said firmly. And I can see how much it means to you, her eyes told him. 'It's just with all these fabulous clothes, and now this...' The words dried up as he took hold of her hand. His expression was lighter, as if a great burden had been removed from his shoulders.

'Thank you,' he said softly. 'I was hoping you'd like it. It has been passed down through my family.'

'Tell me more,' Emily encouraged, forgetting everything else as she surrendered to Alessandro's voice, and his touch...but most of all to the sudden realisation that she wasn't the only one who needed reassurance.

'I know it isn't the usual huge and very valuable stone,' he began, 'and perhaps it isn't the type of thing you might have been expecting. But this ring has a provenance that no other piece of jewellery can boast.'

It might have been made for her, Emily realised as he settled it on her finger. Dainty ropes of rubies and pearls wound around the circumference with a ruby heart as the centrepiece of the design. 'Tell me about it,' she repeated.

'There was a Prince of Ferara named Rodrigo,' Alessandro began. 'He fell in love with a beautiful young girl called Caterina. Rodrigo had this ring made for her...'

As his voice stroked her senses Emily tried to remain detached and remind herself that Alessandro was only telling her a story. But it wasn't easy when her mind was awash with alternative images.

'On his way to ask for Caterina's hand in marriage, Rodrigo's horse shied, throwing him unconscious into the lake. Robbed of her one true love, Caterina decided to join a religious order.'

Emily tensed as Alessandro switched his attention abruptly to her face. 'What happened to her?' she asked quickly, full of the irrational fear that he could read her mind and know it was full of him rather than the characters he was telling her about.

'Caterina's horse shied on the way to the convent,' he said casually, the expression in his eyes concealed beneath a fringe of black lashes. 'When she recovered consciousness this ring was right there by her side.'

The ruby heart seemed to flare a response, making Emily gasp involuntarily.

'So, did she join the religious order?'

'She couldn't.'

'Couldn't?'

'That's right.'

'Why not?'

'I should take you home now, if you are to have an early night before your flight to Ferara tomorrow,' he said restlessly, as if he wished he had never started the story. 'I have another business meeting in about—' He frowned as he glanced at his wristwatch. 'About ten minutes ago.'

All the romance…all the tenderness…had vanished from his voice as if it had never been. Of course it had never been, Emily thought, angry for allowing herself to get carried away. Alessandro's fairy story was just part of the play-acting they were both forced to endure…and the ring was just another prop.

'I'll take good care of it,' she said, closing her fist around the jewel-encrusted band.

'I'm sure you will,' he murmured as he straightened up. 'Shall we go?'

It was an instruction, not a question, Emily realised. 'You don't have to see me home,' she said quickly. 'I've made you late enough already.'

'I'm taking you back,' he insisted in the same quiet determined tone that made it impossible to argue with him.

Alessandro left her at the door to her apartment, refusing yet another invitation to cross the threshold. *'Li vedro in Ferara, Emily,'* he said, waiting until she had closed the door.

'Yes. See you in Ferara, Alessandro,' Emily confirmed softly, turning away from him to face the empty room.

CHAPTER FIVE

IT SEEMED to Emily that everyone in Ferara had cause to celebrate apart from the main characters in the drama that was about to unfold.

From one of the windows in the turret of the huge suite she had been given for her few remaining days as a single woman she had a good view of the cobbled thoroughfare outside the palace walls. Bunting and banners in the distinctive Feraran colours of crimson, blue and gold hung in colourful swathes across the street, along with numerous posters of the soon to be married couple…Emily Weston and Prince Alessandro Bussoni Ferara. Es and As, intertwined.

For once Emily was forced to agree with her mother. It hardly seemed possible!

She had been awake since dawn, when all the unfamiliar sounds of a new day in Ferara had intruded upon her slumbers. Only then had she begun to drink in the unaccustomed luxury of her new surroundings—and with something closer to dread than exhilaration. The setting was everything she might have dreamed about—if she'd been a dreamer. One thing she had not anticipated was how it might feel to be set adrift in a palace that, however fabulous, was full of endless echoing corridors where everyone but she seemed to know exactly what was expected of them.

Ferara, at least, was far lovelier than she had ever dared to expect. On the drive from the airport the countryside that had unrolled before her had been picture-postcard perfect. A landscape of lilac hills shrouded in mist, some crowned with quaint medieval villages shielding fields cloaked in vines, and clusters of cypress trees standing on sentry duty against a flawless azure sky.

The Palace of Ferara was constructed around a sixth century Byzantine tower, and seemed from a distance to be balanced perilously on the very edge of a towering chalky-white cliff face. Rising out of the low cloud cover as they had approached by road, both palace and cliff had appeared to be suspended magically in the air. But as they'd drawn closer Emily had seen that the stone palace was both vast and set firm on towering foundations.

No wonder a Princess of Ferara needed so many clothes, she mused as she retraced in her mind those parts of the palace she had already been shown. The sheer number of rooms was overwhelming.

Tossing back the crisp, lavender-scented sheets, she swung her legs over the side of the bed and headed towards the glass-paned doors leading onto her balcony. Even in the early-morning sunshine the mellow stone already felt warm beneath her naked feet. Staring out across the city, she felt like an excited child, monitoring the progress of some promised treat... Except that she wasn't a child any longer, Emily reminded herself, pulling back. She would have to be totally insensitive not to realise that the people of Ferara had high hopes for this marriage, and all she had to offer them was a sham.

She dragged her thoughts from harsh reality and they turned inevitably to Alessandro, and how long his business would keep him from Ferara. The best she could expect was that he would turn up for their wedding. Then they would get on with their own lives—separately. She would stay on in Ferara, of course, and act out her part as promised. But what did Alessandro have planned? Would she see him at all?

Shaking her head, as if to rid herself of pointless speculation, she reached for the telephone and dialled an internal line. After several rings she remembered that Miranda and her parents would probably have already left for their promised tour of Ferara.

So, what did a 'soon to be' princess do in her spare time? Ring the office, she told herself, trying another number.

'Force of habit,' she explained to the uncharacteristically bewildered Clerk of Chambers who normally organised her working life with unfailing efficiency. 'Yes, OK, Billy. See you at the wedding then.'

She tried to hang on to the familiar voice in her mind, but when she replaced the receiver the room seemed to have grown larger and even emptier than before she placed the call.

Shower, dress, and draw up a plan, she decided, trying to ignore the stab of tears behind her eyes as she headed purposefully towards the lavish marble bathroom. She would have to pull herself together and find a meaningful role for herself if the next couple of years weren't going to be the longest of her life.

She felt better when she came out of the bathroom, hair partly dried and hanging wild about her shoulders, and with a fluffy white towel secured loosely round her hips. She had waltzed herself halfway across the ballroom-sized bedroom, humming her own version of Strauss, before she realised she was not alone. As her hands flew to tug up the towel and cover her breasts she realised there wasn't enough material to cover everything—

'Calm down. I'll turn my back,' Alessandro murmured reassuringly.

It wasn't easy to stay calm when your heart was spinning in your chest!

'Who let you in?' she said, backing up towards the door of her dressing room.

'I apologise for arriving unannounced.'

He could try a little harder to *sound* contrite, Emily thought, conscious that her nipples had turned into bullets. 'I thought you had business to conclude in London.'

So did I, Alessandro mused wryly. But thanks to you, Emily, I couldn't stay away. 'Can I help you with that?' he offered, moving towards her as she debated whether to simply brazen it out and turn to open the dressing room door, or try to manoeuvre the handle with her elbow whilst clinging on to the towel and preserving what little remained of her dignity.

'That won't be necessary,' she said, choosing the latter option.

'Oh, come now, Emily,' Alessandro murmured, moving closer. 'I have seen a woman's body before…'

That was all the encouragement she needed to try and bludgeon the handle into submission with an increasingly tender arm.

'It's not as if anything's going to happen,' he added sardonically, 'remember that "no sex" clause?'

'Yes, thank you, I do remember,' Emily said, conscious that every tiny hair on her body was standing to attention.

'See? I'm not even looking,' he insisted, leaning across her to open the door. 'Your modesty is utterly preserved, *signorina*.'

Launching herself into the dressing room, Emily slammed the door shut and leaned heavily against it as she struggled to catch her breath.

'Don't be long,' Alessandro warned from the other side. 'I've got something to show you…something I think you might like.'

Emily's gaze tacked frantically around the room as she tried to decide what to do next. Dropping the towel, she sprinted naked to examine her daunting collection of new clothes.

Everything was cloaked in protective covers and there were photographs of each outfit on labels attached to the hangers; labels that came complete with directions as to where matching accessories might be found. But her investigations were hampered by too much choice. And just what was the appropriate outfit for after you'd stepped out of the shower only to be discovered naked by possibly the most delicious male on the planet? A male, furthermore, with whom you could anticipate no hanky-panky whatsoever!

Modest enough to prove you weren't the least bit interested in him, she decided, and casual enough to put them both at their ease.

Decision made, Emily dived into the bottom of the wardrobe and tugged out her trusty jeans and tee shirt.

'I hope you slept well?'

'Very well, thank you,' she replied politely, giving Alessandro a wide berth on her way back across the room. 'I had no idea you had arrived home.' Reaching the massive fireplace, she intended to rest one trembling arm on the mantelpiece, but missed when she found she couldn't reach. Acting nonchalant, she leaned against the wall instead, and levelled a bogus confident stare on Alessandro's face.

'Come over here,' he said softly, indicating the cushion next to his own on the cream damask sofa.

As one corner of his mouth tugged up in a smile Emily's battered confidence took a further plunge into the depths, while her heart seemed capable of yet more crazy antics. 'Why?' she said suspiciously.

'Because there's something that I'd like you to see,' he said patiently.

Emily took care to measure each step, so as not to appear too keen.

'Sit down,' he invited, standing briefly until she was comfortably settled on the sofa.

Maintaining space between them, Emily folded her hands out of harm's way in her lap and waited.

Reaching down to the floor at his feet, Alessandro brought up an ancient brown leather casket and set it down on the table in front of her. Releasing the brass catches, he lifted the lid. 'For you,' he said, tipping it up so that she could easily see the contents.

Emily gasped, all play-acting forgotten as she peered into the midnight-blue interior, where a quantity of diamonds flashed fire as the early-morning sunlight danced across their facets.

Reaching into the casket, Alessandro brought out a diamond tiara, together with earrings and a matching bracelet and necklace. 'You will wear these with your wedding dress,' he said, laying them out on the table in front of her.

'Don't you think that's a bit much?'

'To my knowledge, no Princess of Ferara has complained before,' he said, sweeping up one ebony brow in an elegant show of surprise.

'Well, I had planned a more restrained look—'

'You'll do as you're told,' Alessandro cut in firmly. 'The people of Ferara expect—'

'The people of Ferara,' Emily countered, 'are receiving short shrift from us both. And I can't...I won't appear any more of a hypocrite than I already am. They deserve better—'

'You will honour this contract,' Alessandro returned sharply, 'and leave the people of Ferara to me. They are my concern—'

'Shortly to be mine,' Emily argued stubbornly. 'If only for the duration of our agreement. While this contract runs its course,' she continued, 'I intend to fulfil my duties to this county, and its people, in full. And I warn you, Alessandro, I will not be side-tracked from my intended course of action by you.'

'Then you will do as I ask and wear this jewellery,' he insisted, clearly exasperated. 'It's for one day only. That is all I ask.'

Emily mashed her lips together as she thought about it. The royal tiara to hold her veil in place and cement Alessandro's position as ruler of Ferara? She would agree to that. 'I would love to wear the tiara, but this ring is what your people care about,' she said, touching the ruby and pearl band. 'All the other jewellery is very impressive, but, just as you said, no jewel, however valuable, can boast the history of this one modest piece. Why overshadow it? I think your people would appreciate seeing simplicity in their Princess. I've no wish to flaunt your wealth.'

There was a long pause during which Emily couldn't fathom what was going on in Alessandro's mind. His face remained impassive, but behind his eyes myriad changes in the molten gold irises marked the course of his thoughts. Even sitting with his back to the sun, with his face half in shadow, the light in his eyes was remarkable, Emily mused, leaving tension behind as she slipped deeper into reverie.

'You're an exceptional woman, Signorina Weston—'

She started guiltily out of her daydream as Alessandro began putting the fabulous jewels back inside their velvet nest. She could hardly believe what he was saying…doing. She had won her first battle—and so easily— 'You agree?' she said, holding her breath.

'I agree,' Alessandro said, almost as if he surprised himself. 'Everything will be locked up for safekeeping. The tiara will be returned to you on the day of our wedding.'

'Thank you,' she said with relief, getting to her feet as Alessandro stood up to go. 'Will I see you again before then?' It was a question she longed to know the answer to…a question she knew she had no right to ask him.

'I imagined you would be too busy with your preparations,' Alessandro said, looking at her intently. 'I have meetings arranged right up to the morning of the ceremony…I thought I'd give you time to sort through all those clothes,' he added, clearly of the opinion that any woman should be thrilled by such a prospect.

But Emily wasn't impressed. As far as she was concerned, the over-abundance of outfits in her walk-in wardrobe represented nothing more than a selection of costumes for the short-running drama production in which she was about to appear.

'I'd like to do something worthwhile…learn something about Ferara,' she insisted. 'The clothes can wait.'

For a moment Alessandro seemed taken aback. 'Well, good,' he said. 'I'll find someone to have a chat with you—'

As her stomach clenched with disappointment, Emily's lips tightened. 'Don't bother,' she said tensely. 'I'll find someone myself.'

After eating breakfast alone in her suite, Emily knew it was time to make good her boast to find someone who would tell her a little about Ferara. Catching sight of an elderly gardener through one of her many windows, she hurried out of the room.

He was as gnarled as an oak tree and, right now, as bent as one of its branches as he leaned over the plants he was caring for. Emily remained discreetly half hidden as she stared at him, wondering if she had made the right choice.

She needn't have worried about disturbing him. He was oblivious to everything around him apart from the roses he was tending.

Emily smiled as she watched him. The old man's love for his plants was revealed in his every move. He had probably worked in the palace gardens most of his long life. Ferara was that sort of place. Who better to tell her everything she wanted to know? He might not speak too much English, but her Italian was…not too bad, she consoled herself. They should be able to have a conversation of sorts—and anything was preferable to returning to the silence that dominated her ornate, but ultimately sterile rooms.

'*Buon giorno!*' she began hopefully, walking towards the solitary figure. 'I hope I'm not disturbing you.'

'Not at all, *signorina*. I'm delighted to have the company.'

'You speak English,' she said, unable to keep the excitement from her voice.

'I do,' the elderly man replied, leaning heavily on the handle of his fork. 'What can I do for you, *signorina*?'

'Don't you feel the sun?' Emily said, shading her eyes with her hand. 'It's terribly hot out here.'

'Yes, I feel the sun,' he agreed. 'I love to feel the sun. I love to be outside…with my roses,' he elaborated, gesturing around him with one nobly hand whilst star-bright amber eyes continued to reflect on Emily's face. 'Do you like flowers?'

'I love them,' she replied.

'Roses?'

'Especially roses,' Emily sighed, as she traced a petal wistfully. 'They remind me of my parents' garden in England.'

'Do you feel homesick already?' he asked perceptively.

It was as if some bond formed between them in that moment. And as they smiled at each other Emily felt herself relax. 'I'm surprised they flourish here in this heat so late in the summer,' she said, reining back the emotion that suddenly threatened to spoil these first moments with a potential new friend and possible ally.

'My own system of filtered sunlight and judicious watering,' the old man told her proudly. 'Like me, these roses love the sun. And, like me, in this hot climate their exposure to it must be rationed. Otherwise we'd both shrivel up.'

He chuckled, and his eyes sparkled with laughter, but Emily could see the concern behind them, and regretted that she was the cause.

'What's this one called?' she asked, determined to set everything back on an even keel as she pointed to an orange-red, rosette-shaped bloom.

'A good choice,' he commented thoughtfully, stabbing his fork into the ground to come and join her. 'This rose is named after Shakespeare's contemporary, the great English playwright Christopher Marlowe. Here,' he invited, selecting a bloom to show her and holding it up loosely between his fingers, 'inhale deeply, *signorina*. You should be able to detect a scent of tea and lemon. Lemon tea,' he declared, chuckling again, pleased with his joke.

'Mmm. It is a distinctive scent,' Emily agreed after a moment. 'But what is the connection between Christopher Marlowe and roses?'

'You don't know?' he demanded.

It seemed as if she was going to have to learn something about her own culture before starting on his, Emily realised. 'I'm afraid I don't,' she said ruefully.

'Christopher Marlowe pressed a rose inside the pages of a book he gave to a friend after an argument…to express his regret over their disagreement.'

'And did his friend forgive him?'

'Who could resist?' the old gentleman retorted, his eyes widening as he surveyed the array of beautiful blooms nodding in the breeze in front of them.

Before Emily could stop him, he cut one for her.

'Here, *signorina*, take this. Press it between the pages of a book…and always remember that if a rose is shown love and care it will flourish and bloom, wherever it is planted.'

Taking the flower from his hand, Emily smiled. 'Do you work here every day?'

'I intend to,' he told her, eyes shining with anticipation. 'I intend to make this rose garden the most talked about in all of Ferara…all of Europe!'

They talked for some while, and then she left him to his work.

'I'm sure you will,' Emily agreed. 'It's so very beautiful already.'

'Would it bother you if I came here to talk to you again?'

'Bother me?' he exclaimed with surprise. 'On the contrary *signorina*. I should love it.'

'In that case,' Emily said happily, 'see you tomorrow.'

The old man bowed as she started to move away. 'Until tomorrow, *signorina*. I shall look forward to it.'

After her encounter with the elderly gardener Emily felt more confident that she had something to contribute to palace life. A plan was taking shape in her mind: a scheme to improve the living conditions of all Alessandro's employees—though she had to admit to a moment's concern when her private secretary said she knew of no one matching the old man's description in royal service.

Turning it over in her mind, Emily returned to her desk to catch up on some correspondence. On the top there was a large red journal she didn't recognise, and, opening it at the flyleaf, she saw it was from Alessandro. He had written simply, 'For Emily from Alessandro—a record of your thoughts'. And then, at the bottom of the page, he had added the date of their forthcoming marriage.

'Do you like it?'

She nearly jumped out of her skin. 'I love it,' she said bluntly, running the fingers of one hand appreciatively down the length of its spine.

'Your secretary showed me in,' he explained. 'I hope you don't mind?'

'Not at all.' The now familiar surge in her pulse-rate had reached new and unprecedented levels, Emily discovered as she continued to stare at Alessandro standing on the balcony outside her room. Surely there would come a point where she'd got used to seeing him? But how could anyone look that good in a pair of jeans and a simple dark linen shirt? She surmised he was off-duty, and wondered what he planned to do with his free time. 'Is this a gift for me?' she said, glancing down at the journal.

He answered with a grin and a shrug.

'Five years of entries?' she teased lightly. 'I presume you couldn't get any less?'

His silence allowed her to draw her own conclusions. 'Well, I've never had anything like it before.' she admitted frankly, 'so, thank you.'

'May I come in?' he said, leaning on the doorframe.

'Of course.' She wondered if her heart would ever steady again. 'I was only going to write some letters.'

'But I thought you wanted to have a look around Ferara?'

'I do.' She tried not to read anything into the remark, but her pulse rate rebelled again. 'I'm very keen to learn more. Actually, I've already made a friend of one of the gardeners.'

'Did he tell you much about our country?'

'He was a very interesting old gentleman, as it happens. And, Alessandro?'

'Yes?'

Emily waited, noticing how his eyes reflected his thoughts—there was a something in his expression now that suggested this might be a good time to air her idea. 'I know you've been very busy, and that small things aren't always apparent, but…'

'Get on with it,' he encouraged with a gesture.

'After talking to the gardener I got the impression that his apartment could do with some renovation—just some little touches that would make his life easier.'

'And you'd like to take charge of these?'

'Yes. I think it would be worthwhile.'

'I'm sure it would,' Alessandro agreed. 'And as far as learning more about Ferara is concerned—well, I've taken the afternoon off, so I could show you around, if you like.'

A shiver of excitement raced down Emily's spine as she let him wait for her answer.

'The chocolate festival,' he prompted, 'the one I told you about? It's usually held in February, but there's to be a special demonstration in celebration of our marriage.

Because of the heat at this time of year it's taking place inside the grand hall of one of the municipal buildings.'

So, his talk of a chocolate festival hadn't been a wind-up after all, she realised, feeling a rush of anticipation. 'I'd love to go.'

'That's settled, then,' he said. 'We'd better leave right away if we want to catch the best demonstrations.'

When they arrived, Emily was amazed to find the streets of Ferara had been recreated within the cool, vaulted interior of the ancient building, complete with chocolate stalls, chocolate sculptures in various stages of completion, and crowds milling about. There was a ripple of excitement when Alessandro was spotted with his bride-to-be, but after the initial surprise they were able to move around the vast marble-floored exhibition area quite freely. It was Emily's first real exposure to her new countrymen, and at first she held back a little self-consciously, but Alessandro grabbed her hand, drawing her forward, giving every indication of being proud of his choice of bride.

He was either a very good actor, Emily decided, or—a very good actor, she told herself firmly, knowing how easy it would be to let her imagination get the better of her where Alessandro was involved.

'Let me get you some chocolate,' he offered, weaving through the press of people, towing her behind him. He took her to stand beneath one of the towering pillars where an artist was already busy at work, then reached out and caught some of the glossy flakes as they showered down. He began feeding them to her, until Emily had to beg him to stop.

'Stop? Are you sure?'

'No,' Emily admitted, laughing because she was sure her face had to be smeared with chocolate.

To anyone unaware of their tangled relationship they would have passed for two people in love, laughing and enjoying the festival for what it was—an explosion of happiness and goodwill to celebrate the marriage of a man who was clearly much loved by his fellow Ferarans.

Freed from the tensions imposed by their arranged marriage, they actually enjoyed each other's company, Emily realised, smiling ruefully as she accepted the clean handkerchief Alessandro produced from his pocket.

'Is there anything else you should have warned me about?' she probed cheekily. 'Cream bun fights, perhaps?' She gazed up at him as she tried to wipe some of the chocolate smears off her face, loving the feeling of closeness that had sprung up between them.

'I think I can safely promise you one or two more interesting customs throughout your time here.'

Emily's smile faltered. Trying not to spoil the mood, she shook herself out of the doldrums. 'Tell me about these different traditions,' she pressed with another smile.

'If you haven't guessed already, our wedding's a great excuse for giving some of the best a second airing. Everyone in Ferara loves a carnival. You'll definitely be seeing my country at its best.'

'I'm looking forward to it,' she said. And she was, especially if Alessandro was to be her guide.

'You're still covered in chocolate,' he commented as she made another attempt to clean her face.

'Well, if I am it's all your fault,' Emily countered with a laugh that swiftly turned into an uncertain silence.

That remark was the closest she had ever come to flirting with him. And in view of his comment that seemed to remind her of the time limit on her visit, flirting was out. Not only that, but her teasing manner was attracting quite a bit of interest. 'I must look a mess,' she said self-consciously.

'You look lovely,' Alessandro argued, removing the handkerchief from her hand. Dampening one clean corner with his tongue, he very gently wiped her face for her. 'There's—that's better,' he declared at last with satisfaction.

Emily fought the urge to stare into his eyes, suddenly terrified that what she might see there would not match her own feelings. 'I suppose we'd better be getting back.' She broke free and went to stand some distance away before he had the chance to put distance between them.

This was crazy, Emily realised. When all she wanted was to be with him here she was calling an end to the day almost before it had begun! How had she ever imagined she could throw herself in the path of a man like Alessandro and walk away unscathed? Suddenly she couldn't wait to get away. The smell of the chocolate, the heat of the crowd and the noise reverberating round the lofty building stabbed at her mind, and she was almost running as she burst out through the imposing double doors that led to the open air. Shielding her eyes against the unforgiving rays of the midday sun, for a moment she was completely disorientated. Starting down the broad sweep of stone steps, she nearly stumbled.

'Emily! Are you all right?'

The voice was unmistakable—deep, and concerned. Tears sprang to her eyes as he caught hold of her, and she hated herself for the weakness. Somehow she had to get back her pre-Alessandro control, Emily raged inwardly. But she needed his steadying arm to guide her down the steps...

'It's hot, and you've consumed vast quantities of chocolate,' Alessandro said soothingly. 'I think we should take a gentle stroll back to the palace. I'll organise a light lunch—'

'Oh, no. I couldn't eat anything,' Emily said truthfully, though her lack of appetite was a direct result of the ache in her heart; nothing at all to do with the sunshine or an over-abundance of chocolate.

'I think for once you're going to do as I say,' Alessandro said sternly as he led her carefully down the steps. 'You almost fell up there. Then what would I have done? I can't have a wedding without a bride.'

'I'm sure you'd find someone without too much trouble.'

'But they wouldn't be you, would they?' he said tolerantly.

'Does that matter?'

'Yes, it does. So you're just going to have to humour me. The sun is strong and you're not used to it. Here, lean on my arm. We'll take it slowly…walk in the shade. I don't suppose you've eaten properly.'

'I've had lots of chocolate,' she pointed out mutinously.

'An unrelieved diet of chocolate might get a little boring, even for you. A light salad, some iced water—'

She hoped he was right. Maybe the heat *was* getting to her…the heat, and feelings she was sure he didn't reciprocate. Alessandro was simply making the best out of a difficult situation, she thought, flashing a look up at him…while she was falling in love, she realised with a stab of concern.

Alessandro returned Emily's troubled glance with a smile and a reassuring squeeze. He had been right to take her out of the heat. He should have anticipated how many people would attend the event, but he had just wanted an excuse to be with her. The chocolate festival had been the perfect opportunity.

Falling in love had been the last thing on his agenda, he realised as they made their way slowly back to the palace. But here, under the centuries-old shade of the cypress trees, the warmth of the sun was like a balm that enveloped them both in its healing rays. If he could have done, he would have willed all the mistrust, all the uncertainty that had tainted their relationship to float away on the light breeze that sighed through the branches over their heads…

Emily was perfect, and the mood of his people was wholly supportive, he realised with pleasure as he courteously returned several greetings. She would make a wonderful first lady: a true equal to stand beside him and care for these people he loved so much. She could hardly wait to make a start on improving the lot of those around her...sharing her own happiness with others. He snatched a look at the woman who in one short week would be his bride. She was deep in thought, but not so preoccupied that she couldn't take account of every smile that came her way and return it with sincerity. He felt a rush of deep affection for her...something that transcended physical attraction and looped a band of love around his soul.

He had never once felt like this, Alessandro realised, relishing the simple trust she placed in him, linking her arm through his. The privilege of being allowed to care for her made him happier than he could ever have imagined. It fulfilled him...completed him. Falling in love with Emily was the most natural, the most inevitable step he had ever taken. But if he rushed things he knew he ran the risk of damaging their relationship, perhaps irrevocably. He would have to take things easy...take it slowly, give them both time to get to know each other.

It wasn't enough that the chemistry between them was almost frightening in its intensity and that every male instinct he possessed insisted he take her straight to his bed. He knew with utter certainty that if he wanted more, he had to wait—

'D'you know, Alessandro?'

She captured his attention so easily, he realised happily. 'Tell me,' he prompted softly.

'I love Ferara...I love your people... They're all so friendly, so genuine and so welcoming...' She hesitated.

'And?' he said gently, sensing there was something more she wanted to say.

'I really think this might work...between us,' she elaborated awkwardly, though there was no need, Alessandro thought with an inward smile as he drew her a little closer. He had already come to that same conclusion himself, some time ago.

CHAPTER SIX

FOR the next couple of days Emily hardly saw Alessandro, except in passing. But she knew he was swept up in protocol, and fine-tuning their wedding arrangements. Her own family was busy with last-minute preparations, too, so any spare time she had she spent talking to her new friend.

With only one night to go before the wedding, she finally found the courage to ask him more about where he lived. Now that she intended the welfare of the palace staff to be one of her main areas of interest while she was in Ferara, this looked like as good a time as any to make a start. 'Does it suit you?'

'Suit me?' he asked with a wry grimace.

'I'm sorry,' Emily said, realising he probably didn't have much choice. 'I suppose your accommodation comes with the job.'

His nod of agreement suggested she had hit the mark. Emily decided to press on. 'Are you comfortable there?'

'Not bad,' he agreed, after much thought. 'Though the kitchens are a long way from my apartment. By the time I get my food it's usually cold.'

'Don't you have your own kitchen?'

'My own kitchen?'

'A kitchenette?' she amended quickly. This new turn in her career was proving to be harder than she had expected. 'Somewhere to prepare yourself a bite to eat…a drink?'

'No. Nothing like that,' he told her, rubbing the back of his neck with his hand as he thought about it. 'Sounds like a good idea, though.'

'I'm sure I could arrange something for you.'

'Could you?'

'Would you let me try?'

'Only if you agree to give me cookery lessons as well,' he said, dismissing the idea with a wry grin and a flick of his hand.

'I'm not thinking of anything very elaborate,' Emily said encouragingly, 'just a small fridge, and perhaps a kettle and toaster to start with. If you had those, at least you'd be able to make yourself a quick snack whenever you felt peckish.'

'Good idea!' her new friend said enthusiastically. 'I'll leave it with you, then.'

'Excellent,' Emily said enthusiastically. 'I'll let you know what progress I've made when I see you tomorrow—'

'Tomorrow?'

Emily's hand flew to her mouth. 'My wedding day—' Her stomach churned with apprehension. How could time have passed so fast?

'So, where is your husband-to-be?'

'Prince Alessandro?'

'Yes, yes,' her elderly friend retorted impatiently. 'My son. Where is he? Why has he left you on your own?'

'Your—' Emily's mouth fell open as the full extent of her blunder overwhelmed her. 'You didn't say!'

'And would you have been so open with me if I had?' Alessandro's father demanded as he levelled a shrewd look on her face.

'Well…I…I don't know,' Emily admitted frankly. 'You must think me a terrible fool—'

'On the contrary,' he replied. 'I think you anything but a fool. My son, however—'

'Oh, no, please,' Emily said, shaking her head. 'You don't understand—'

'What don't I understand?' the old Prince demanded, straightening up so that even in his gardening clothes Emily could be under no misapprehension as to his status.

'I… Well… This is not the usual sort of wedding.'

'You love him?' he asked her directly.

'Well, I...' Emily paused, unsure of what to say.

'I said,' he repeated sternly, 'do you love my son?'

'Causing trouble again, Father?'

The deep, familiar voice went straight to Emily's heart. 'Alessandro!' she exclaimed breathlessly. Who said a prince could descend on you unannounced, wearing snug blue jeans and a close-fitting white top, looking as if he had just climbed out of bed? And his hair was still damp from the shower, she noticed on closer inspection.

'I see you've met my father,' he said, shooting her a wry grin.

He betrayed nothing of their developing friendship, but, remembering his concern for her after the chocolate festival, Emily felt a shiver of awareness shimmer over every part of her as he moved past her within touching distance. He had been more than tolerant. He had been... As she struggled to find the right word she watched him throw his arms around the older man and kiss him warmly on both cheeks several times before hugging him again. To be the object of such fathomless affection—to be capable of bestowing it—

She looked at Alessandro as if seeing him for the first time, and knew without question that she loved him.

'*Papa! Mi sei mancato!*'

His father's voice was equally fierce as he clutched his son to him. '*Anche tu, Alessandro.* I've missed you, too, *vagabondo*!'

Another hug and they were done, leaving Emily still gaping.

'You have neglected your bride so badly she has forgotten that tomorrow is her wedding day,' the old man accused, wiping his eyes on his sleeve. 'You are a bad boy, Alessandro—neglecting us both like this.'

'I never neglect you, Papa,' Alessandro argued, flashing

a glance at Emily as he tightened his arm around his father's shoulder. 'It's just that business sometimes—'

His father pressed his lips together in a show of disapproval. 'Business, business, business,' he proclaimed with a dismissive gesture. 'And your bride, Alessandro? What about your bride?'

Emily was forced to laugh as Alessandro executed a deep bow, flashing her a smile as he straightened up. 'I can only offer you my most humble apologies, Signorina Weston. Whatever punishment you decide to exact, I shall accept without question.'

Don't tempt me, Emily thought, feeling the effects of his statement reverberate around her senses.

'Once again,' Alessandro continued easily, tossing her an amused and comprehending look, 'I regret that unavoidable matters arose, demanding my immediate attention—'

'Your *bride* demands your immediate attention,' his father broke in sternly. 'Your wedding is tomorrow, in case you had also forgotten that, Alessandro.'

'I had not forgotten, Father,' Alessandro responded softly, glancing at Emily.

'It doesn't matter,' Emily insisted, shaking her head to hide her confusion. 'Alessandro is very busy, Your Royal Highness. And I have plenty to occupy me,' she managed vaguely. 'I'll leave you two together—'

'You will do no such thing,' the old Prince informed her imperiously. 'You will stay here with me and talk a while longer. After tomorrow Alessandro may begin the process of taking precedence over me. But today, as far as I am aware, I am still the undisputed ruler of Ferara, and I wish to talk with my future daughter-in-law. Alone,' he added pointedly. 'Make yourself busy somewhere else, Alessandro. Emily and I have much to discuss.'

'Father,' Alessandro said, executing a small formal bow. 'Your wish is my command.'

*　　*　　*

The wedding had more similarities to a big-budget film than any ceremony Emily had ever attended before. And, in true cinematic fashion, preparations for her starring role began just before dawn, when her private secretary called to inform her that the beauticians and hairdressers had started to arrive.

Breakfast was delivered on a tray with legs, presumably so that she could enjoy her last breakfast as a single woman safely tucked up in bed. But Emily was already out and about when the young maid knocked timidly on the door. Together they decanted the fruit juice and croissants onto a table overlooking the rose garden.

'You can take the rest away. I shan't eat it,' Emily insisted ruefully, scanning the cooked delicacies and plates of cold meats and cheeses, knowing she couldn't face them. 'Oh. Leave me an orange,' she said as an afterthought. She knew they had come from the palace orchard and were absolutely delicious.

'Yes, *signorina*,' the maid said with a courteous bob.

Just as Emily had thought, her simple breakfast proved to be the only oasis of calm in a day that was testing in the extreme. Pulled from pillar to post, she found herself constantly surrounded by strangers all charged with seeking perfection. The unfamiliar attention was daunting, and what made it worse was being treated suddenly as if she was on a higher stratum from everyone else. It made normal conversation impossible.

As her hair was dressed up, ready to hold the weight of the tiara, and the finest film of coral rouge was applied to her cheeks, Emily began to feel increasingly like an inanimate object. No one seemed able to meet her eyes. No one spoke unless she instigated the conversation. And no one seemed prepared to volunteer an opinion on anything, preferring to wait for her to state her own views as if they were the only ones worth listening to. The lack of verbal interplay was driving her crazy. And her nerves were building to crisis level as what had been a theoretical exercise became all too real.

Just when she thought she couldn't stand one more minute of it, her face broke into a smile.

'Dad! Mum! Miranda!' Breaking free of the posse of primpers, Emily fled across the room towards her family.

'But, *signorina*…your veil,' the designer called after her.

'Give me a moment, please,' Emily said, keeping her head firmly buried against her father's shoulder.

'Five minutes,' her father bartered, keeping her close as he encircled Miranda's shoulders with his other arm. 'Then you can have her back, I promise.'

There was such quiet determination in his voice that even the highly-strung designer was forced to concede defeat.

Her father sounded just like Alessandro, Emily thought fondly, raising her head to watch the couturier make an imperious signal and lead his group out of the room.

'There's still time to change your mind, Emily,' Miranda whispered, looking around anxiously at their mother, who nodded agreement.

'It's not too late,' her father agreed gruffly. 'I can have you out of here in a jiffy—'

'No, Dad,' Emily insisted firmly. 'There's too much at stake here—for everyone concerned. I'm going ahead with it.'

'Oh, the violin arrived! It is absolutely—' Miranda's hand flew to her mouth. 'How could I mention that?' she asked herself distractedly. 'When you're having to put up with all this?' She made a wild gesture to encompass the various stations dotted around the room set up by hairdressers, beauticians and designers.

'It's not so bad,' Emily teased. 'No, honestly,' she said sincerely, catching hold of Miranda's hand. 'Nothing would induce me to stay here if I didn't want to. It's not so bad living here at the palace with Alessandro.' She raised her eyebrows a fraction as she looked at her sister.

'You mean—' Miranda flashed a glance at their mother and father, who quickly pretended interest in the view outside the window.

'No, I don't mean what you're thinking,' Emily said softly. 'But he's great fun to be with when you get to know him. And he's so kind.'

'Is that all?' Miranda said, sounding disappointed.

'It was never meant to be anything more,' Emily pointed out, working at her smile. 'And you look beautiful,' she said, desperately trying to turn the direction of the conversation. 'And Dad, Mum, you look fantastic,' she added for good measure.

'You're absolutely sure about this?' her father said, looking at her again with concern.

'Yes,' Emily said, raising her eyes to his to prove that her composure really was restored. 'You can call everyone back in again now. I'm ready.'

The ancient cathedral in Ferara was on so vast a scale it might have been built for some lost race of giants. As Emily arrived beneath the towering stone archway that marked the entrance a murmur rose from the congregation like a collective sigh.

'This situation is about as real as a film,' her father murmured, echoing Emily's thoughts. 'The only difference is, I doubt any of us will be able to forget this once the show's over.'

'Courage, Dad,' Emily replied as she squeezed his arm. 'We'll get through this together.'

'I'm supposed to be supporting you, remember?' he growled out of the side of his mouth as the opening chord burst from the organ and an angelic choir soared into the first anthem.

Emily was about to move forward when one of the several attendants who had joined the procession from the palace attracted her attention.

'*Signorina, scusami l'interrruzione,*' he murmured, bowing low. 'This is an ancient custom in our country. The bride's flowers are traditionally a wedding gift from the groom's family.'

'How lovely,' Emily said, exchanging her bouquet with a smile.

'His Serene Highness is most keen that traditions should be upheld,' the attendant added, backing away from her in a deep bow.

As Emily's curled her fingers around the slender stems of the roses she knew they were more than a gift. The fragrant arrangement signified the approval of Alessandro's father, and that mattered to her more than any one of the fabulous wedding presents that had arrived at the palace.

She could not remember ever feeling so keenly aware…so alive. And as she steadied herself for the walk up the aisle she found she could identify each strand of scent—incense, the roses resting in her arms, and the heady mix of countless exclusive perfumes. And above all the dazzling sights and sounds and scents, even though she never looked directly at him once, she was aware of Alessandro, waiting in silence for her at the end of the vast sweep of aisle.

Moving forward, Emily felt the burden of her long train ease as the squad of young train-bearers, chosen from schools in Ferara at her own request, took up the weight. And after a few brief moments of adjustment, when she feared she might lose the priceless tiara as the veil was tugged this way and that, they managed to keep pace with her perfectly.

She walked tall and proud at her father's side between the massed ranks of European royalty, wearing the slim column of a gown she had insisted upon. Only the splendour of the diamond tiara denoted her rank—that, and the floating pearl-strewn veil that eddied around her like a creamy-white mist. The only real colour was in her cheeks and in the coral-tinted roses her old friend had provided—Christopher Marlowe roses from the palace gardens, with every thorn removed, simply arranged and tied with silk ribbons in the colours of her new country: crimson, blue and gold.

She was aware of her mother in deep blue velvet, and Miranda, ravishing in palest lemon, as well as some other bridesmaids whom she had met only briefly. And then, as the organ sounded a fanfare of celebration, Emily focussed on the long walk ahead of her—the walk to join Alessandro, who stood waiting for her at the foot of the steps to the high altar.

The aisle itself was a work of art, paved in marble and carved by long-dead artisans to such effect that the scenes portrayed appeared more like faded photographs scanned onto the cool surface rather than the painstaking work of supreme craftsmen.

In front of her a vast window of such intense blue it appeared to be backlit by a power even greater than the sun threw splashes of colour across the faces of the dignitaries, some of whom Emily recognised, but she only sensed rather than saw every head turn her way, because her own gaze had found Alessandro's.

Even though she knew he was entering into marriage with no thought of love or romance, his strength lent her courage, and, seeing a flicker of concern in the eyes of his father, when Emily dropped her curtsey in front of him she smiled reassuringly as he reached forward to bring her to her feet.

Then she was standing next to Alessandro, with every fibre of her being pulsing with awareness… Alessandro, who appeared a daunting figure even in such a setting, where the scale of the building challenged normal perception. She matched her breathing to his, steadying herself, willing herself free of expectation, knowing that if she harboured none she could never be hurt.

But as the ceremony reached its climax a heady sense of destiny overcame her. Too much incense, she told herself firmly. But, whatever happened, she would do her best for the people of Ferara during her tenure as their Princess.

'You may kiss your bride.'

Reality struck home like a real physical blow. Would he kiss her? Or would he humiliate her in front of everyone? Was this hard for him? Impossible?

Too churned up to interpret anything, let alone the expression in her husband's eyes, Emily tensed as she waited. She didn't know what to expect.

He smiled, as if he was trying to imbue her with some of his own confidence. Alessandro, always considerate…thanking her for keeping her part of the bargain, Emily reasoned, wishing against her better judgement that it could be more. She felt his firm lips touch her mouth, pressing against the soft yielding pillow of her lips as she sighed against him—then a chord from the organ broke the spell and he linked her arm firmly through his.

And they were walking down the aisle together, man and wife, smiling to the left, and then smiling to the right—but never once smiling at each other.

They had their first row on their wedding night.

Elevated to a magnificent suite of rooms adjoining Alessandro's own, Emily prepared for bed alone. Her head was ringing with the effort of maintaining a front for so long. But at least she could console herself with the knowledge that she had begun to fulfil the requirements of their contract.

Who was she trying to kid? Emily wondered angrily as she sat down in front of the gilt-embossed dressing table mirror. A ceremony couldn't plug the chasm in her heart, or blot out her certainty that everything she had planned—so carefully, so meticulously—was already falling apart around her ears because she had made the classic mistake of allowing feelings to get in the way.

The fact that Alessandro was a prince didn't matter at all—the fact that they had a business contract between them rather than a love affair mattered more to her than she could ever have imagined. It hurt like hell, she realised wistfully.

Plucking out the last of the pins holding her hair in place, she allowed it to spill over her shoulders and began to brush it with long, impassioned sweeps.

It was hard to believe she had been naïve enough to think she could simply pick up the pieces of her carefree single life and transfer them to Ferara with the rest of her luggage. Naïve? Her naïvety had been monumental, Emily thought, shaking her head angrily and then tossing the brush aside.

The wedding changed everything she realised, remembering the solemn vows she had made. Alessandro was her husband now, and she was his wife. And with those simple facts came hope, desire, expectation—and, most pressing of all, she thought, ramming her lips together as she tried not to cry, was the need to spend at least your wedding night with your husband.

Once they'd left the cathedral there had hardly been a chance for her to speak to him. And even when they had opened the reception by dancing together there had been constant interruptions. And she hadn't helped matters, Emily thought, remembering how stiffly she had held herself. There had been a moment when the toasts were made—Alessandro's hand had closed over her own as they'd sliced through a tier of the wedding cake and she had felt her whole body rebel and strain towards him. But she had clenched her fist over the handle until her knuckles had turned white and hurt...and apart from that—

She started at the knock on the door.

She had sent everyone away, taking the chance, once she had showered, to slip into a clean old top that had somehow found its way into the bottom of her suitcase. It didn't matter what she looked like. It could only be the maid with some hot milk, she reasoned, hurrying to the door.

'Alessandro!'

She felt foolish, standing there with bare feet, wearing nothing except an old faded top while her husband looked every bit as resplendent in a simple black silk robe as he had in full dress uniform, with medals and sash of office.

'I just came to see if you were all right…if you had everything you need,' he said, appearing not to register her choice of clothes as he scanned her sumptuous quarters as if running a mental inventory.

'I'm fine,' Emily replied. 'Just a little tired.'

'You looked beautiful today.' As he turned to look at her his gaze was steady and warm. 'Thank you, Emily.'

'It was nothing,' she lied, forcing a smile. But her glance strayed to his mouth as she remembered his kiss at the culmination of their marriage ceremony…chaste and dutiful maybe, but it still possessed the power to thrill her like no other kiss could ever hope to again. Recklessly she re-lived it now, briefly, self-indulgently, closing her eyes for just an instant as faint echoes of sensation shimmered through her frame.

'I think it all went well,' Alessandro said, breaking into her reverie.

'Yes,' she managed tightly. 'It all went very well. Miranda is in seventh heaven. The violin is everything—'

'Can we talk about us for a moment?'

His expression was hidden in shadow as he moved away from her towards one of the heavily draped windows, but Emily knew something had upset him. Perhaps he thought the violin too high a price to pay for a woman for whom he felt nothing.

'There's no reason why it should be awkward between us—' he began.

Awkward between them! What the hell was he talking about? Alessandro thought angrily, balling his hands into fists while in his mind the image of some rare bloom over-laid the fever. He swung around to look at her. Petals bruised easily, too easily—

'Are you all right?' Emily said, reaching out a hand. Then, remembering her position, she let it fall back again by her side.

He was completely naked under the robe; she was sure of it. Her speech had thickened as erotic possibilities crowded her mind... No one need ever know. They could be lovers and still end the contract as agreed. Just the pos-sibility was a seduction in itself... The walls were twelve feet thick in this part of the old palace, she remembered. And their rooms were interconnecting. Most of the servants were still celebrating at one of the many parties in the pal-ace grounds—she could still hear periodic explosions from the fireworks outside.

'I'm not aware of any awkwardness between us,' she said, in an attempt to prolong the conversation, trying not to stare too blatantly at the outline of his hard frame so clear in silhouette as he stood with his back to the window.

She was standing close to him now...close enough to detect the tang of the lemony soap he must have used in the shower. Closing her eyes, she inhaled deeply, then mur-mured dreamily, 'Don't worry, Alessandro. I'm completely at ease—'

She gasped in alarm as his fist hit the wall.

'"Don't worry, Alessandro"?' he mimicked softly, dan-gerously, and so close to her lips she could feel his warm breath on her face. 'How can you ask me not to worry? Am I the only one tense here? Don't lie to me, Emily,' he warned, pulling back. 'You're about as at ease with all this as I am.'

He took a couple of steps away, as if he couldn't bear to be close to her any more than she could bear to be parted from him.

'Please don't waste your breath on innocent protestations,' he said. 'I know you're lying to me. We're both in this over our heads, and you know it.'

'We knew what we were getting into—'

'Oh, did we?' He cut in sceptically. 'You're quite sure about that, are you, Emily? You're quite sure nothing's changed between us now that we're man and wife?'

He had taken the same mental journey she had, Emily realised with surprise. And each nuance in his voice betrayed the fact that he was every bit as disturbed by his thoughts as she was by her own.

'It's our wedding night—'

'So?' he demanded harshly.

'My no-sex clause—' She felt so foolish, so exposed. 'We could—'

'Forget it?' he suggested.

His gently mocking tone nudged her senses until she was unbearably aroused; the wet triangle of lace between her legs stretched taut in the struggle to contain her excitement.

'I don't think so, Emily,' he said harshly.

Every last remaining strand of common sense told her he was right, while her instinct, her desire, every hectic beat of her heart said she would stop at nothing to change his mind... But once the terms of their contract were satisfied he would need to move on, Emily reminded herself. Marry a woman of his own choosing—someone, as he had already intimated, who could shoulder the responsibilities of Ferara as an equal partner. There would be no place for her in Ferara then, so she would just have to find some way to rein in her hunger for that country's prince sooner rather than later.

Switching on the smile that had served her so well throughout the day, she agreed tonelessly that she did have everything she needed. But, just when she was complimenting herself on the cool way in which she'd handled the situation, Alessandro threw everything into confusion again.

'I suppose we could do as you suggest—keep the terms of our contract and yet have an affair,' he suggested bitterly.

There were a few moments of stunned silence, then Emily laughed nervously—as if to show she knew he couldn't possibly be serious.

'What do you think, Emily?'

'What do I think?'

What *did* she think? She wasn't incapable of any thought, Emily realised as she watched him caress the door handle. Her belly ached with need for him. She was utterly beguiled by his strength, by the subtlety in his hands and by the strong, flexing power in his fingers... She wanted to know how all that would feel, transferred from hard steel to soft flesh—

'Well?' he said harshly.

Could he be serious? Her body seemed to think so.

Even as he watched her eyes darkening, and saw the tip of her tongue dart out to moisten her lips, Alessandro knew it wasn't enough. Even if Emily agreed, a sexual relationship with his beautiful new wife would only leave him more frustrated than ever. And he wanted more. He wanted much more. He wanted her love. He knew he had to do something...say something...or he might tip them both headlong into a situation from which neither of them would ever recover. He lifted his hands in a gesture of surrender.

'Forgive me, Emily. I don't know what I'm saying. I'm very tired—'

Yes, he was tired, Alessandro acknowledged. He was tired of all the play-acting, tired of pretending he didn't feel the most urgent need to consummate their marriage and ease the physical torment he was certain now that she felt every bit as much as he did. He longed to make Emily his wife, and in more than name only. He wanted them to be bound together, body and soul, for the rest of their lives.

But the weariness dragging at his mind had another

cause, he accepted restlessly as he started to pace the room. What exhausted him the most was the secret he was forced to keep. The secret he bound so close because it was the one thing in the world that could take her away from him. And, in spite of the physical desire that raged through his body, he couldn't—he wouldn't—run the risk of losing her.

'We're both tired—and no wonder,' Emily observed gently, trying to hold her husband still from his angry pacing when she knew she had little more to soothe him with than her voice.

'I know,' Alessandro said, shaking his head as he stopped dead to look at her, as if for the first time. It was as if she understood everything…and nothing, he realised, passing a single finger down the side of her face. But it wasn't her fault…none of it was her fault.

Emily longed to grab hold of his hand then, and kiss it, and hold it against her cheek to warm him with her strength…her love… But the moment had passed, and now he was tense again. She could feel it in the air without looking at him.

'My behaviour just now was unforgivable,' Alessandro said, moving away from her. 'I'm sorry if I frightened you. The last thing I want is to make this any harder for you than it already is.' Reaching the door, he turned to face her again.

'Is there anything…anything at all, Emily…that I could provide for you here in Ferara to make you happy?'

'I am happy,' she protested quickly.

'Don't give me a glib answer because that's what you think I want to hear,' he warned. Leaning back against the door, he said softly, 'I mean it, Emily. Whatever you want—whatever it takes to make you happy—just name it.'

You, she thought, meeting his gaze steadily. That's all I want…you. First, last and always.

'You mentioned an idea for upgrading the palace apartments for staff—we could set up weekly meetings—'

'Yes,' she said quickly. Even a regular business meeting with him would be better than nothing at all. 'I think that's a wonderful idea.'

'I'm pleased you think so.'

Emily returned his smile. The first real smile she had seen on his face all day. But if he'd wanted her half as much as she wanted him they would have been setting up a very different sort of assignation, she reminded herself sadly.

One thing was sure: he wouldn't have been leaving her to spend their wedding night alone.

CHAPTER SEVEN

ALESSANDRO'S father sat up in bed to stare at his son in tolerant mystification.

'You come to my rooms at dawn to ask an old man like me what to do about the state of your marriage? Is this really my son Alessandro talking? I would hardly have believed it possible—before Emily came into your life,' he added, shaking his head. 'And had it not been for the nonsense you have told me about this—*contract*—' he spat out the word '—had it not been for that misplaced kindness to me, you would never have found yourself in this mess in the first place. How could you do such a thing, Alessandro? And how could you imagine such a travesty would work?'

I did it for you, Father...only for you, Alessandro thought, taking the rebuke in silence. And in spite of everything he couldn't find it in his heart to regret a thing...except that by trying to help his father it seemed that he had only succeeded in causing him more pain.

'Emily is like a tender bud—'

'I know, Father! I know!' Alessandro exclaimed impatiently, swiping the back of his neck with his hand as he sprang to his feet to pace the room like a tiger with a thorn in its pad. 'She is like no other woman I have ever met,' he went on, shaking his head in utter incomprehension. 'She shows no real interest in the priceless jewels she is entitled to wear, or the designer clothes I arranged to please her. She chooses instead to devote herself to the needs of our country, and to the small improvements she can make here at the palace. These...these are her passions.'

'Are you complaining, Alessandro?'

'No, Father! No. It's just that I am having to learn a

whole new way of dealing with a woman. I feel like a youth embarking on his first love affair—'

'Perhaps this *is* your first love affair,' the old Prince murmured sagely.

'So, help me, Father. Tell me what to do.' Alessandro stopped, and levelled a blazing stare on his father's face. 'You must help me. Before I lose her.'

'You know what to do,' his father told him calmly. 'You know in your heart what is right, Alessandro. And if you want to make *me* happy, you will forget all about this foolish contract. Make this marriage work, Alessandro, or spend the rest of your life wishing that you had. It's up to you.'

Alessandro stopped pacing and stared unseeing into the distance. 'Monte Volere,' he murmured to himself. 'I shall take her to Monte Volere.' Then he turned around. 'Monte Volere, Father!'

'September…harvest-time in Monte Volere,' his father commented thoughtfully. 'A very good place to recharge the batteries of the heart.'

Alessandro felt the tension leave him as he watched a smile of contentment curl around his father's mouth.

'I think you've redeemed yourself, Alessandro. It's an excellent idea,' the old Prince declared with satisfaction.

'How soon can you be ready to leave?'

'Leave?' Emily said, still reeling from being shaken out of her slumbers by an Alessandro she had never seen before—black jeans, black tight-fitting top, black leather jacket slung across the broad sweep of his shoulders, tousled hair and yesterday's beard throwing shadows across the harsh planes of his handsome face.

But they were man and wife now, and her husband seemed to need her. 'Is everything all right?' she asked, instantly alert. 'Is it your father? Has something happened?'

'Yes. No. And, no—not yet,' he said, warming to her concern. 'My father's fine; don't worry.'

Alessandro was all tension and energy, like a coiled spring about to unwind—fast, Emily realised. 'So...?' she began curiously.

'How long?' Alessandro repeated, not troubling to hide his impatience now.

'Er...not long,' Emily admitted. 'I'd have to shower and—' She broke off uncertainly. 'Do I need to pack anything? Bring anything with me?' she elaborated, drawing up the sheet when the intimacy of his stare brushed something savage in both of them.

'You can shower when we get there. Come as you are.'

'In my nightclothes?'

'Why not?'

'Because it might cause a scandal?' Emily ventured cautiously.

Alessandro's look suggested that throwing her over his shoulder and storming off might cause a far bigger one.

'You're probably right,' he conceded reluctantly. 'So be quick. Just sling on your jeans and let's go.'

Jumping out of bed, Emily tore into her dressing room and, reaching into the very back of the wardrobe, where she had managed to conceal them from the army of wardrobe mistresses who had taken control of her clothes, she pulled out her jeans.

But the position of Princess came with conditions attached. One of the most onerous was that her appearance should never give cause for gossip or alarm. Discounting the crumpled denims out of hand, she grabbed a smart pair of navy trousers and a short-sleeved white blouse. They would do, Emily decided, gathering up her hair and securing it with a band and a couple of clips.

'Ready?' Alessandro said, barely looking at her as he grabbed hold of her forearm and dragged her with him.

'Ready,' Emily said, trying to catch her breath as she settled back in the passenger seat of a flame-red Ferrari.

'Good,' Alessandro said, narrowing his eyes as he concentrated on the road, his foot flat to the floor.

With the palace disappearing into the distance behind them, Emily was relieved to find Alessandro's driving fast but a good deal smoother than his chauffeur's. He drove without speaking, and finally, when she was almost bursting with curiosity, he announced that they would be stopping for lunch at a small village in the hills.

The Prince of Ferara's arrival with his new wife at an unpretentious café in the main square caused disbelief, followed swiftly by purposeful activity. And that was thanks largely to Alessandro's manner, Emily realised as she watched him putting people at their ease. He had barely finished introducing her around—and giving a pretty good impersonation of being proud of his choice of wife—when several women emerged from the kitchen, bearing local delicacies which they placed on the freshly scrubbed outdoor tables.

'You will need your strength,' one of them informed Alessandro coyly, nodding encouragement as she held out one of the first large oval dishes of pasta for him to taste.

'My strength?' he queried, making a point of not looking at Emily, though she noticed the smile he was gracious enough to hide behind a huge red-chequered napkin.

'*Si*, Principe,' all the other women chorused gaily, much to Emily's embarrassment.

Then one of the men threaded his way through the women, flexing a battered cap in his hand. 'Today is the Palio del Timone, Principe,' he explained. 'Each year we have a tug o' war with the neighbouring village; you have arrived just in time—' He stopped, as if he felt he had gone too far.

'Go on,' Alessandro encouraged, putting down his fork to listen.

'If you took part…' The man hesitated again.

Alessandro got to his feet and clapped him on the shoulder. 'Of course I will take part.'

'Federico,' the man supplied, flashing up an expectant glance.

'Federico,' Alessandro said, shaking him by the hand, 'you have just recruited a new member to your team. I am honoured to serve with you.'

Rubbing his hands together with glee, Federico turned. 'Did you hear that? I believe this year we may just have the edge!'

As the excitement rose to fever-pitch, Emily remembered Alessandro had been in a rush when they left the palace. 'Are you sure there's time for this?' she murmured with concern as she joined him.

'Why not?' he demanded, looking at her in amusement. 'How much of a hurry are you in, Principessa?'

As she went after him Emily's face was bright red, provoking delighted smiles and knowing looks from those women close enough to observe the exchange.

If their marriage had been consummated, Emily reckoned, a little embarrassment would have been a small price to pay. But as it was it seemed particularly unjust—especially as the women were still nudging each other and winking at her.

The news that Alessandro was to take part in the competition had spread like wildfire, and it seemed as if the entire population of the village had managed to crowd themselves into the small paved area around the café. Silence fell as he crossed the square to greet the opposing team. It was obvious that his side was at a considerable disadvantage, as most were older than their rowdy young opponents from the neighbouring village.

'Do you think you can redress the balance?' Emily asked anxiously, as she watched him strip to the waist. His naked torso was all the answer she needed, and a murmur of approval rose around them as he handed her the black top.

'Take up the slack,' the man from the café ordered, pointing to the thick rope lying on the ground. 'Principessa,' he added, 'when you drop the flag, the men must put their weight and their strength behind that rope. The first team to haul the others across that white line wins the Palio.'

Emily tried to concentrate—but was there anything more delicious than seeing Alessandro put his weight and his strength behind that rope? she wondered, watching the flex of muscles on his sun-bronzed body. If there was, she could only imagine it would be Alessandro completely stripped of his clothes.

His glance flashed across at precisely that moment, filling Emily with a very different kind of excitement from the rest of the spectators. And as she dropped the flag he gave a slight smile that seemed to promise her a contest no less involving than the one he was embarking upon.

Emily watched the denim mould around his impressive thighs as he dug his heels into the ground, gravel spitting up either side of his feet as he heaved. Each muscle and sinew was clearly defined as he threw every bit of his strength behind the rope, working to drag the other side closer to the line.

It was all over very suddenly. A groan from the losing side and a triumphant shout from Alessandro's who, brandishing the rope, punched the air with their fists. Then there was a noisy round of back-slapping and congratulations, as well as good-natured banter before Alessandro came back to reclaim his top.

'I'll just take a shower, then I'll be right with you,' he promised, wheeling away to accompany Federico. 'Then we'll go,' he called back to her over his shoulder. 'Be ready.'

The villagers wanted Alessandro to share in their celebrations, and were disappointed when he told them he had to leave. But, having exacted a promise from him to return the following year, they accepted his decision and fell back.

'If we are to reach Monte Volere before bedtime, I must go now,' he explained, provoking another round of nudges and tempting Emily to disillusion everyone on the spot. Her husband's hair might have been still wet from the shower, and his top clinging damply to the water droplets around his neck—giving the impression that he was in such a hurry to get back to her he hadn't troubled to dry himself properly—but she knew he only wanted to get to his country estate before dark.

Beyond the narrow streets and close-clustered village houses the countryside opened into a vast, sprawling plain. As the tawny volcanic soil paled to blonde they sped on through the pale, freshly tilled earth on an arrow-straight road, until another range of hills, even higher than those they had left behind, loomed in front of them.

'Not long now,' Alessandro promised as he began to negotiate a series of tortuous hairpin bends. 'I'm going to stop when we get to the top,' he informed her. 'Then you'll see one of the most spectacular vistas in all of Ferara.'

Emily formed a sound of appreciation in her throat. But the last thing on her mind after the events in the village was a sightseeing trip. And even if Alessandro's suggestion of an affair between them had been his idea of a joke, she had believed this trip to his country estate signalled his intention to bring them closer—if only for the sake of appearances. Now she knew the visit was nothing more than proof he intended to keep his word and show her around. And, keen as she was to learn more about Ferara, she was keener still to learn more about her husband.

'Save it,' she muttered ungraciously.

As Alessandro shot her a curious glance Emily regretted the outburst. He was only doing what he thought was right—what he thought she would enjoy.

'No. I insist,' he said firmly.

She had to admit he was right about the view. As she climbed out of the car Emily felt like an eagle staring down at the lake, tiny below them, shimmering in the heat haze like a panel of jewel-encrusted silk.

'It's absolutely stunning,' she murmured, fighting off the insane urge to move close enough to slip her arm through his.

'This region of Ferara has many similarities to the fiords of Norway,' Alessandro said. 'Don't stand too close to the edge,' he warned, coming to stand between Emily and the sheer drop only a metre or so in front of her feet.

Emily smiled, then felt unaccountably bleak when he started back to the car as if there was some other fabulous camera opportunity waiting just around the next bend for them.

'You will find there is a lot of variety in Ferara,' Alessandro remarked as he turned the car back onto what was now little more than a steep mountain track. 'I hope you will eventually come to love it as much as I do.'

And the point would be…? Emily thought his remark strange, bearing in mind the peculiar circumstances of their marriage. 'Mmm,' she managed non-committally.

But if the view he had shown her had been the eagle's perch, then his estate at Monte Volere was the eagle's eyrie, she discovered as Alessandro turned in beneath a narrow stone archway. Set on the highest point of a hill cloaked with vineyards, the pink and cream stone of the old manor house glowed rose-red where shadows were painted by the failing light.

'Why have you brought me here?' she said curiously.

Alessandro turned to stare at her, an amused expression tugging at his mouth. 'Rest and recreation—'

'No. Really,' Emily insisted.

'Really,' Alessandro replied steadily as he drew to a halt

in front of the old building. 'I thought you needed to get away from everything…everyone…for a few days.'

'To be alone?'

But Alessandro had already climbed out of the car.

'I'll show you to your room,' he called over his shoulder as she followed him up the steps. He opened an oak door and beckoned her inside.

My room? Emily thought, banishing the sense of disappointment. She stared across the stone-flagged hall as Alessandro sprinted up the stairs.

'Well?' he said, leaning over the carved wooden banister. 'Aren't you coming?'

The room he showed her into had been made cosy with throws, rugs and cushions in a variety of warm colours. One wall was almost completely devoted to a huge fireplace, carved from a single block of mellow honey-coloured sandstone. This housed a black wrought-iron grate and, because there was no need for a fire, an earthenware dish containing dried pot pourri to provide a splash of colour on the terracotta tiles. A wide-armed fan whirred lazily on the ceiling, stirring the scent of dried rose petals into the air. The thin coating of yellow ochre paint on the rough plaster walls had paled to lemon where the sunlight had faded it over many years, and exposed oak beams supported the high, sloping ceiling over the vast four-poster bed. Dressed with crisp white bedlinen, this offered a breathtaking view over the surrounding countryside—something Emily discovered when impulsively she flung herself down on it and bounced up and down.

'I'll be right across the landing if you need me,' Alessandro said, closing the door quietly behind him before she had a chance to say a word.

Suddenly Monte Volere didn't seem so appealing—she didn't even want to be there any more. Gusting a long, shaky sigh, Emily stared around the empty room. If this was Alessandro's idea of a honeymoon— She mashed her lips together, remembering he wasn't much good at wedding nights either. But she wouldn't let it get her down. No expectations, no disappointments, she reminded herself—and at least the bed looked comfy.

As Emily had anticipated, the high bed was extremely comfortable. The ceiling fan turned rhythmically over her head, soothing her while it kept everything airily pleasant. Over and above all this, she had taken a leisurely bath to ensure she got a good night's sleep—but, glancing at the clock, she saw it was three o' clock in the morning.

Safe to say success has *not* crowned my ventures, she thought, staring across at the closed door onto the landing. Irrationally, she felt an overwhelming urge to open it. Open it, and then what? Emily asked herself impatiently, giving her pillows an extra thump. And then leave the rest to fate, she decided, after another period of restless thrashing. Swinging her feet onto the cool tiled floor, she padded silently across the room. With care, she managed to lift the heavy wrought-iron latch without making a sound. Cautiously, she tested the door. The hinges were well oiled, and the movement was squeak-free. Opening it a little more, so that it looked like an invitation rather than an oversight, she hurried back to bed with her heart thundering in anticipation.

Above the sound of the fan she thought she could hear something…footsteps, maybe—measured, rhythmical—pacing, she decided. It had to be Alessandro, since he had already told her that the staff at Monte Volere came in on a daily basis, so she knew they were all alone in the house.

Arranging herself on the pillows, Emily fluffed out her long hair, moistened her lips, listened—and waited.

Across the landing Alessandro, after tossing and turning all night, found himself pacing the floor like a pent-up warrior on the eve of battle. Emerging from his angry introspection for a few moments, he noticed Emily's door open.

Feeling sure that he had closed it behind him earlier in the evening, he felt a rush of concern for her. Pulling on his jeans, he crossed his room to investigate.

Leaning against the wall just outside his bedroom, he paused, consciously stilled his breathing, and listened. They were still alone in the house; he was sure of it. The only noises he could detect were the typical muted creaks and groans of old timber as it cooled and relaxed after the heat of the day.

But, just to make absolutely certain Emily was safe, he crossed the landing, taking care to move silently, and stared into her room.

With her senses on full alert Emily detected the movement even though she heard nothing. Licking her lips one last time, she closed her eyes and concentrated on taking deep, calming breaths. Her limbs felt deliciously suspended and a seductive lethargy rolled over her…her nerve-endings grew increasingly sensitive as she lay still and contemplated Alessandro's imminent arrival.

Emily…his wife, Alessandro mused, incredulous that it was so as he gazed at her still figure. Could it be possible that she was even more beautiful asleep than awake? Then, remembering the strength of character that burned in her eyes, and the firm set of her mouth whenever she was angry with him, he smiled and shook his head in a quick gesture of denial. And she was lovelier still when she smiled, he remembered. And when she laughed…

His gaze lingered on her mouth. The temptation to cross the room, to match his length to hers and to tease open those full, sensuous lips…lips he was sure waited like the rest of her to be awakened—

He stopped himself. The open door was her protection, he realised. How could he surprise her when she was beginning at last to trust him? He could not take advantage of the open door. He would not frighten her by entering the room when she was asleep. Spinning around, he returned to his own room after making sure that his wife's bedroom door was closed securely behind him.

Breakfast was a tense affair. Cursing herself for behaving like a lovesick fool, Emily accepted that she had received no more than she deserved…which was precisely nothing.

Alessandro seemed cool and distant, though as polite as ever. Dismissing the cook who had come in to prepare the food for them, he insisted on waiting on her himself at breakfast.

'This really is far too much for me,' Emily protested, when he handed her a dish piled high with freshly peeled and sliced peaches, and a second plate covered in a selection of cold meats and cheeses.

'Eat,' he commanded impatiently, returning to the table where their breakfast buffet had been laid out only to return with some warm bread rolls. 'You'll need your strength today.'

'Need my strength?' Emily said suspiciously. 'For what?'

'We've got a busy day ahead of us.'

Watching him tear into his own roll, and stab at a plate of cheese with the energy of ten, Emily felt her spirits take a dive. Hiking, she guessed—at the very least. Mountaineering, probably—both of which filled her with dread. 'You mean a day of physical activities?'

'Mmm,' Alessandro confirmed gruffly, his eyes glittering with a dangerous light. Draining his coffee cup fast, he pushed it away. 'Grape-treading,' he rapped purposefully.

'Grape-treading?' Emily echoed, following him with her eyes as he strode to view the massed fields of vines through the open window. The occasion was sure to be fascinating to watch, she thought. Her glance embraced Alessandro's powerful forearms and the broad sweep of his chest. What part would he play in the proceedings? she wondered, hoping it would require him to strip to the waist again.

'What?' he demanded, thrusting his fingers into the back

pockets of his jeans as he turned around. 'What are you staring at?' he repeated, more insistently.

Emily tore her gaze away from the well-muscled thighs so tantalisingly defined in snug-fitting denim. 'Nothing,' she said dismissively, with a flip of her hand. 'I'd like that very much. For you to take me to the grape-treading, I mean.'

'Good.'

That voice again, she realised, turning her face away so that he couldn't see her reddening under his calculating and extremely disturbing gaze. 'I had no idea that such archaic practices survived,' she said, rustling up her most professional manner.

'Just about everything is mechanised these days.' Alessandro said, accommodating her approach. 'But for the highest quality wines only an experienced eye can judge the grapes. So we keep our vines low and pick by hand. It is hard work, and must be completed quickly before the heat of the sun raises acidity levels.'

She tensed as he prowled closer. 'I see…'

'Oh, do you?' he murmured sardonically, somewhere very close to her ear.

'But surely you can't tread all those grapes out there?' she said edgily, staring fixedly out of the window as she waited for her face to cool down.

'Of course not, ' Alessandro said, standing right beside her. 'The grape-treading is purely symbolic. It marks the start of the harvest.'

He refused to take the hint as she moved away, and suddenly was right in front of her again.

Glancing from side to side, Emily realised she was boxed into a corner between an old oak dresser and a bookcase. How on earth had that happened? she wondered, sagging with relief when he moved away.

'Different varieties of grape ripen at different times,' he continued evenly, as if their game of tag, at which he was clearly a master, had never taken place. 'And when they are all safely gathered in we celebrate, with a proper Festa del Villaggio. The custom of treading some of the grapes the old way after the first picking is said to placate the forces of nature.'

Emily began to relax. The history of the grape was surprisingly interesting...or perhaps it was more relief that, having distracted them both by explaining it, Alessandro was allowing the sexual tension between them to ease. She inclined her head to demonstrate her fascination with the subject, hoping her body would take the hint and calm down, too.

'It is also carried out to ensure good weather,' Alessandro went on, in the same soothing tone. Without any warning, he crossed the room, seized her arms, and held her close. 'So, Emily,' he demanded impatiently, 'will you come?'

'I'd love to.' After all, she persuaded herself as his hands relaxed, the chance to get to know her husband a little better, to see him interacting with the villagers, was an opportunity that might never come again.

'Great. You'll have to get changed first.'

'You mean it's today—right now?' She should have guessed! 'Why can't I go like this?'

'Well, if you want to look like you're heading for court—'

'Without a jacket—?' As she pulled a face his lips tugged up in a half-smile. 'You're teasing me.'

'Am I?' he murmured provocatively.

'OK, so now what? Point me in the direction of the nearest shops?' Emily demanded, confronting Alessandro, hands on hips when he started laughing. 'Please, Alessandro. Don't be difficult. I want to go with you. Just tell me where the shops are and I'll go and buy something suitable to wear.'

'OK. I'll take you.'

'Thank you,' Emily said graciously.

'We can walk there,' he said, when she stopped at the passenger door of the four-wheel drive he'd told her he used to get about the estate.

'Walk?' Emily couldn't imagine how she had missed a dress shop as they drove through.

'Certainly,' Alessandro said, striding away in the direction of the fields. 'It will only take ten minutes or so to reach Maria Felsina's cottage.

'Cottage?' Emily demanded, increasing to a trot to keep up.

'You'll see. Come on,' he urged, speeding up again. 'We haven't got all day. You don't want the grape-treading to start without us, do you?' he called over his shoulder.

A suspicion had taken root in Emily's mind. 'You mean we'll actually be taking part?'

Alessandro's loafers slapped rhythmically against the hard-baked earth. 'Of course,' he called back. 'Why else would we be going?'

'I don't know...I'm not—'

'Not what?' Alessandro demanded impatiently. He blazed a stare at her. 'Do you want to come with me?'

'Of course I do. But—'

Taking her arm in a firm grip, Alessandro marched on in silence.

As they stood in front of the modest dwelling, waiting for the door to open, Emily still felt bemused at the possibility of shopping for clothes inside such a tiny cottage.

'Don't look so worried,' Alessandro said as he turned to look down at her. 'Maria will find you something to wear.'

Emily made a conscious effort to relax. 'I'm fine,' she said.

All the signs of a much loved home surrounded them. There wasn't a single weed to be seen in the garden, and the colourful flowerbeds to either side of the newly swept path were crammed with blooms. The shuttered windows beside the front door were underscored with planters overflowing with blossom, while heavily scented climbers jostled for space around the doorframe.

Closing her eyes, Emily tried to concentrate on the sounds of the bees buzzing and the birdsong; the mingled perfume of flowers, all so delightful and distinctive. Had she been alone, she might have succeeded. But Alessandro was standing very close, claiming every bit of her notice—and why was he making such a fuss about kitting her out for the grape-treading? Surely she would only need to roll up her trouser-legs and don some sort of overall—?

She came to full attention as the door swung open. A short, generously proportioned woman, as creased and as brown as a walnut, slapped her hands together when she saw Alessandro and cried out with pleasure, 'Alessandro! *Piccolino!*'

'My nanny,' Alessandro explained, swinging the old lady off the ground with an answering shout.

Emily watched as a frantic exchange of questions and answers ensued between them.

'Maria apologises for being at the end of the garden tending her geese,' Alessandro translated. 'Her favourite, Carlotta, is to take part in the annual goose race and must have extra care. True,' he assured Emily when he saw the look on her face. 'One day I'll take you to see the race. These birds are treated like favoured members of the family. And the winner...' He gave a low whistle of appreciation.

'Fed to the family?' Emily guessed wryly.

'Certainly not!' Alessandro said with a grin. 'There is a substantial cash prize at stake—to keep the winning goose in luxury for the rest of its life. It is up to the owner to ensure that this is the case. A matter of honour,' he explained, pinning a serious expression on his face. 'And now Maria invites us into her home.'

'*Si,*' Signora Felsina insisted, nodding her head enthusiastically as she beamed at Emily.

Stepping over the stone threshold, Emily looked around curiously. The tiny cottage windows allowed in little natural light, but several old-fashioned oil lamps had been lit so that everything was softly illuminated. She could smell something delicious cooking on the old black range, and noticed that the best use had been made of the narrow window ledges, which housed an array of pungent green herbs flourishing in terracotta pots.

Contentment was contagious, she discovered, hoping they could stay for a little while. Everything was ordered for comfort. Every object had been arranged to please the eye. And all of it gleamed with the unmistakable patina of regular attention. A bolt of desire pierced her heart as she glanced across at Alessandro—desire that went way beyond the physical to claw at her soul. Did he feel it, too? Did he long for a sanctuary like this to call his own? Could he feel the tug of a real home? The longing to create a similar haven was overwhelming her—

'Sit, Principessa, sit—'

The heavily accented voice of the older woman interrupted Emily's reveries.

'Here,' she insisted, tossing rugs and cushions aside. 'Sit here, Principessa.'

'Emily. Please…call me Emily.'

Something in Emily's voice must have troubled the older woman. Her hand lingered on Emily's arm as she turned to confront Alessandro.

'Alessandro,' she said, her voice mildly chastening. 'Your bride is not happy. What is wrong, Alessandro?'

Emily tensed at the bluntness of the remark, but Alessandro seemed not to have taken offence.

At his non-committal grunt Maria shook her head, and took herself off to pour out three fizzing glasses of homemade ginger beer from a vast stone flagon. 'You sit, too,' she said, turning around to face Alessandro. 'You take up too much space,' she complained fondly as she transferred the squat glasses onto a wooden tray.

'Here, let me,' he said, ignoring her instruction and removing the tray from her hands. 'Now, *you* go and sit down, *tata*.'

Emily watched as the old lady hurried to obey his instruction, noticing her beam of delight when Alessandro used what surely must have been his childhood name for her.

Settling herself down into a chair so plumped up with cushions her chubby sandal-clad feet barely touched the ground, Maria Felsina held her glass aloft as she made a smiling toast to Emily.

'Emily,' Alessandro echoed softly.

Draining her glass with relish, Maria leaped to her feet and declared, 'And now you must eat—'

'Oh, no—' Emily protested. She was still full from breakfast, but Alessandro's glance warned her to stay silent. 'Thank you,' she said, seeing she might cause offence by refusing one of the sugar-frosted buns. 'These look delicious.' And they were, she realised, as the moist, feather-light sponge slipped down her throat.

In spite of the warm late-summer weather, there was a low fire in the grate, and as she ate Emily longed to open some buttons at the neck of her tailored shirt. She went so far as to toy with the top one—but when Alessandro caught her glance for some reason, the innocent action suddenly struck her as irredeemably provocative. She looked away, but not before she saw one of his sweeping raven brows rise minutely in an expression that was both accusing and amused.

'My wife has come to you for clothes, *tata*,' he said, turning his attention back to his old nurse.

'Will they fit?' Emily murmured discreetly.

Alessandro must have translated this, Emily thought,

judging by their peals of laughter. Before she could feel embarrassed, Maria took her hand and stroked it gently, as if to atone for the outburst. Then, confirming Emily's reading of the situation, she turned a face full of mock reproach on Alessandro and wagged a blunt-nailed finger at him.

'Maria is the best dressmaker on the estate,' Alessandro explained. 'She'll soon sort you out with something to wear.'

'In time?' Emily said anxiously.

Her concern crossed the language barrier, and with a vigorous nod of her head Maria indicated that she should follow her into the next room. Taking her through a low door, Maria pointed to some bolts of cloth stacked in one corner of the room, and then at the old treadle sewing machine standing against the wall.

There was a makeshift gown-rail—just a piece of rope suspended between two hooks on a low joist—and crammed onto this were cotton skirts in a startling profusion of colour and pattern, together with white puff-sleeved tops, all with the same scooped necks and tie fronts.

'*Ecco*, Principessa!' Maria exclaimed. And then, after viewing her thoughtfully for few moments, Maria swooped on the rail and unhooked an armful of clothing.

'Oh, no! I couldn't possibly!' Emily protested, seeing the top was so low her belly button would get an airing, never mind anything else. When Maria pressed it into her hands she bundled it behind her back, hoping Alessandro, who had just appeared at the door, hadn't noticed.

His eyes sparkled dangerously in the dim light. 'Well? Go and try them on,' he urged softly.

'Will you—?'

'I'll come back when you're changed,' he said reassuringly.

Next, Maria held out a selection of skirts for her to choose from, and Emily surprised herself by selecting the gaudiest one.

Maria smiled, nodding approval of her choice, shaking out the fabric equivalent of a sunset.

The prospect of wearing something so showy…so decadent…was exciting. Pulling on the skirt, Emily began to do battle with the blouse, managing at last to adjust the front into something approaching respectability.

'No, no,' Maria protested, waggling her finger. 'Like this, Principessa,' she said, with a broad grin on her face.

Before Emily could stop her Maria had tugged the elasticated top below her shoulders until there was more cleavage on show than ever. But the older woman still wasn't satisfied, and, plucking at Emily's bra strap, she shook her head in disapproval.

With a rueful laugh Emily finally capitulated and, reaching behind her back, freed the catches on her bra. As the last restraint was removed even she had to admit the result was impressive.

Indicating there was one last thing to be changed, Maria darted down to reach beneath an old wooden chest. Pulling out a pair of simple brown leather sandals, scarcely more than a thong to stick between the toes on strips of toughened leather, she pushed them across the stone-flagged floor towards Emily.

'Grazie,' Emily said, flashing up a smile as she slipped them on. They were surprisingly comfortable, she found, wiggling her toes and relishing the freedom. As she straightened up, Maria reached for the pins that were already finding it a struggle to contain Emily's heavy mane of shiny black hair. They were cast aside, and with a final flourish Maria carefully drew her fingers through the resulting cascade, arranging it like a gleaming cloak around her protégée's shoulders.

Standing back, she beamed with satisfaction and, taking hold of Emily's arm, turned her around to view her reflection in the mirror.

Even the short time she had been in the hot climate had

warmed Emily's skin-tone to gold, and the brazen hussy staring back at her bore no resemblance whatever to the tight-laced professional she was accustomed to seeing. Instead, a full-breasted woman, with wild, untamed hair streaming across her shoulders, gazed back proudly. Toned legs, full lips, and dark up-tilted eyes suggested endless possibilities…endless fantasies…

As Maria gusted with approval. Emily started to move towards the door. At the last moment she hesitated; dressing up, play-acting, was one thing, but her husband was all too real—and she didn't know him well enough to be able to predict how he would react when he saw his wife parading about like some fugitive from a bawdy etching. There was a distinct possibility she might unleash a whole lot more than she could cope with.

At the sound of a low, appreciative whistle she froze.

'That's quite an improvement.'

Leaning up against the doorframe, his arms loosely folded, Alessandro made no attempt to hide his interest in her newly adopted persona. 'You really look the part,' he murmured, giving Maria a wry nod of approval.

Raising her head defiantly, Emily stared him square in the eyes. What part was that? she wondered suspiciously.

'Leave the rest of your clothes here,' he said, straightening up. 'We'll pick them up later. Come on,' he pressed, 'everyone will be waiting for us.'

And, before she could refuse, he stretched out, caught hold of her, and swept her out of the door.

CHAPTER EIGHT

THEY were in a huge barn filled with the young men and women of the village. The contrast to the dappled light of the afternoon was apparent the moment Alessandro slid shut the huge wooden door behind them. Inside the barn Emily was conscious of a heady, sensuous quality to the heavy golden air that was lacking on the outside.

Ribbons of sunlight slanted across a sea of smiling faces, while the scent of young, clean bodies merged with the more pungent aroma of ripe fruit. There was an air of expectancy, and even sound seemed in thrall to the mellow mood, Emily discovered, when a murmur of welcome rose like a wave, subsided first to a whisper, and then to silence as Alessandro raised his hands.

She saw that here there was no protocol; her husband was greeted as warmly and as naturally as if he was just another man from the village, come to show off his new bride. His loud greeting was matched by the shouts of the other men present and then, turning to Emily, he urged her forward.

There was complete silence as everyone waited to see what she would do.

She felt her cheeks grow hot, and for a moment she held back. But the firm touch of Alessandro's hand on her arm gave her no choice and, stepping forward, she executed a smiling curtsey to the assembled crowd.

'Thank you,' Alessandro rasped, very close to her ear.

Emily turned and smiled back at him, the cheers resounding in her ears. She felt a warm rush of happiness to know that her action had pleased him.

She watched as he tugged his shirt over his head, and

117

then saw that she wasn't the only woman looking at him with naked appreciation.

And some of the village girls weren't afraid to move closer. Instinctively, Emily moved onto the offensive. Almost before she knew what she was doing she had placed herself between Alessandro and his admirers.

As he toed off his shoes he saw what she was doing, and threw her a half-smile that rippled through her body with startling consequences.

Was it a challenge? Emily wondered, conscious that the other women had backed off. Keeping her eyes locked on Alessandro's, she kicked off her own sandals.

Matching her stare for stare, he leaned forward and rolled up the legs of his jeans.

Holding his gaze, Emily tossed back her hair, then, emulating all the other women, she picked up the hem of her skirt and secured it into her underwear. She had never been consciously proud of her legs before, but now she was—especially when Alessandro's eyes broke their hold on her own to lavish a lingering and frankly appreciative gaze on them.

He was naked apart from his jeans, and his hard, muscled torso gleamed like a priceless bronze in the sultry haze, setting him apart from all the other men. It wasn't simply the power in his body, Emily realised as their eyes locked again, or even his extra height. It was that bone-melting menace in his dark, angled stare.

Prowling the floor around her, it seemed almost as if it was now Alessandro's turn to draw an invisible barrier between Emily and the rest of the men, so that even amidst the crowd she was undeniably and unmistakably his.

Emily's breath caught in her throat. Involuntarily, she touched her tongue to her lips, and one of the young women, misreading her expression, took it for uncertainty. Leaving her partner on the outskirts of the crowd, she alone dared to breach the invisible circle her Prince had drawn around his wife.

Taking Emily by the arm, she drew her across the saw-dust-covered floor towards the huge open vat that stood at one end of the barn. Leading her up the steps, she brought her onto the high platform of seasoned oak.

'Come,' she said softly, in lightly accented English. 'You must be the first to climb in, Principessa.'

A low murmur of approval rose from the men, then died the instant Alessandro shifted his position and started moving towards her.

'I'll lift you in,' he murmured, just as she was about to climb over the side.

Convincing herself that the only reason she would allow him to do that was because there were so many people watching and she couldn't refuse, Emily proudly inclined her head. There was something about the very special atmosphere surrounding them that made her acutely aware of the power of her femininity. It was a force she could use, or not, as she chose...

But she had overlooked the fact that she had not felt Alessandro's arms around her since they had danced together at their wedding reception. And now, thanks to her own reckless choice of clothes and the sensuous ambience in which they found themselves, she was intensely aroused.

The touch of his hands around her waist was electrifying. She closed her eyes and told herself not to read anything into it. But Alessandro took delight in lowering her as slowly as he could, so that it seemed to Emily as if a lifetime of pleasure was encapsulated in the few seconds it took to sink down into the mountain of grapes. The silence around them had thickened and taken on a new significance, as if everyone in the barn was holding a collective breath. As she sank lower she could feel the swollen fruit bursting beneath her feet, until her legs were completely submerged to the very top of her thighs.

When Alessandro vaulted over the side to join her a great cheer went up, temporarily diminishing the sensuous mood. It seemed his presence in the vat was the sign for everyone else to climb in, and a mad scramble ensued as tiny spaces were claimed; couples were so closely entwined it was impossible to see where one handsome youth ended and his pretty young partner began.

In the melee, Emily was thrust up tight against Alessandro, her feet struggling for purchase on the warm, slippery juice and split skins. She was forced to cling onto him just in order to remain standing. Relaxing gradually, as he steadied her, she became aware of his heart thrumming rhythmically against her breasts and his naked chest like warm marble beneath her hands.

The air was intoxicating, and stimulating, filled with the perfume of grapes and juice and heightened emotion. There was so much noise, so much covert—and not so covert—activity between the couples, that Emily felt shielded by it, free to indulge in her wildest fantasies, to become someone else altogether, someone far more daring and provocative than she could ever hope to be...

Then, as if at some silent signal, the noise stilled as suddenly as it had begun. Out of the silence rose a moistly slow and regular beat. It was impossible to ignore and useless to resist, and, after missing only a couple of the moves, Emily found herself joining in with the rest and stamping her feet in a rhythmical pattern.

As the pace increased the atmosphere became charged with a new and primal energy, and, clinging on to Alessandro, Emily felt her senses respond urgently. She softened against him, each of her muscles yielding in turn, until finally she was moulded into him, moving to his rhythm, their rhythm, to the insistent, unavoidable rhythm that consumed them both.

As she abandoned herself time stood still and meant nothing. She no longer knew where she began and he ended. The only certainty was that she was safe in his arms, and it was to his eyes that her overheated glance flew for approval.

Soon her clothes were drenched and she was coated all over with the sweet, sticky juice. She noticed that some of their companions were already beginning to peel away, clambering out over the sides of the vat in untidy, exhausted groups. She noticed too how a haze of passion seemed to linger behind each departure, hovering in the air around her and in the lingering exchange of slanted glances as couples retired silently into the shadows, arms intertwined and bodies fused in tense expectation.

Quite suddenly she was alone with Alessandro.

Leaning against the side of the great vat, his arms outstretched and resting lightly on the rim, he studied her calmly. Emily felt as if even the air she breathed was saturated with sensuality. She was trembling as he moved towards her, remained quiescent when he swept her into his arms, and felt bereft, even for those few moments of separation, after he had lowered her down over the side of the vat...

Vaulting over to join her, Alessandro twined his fingers through hers and drew her quickly down the steps with him, across the floor of the barn towards another door she hadn't noticed before. From there he took her across a small cobbled yard, made shady by a roof of densely intertwined grapevines, and, unlatching another door, he brought her inside the facing building, and shot home a sturdy black bolt.

They were locked in together, closed off completely from the outside world. Streamers of sunlight strung from the roof trusses high over their heads brightened the honey gold air humming around them, and as Alessandro mounted some open wooden steps with Emily in his arms she registered hazily that he was carrying her up to the hayloft.

Alessandro brought her to a mezzanine level, where the

floor was hidden beneath a deep, soft carpet of sweet-smelling hay. Setting her down gently, he sat beside her and drew her onto his lap, stretching out his long legs as he eased back against the bales of hay.

Emily felt as if she might drown in his eyes, as if the depth of expression had been there all the time, waiting for her, if only she'd had the courage to see it. There were no divisions between them now, only the gasping, pleading murmurs escaping her lips that left Alessandro under no illusion as to how much she wanted him and how hard it was for her to wait.

Pausing only to snatch apart the grape-stained ties of her blouse, he dragged the fabric away and plunged his tongue between her breasts to lick the sticky juices off. Feasting on sweetness, his questing mouth found first one succulent extended nipple and then the next, while Emily, meshing her fingers through his hair, could only beg him not to stop.

'I have no intention of stopping, *cara mia*,' Alessandro husked, holding her firm beneath him. 'Not until every last drop of juice has been licked from your body.'

And as he moved back to his task Emily found her pleasure increased when she could watch her body responding to his touch. The sound of her own rapid breathing, coupled with the deeper, throaty sounds of contentment from Alessandro, added a piquancy to her enjoyment she could never have anticipated as he fulfilled his pledge with devastating thoroughness. And, in spite of her impatience, Alessandro continued to prepare her with the utmost care, as if he knew how inexperienced she was.

When at last his hands reached down to throw back her skirt, she thrust up her hips in desperate haste, willing to go to any lengths now to make it easier for him. But he broke away, swinging to his feet as he reached for the buckle on his belt. Then, dropping back to his knees by her side, he took her face between his warm hands and kissed her very slowly, so that she was in no doubt how deep his feelings ran.

'Don't be frightened,' he murmured, reaching to strip off the rest of his clothes.

Emily gave an involuntary gasp and looked away. Nothing could have prepared her for the sight of Alessandro naked, and aroused. 'No,' she gasped instinctively, pulling back.

'No?' he queried softly, reaching up inside her blouse. His slow, seductive strokes soothed her, and then he took each engorged nipple-tip between his fingers and tugged a little. Smiling down at her, he murmured, 'Are you quite sure about that, Emily?'

The only answer possible was a series of small gasps—gasps that became cries of delight as he replaced the touch of his hands with his mouth.

'Do you still want me to stop?' Alessandro taunted her softly, whispering the words against her neck, so that she shivered with pleasure and pressed against him all the more.

'No,' Emily moaned, wanting only his touch and his kisses, not his questions.

'Are you sure?'

She reassured him frantically with every persuasive phrase she could think of. He would be a wonderful lover, she was sure of it, and that certainty increased her desire for him until it filled her whole world.

'So, you're not scared of me now?' he pressed gently.

'Scared?' Emily scoffed faintly, turning her face away so that he could not see how brazen he had made her…how she longed to be full of him, stretched by him, pleasured endlessly only by him.

'There's nothing to be ashamed of if you are,' he pointed out softly. 'At one time it was quite usual for women to save themselves for their husbands—'

'Don't tease me,' she warned huskily.

'I'm not teasing you,' Alessandro assured her, kissing the top of her head while his hands moved over her with long, calming strokes.

'I'm not very experienced,' Emily admitted, wanting more as she moved sinuously against him. 'And I'm twenty-eight,' she breathed provocatively, as if the time had come for him to remedy the situation.

'As old as that?' he growled, attending to her breasts.

Emily let out a soft cry as he began to suckle greedily whilst rolling the other nipple between a firm thumb and forefinger. He knew exactly how to tantalise her to the point of reason and beyond, until her body, her mind, her whole being craved only one thing.

'So what if you're not experienced?' Alessandro demanded, stopping to gaze at her. 'I think I know what you need…'

'Alessandro—'

'"Alessandro,"' he mocked softly, positioning her beneath him. She felt his breath fan her neck, and sighed as the shivers raced and competed with every other sensation delighting her senses.

'What's wrong, Emily?' he demanded, easing her thighs apart. 'Is it time to stop teasing you?'

'Alessandro,' Emily whispered putting her finger over his lips, 'don't hurt me…'

'I would never hurt you—'

'I don't mean that…I mean don't do this unless—'

'Unless?' He drew her hand to his lips to drop kisses on her soft palm. 'Tell me, Emily,' he insisted softly.

'I know this is just a marriage of convenience—'

He leaned back a little and stared at her thoughtfully. 'Is that all it is for you, Emily?'

'What is it for you?' she persisted, still craving reassurance.

'Our marriage is anything we choose to make of it,' Alessandro said, kissing each fingertip in turn. 'And in answer to your question, I would never hurt you...not intentionally.'

A starburst of emotion clouded her thoughts as he kissed her lips. His hands were growing more demanding, so she couldn't marshal her thoughts except to know that Alessandro was so skilled a lover... And she was lost.

Tugging off her skirt, he tossed it away and then returned his attention to her nipples. He began teasing them again with light passes of his fingertips, watching with satisfaction as she moaned and writhed beneath him.

Holding him captive with her fingers meshed through his hair, Emily savoured the touch of his mouth and his tongue, the nip of his teeth on her own swollen lips as his hands moved over her body transporting her to a fierce, elemental place where thought was nothing more than the slave of sensation. And now when he held back she played him at his own game, rolling away, luring him on.

But Alessandro was too fast and caught her easily, bringing her back beneath him and holding her firm between powerful thighs that seemed banded with steel. And now all that lay between them was a tiny white lace thong.

He had brought her to a highly aroused state, and Emily knew that it pleased him to see her so eager for his possession. Coaxing her thighs apart, he encouraged her to lift them for him, his amber eyes glittering with satisfaction as he used one hand to secure her arms above her head and the other to trace with a tantalisingly light touch the damp contours of the swell between her legs. She felt as if her whole being was concentrated in that one small area, as if every sensation she had ever experienced was magnified and centred there. Long, shuddering sighs told him how good it was, that it was the most intense sensation she had ever experienced, while Alessandro's murmurs to her in his own foreign tongue encouraged and enticed her all the more as he trailed his fingertips across the pouting site of her arousal.

When he tugged the thong off and she lay naked beneath him, wanting him so badly, there was a part of Emily that still held back at the thought of what such a powerful man might do to her. But even now Alessandro could sense her fear, and his hands were skilful and persuasive, making her forget everything but her desire for him. And when he dipped his fingertips between her wet swollen lips, the last of her doubts was erased by an intensity of sensation she could never have imagined. Crying out shamelessly, she begged him to take her then, but he refused to be hurried, only tempted her with the tip of his erection, pulling back just before she had a chance to draw him inside her. And then, releasing her hands, he gave her absolute freedom to decide the pace.

But once he was inside her Alessandro reclaimed control, increasing the pressure to fill her completely, stretching her beyond anything she could ever have imagined, until pleasure blanked out every thought but her craving for fulfillment. Holding her firm, he murmured reassurances, repeating her name when her sobbing cries marked the onset of the powerful spasms he had set up with such care.

Could anything ravish his senses more than this? Alessandro wondered, as he savoured the sight of Emily bucking beneath him.

Only one thing, perhaps, he realised as he plundered the moist, hidden depths of her mouth to taste her sweetness— and that would be the sight of his beautiful wife holding their child at the moment of its birth.

'I don't know if I like them,' Emily protested as Alessandro held out a linen cloth sagging with the weight of warm green figs plucked straight from the tree.

He made a sound of encouragement as he gave his collection a little shake. 'But ripe figs don't travel well,' he insisted. 'I promise you, Emily, you have never tasted anything like this before.'

It was so hard to resist him… No, impossible, Emily realised as she gazed up into golden eyes whose beloved intensity had become so familiar to her over the past few days at Monte Volere. Did they only burn with fire like that when he looked at her? she wondered, smiling up at him as she picked out one of the plump ripe fruits and raised it to her lips. Even that innocent gesture seemed redolent with meaning now. She heard herself sigh, felt her body quiver with awareness…anticipation. She seemed to be in a permanent state of arousal…

After taking her to his bed in the homely old manor house Alessandro had introduced her to physical love in a way that made her want him all the time…every moment of every day, waking and even sleeping…so that she reached for him unknowing in the middle of the night, and then woke to find him making love to her again.

'Well?' he demanded softly as she sank her teeth into it.

Savouring the mouthful of intense, perfumed sweetness, Emily made a sound of contentment deep in her throat. 'It's the second best thing I ever put in my mouth,' she admitted, flashing him a glance.

Alessandro threw his head back and gave a short, virile laugh. 'Wait until you taste the wine from my vineyards,' he murmured provocatively. 'There are several contenders that should be considered before you make your mind up.'

'I won't change my mind,' Emily promised, slanting him a look as she linked her arm through his, relishing his strength and his body warmth through their light, summer-weight clothes.

'Ah, but my wine contains the essence of life,' Alessandro declared, laughing at her puzzled expression. 'You'll see what I mean when you drink it.'

He wasn't joking, Emily realised later, as she watched him select a bottle from the rack. She was even more surprised to see him moving about the well-equipped kitchen with a familiarity that suggested he was accustomed to fending for himself.

'Who taught you all this?' she demanded softly, linking her arms loosely around his waist as he whipped up an omelette. Leaning her face against his strong, muscular back, she inhaled his warm musky male scent... Being with him like this felt so wonderful...so right.

'Maria Felsina,' he said, reaching for the olive oil. 'Before she became a most sought-after dressmaker, specialising in traditional clothes, she lived with our family. She was the one who greeted me when I returned home from school for the holidays—from university, too. We spent more time together here at Monte Volere than at the palace. This is the one place where I can relax and be myself.'

'I can see that,' Emily agreed. 'Even at the grape-treading I noticed the way the people accepted you as one of them.'

'I am one of them,' Alessandro said simply. 'We all call Ferara home.'

'Did you see much of your parents when you were a child?'

'My parents were swept up in their duties at Court—'

'I hope you will find time for your own children—' Emily stopped, aghast, wondering how such words could shoot out of her mouth having made no connection first with her brain. She had no plans to have children, and was quite sure that Alessandro felt the same. Her cheeks were still on fire when he turned to look at her, and there was an expression on his face that seemed to confirm it would have been better to keep her opinions to herself. 'That is, when you have children eventually yourself—some time in the future,' she said, stumbling over the words.

The look of bewilderment, of sheer panic, on his wife's face pierced Alessandro's heart. 'Don't look at me like that, Emily,' he insisted, sweeping her into his arms. 'You've said nothing wrong.' Dipping his head, he stared deep into her eyes to assure her, 'I plan to have lots of children with the woman I love—and sooner rather than later.'

Alessandro forced back the urge to tell Emily about the final requirement before his father could retire. His desire had never been stronger, he realised as he pressed her to him. But now was not the time. Their love was little more than a tender shoot, and she was at her most vulnerable. He didn't know how she would react when he told her, and crucial business meetings were about to take him away. When he told her, he wanted the time to be right... He had to be there, to reassure her...

'Alessandro?' Pressing him away from her, Emily stood back. Did his silence mean some woman had been found for him...some woman who would bear his children...a fitting partner to rule Ferara alongside him?

'I wish I didn't have to go away,' he said tensely. 'But as you will discover, Emily, with great privilege comes great responsibility. You know I wouldn't think of leaving you unless there was absolutely no alternative.'

Did she? Emily wondered, staring up at him. But then he dragged her back into his arms, as if he couldn't bear to watch the doubts scudding across her face.

'Stop this, Emily!' he told her fiercely. 'When I am a father I will be with my children; I will take equal part in their upbringing and I will spend as much time with them as any father, possibly more.'

'I believe you—'

'That's better,' he said, tipping the creamy egg mix into the pan. 'I cannot bear to see you upset. You'll feel better when you eat.'

If only it was that easy, Emily thought as she poured out two glasses of wine while Alessandro slid a delicious looking golden omelette onto a plate and dressed it with salad for her.

'You must promise me that you will stop worrying,' he insisted, nodding towards the table. 'I don't want to come home to a waif who has pined away. Haven't I told you, *cara mia*? Everything's going to be all right. My wife will take an equal part in everything I do.' He stopped in the act of pouring his own egg mix into the pan. 'What's wrong, Emily?'

Fork suspended, Emily could only stare at him. The idea of some other, unknown woman sitting so close to Alessandro, living with him...bearing his children...was insupportable.

'I promise you,' Alessandro said steadily, bringing his own food across to the table, 'we will share everything, and that's a promise.'

'Good,' Emily said, swallowing a huge mouthful of food, effectively staunching her end of the conversation. She tried not to choke on it as she considered the possibility that negotiations between Ferara and Alessandro's bride-to-be might be going on right at this very moment—even as they ate.

When was she ever going to accept that as soon as their contract came to an end Alessandro would want a proper marriage?

No time soon, she realised as they chinked glasses. But it was too late for regrets. She couldn't turn the clock back, and the truth was she was in love with her husband— deeply, passionately and ultimately, though she wished desperately it could be otherwise, hopelessly.

CHAPTER NINE

IT SEEMED no time at all since they had driven beneath the stone archway that marked the entrance to the Monte Volere estates to share their magical time, and now they were back in the Feraran capital, faced with reality. Even though Alessandro had reassured her about their impending separation, Emily felt as if her worst fears were taking on a darker, clearer shape. Alessandro had assured her that their parting would be for a couple of weeks at most. So why did she feel so sure it would be longer…?

This morning he would leave. The time for his departure had come around before she'd even had time to complete her move into his apartment at the palace, let alone discuss the worries that were now occupying her mind every waking moment. The little she had managed to glean about his trip left her in no doubt that it would be arduous, maybe even dangerous, and the last thing she wanted was to burden him with personal concerns…

Dressed casually for what she knew would be a rushed farewell, she waited in her old apartment, surrounded by all the chaos associated with her move. Pottering about aimlessly, she tried to concentrate on practical matters, picking up one thing, and then another, and switching their positions haphazardly in between glancing at her wristwatch as she counted down the minutes to his departure and wondered how much time they would have left together. Alessandro was already overrunning his schedule, and at the palace his daily life ran to a remorseless timetable.

'Emily, I'm so sorry.'

She nearly jumped out of her skin when he breezed into

131

the room, but he came straight over to her and, seizing both of her hands in his, raised them to his lips.

'Forgive me, *cara sposa*—'

'Matters of State?' Emily teased softly, forcing a smile through the foretaste of loneliness that was already stealing into her mind. The last thing she wanted was to worry Alessandro in the last few moments they had together. She needed to know that he was oblivious to the undercurrents chipping away at her happiness, and felt a rush of relief when he grinned back at her.

'How I hate these distractions,' he murmured, tugging her towards him.

'What? Me?' Emily demanded fondly, staring into his eyes.

'Everything but you,' he growled softly. Pulling her over to the sofa, he insisted she sit down.

'You'll be late,' Emily reminded him, glancing at the delicate ormolu clock on her mantelpiece.

'So I'll be late for once. It's not something I make a habit of.' He paused and looked down at her, his dark golden gaze direct and full of warmth. 'But this is special.'

'What is?' Emily said curiously.

'You,' he said wryly, brushing a strand of hair away from her face. 'For you I would make the whole world stand in line and wait, because I love you. I love you more than life itself, Emily. Forgive me for leaving you, but know that, however much you miss me, I shall miss you more.'

Tentatively Emily traced the line of Alessandro's claret-coloured silk tie from the point where it secured the crisp white collar around her husband's strong, tanned neck, down his toned torso to the slim black leather belt on his midnight-blue suit.

'And I love you more than I ever thought it possible to love anyone,' she whispered. 'I have never trusted anyone so completely in my life—with my life—you are my life.'

Bringing her hands to his lips, Alessandro turned them

and kissed each palm in turn. 'For ever, Emily,' he murmured, looking deep into her eyes. 'And now...' The corners of his mouth were starting to tug up in a grin. 'I've got something for you.'

Shifting emotional gears in tandem, Emily threw him an amused look. 'A crown?' she teased, remembering the last occasion on which he had said something similar.

'Not a crown,' he said with a wry shrug. 'I could get one for you, but I thought you weren't so keen on that type of thing.'

She loved the way his eyes crinkled at the corners when he grinned at her like that. 'OK, so don't keep me in suspense.'

Reaching inside his jacket, Alessandro drew out a slim volume of poetry. 'Christopher Marlowe,' he murmured softly as he pressed it into her hands. 'Well, Emily, do you like it? Does it please you?'

'It pleases me very much,' Emily whispered as she traced the worn binding reverently with her fingertips. He couldn't have brought her anything she would have liked more, she realised. 'I love it,' she whispered. 'It's the most beautiful...the most special thing I've ever been given.'

'I was hoping you would say that,' he said, cupping her chin to draw her forward for a tender kiss on the lips. 'Because I want you to read a page every day while I am away, and then you will know how much I love you. And now—'

'You must leave?' Emily said, trying to be brave about it.

'Soon,' he agreed, putting his finger over her lips.

She pulled away. 'I'm sorry, Alessandro. I feel so—'

'How?' he demanded softly. 'Emily, speak to me.'

'Once the terms of our contract are satisfied—' She shook her head, unable to go on.

'You can't stop there,' he warned.

'Has a bride been found for you?' She spoke so softly she couldn't be sure at first that he had heard.

'A bride *has* been found,' Alessandro confirmed. 'But I found her myself, and she is sitting here in front of me now.'

'So, you really do love me?'

Alessandro's brows rose as he stared at her, and when he spoke again his voice had adopted the low, teasing tone she loved so much. 'You guessed,' he teased gently with a heavy sigh. 'I guess that means my secret's out.'

As he brought her into his arms Emily felt safe again, as if her fears had been of her own conjuring—and all for nothing.

'I love you,' she murmured against his lips. 'But I don't know how I am going to live without you.'

He put his finger over her lips and smiled into her eyes before replacing his finger with his lips. 'You don't have to live without me, *mio tesoro*,' he said at last. 'This will just be a very brief separation.'

'Promise?'

'I promise,' he vowed softly, wrapping her fingers around the book of poems as he got to his feet. But at the door he stopped, and dragged her to him. 'I'd take you with me, but—'

'I'll be fine. Go,' she whispered fiercely, 'before you change your mind.'

'I have already changed my mind,' Alessandro confessed, raking his fingers impatiently through his hair.

'But you're running late,' Emily murmured without much conviction as he dragged her back into his arms.

'One of the privileges of being a prince is that I set the agenda,' he husked against her ear. 'And I have just remembered something very important…something that cannot wait…'

'Here?' Emily breathed, feeling her heart pound against his chest as he pressed her back against the door.

Miming that she should be quiet for a moment, Alessandro dug in his pocket for his mobile phone. 'File a new flight plan,' he ordered briefly when the call was connected. 'I have been unavoidably delayed.'

In the short time since Alessandro had been away, Emily had to admit that one of her greatest successes had been his father's apartment. With his approval she had transformed it, relegating the angular, uncomfortable furniture to the areas of the palace she thought might eventually be opened to the public and replacing it with a selection of well-padded armchairs, cosy throws and rugs. A small kitchen had been created, and a supply of fresh fruit, cakes and other delicacies were ordered to be delivered on a daily basis.

'You've done too much for me already,' he protested one day, while Emily was balanced on the top of a pair of stepladders, fixing some dried autumnal arrangements to the wall.

Turning quickly to reply, she paused and put a hand to her forehead. She never usually felt dizzy…

'Why don't we call one of the servants to do that for you?' he suggested.

Hearing the anxiety in his voice, Emily hurried to reassure him, realising he had been on his feet helping her for most of the morning. 'I'm fine,' she said. 'Are you getting tired?'

'No, it's you I'm thinking about,' he said. 'Why don't you come down from there? You look pale.'

'Don't worry about…' As her voice faded Emily blinked her eyes several times, fighting for equilibrium. She had never fainted in her life before, or been sick, but all at once it felt as if she was going to do both.

'I'm sorry, I think I'm going to be—' Hand over mouth, she slid cartoon-style down the stepladder, and made a dash for the bathroom.

She got there just in time. Turning on the cold tap, she filled the basin and immersed her face in the icy water.

Then, pulling back, she looked at herself in the mirror. Wet-faced and ashen, she steadied herself against the wall. She was no fool, she knew all the signs: she was pregnant. The only problem now was how was she ever going to bear the wait until Alessandro returned.

'Are you all right in there?'

'Yes, I'm fine,' she called brightly. Hurriedly wiping her face on a towel and arranging her hair as best she could in just a few seconds, she swung open the door, making sure she had a reassuring smile on her face for Alessandro's father. 'Let's get back to those catkins and hazel twigs,' she said as she walked past him.

'No, no,' young lady,' he said, waggling his finger at her. 'You've done more than enough for one day in your condition—'

'My condition?'

He couldn't conceal the sparkle in his eyes as he looked at her. 'You know what I mean,' he insisted, ushering her to a chair. 'I'm only surprised my son hasn't thought to inform me.'

'Inform you? What should Alessandro have told you?'

The old Prince considered this in silence for a few moments, then his face crumpled with concern. 'You mean he doesn't know yet?'

'That I'm pregnant? Emily said with a shy smile. 'No, Alessandro doesn't know about our baby yet. I've only just found out myself. But I'll tell him the moment he returns—'

'He should have been the first.'

'These things happen,' Emily said with a shrug as she smiled back at him.

'He'll return soon—immediately,' Alessandro's father amended thoughtfully. 'I'll have a messenger dispatched to bring him back here at once.'

'Could you do that?' Emily said, hardly daring to believe that Alessandro might be back with her so soon.

'Of course. And as soon as Alessandro knows about the baby we can make the announcement.'

'Won't it be a little early to go public with the news of my pregnancy?' Emily said with concern.

'Excuse my eagerness, but as well as celebrating my first grandchild I shall be celebrating my freedom.'

'Your freedom? What do you mean?'

'I shall be free…free to concentrate on my roses,' he explained excitedly. Now that you are expecting the heir I can abdicate formally. Forgive me, Emily. I am so eager to renounce the throne and pass it on to Alessandro I can hardly think straight.'

'What did you mean about making the announcement of my pregnancy official…before you can abdicate?' Emily said carefully.

'Alessandro must have explained—'

'Of course,' she said quickly. 'But it's always good to hear it again. I have so much yet to learn about my new country.' She felt as if each separate word was being wrenched out of her, and each one of them caused her pain—pain that only increased when she saw the expression of suppressed excitement, of longing, and of a dream so close now he could almost touch it written clear across her father-in-law's face.

'Well, as you know,' he began, struggling to keep his excitement under control, 'the first condition was that my son should marry before I could contemplate abdication—'

'Contemplate…' Emily murmured.

'That's right. Marriage, of course, was the first step. And the announcement of your pregnancy…the birth of your child, Alessandro's heir…is what my country's archaic legislation requires before I can abdicate in his favour. I never mentioned it before…for reasons of delicacy,' he explained gently. 'I know you can't force these things—'

Oh, can't you? Emily thought, feeling as if her heart had

just splintered into a thousand little pieces. 'No,' she agreed huskily. 'That's true.'

'But now, with this wonderful news…wonderful for all of us,' he said expansively, opening his arms in an embrace-the-world gesture. 'Emily, come to me. Let me thank you for this gift of life.'

Like an automaton, Emily accepted the old Prince's arms around her shoulders and even managed to return his kiss. He had done nothing wrong, she reasoned. She couldn't blame Alessandro's father for his son's *oversight…*

Oversight, Emily thought incredulously, much later alone in her own room. She hadn't even moved fully into Alessandro's apartment at the palace and now she was pregnant with his child. Everything that seemed to have been built on firm foundations between them had been founded on a lie. There was only one thing left to do now— and it didn't involve staying a minute longer than she had to in Ferara.

Picking up the telephone, she called her sister's mobile.

'What do you mean, she's gone?'

His father looked at him in anguish. 'I said she should tell you—'

'Tell me what?' Alessandro demanded in a clipped voice devoid of emotion. 'I'm sorry, Father,' he said, shaking his head as if he had never been more disappointed with himself. 'None of this is your fault. If I hadn't been visiting such a volatile place I would have taken Emily with me and none of this would have happened.'

'I think it's more complicated than that,' the elderly Prince ventured cautiously.

'What do you mean?'

Clapping his son on the shoulder, the old man let his hand linger for a squeeze of paternal affection. 'I'm sorry, Alessandro. I can't tell you—'

'Can't tell me!' Alessandro exploded. 'What can't you tell me about my wife? Has she been unfaithful to me?'

'No!' the old Prince exclaimed with outrage. 'She has not.'

'Then what?' Alessandro demanded angrily. 'Why else would she leave me?'

'You left her…*here*…*alone*,' his father reminded him. 'A stranger in our country, young and vulnerable. She was lonely—'

'We had an arrangement,' Alessandro reminded him bitterly.

'An arrangement?' his father exclaimed incredulously. 'If that's all you think of your marriage, Alessandro, then perhaps Emily was right to go.'

'Right! She is my wife!' Alessandro thundered. 'And whether you like it or not, Father, we have an arrangement—'

'Bah! Don't talk to me of arrangements, Alessandro,' he warned. 'I'll have none of it. I will not have my happiness at Emily's expense…or yours,' he added, seeing the torment that was fast replacing the anger on his son's face.

Mashing his lips together in impotent fury, Alessandro turned his back and stalked to the window. 'Then where is she?' he growled in an undertone.

'Somewhere where she is appreciated, I imagine,' his father told him mildly.

'And where might that be?' Alessandro said, turning slowly on his heels to confront him again.

'I'll leave you to work that out. But don't take too long, Alessandro. Don't let her slip through your fingers.'

Grinding his jaws together, Alessandro sucked in a breath as he made his decision. 'If she really wants to go, Father, there is nothing I can do to stop her. But if there is even the slightest chance—'

'You're wasting precious time, Alessandro.'

Inclining his head in a curt show of silent agreement,

Alessandro paused only to give his father a brief, fierce embrace before setting off for his own rooms, where he would pack an overnight bag and ring the airport to file his flight plan for London.

'As it happens, Emily, I do have something for you. Something I think you'll like—the fallout from a nice juicy bankruptcy. Your clients are major creditors—after the usual banks and Inland Revenue et cetra. Respectable elderly couple, allegedly fleeced out of their life savings by some toff from the Shires.'

'Billy, you're a diamond,' Emily said gratefully, playing to her Chief Clerk, whose thick Cockney accent and market stall *joie de vivre* masked a mind of Brobdingagian scope and efficiency. She had been expecting to pick up the dregs on her return to Chambers—the cases no one else wanted. But this was right up her street. 'Do we have all the papers?'

'Do pigs have wings? But your clients are available for a conference this morning.'

'Good. Give me what we've got. Set up the meeting. Oh, and Billy?'

'Yes?'

'If any personal calls come through for me...I'm not available.'

'I understand,' Billy said non-committally, straightening his impeccable tailor-made waistcoat on his rapid passage out of the room.

Collecting up her things, Emily went to settle herself into the office Billy had allocated to her. She was back to being a 'door tenant' for the time being—a part-timer in Chambers—and would have to submit to being shuffled about wherever there was available space.

Across Europe the new generation of young royals all combined professional careers with the responsibilities of their rank, so there hadn't been a single comment when she'd returned to work. And by using her maiden name she was largely assured of anonymity. So far, at least, the paparazzi had failed to mark any change in the blissful state of the Crown Prince of Ferara's marriage.

It had been Miranda's suggestion that she return to work and take time to think things through. They stuck by each other through thick and thin, Emily mused, knowing she needed her sister's support like never before. She knew Miranda would never suggest she should try and forget there had ever been a man called Alessandro...but that wasn't going to stop her trying, Emily thought as she reached for the intercom button.

'Billy, can you bring those papers in right away, please?'

The meeting with her elderly clients went well. As Emily had anticipated, they were both dressed in their Sunday best, and trying their hardest to appear at case, when in fact, after planning carefully all their lives to enjoy a well-earned retirement, they were now staring into the abyss. Fortunately they had kept a meticulous diary of events, and with that she could build a case.

Emily found nothing unusual in taking over a case at the last minute, but it did mean that crucial parts of the thick file had to be read and assimilated before the first court hearing that same afternoon. Fortunately she thrived on the pressure; cases like these were what had attracted her to law in the first place.

She broke concentration reluctantly when a knock came at the door, knowing it could only be one person.

'Sorry to disturb you, Emily,' said Billy. 'I thought you should know you've had one call.'

'From?'

'Your sister.'

'Oh?' Emily said with concern.

'She said not to worry you.'

But the way Billy had delivered the message suggested

she should look deeper into the matter without delay, Emily thought, automatically scanning her diary. 'Could you get hold of her for me, please, Billy?'

'Already on line one,' he announced briskly, on his way out of the door.

'Miranda?'

'Sorry to trouble you at work, Em. I know you left a message with Billy to say you were too busy to speak to anyone, but I thought you should know—'

'You don't have to apologise.'

'Alessandro's in town. He wants to see you. I didn't know what to say.'

Emily's heart must have stopped. She only knew she had never been more grateful for her sister's support at the other end of the line. 'Did you tell him?'

'Where you'll be? No. I'm waiting for you to give me the go-ahead on that. But, Emily?' Miranda added anxiously.

'Yes?'

'I really think you should see him. At least give him a chance to explain.'

'I don't know.'

'Please, Em. If you'd spoken to him, heard how worried he sounds, you wouldn't be so hard on him. He knows you're appearing in court today; he just doesn't know which one…'

The silence hung between them and deepened, until finally Emily said softly, 'I can't keep running away from him for ever, can I, Miranda?'

Dragging the documents she had been reading before the call back towards her, Emily read the name of the man she would be accusing in court that day—the man who had tricked and betrayed an elderly couple. Alessandro had betrayed and tricked *her*, she remembered bitterly—and into a marriage of convenience that included an innocent child. What sort of man did that?

Alessandro managed to slip into the visitors' gallery just as the court usher called out, 'All rise,' and the judge walked in and took her seat.

He missed the first few moments of procedure—case number, names, et cetra—and was barely aware that another man, seeing him arrive, had also moved into the gallery a couple of rows back, and was desperately trying to catch his attention. The only thing he saw, the only thing he cared about, was Emily, fully robed and bewigged, standing in front of the judge.

He drank her in like a life-restoring draught, feeling his resolve and his determination increase with every second that he gazed at her. Just being so close was like a healing process, and he hadn't even realised how heartsick he was until this moment. He was in such agony he had to clench his fists to stop himself calling out to her. Taking a deep breath, he battled to compose himself. He would win her back. He had to…

His heart sang with pride while his mind seethed with questions as reason and logic made a steady return. Staring at her, he found it impossible to equate the woman he'd thought he knew—the clear-faced, intelligent woman below him now in the well of the court—with someone who could give herself to a man as freely and as lovingly as Emily had and then simply disappear without a word. Had she fallen out of love with him? His guts churned as an ugly worm of suspicion burrowed into his mind.

He had been so sure that she loved him—but then how could she have left him so abruptly if that was so? And, feelings apart, she had broken the contract that meant so much to her—to her sister. His father was heartbroken by their split, yet Emily had said she loved him, too. What could have taken her from them without even the basic courtesy of a note…something…anything to explain her behaviour? It had to be something so momentous, he reasoned, that only a face-to-face meeting would allow it to be brought out into the open. Yet a face-to-face meeting was the very thing Emily seemed intent on avoiding—but she *would* meet with him, he was determined on that…

The efforts of the man sitting behind Alessandro to attract his attention failed until the judge called a mid-morning recess. The very last thing on Alessandro's mind was a reunion with someone from his old school. Let alone Archibald Freemantle, he realised, grinding his jaw as he fought to remain civil.

His whole mind was focused on one thing and one thing only, and that was making things right with his wife. Maybe his pride had taken a battering when she deserted him, but the overriding emotion he had felt then, as now, was one of loss. Loss so insupportable he had no strategy to cope with the devastating effect it was having on every aspect of his life. Without Emily he had no life, Alessandro thought bitterly, forcing his attention back to the irritating individual in front of him.

'Archibald,' he said coolly, extending his hand as courtesy demanded, then removing it as fast as good manners allowed. 'What brings you here?'

'This case, old boy,' Archibald exclaimed, with such a heart-felt sigh it threatened to mist up his gold-rimmed spectacles.

'Oh?' Alessandro said vaguely, trying to be discreet about his desire to spot Emily…if only for a moment…just a glance would do, he realised, cursing himself for being a lovesick fool.

'You must have realised it's m'brother,' Archibald said, huffing again. 'Freemantle Minor,' he clarified, reverting to the argot of school.

Alessandro tensed. It didn't seem quite the moment to comment, *Oh, that rat,* so he confined himself to a murmured, 'Ah, now I recognise him.' The man in the dock, he realised, and a flash of amusement briefly eased his torment. Toby Freemantle had started his career as a small-time crook, going through coat pockets at school—until he was asked to leave. It appeared he had pursued his calling into adult life.

'Would have got off,' Archibald said hotly, clearly determined to elicit Alessandro's support, 'had it not been for that bitch barrister the wrinklies hired. Apparently she's hot stuff—said to be one of the best legal minds around. For a woman,' he added scornfully.

Rage powered up through Alessandro's frame at this casual dismissal of Emily's abilities, but only a muscle flexing in his jaw threatened to betray his feelings.

'I'm sure the judge presiding would be delighted to hear you make such a remark,' he commented laconically. 'Oh, and by the way, Archibald…'

'Yes?'

'That woman is my wife.'

Making a hasty exit, Emily was keen to escape to Chambers, where she could forget her personal problems and immerse herself in the case ready for cross-examination the next day.

Head down, arms encircling her bundle of papers, secured with the traditional pink ties, she failed to see the tall, imposing figure waiting at the head of the broad sweep of marble steps… Until an arm reached in front of her to grab hold of the mahogany banister and block her way.

'Emily—can we talk?'

Her mind locked with shock, even though she had expected Alessandro to find her. Unable to cope with the thought of seeing him again, she had simply banished it from her mind.

Seeing the security guards on alert, and moving towards them fast, Emily nodded them away first before she spoke. 'Alessandro. I didn't expect to see you here.'

Why was she lying to him? She bit down on her lip. All

her cool, all her reserve, every bit of the calm logic that guided her in the courtroom had vanished.

It was useless reminding herself that this was the man who had lied to her, who had used her like a breeding mare to gain an heir for his country, when the need to feel his arms around her instead of having one of them obstruct her path in such a stiff and telling way was all she cared about.

She could hardly breathe. She couldn't bring herself to look at him. But then, she didn't need to, she realised wretchedly. She could feel him, sense him, scent his clean male warmth and imbibe his very essence without using her eyes.

If she didn't keep his betrayal, his lie of omission at the forefront of her mind, she might just go mad from wanting him.

'Emily, please…won't you even speak to me?'

She wouldn't survive if he hurt her again. 'This is a difficult case—'

'I can see that. I'm sorry to intrude on your work, but your phone is always switched through to your answering service.'

'I don't have much time—'

'As I said, I apologise for approaching you like this, but I could think of no other way.'

The whole situation was a catastrophic mess, Emily realised tensely. Leaving aside her own feelings, Miranda's first solo concert was coming up in the New Year—a concert where she would be playing the violin Alessandro had loaned to her.

'Emily—' Alessandro's voice had roughened, and was considerably louder. It brought her back to full attention. 'I have to talk to you,' he insisted. 'But not here; not like this, please.'

Emily's face flushed red as she stared up at him. She had never thought to hear so needy, so desperate a note in his voice.

'I know I've let you down—'

He had found out she knew about the baby clause; she could hear it in his voice...in what he didn't say. She had to hear his explanation. 'I feel as if I hardly know you any more,' she murmured, speaking her thoughts out loud.

'Well, I only know that I've hurt you, Emily. And that I can't let it end like this. I can't go on any more without your forgiveness.'

My forgiveness...my forgiveness, Emily thought wretchedly as her hand moved instinctively to cover her stomach. 'If you could give me the rest of the afternoon...'

'You have to eat,' he said instantly. 'Why don't we meet at my hotel for dinner? Eight o'clock? You won't want a late night.'

'Yes... Yes, please.'

'Shall I send a car for you?'

Her mind was in freefall. She needed time to think, to prepare, to plan how she was going to tell him about their baby. 'No, that's fine. I'd rather you didn't.'

Emily stood motionless, watching Alessandro take the steps down to the foyer. He moved with long, purposeful strides, his head held high, and the gaze of every woman, and not a few of the men, zoned in on his rapid departure.

Only when he had gone through the doors that led to the street did she begin very slowly to follow after him. He was still her husband...and in spite of everything she knew without doubt she still loved him.

She fought hard in court...wasn't her marriage worth fighting for, too?

The invisible men, as Emily had learned to call them, had obviously telephoned ahead, as the door to Alessandro's suite swung open before she could even knock.

As he stood back to let her pass the temptation to touch him, to look into his eyes, was almost irresistible. But she could feel remoteness coming off him in waves, pushing her away.

Shrugging off her winter coat and scarf, she put them on a chair first, and then, having first drawn a deep, steadying breath, she turned around. 'How are you, Alessandro?'

He looked amazing. Black trousers, black round-necked cashmere sweater framing his tan…

'How am I?' he said, dipping his head to give her a keen look. 'That's an interesting question, coming from you, Emily.'

Picking up her coat and scarf, he walked across the room and deposited them inside what must be a cloakroom.

'Apparently I'm some sort of monster,' he said with his back to her, 'since my wife walked out on me without a word of explanation.'

CHAPTER TEN

THE expression in her husband's eyes frightened Emily. It was as if all the angry frustration, all the bafflement possible had been captured and condensed in his gaze. And as for herself... She took a steadying breath and struggled to find the words she had so carefully rehearsed in the taxi from her apartment. But she was in too much pain to speak—pain so bad it felt as if her heart had been ripped out of her chest and stamped on.

It seemed like several lifetimes before she managed to say, 'I spoke to your father—'

'And?'

She had never heard him sounding so curt, so cold. And she wasn't doing much better. Her own voice was strangulated, false. She had to wait and take a few deep breaths before she could relax enough to start again. 'He told me—'

'Told you what?' Alessandro cut in harshly. Why was it that angry words hung in the air longer than any others? he wondered furiously. The very last thing he had intended to do was shout at Emily the moment she arrived, but his emotions were in turmoil. No one knew better than he that the rest of their lives depended on what happened between them in the next few hours. 'Go on,' he said, making a conscious effort to soften his tone.

Emily knew she had to set him straight about his father's role, if nothing else. 'It was something he thought I already knew...something he believed you would have told me,' she went on, trying to stay calm. 'He said he couldn't abdicate until you...until I had your child.'

Alessandro's face went blank and unreadable—like a stranger's, Emily realised with an inward shudder. She saw the change come into his eyes first: a slow infusion of pain, then guilt, and finally something approaching fear.

'I thought I'd lose you,' he said, so softly she could hardly make out the words. 'I believed it was too much for you to accept all at once. You would never have agreed—'

'You're right about that,' Emily flared, her own voice shaking with emotion. 'I would never have agreed to barter the life of a child—even for the sake of my own sister's happiness.' She stopped. There was an iron band around her chest; she could hardly breathe. She wheeled away from him in bewilderment. 'I thought you loved me,' she cried accusingly.

In a couple of strides Alessandro had crossed the room and grabbed her chin, forcing her to look up at him.

'Don't you understand anything, Emily? I do love you. More than you will ever know. No! Look at me!' he insisted when she tried to turn her head away. 'I love you,' he repeated fiercely. 'I have loved you from the first moment I set eyes on you. I don't suppose you believe in love at first sight; neither did I, before I met you—' He shook his head and looked away, as if the emotion was too much for him to bear. 'I was frightened I might lose you if I told you the truth. I can see now that I was wrong. But if you won't accept my apology then I don't know what I can do…what I will do without you…'

'When would you have told me?' Emily demanded tensely when he'd let her go.

'If you had become pregnant there would have been no need to tell you,' he admitted with a short, humourless laugh.

'That's very blunt.'

'Yes,' he agreed bitterly.

'And if I hadn't become pregnant?' She needed to choose her words with more care, Emily realised distractedly, still agonising over her own startling news and wondering how she was going to break it to him. 'When…when would you have told me?'

'I'm not sure,' Alessandro admitted bluntly. 'I needed time…time to be sure you trusted me before I could identify the *right time*.'

'I see.'

'No, you don't,' he said, taking hold of her again. 'I was wrong. I can see that now. I should have told you right away. I need you to forgive me, Emily. I need you to accept my apology so that we can rebuild everything I have damaged, however long it takes… Emily?'

When she told him about their baby—what would he think of her then? Emily wondered numbly. He had been so honest, so frank and giving in his own apology, while she harboured the greatest secret of them all, jealously guarding it inside her like some precious gift she had not yet chosen to bestow. Instead of making it easier for her, Emily realised, Alessandro's openness had only made it all the more difficult.

'This isn't easy for you,' he said. 'I realise that. You need time to think. I'm going to take you home. No, I insist,' he said, holding up his hands. 'I'll keep in touch, and when you're ready—'

'No,' Emily said urgently—this wasn't supposed to happen. 'I don't want you to take me home.' This was the moment. She needed to tell him…whatever the consequences might be for herself.

She could see how pale he was beneath his tan, hear the enormous pressure he was forced to endure because of her reflected in his voice. She couldn't bear it. She couldn't bear to see him suffering and know that she was the cause.

'Don't apologise to me. We're both at fault,' she said, the words all coming out in a rush. 'We had no chance to get to know each other—'

'Listen to yourself,' he said. 'You're half-frantic with worry, and all because of me. There's no excuse for my behaviour,' he said harshly, cutting off any chance she might have had to say more. 'I'm going to get your coat—'

'No, Alessandro, wait—'

But he was already back, and helping her into it. 'I'm taking you home, Emily. I've upset you enough for one night. I won't hear any arguments.'

But her home was in Ferara, Emily thought as he ushered her out of the door. With Alessandro...

'I don't want to pressure you,' he said, releasing his hold on her arm at the door to her apartment. 'I've put you through enough. If you come back to me, Emily, it will be for ever, so I want you to be sure.'

'We never expected it to come to this.' Emily shivered suddenly as he kissed her on both cheeks, as if in that moment the shadow between them had made itself visible.

'We never expected to fall in love,' Alessandro countered softly, shooting her a wry half-smile as he turned to go.

Emily had thought she'd had sleepless nights before, but she'd been wrong. *This*...this was a sleepless night.

Finally she gave up on sleep altogether, and, clambering out of bed, crossed the wood-strip floor to the enclosed balcony that had been one of her main reasons for buying the riverside flat.

She could never have anticipated that her meeting with Alessandro would go so badly wrong...that she would be so lacking in force, in ability to put her point across. She was ashamed of the way she had caved in, Emily realised tensely. But the atmosphere had been so fraught, their reunion so fragile... If Miranda had been at home they would have talked things over. But Miranda had already embarked on a tour of the provinces that preceded her debut in the capital... And, though she had lost track of time, Emily knew it was the middle of the night—Miranda would be asleep.

Wrapping herself in a mohair throw, she curled up on one of the sofas and stared bleakly out at the river, stretching darkly into the distance like an oily rag. The main road was freshly salted with icy sleet and made her long all the more for the mellow colours and warmth and sunshine of Ferara.

Whatever time it was, her mind was still buzzing. She hadn't managed to sleep since Alessandro had left a little after twelve. Burrowing deeper into the soft throw, she squeezed her eyes tightly shut and wished harder than she had ever wished for anything in her life that things could be different... Wasn't cheating a man out of his child on a par with cheating a defenceless elderly couple out of their life savings?

The unmistakable sound of her laptop signalling incoming mail broke into that disturbing thought, and, peering at the clock, she saw that it still wasn't quite four-thirty in the morning.

Racking her brains for friends in the Antipodes, or even late-working New Yorkers, she padded across acres of wood-strip flooring into the open-plan space that constituted her living area. Leaning over her desk, she clicked the mouse and brought up the screen.

Tight schedule—now leaving first thing tomorrow— make your decision about returning to Ferara—let me know soonest—Alessandro.

Her heart gave a little flurry just to know that he was awake—and thinking of her. But, reading the e-mail again, she went cold. She couldn't leave London. There was still the court case to settle. And it wasn't going well; there were all sorts of outstanding issues.

Fingers flying, she typed a reply and sent it straight back.

I can't make that sort of decision yet. I have a tight schedule, too.

She hovered anxiously over the machine, realising that he couldn't read her mind and know all the difficulties she was facing at work. Out of context the message would just seem petulant.

His reply came through right away.

I understand you need more time.

Frowning a little, Emily pulled out her chair and sat down in front of the computer.

The case I'm involved in is proving more complex than I had anticipated.

This time she gave herself a little more space before touching 'send', and checked what she had typed again for possible misunderstandings. She hugged herself as she waited for Alessandro's reply. It didn't take long.

When will your case be completed?
Difficult to say. Two weeks max, at a guess.
Before the holidays?
Hopefully before the holidays.
I'll send the jet.
No need.
But that's a yes?

She hesitated about ten heartbeats—a split second.

Yes.
I'll send the jet.

Emily sat staring at the screen until dawn sketched rosy fingers across a sullen, snow-laden sky, but there was no more mail that night from Alessandro.

Touching the screen by his name before she switched off, she wondered what lay ahead for them both with the holidays approaching fast. The possibility of seeing him again was the only present she had on her Christmas list.

Unforeseen delay in resolving case—no chance I can make it for Christmas.
Sorry.
Emily

Alessandro took out his frustration on his desk with a blow so hard he found himself nursing his fist, wondering if he had broken anything.

He had chosen e-mail specifically as a mode of communication to give them both a breather. A voice on a telephone could reveal so much…too much. E-mail was brief and to the point. And utterly without emotion—or should be…had always been…up to now.

Hating himself for putting his heart on the line, he stabbed back.

What's the problem?

Sitting in her office, surrounded by papers, Emily rested her forehead on the heel of her hand and stared at the screen. She felt sick from early pregnancy blues augmented by a very real concern for her clients. It was beginning to look as though she would win the case, but the chance of securing some money for the elderly couple was appearing increasingly unlikely.

The likelihood of reaching any type of satisfactory conclusion before the long drawn-out holiday season interrupted everything was negligible.

She touched the screen by Alessandro's question, as if it was possible to draw some comfort from him by doing that, then pulled her hand away. Having him at the other end of the line, waiting for her reply, was no compensation for having him with her. And knowing he was out there somewhere, but not knowing where, made her feel lonelier than ever. It made her feel weak and vulnerable—something she could have done without. Because that was no help to her elderly clients, whose future peace of mind lay in the scrambled mounds of documentation scattered across her desk. But the least she owed Alessandro was an explanation for staying in London over Christmas…

Freemantle has no money—no assets—no nothing. Can't leave my clients in the lurch—have to keep trying.

Try what? Emily thought, absentmindedly dispatching the message before she had quite finished it. If Toby Freemantle was stony broke—

Her eyes flashed to the screen as Alessandro's reply came up.

Trace his maternal grandmother's will. She left him all her art treasures. His brother boasted to me that whenever creditors came to call the paintings were stored in their mother's attic. Keep me informed. Alessandro.

Instantly alert, Emily straightened up, and tapped in. *Thank you—I will.*

And then, not because she thought it was prudent, or that he would even care, but because her heart took over, she lapsed into a personal style.

*I hope you have a good Christmas, Alessandro—say
sorry from me to your father. Emily.*

Making a sound close to a tiger in a rage, Alessandro
replied.

*Sure to—Father in South Africa, looking at rose gar-
dens—signing off, Alessandro.*

Alessandro had been right, Emily thought, waving off two
very happy elderly people, her hands clutching tight the
bottle of champagne they had insisted on buying for her.
She wouldn't drink it now, because she was almost four
months pregnant, but it signified their peace of mind, and
that was all that mattered. She would take it to the
Christmas gathering at her parents' house.

Thanks to Alessandro, the works of art she had tracked
down with the help of the fraud squad had raised millions
at auction, brightening the London scene on the run-up to
the big Christmas shut-down. There had been more than
enough money to satisfy all the creditors and even set Toby
Freemantle up for life—when he came out of jail.

As the elderly couple disappeared around the corner, arm
in arm, she knew her first e-mail had to be to Alessandro.
She had to thank him, let him know the outcome of the
sale.

Great news—do you ski?

Rocking back on her chair, Emily stared at the screen
again.

Almost as hesitantly as she might have said the words,
she tapped in, *Yes—why?* then clicked the mouse and
waited.

We have issues to resolve sooner rather than later. I plan to spend Christmas in a small village called Lech, in the Arlberg region of Austria. I'd like you to join me.

Emily's heart leapt at the invitation. But she had promised to attend her mother's famous Christmas lunch, she remembered, frowning.

'Of course you must go with Alessandro,' Miranda insisted, when Emily telephoned her twin to run the idea past her. 'You don't think Mother will try and make you stay in England if she thinks there's a chance of a *rapprochement* with Alessandro, do you?'

'No, but—'

'But what?'

'I haven't told him yet,' Emily said tensely, tracing her still flat stomach.

'Are you going to wait until he can see for himself?'

'I don't know. I—'

'Look, Emily,' Miranda said, beginning to sound impatient. 'I've got to go to rehearsal. You're the one who always knows what to do. You know what you have to do now. You're just allowing emotion to get in the way of clear thinking.'

Emily allowed herself a wry smile. 'Are you surprised?'

'That you've let things go this far? Yes. It's a fact that Alessandro wasn't entirely open with you. Get over it. Aren't you doing just the same to him now? If you want the truth, it looks like a bad case of double standards.'

'Please don't be angry with me. You know I've forgiven him. But he wouldn't give me a chance to explain—'

Miranda heaved a heavy sigh down the phone, cutting her off. 'I'm not angry with you, Emily. I'm just worried about you—and Alessandro. Please say you'll go.'

'I can't just turn up pregnant in Lech.'

'No, you can't,' Miranda agreed thoughtfully. 'So maybe I'll—'

'No! Don't you dare say a word to him,' Emily warned. 'This is something I have to handle by myself.'

'Promise?'

'Have I ever let you down?'

'This would be one hell of a time to make it a first,' Miranda said bluntly.

Emily could feel her sister's concern winging down the phone-line. 'I won't let you down, Miranda. I promise.'

After doing her research, Emily knew why her husband had chosen Lech for his winter retreat—the townsfolk were so used to visiting royalty no one paid the slightest attention to one more prince arriving for the winter sports. She realised now that any type of anonymity was preferable to none.

It wouldn't take her long to pack a suitcase, book a flight—

She swung around in surprise when the doorbell rang. She wasn't expecting anyone and, apart from kicking off her high-heeled shoes, she hadn't even changed her clothes after the final meeting with her clients. Checking her appearance in the mirror, she pulled a face and made a vain attempt to capture some of her long hair into the slide at the back of her head. Reaching the door, she opened it and gasped.

'Alessandro! Wh—?'

'May I come in?'

'Yes, of course. But—' Her bewildered gaze followed him across the wide expanse of floor to the picture windows, where he turned and stood looking around him, the corners of his mouth pressing up in an appreciative grin.

'This is very nice,' he said, looking around the apartment.

'Thank you,' she said. Shutting the door, Emily leaned back against it. Her heart-rate had gone into orbit...she needed a minute. No, a minute wasn't nearly long enough, she realised, staring at her husband.

His charcoal-grey vicuña overcoat had been left open to reveal a black V-neck cashmere sweater and black trousers, and his inky-black hair in its customary off-duty disarray fell over familiar dark gold eyes—eyes that were presently trained on her with amused speculation.

'I don't understand—I was just e-mailing you—'

'And you presumed I was in Ferara?'

She could see he was trying not to smile. 'Well, yes. I wanted to share the good news with you the moment I found out myself.' Even as she spoke the words it was as if a double helping of conscience had reared up to mock her.

'Good to know you were thinking about me,' Alessandro commented, slanting her a look.

He didn't miss a thing, she realised edgily, moving away from the door.

'I was just around the corner in my hotel at the time,' Alessandro said, clearly trying to put her at her ease. 'What about Lech? Are you packed?'

'I haven't booked a seat yet.'

'Booked a seat?'

It took a whole new mind-set to deal with Alessandro, Emily reminded herself. Of course he would have flown to England in his own jet. 'You came for me?' she said hesitantly.

'Looks like it,' he agreed dryly.

'Can you give me half an hour? Here—let me take that for you,' she said as he began to shrug off his overcoat. 'Can I get you anything while you wait? A drink?'

'Just get ready,' he said. 'I'll wait.'

'Wait out here, then,' she suggested, opening the window to the balcony. 'It's got a fabulous view, and—'

He caught her to him as she went past, dragging her close and shutting her up with a long, deep kiss that wiped her mind clean of everything but him. But even as she softened against him he gently but very firmly pushed her away.

'Go,' he whispered. 'We have a non-negotiable take-off slot. It's nearly Christmas—or had you forgotten?'

Alessandro took her through a sumptuous wood-panelled entrance hall into a quaint reception area decorated in typical Austrian alpine style, with red gingham curtains edged with heavy ecru lace. Garlands of dried flowers hung on the walls, and in a huge stone grate a roaring log fire acted like a magnet to the people clustered around, exchanging tall stories from their day on the slopes.

There wasn't a photographer in sight, Emily noticed with relief as she watched her husband complete the formalities and return to her side with a huge old-fashioned carved wooden key-fob.

'When we get to the room I suggest you take a bath,' he said as they strolled through the hotel to the guests' accommodation. 'It's too late to sort out skis for you tonight, and mine are already here. So we'll take it easy—have dinner, chat...'

Chat. Emily nodded and smiled, but her insides were churning. There would be no more running away from the truth now. But at least he was giving her time to prepare.

As he propelled her into the lift Alessandro's hands were around her waist. His touch was electrifying. And suddenly all Emily knew, all she could think of, was that she wanted him...

'Are we going to eat in the restaurant or our room?' she asked as he pressed the button for their floor.

As an attempt to kick-start the logical side of her brain it was a pretty pathetic gambit—and she knew it—but with Alessandro so close, and no one else around, it was all she could manage.

'Why, Principessa,' he murmured softly, letting his

hands slip down slowly over her thighs as the lift began to rise, 'are you hoping to seduce me?'

Resisting the temptation to lean back into him, Emily made a soft, double-barrelled sound of denial. And when he moved to drag her close she turned to face him, warning him off with her eyes. 'We have things to discuss,' she said, realising uncomfortably that he didn't know the half of it.

'Of course,' he agreed, with a small mocking bow.

But she could see the dark, smouldering desire in his eyes and the arrogant twist to his lips that proved he was remembering other occasions when the secrets between them had lain dormant and could not douse their passion.

She was relieved when the lift slowed at their floor. The atmosphere in the confined space had grown so thick with sexual tension she could feel herself drowning in it—and losing all sense of what she had come to do...to say to him. But when he stopped outside one of the heavy oak doors he rested his hand on the wall, trapping her.

'We have to share, I'm afraid. I could only get one suite because—'

'It's Christmas?' she supplied crisply, channelling all her apprehension into one snippy remark.

But he wouldn't be provoked, only stared at her lazily, forcing Emily to wonder how long she could remain immune to his unique scent...sandalwood, musk...man. And his slow smile was producing a sensory overload that made her want to drag him into the room and to hell with everything else.

But if he was in the mood for playing games... 'As we still have issues to resolve, I hope there's more than one bed in the suite?'

'Didn't I just say we'd have to share?'

'A suite...you said we had to share a suite. You didn't say anything about sharing a bed.' How come that had come out in a provocative murmur, sparing him the scolding she had intended?

'Why shouldn't we share a bed? After all, we are man and wife.'

'I hope for your sake the sofa's comfy,' Emily said, fighting to keep her voice steady as she took the key from his hand.

Just as she had feared, when she opened the door one large bed dominated the room. Spying her luggage in one corner, she hurried over to it and picked up the smallest bag. 'See you after my bath, Alessandro—'

The heel of his hand shot out, slamming into the bathroom door as she tried to close it.

'Perhaps I'd better warn you—these doors don't lock.'

'I'm sure I can trust you to be a gentleman.' Their faces were so close she could have kissed him. But, giving the door one final push, she almost sank to her knees with relief when Alessandro allowed it to close.

Inside the privacy of the marble-clad bathroom, Emily let out a long, shaky breath. With every hour that passed it became harder to tell Alessandro about the baby. She stabbed a furious glance at herself in the mirrored wall. Just when had she become such a coward? If she couldn't face up to it by the time she'd had her bath she didn't have anything to offer him—or their unborn child. It would be better for all of them if she took the next flight out of Austria…

Dinner was conducted with every outward show of restraint, whilst inwardly fires raged inside the two people facing each other across the cosy country-style table.

There was nothing remotely cosy about the workings of Emily's mind as she forked up the last scrap of home-made *sachertorte*, but she managed to hide her angst behind enthusiasm for the food.

'I've never tasted a better chocolate cake in all my life,'

she said, as if they were two friends on a casual outing. 'If I stayed here for long I'd be huge.'

'You have put on a little weight,' Alessandro commented, slanting her a look as he laid down his own fork with his own cake half-eaten. And she looked better for it, he thought. She looked like some luscious fruit that was ripe and ready for eating. He swiped the linen napkin across his lips to hide his smile at his mind's meanderings. 'Not that it's a bad thing—in my opinion the extra weight suits you.'

Emily remained silent. She hadn't noticed any changes to her body—not yet. She hadn't weighed herself for a while, but…'

'Have you finished?' Alessandro said, easing his position on the carved wooden chair. 'I thought we'd have coffee sent up to the room. That way we can talk in private.'

'Fine,' Emily said quickly. She wanted to confide in him—tell him everything—and this was the best opportunity there'd been. She was already moving to her feet before Alessandro realised she meant to go right away.

'OK, OK,' he said with amusement, reaching the door a pace in front of her to open it. 'I get the message.'

Emily turned to him as they stepped into the lift. 'Do you, Alessandro?'

'I think so.'

And this time when he dragged her close she hadn't the will to resist.

Binding her hands around his neck, Emily dragged him to her with a harsh, unguarded sound of need, opening her mouth against his lips, begging for possession.

His kisses weren't enough. But as her hands flew to the buckle on his belt he dragged them away. Ramming her into the corner of the lift, he kept her wedged there while he reached across to push the lever that would stop the antiquated contraption between floors. Then, wrenching up her slither of a skirt with one hand, he tugged off her tiny lace thong with the other.

Swinging her up, he wrapped her legs around his waist and, supporting her buttocks in hands grown firm and demanding, he entered her in one thrusting stroke, pausing only to utter a contented groan as the moist heat of her body enveloped him completely. Then, pounding into her, he answered her calls for more, increasing speed and force until she let out a long, grateful, wavering cry as the violent spasms engulfed her in sensation.

'And that's just the appetiser,' he murmured, nuzzling his face into her hair as he lowered her to the ground. 'Now get dressed,' he added sternly, bending to scoop up her discarded clothing. 'It wouldn't do for the Princess of Ferara to be seen without her knickers.'

This wasn't quite how she had pictured their first confrontation, Emily realised. But it wasn't easy to resist, when Alessandro could make her laugh at the most inappropriate moments…make her feel happy, and safe, and desired.

He hit the start lever while she struggled into her clothes. And when they reached their sumptuous suite, he slammed the door shut behind them with one hand and dragged her against him roughly with the other.

'One bed OK for you now?' he demanded huskily.

'Bed, floor, lift…' Emily breathed seductively against his mouth. 'It's all the same to me, *mi amor.*'

As he backed her towards the fluffy cream sheepskin rug in front of the roaring log fire she almost forgot what had driven her from the restaurant at such speed. But, sensing her minute mood-shift, Alessandro drew to a halt in the middle of the room.

'Coffee? Talk? Or…?'

Or would be nice, Emily thought, wavering a little, still reeling from the aftershocks of his attentions in the lift. But her rational mind insisted they couldn't go on like this. She had to tell him…tell him now.

'Coffee, please,' she managed.

'Sure?'

'No. Yes. I—'

'Coffee it is,' Alessandro said, as if nothing untoward had occurred between them since leaving the restaurant. Releasing her to switch on some subdued lighting, he poured out two cups from the coffee tray that had been left for them some time during their extended journey between floors.

How to begin? Emily wondered, murmuring thanks as she took the cup and saucer from him.

'So. What do you want to do about these baby issues? The contract?' he prompted. 'I presume that's what all this is about?'

Emily sank down onto a small leather sofa to one side of the inglenook fireplace, stunned into silence by his remark. There were no *baby issues*. There was only a small and very vulnerable child, growing a little more inside her each day.

CHAPTER ELEVEN

THE phrase *baby issues* would not have offended her so deeply had she not been pregnant with Alessandro's baby, Emily realised. Impending motherhood had already imbued her with an overwhelming desire to protect their unborn child from everything—even the most innocent remark. And she was sure Alessandro's remark was innocent. It hadn't taken her long to discover that pregnancy hormones equalled emotional incontinence, and right now she didn't trust herself to speak in case something irrational and angry burst from her mouth.

'Well, if you won't speak to me,' he said, butting into her thoughts, 'I don't know what else I can say.' Throwing up his hands in frustration, he crossed to the window, where he stood staring out at the ghostly shadow of the snow-capped mountain that loomed like a sentinel over the village at night.

And now he was angry—and her silence was to blame, Emily realised, sensing tension so thick in the air it hung like smog, keeping each of them isolated in their own lonely space. But how could she discuss their baby as if it was nothing more than a clause in a contract? She stared in dismay at the huge double bed that only seemed to mock her desire to resume normal relations with her husband.

'Alessandro—'

He turned and looked at her, his head slightly dipped and a furrow of concentration scoring a deep line between his eyes.

It was as if his vision cleared and he had time to study his wife properly for the first time in weeks, Alessandro realised. She looked so weary—exhausted, he amended. Why hadn't he noticed that before?

'Don't be angry,' Emily said softly. 'I really need to be with you tonight.'

His head jerked in surprised response, but he hid his feelings quickly. How had it come to this?

'Where else would you be?' he said gently, reaching out his hands. And when she took them he drew her into his arms.

He held her in his arms all night, dressed in the bizarre outfit it turned out was all she had brought with her—a long baggy tee shirt, with the logo showing only faintly on the front after too many washes, and a pair of stripy pyjama bottoms that trailed over her feet.

He had made no comment when she came out of the bathroom after her shower. And said nothing more when she climbed into the high, comfortable four-poster-bed and pulled the sheets up to her chin. He just climbed in after her, wearing a pair of boxer shorts for the sake of decency, rolled onto his back, and switched out the light.

He wasn't sure exactly when she edged towards him, only that she had...and he stroked the hair back from her brow and kissed her while she was sleeping, as she whimpered in his arms from some deep-seated despair.

He must have dropped off some time during the night, because he woke to find her at the window, staring out, peering from side to side as if there was something quite extraordinary happening outside.

Turning, as if she felt his waking presence as keenly as if he had spoken, she said,

'Alessandro, I think we're snowed in.'

Emily waited as he stretched and yawned noisily, then sat up and raked through his wayward black hair in a hopeless attempt to tame it.

Padding across the room to join her, he leaned his fists

on the windowsill and gazed out across what had become in a few short hours a featureless snowscape.

'No chance of anyone leaving Lech today,' he murmured.

Where there had been pavements and cars and railings, marking the banks of the river that wound its way through the village, there was only a uniform blanket of deep white snow.

'Hungry?' he said, not appearing too concerned by this turn of events.

'A little,' Emily admitted, trying to ignore the fact that her husband was naked, apart from his hip-skimming boxer shorts, and standing very close.

'I'll ring down—have them send something up to us. I feel lazy today. We might as well take it easy…after all, we're not going anywhere.'

Emily moved away to put on some more logs and stoke the dying embers of the fire. The fact that they had slept in the same bed together and he hadn't attempted to make love to her had left her feeling restless and uneasy. Was he still angry with her? Maybe he didn't want her any more. Maybe he was going to reinstate the celibacy clause in their agreement. Maybe he would find that all too easy.

'How long do you think we're here for?' she said, pulling herself together, knowing she sounded edgy, as if she didn't want to be snowed in with him, when nothing could be further from the truth.

But Alessandro seemed not to notice. He had the phone in his hand and was gesturing for her to wait as he got through to Room Service. He spoke rapidly in German…something else she hadn't known about her husband, she realised, feeling panic sweep over her. The fact was, she didn't know much about him at all.

'That's settled,' he said, replacing the receiver. 'Relax, Emily. There's nothing we can do. We might just as well settle back and enjoy the break. Why don't you stop prowling around the room? Go and have a nice long soak in the bath while we're waiting for breakfast to arrive.'

Did he want to put distance between them? Emily swallowed down the fear that had lodged in her throat. All her emotions seemed to be in turmoil—all the time; every little thing seemed to assume crisis proportions. 'How long?' she said again.

'Breakfast? Or—?'

'No, not breakfast,' she flashed back. 'You know what I'm talking about, Alessandro.'

'Do I, Emily?' he said. 'I know you're very prickly this morning, and over-sensitive. Is it something I've done—or not done?'

Her face flamed as the thought of what he had not done. And when she saw the faintly ironic shadow in his slanting amber gaze she knew for sure he was reading her mind.

'You seem to be in a great hurry to leave Lech,' he pressed. 'Do you have an urgent appointment to keep elsewhere?'

'No, of course not.' Emily's mind lurched back on track. 'I came here to be with you—to thank you properly for helping me with that case.'

Is that all? Alessandro thought as he snatched up his robe. Thrusting his arms into the sleeves, he threw her a cynical look. So, Emily only wanted to thank him for his help with her case? It was almost worse than being told she had only come for the sex. 'To answer to your question,' he said coolly, securing the belt, 'walking parties may be able to leave here quite soon with a local guide. Others, who are not quite so desperate to return to reality, can stay on at the hotel until the road down to Zurs is cleared.'

'Oh...' Emily said, peering distractedly out of the window.

'Which category of snowbound guest do you fall into, Emily?'

She moved back towards the fireplace, where the logs were well ablaze. 'I'm staying,' she said without hesitation.

'And we'll do what?'

Now it was Alessandro's turn to sound as if he was having difficulty reining in his feelings—as if he was determined that the emotional rollercoaster ride she had subjected him to had made its final run. It was time to build bridges between them, Emily realised, before the moment was lost for ever...

'I don't know,' she said, determined to find something that would bring them close again. 'Tell each other stories?'

His gaze narrowed thoughtfully, and then, to her relief, softened a little.

'For instance?'

'How about the one you never finished...the one about this ring,' she suggested, holding out her hand so that the central stone in the beautiful old piece of jewellery glowed like a drop of crimson blood in the firelight.

Their relationship was like a ball of wool that had become hopelessly tangled, Emily thought as he came to sit down on the sofa while she chose a spot on the rug. Telling each other stories wouldn't have been her first choice for Christmas Eve activities, but it was somewhere to start teasing out the knots.

'You reached the point where Caterina found the ring and believed it was a sign from Rodrigo,' she prompted.

'OK,' Alessandro said, settling back. 'So Caterina was forced to accept that her lover had drowned. But she decided she couldn't lock herself away in a religious community after all, and would live her life as Rodrigo would have wanted her to.'

'How could she know what he wanted?'

'Because that was the moment she realised she was pregnant with his child.'

Emily's glance flashed up, but there was no separate

agenda, she saw thankfully—he was only recounting a much-loved story.

'Caterina put Rodrigo's ring on her finger and returned to Ferara to fulfil her destiny. And every Princess of Ferara has worn the ring you have on your finger since that day.'

'That's the most romantic thing I ever heard,' Emily admitted, turning the ring around her finger so that the flames from the fire seemed to imbue it with life…or with challenge, maybe… And now it was her turn to come up with an equivalent tale. How would she begin? *Alessandro, I'm going to tell you the story of a baby*?

'I'm sure the history of that ring has been embellished over the years until it's little more than a fairytale,' Alessandro said, misreading the questions in her mind. 'Emily? Where are you going?'

'To have that bath you suggested.' To give herself time.

'You don't get out of telling your story that easily,' Alessandro warned. 'I'll order breakfast while you're reclining in bubbles, then it's your turn.'

Putting a CD on to play, Emily slipped the slim volume of poetry Alessandro had given to her, with the Christopher Marlowe rose from her wedding bouquet pressed inside it, between his jeans and jumper, where he was sure to find it, before heading for the bathroom.

'What are you doing?' he said suspiciously as she darted about the room.

'Nothing.'

'This music—?'

Her shoulders dropped with relief that the first part of her plan hadn't failed. 'Miranda's first commercial recording.'

'It's quite remarkable,' Alessandro murmured, remaining very still as he listened.

'It was brought out in time for Christmas. This is the first copy off the press. Miranda wanted you to have it…she signed it for you.' Hurrying to his side, Emily pressed the empty case into his hands. 'I suppose I should have wrapped it up—'

'No, this is perfect,' Alessandro insisted. And before she could get away he caught hold of her hands and raised them to his lips. 'Go and have your bath, Emily—and don't be long.'

The message in his eyes was unmistakable...irresistible. Emily held his gaze. Her heart was thundering in her chest. It was going to be all right. Everything was going to be all right...

'Do I have to?' she protested after her bath, when they were both sitting by the fire again. 'I'm fine with facts, but I'm absolutely hopeless at telling stories.'

'Then if you can't play the game,' Alessandro warned, 'you'll have to pay a forfeit.'

There was only a glint of humour in his eyes, but it was enough for Emily to feel as if the whole world had revolved on its axis and returned them to a moment in time before secrets had driven a wedge between them. 'A forfeit?'

'Certainly,' he murmured, in a voice that hovered between stern and seductive. Reaching towards her, he brushed a wayward strand of hair back from her face with one finger. 'And I get to choose what that forfeit should be.'

Emily's nerves were jangling with awareness.

She was acutely conscious of the crackling of the logs in the grate and the barely discernible patter of snow against the window as his hand moved to cup the back of her head and draw her close. As his warm, musky man-scent invaded the clean air she made no move to resist when he gathered her into his arms.

'Thank you for the rose,' he whispered against her lips, and even though his eyes were half closed Emily could see how bright they flared with passion, and with love.

'And for the gift of music. I can't think of a better Christmas present.'

'Except this,' she murmured seductively, drawing him down with her onto the soft rug in front of the fire. It felt like a homecoming, a long awaited return. She was lost from the moment his lips touched her body. And when his tongue began to work on her nipples there was no possibility of turning back.

Moving lower, Alessandro freed the fastenings on her jeans and took them down, together the tiny thong she was wearing. Naked now, Emily moved sinuously beneath him as he covered her waist and her belly with tiny teasing bites, before moving on to the insides of her thighs. Running her hands appreciatively over his back, she felt bereft when he left her briefly to tug off his clothes.

There was nothing wrong in having your husband make love to you, Emily reassured herself when something dark and unfathomable niggled at the back of her mind—nothing but the knowledge that you were really four months pregnant with his child and he didn't know yet! She pulled away as his kisses grew a lot more intimate.

'What?' he said, but there was already a hard look in his eyes—as if he knew, Emily saw apprehensively. But how could he know? 'You taste different.'

She was so thrown by the comment that it took her a few moments to rally her thoughts. 'Different?' she muttered.

'You heard what I said.'

The change in Alessandro's voice, in his mood, was frightening. Backing away, Emily sat up and hugged her knees to her chest. 'How do you mean, different?'

His eyes had narrowed and his gaze was calculating. 'I can't list the contributory factors like a recipe—'

'The *contributory factors*?' Emily demanded, reaching nervously for her clothes. 'Don't ever accuse *me* of lawyer-speak again!' Her attempt to lighten the mood skittered across the frigid silence between them, making no improvement. Stumbling awkwardly around, she pulled on her clothes. 'I should never have come,' she exclaimed when Alessandro made no response. 'I'm going to call down to Reception and find out when that guide will be leaving the village—'

'Put that down!'

One minute he was on the rug gazing up at her; the next he was standing beside her with the telephone in his hand.

'I think you owe me an explanation, Emily.'

'No—why—?' she said, backing away from the look in his eyes.

'I think you know. How many months pregnant are you, Emily? Why didn't you tell me the moment you found out?'

Emily's head spun and the ground seemed to come up to meet her. This was the very last thing she had wanted. The hurt in his voice jabbed at her mind like so many thorns.

'How long were you prepared to wait before you told me?'

'Stop!' She put her hands over her ears, as if she couldn't bear to hear another word. 'Please, Alessandro, stop firing questions at me. I can't think—'

'That's perfectly obvious.'

She glanced at him, then quickly looked away. Everything that had been between them minutes earlier had been replaced by an expression on his face that chilled her to the marrow. 'I'm sorry—'

'You set a great scene; I'll hand you that,' he said bitterly, swiping one angry hand across the back of his neck.'

'A scene? What do you mean?'

'The music, the poetry, the rose,' he flashed accusingly. 'I would have preferred honesty…and from the start. Why couldn't you just trust me?'

Silence swooped down between them, holding them

apart, until finally Alessandro said in a voice so low she could hardly be sure he spoke at all, 'It's my fault. That damnable clause in our country's constitution—I should have told you—'

'Stop it!' Her cry rang harshly round them after his murmured confession. 'I'm at fault, too, Alessandro,' Emily insisted desperately. 'But I was frightened—'

'Frightened?' He looked stunned. Wheeling away from her, he raked stiff fingers through his hair, and then stopped again, as if he hardly knew what he was doing. 'I can't stand this,' he admitted, shaking his head distractedly. 'I can't bear what's happening between us—and most of all I can't bear to think you were frightened of me.'

'I was never frightened of you,' Emily admitted softly. 'I was frightened of losing you...frightened of what it will mean to all of us...you, me, and especially our child...when that wretched contract comes to an end.'

'Contract!' He made a sound of disgust as he turned his face away. 'I should never have put my name to it in the first place.'

'We both entered into it in good faith,' Emily pointed out. 'We just didn't expect to have feelings get in the way of a business deal.'

'Can you ever forgive me?' he demanded tensely, staring at her as if his very life depended on her answer.

'Easily,' Emily said as she touched his arm. 'We've both made mistakes. Neither of us was prepared for how our feelings would grow. That contract was drawn up to satisfy our business instincts, not our emotions. I know I should never have left you...but when I found out about the clause in the constitution that demanded an heir before your father could abdicate I couldn't think straight—'

'And no wonder,' Alessandro admitted, very slowly drawing her into his arms, as if he needed to be certain she knew that was where she belonged. 'And now?'

'Now?'

'Can you think straight now?' he demanded softly.

'I hope so…I don't know.' She shrugged with exasperation. 'I'm just so—'

'Pregnant?' he supplied gently, a wry smile playing around his lips as he looked at her. 'This is the first time for you and the first time for me…and I am totally overwhelmed to know we are expecting a child. Your hormones must be in turmoil. Don't be so hard on yourself, Emily.'

As he dipped his head to kiss her Emily made herself pull back. 'Are you quite sure that marriage to a commoner is what you really want, Alessandro?'

'What on earth do you mean?' He drew his head back to stare at her in bemusement. 'How can you even ask me a question like that?'

'There must be so many women of noble birth who would jump at the chance—'

'And none of them is you.'

'But it can't have been easy for your father when you told him.'

Alessandro placed his finger over her lips. 'My father loves you, Emily.'

'You can trace your ancestors back thirty generations—'

'And half of them were warlords,' Alessandro broke in firmly. 'Brigands who snatched power from those weaker than themselves. They would be considered beyond the pale in today's society.'

'But still—'

'No, Emily,' he said firmly. 'Stop this right now. Did you know that Christopher Marlowe was the son of a shoemaker? No?' he said, staring at her intently. 'And yet he was a far greater prince than I. We quote his words more than four hundred years after his death. Who will remember my words?'

'You share your father's passion for Tudor playwrights,' Emily exclaimed, her face breaking into a smile as she relaxed at last.

'It would be impossible to live under the same roof as my father and not share his passions,' Alessandro admitted wryly. 'And one of his most profound, my love, is you.'

'And yet I've been so unreasonable—to both of you.'

'No,' Alessandro argued gently. 'You're a woman in love, a pregnant woman in love, and with a man you're still getting to know.'

'So, where do we go from here?' she said anxiously, scanning his face.

'That's the easy part,' he murmured, kissing her again.

When Alessandro insisted they should both dress for dinner that evening Emily didn't have the heart to refuse him, even though she expected the small, exclusive hotel festivities to be low-key.

The floor-length gown, packed into her suitcase at the last minute in a moment of whimsy, was of crimson silk, and emphasised the creamy whiteness of her skin. She felt particularly comfortable in it because it draped elegantly over her fuller figure. Leaving her hair to fall loosely around her shoulders, she wore the minimum of make-up—just some lip-gloss and soft grey eyeshadow to point up the brilliant jade-green of her eyes.

Wondering what Alessandro had planned, she found herself ready before him, and had to keep reminding herself that this was the man who loved her while she watched with naked appreciation as he dressed after his shower.

As he slipped into his dinner jacket, and made final adjustments to his hair in the mirror, he smiled back at her. 'I think it's time for your Christmas present,' he said, shooting her the type of look that always made her melt.

'But we've just got dressed—' She stopped at his amused glance of male awareness. The sound of his voice was enough to arouse her, she realised self-consciously. But he instead of moving towards her he made for the door.

'Alessandro?' Emily called after him anxiously. 'Where are you going?'

'I said it was time for your Christmas present now,' he reminded her. Removing what looked like a single sheet of paper from his jacket pocket, he left it on the oak dresser by the door. 'While I'm gone, you might like to cast your eyes over this,' he suggested. And then, before she had a chance to say a word, he left the room.

'Alessandro, wait—' Emily's heart gave a sickening lurch as she rushed towards the door. Swinging it open, she stared both ways down the corridor. But everything was silent. He was nowhere to be seen. Coming back into the room, she closed the door behind her. Biting her lip, she snatched up the sheet of paper and began to read.

Alessandro's bold pen-work leaped off the page at her, his blue ink resonating purposefully against the thick ivory-coloured sheet.

> *'Come live with me, and be my Love,*
> *And we will all the pleasures prove...*
> *If these delights thy mind may move! Then live with me, and be my Love.*

Two minds with but a single thought... When would she ever learn to trust him?

'Alessandro—' She whirled round as he came back into the room. 'I read the poem.'

'Did you like it?'

The confidence in his eyes thrilled her. 'Of course.' She wondered if they would ever make it down for dinner...

'So, I chose well?'

'How can you ask?'

'I apologise for leaving you so abruptly,' he said, crossing to her side. 'I just wanted to check everything was ready.'

'Ready?' The restaurant table, she surmised, imagining how busy the hotel would be on Christmas Eve.

'Yes. We have to go out onto the balcony.'

'The balcony?'

'Do you have a wrap? Here, take this.'

Before she could stop him, Alessandro had shrugged off his own jacket and was wrapping it around her shoulders.

'You'll freeze,' Emily said, looking at him with concern. 'And why the balcony?'

'Stop asking questions,' Alessandro said, snatching up another jacket from the chair. 'We'll miss everything.'

'What?'

But Alessandro was in no mood for conversation as he hurried her outside.

The balcony overlooking the immense, mountain peaks in front of them was beautifully lit, and there were heaters, strategically placed by the hotel, so that instead of feeling cold, as she had expected to, Emily felt positively cosy as she sank into the comforting warmth of Alessandro's jacket.

The particular balcony on which they were standing went right around the hotel, and more people were joining them, Emily noticed, trickling out of their rooms in twos and—

'Mum? Dad!' she gasped, seeing who it was. Bolting towards them, she gave them each a hug, laughing with surprise. Then, at her father's gentle prompting, she turned. 'Your Royal Highness—' Turning to Alessandro, she could only shake her head in speechless delight.

'Happy Christmas, my darling,' he whispered, drawing her close to plant a tender kiss on her lips. 'Look—' he said, including everyone as he gestured towards the mountain. 'They're about to start.'

'What…what's happening?' Emily demanded softly, looking for answers to Alessandro.

'Watch the top of the mountain,' Alessandro instructed, holding her in front of him as everyone else gathered round.

At first all Emily could see was a cluster of light, right at the top of the tallest peak. 'Where's Miranda?' she whispered, as her mother came to stand next to her at the front rail of the balcony.

'Listen,' Alessandro commanded, silencing everyone.

As she waited, Emily noticed that the whole village seemed to be out on the streets; people were standing on the wall by the river and on the parapet of the bridge to get a better look. But the silence was absolute as they all stood staring at the top of the mountain.

Emily jumped closer to Alessandro when she heard a cannon being fired, somewhere far away. The loud report echoed several times, fading with each repetition as the shots bounced off each majestic rockface in turn. As it fell completely silent again a haunting melody shimmered through the crisp mountain air.

'Miranda!' Her sister's playing was uniquely beautiful and Emily would have known it anywhere. Alessandro's hold around her waist tightened a little as he burrowed his face into her neck to give her a kiss of confirmation.

The limpid sound of the solo violin was completely suited to the magical occasion, and as the sound rose through the speakers judicially placed throughout the village a murmur arose from the crowds on the streets, and then applause.

As Alessandro pointed up towards the jagged peak again Emily could see that the tiny cluster of light at the top of the mountain had split up to form a chain, and was now beginning to stream down the slopes in a long, curling ribbon of light.

'The ski instructors—each holding a torch,' Alessandro explained, and the shimmering line took its cue from the waltz Miranda was playing and swung in giant rhythmical loops across the mountainside as they came down towards the village.

'It's magical!' Emily murmured, leaning back into

Alessandro. 'The best…the very best Christmas present I could ever have.'

'Don't speak too soon,' Alessandro murmured close to her ear, so that her whole body ached for him.

After the display they ate a light meal together. Miranda joined them, flushed and happy with success, and accompanied by a rather striking-looking man who, Emily learned, having won a gold medal in the downhill ski race at the Winter Olympics, had been granted the honour of leading the torchlight procession of skiers down the mountain.

When they had finished eating Alessandro led everyone back onto the balcony, to see a barrage of fireworks screaming into the night sky, illuminating the inky blackness with endless plumes of exploding light.

'Happy Christmas, *belissima*,' he murmured, as every clock in the village struck midnight.

'Happy Christmas, Alessandro,' Emily whispered in return, wondering if anyone in the world had ever been as happy as she was.

'Alessandro! Emily!'

Releasing their hold on each other, they turned to share their happiness with Alessandro's father.

'Tonight you have made an old man very happy,' he said, opening his arms wide to embrace them both. 'This—this is what I have wished for since our first meeting in the garden,' he added, turning to address Emily. 'I would gladly cede all the privileges life has granted me to see my son Alessandro as happy as he is now—with you, Emily. And to know,' he added archly, 'that for the very first time in his life he has met his match.'

Was that a wink? Emily wondered, laughing back. She was so happy. 'I will do my best to keep things that way,' she promised, matching his conspiratorial tone.

'I know you will,' the elderly Prince declared confidently. 'And as for you, Alessandro—' He turned to face his son. 'You are a very lucky man. And now…' He turned around to draw Emily's family into the conversation. 'I think it's time we left these two lovebirds alone. I would be honoured if you would all join me in my suite for a nightcap before we retire to bed.'

Giving her mother and father a warm kiss each, Emily saved a special hug for Miranda, taking the chance to murmur, 'I like him,' when she sensed Miranda's handsome new conquest was uppermost in her twin's mind. Embracing Alessandro's father, she kissed him on both cheeks and whispered, 'Thank you for everything…and thank you especially for Alessandro.'

With a last squeeze, he released her back into the arms of her husband.

'Goodnight to you both, and a happy Christmas to everyone.' With one last expansive gesture he led Emily's family away.

Under protection of the darkness Alessandro's lips brushed lightly against Emily's neck, and then moved on to her cheek, her mouth, always light, almost testing—as if they were on a first date. The thought excited her, and she turned her face up to him to whisper, 'Don't stop.'

'You're very forward, Principessa,' he growled softly. 'Do you think we had better go inside?'

Emily's limbs felt as if they had turned into molten honey as he swept her into his arms and carried her back into their suite.

Glimpsing her reflection in the mirror at the side of the bed, she watched Alessandro release the hooks on the back of her dress. As his hands moved lower he began to kiss the back of her neck and her shoulders, until she was leaning into him, sighing with pleasure. The jewelled pins in her hair made it seem scattered with stars, and he released them so that the ebony waves tumbled over her shoulders. Her breasts were creamy against the crimson silk bodice, the shadow of her cleavage deep and dark—

'Stop looking in the mirror,' he murmured. 'I want all your attention on me.'

'That's not so hard,' Emily admitted softly as the dress fell away and he eased it over her hips.

'Beautiful,' he murmured, looking at her admiringly as his hands moved to cup her breasts. 'I should like to keep you here for ever.'

'I should have to leave the bedroom some time,' Emily teased, but she gasped as his thumb-pads stroked firmly against her nipples.

'Don't worry, I would never stop my wife doing the job she loves,' he insisted, his gold eyes darkening to sepia as he observed her arousal. 'But not tonight,' he continued softly, sternly. 'I have never wished to narrow your horizons, Emily...only to broaden them.' And then, allowing her to sink back onto the soft pillows, he stood up and pulled off his clothes.

She was definitely ready to have her horizons broadened again, Emily thought, watching him strip. A familiar lethargy was already invading her limbs, and before he even touched her shafts of sensation were streaming through her body. As he lay down beside her she feared she was about to discover if it was possible to climax from anticipation alone.

Coming closer, he caressed her ear with his lips, moving on to nibble the tender lobe. And all the while his warm breath fanned her pulse, making her long for the firmer touch of his hands, a touch he knew just how long to deny her. Then his weight was controlling her, his hands positioning her, until she could do no more than submit—a licence he made full use of until she lay calm and sated in his arms once again.

And later, much later, when Alessandro was tracing the gently curving swell of her belly with awe, he murmured, 'No more separation for us, Emily—ever. When you have a case in London we will move Court over there, so that I can be with you…the baby, too, of course,' he said, a smile coming to his face as he looked at her. 'We will buy a suitable property. I don't see a problem.'

'I'm sure you don't,' Emily said, smiling as she ran her nail-tips gently through his tousled hair, making him gasp aloud with pleasure at her touch. 'But when have you ever seen a problem that you couldn't solve, Alessandro? I don't believe a problem ever existed that could defeat you.'

'I almost met my match with you, Emily,' he admitted wryly. 'That is, of course, until I found the perfect way of dealing with you…'

She sucked in a swift breath as he entered her again, smoothly and firmly, filling her completely.

'I can't argue—' She couldn't speak. Pleasure had stolen her words away. And then his lips and tongue claimed her mouth, finally completing the task.

Could there be more happiness in all the world than this? Emily wondered late on Christmas morning, when Alessandro swung out of bed and left her briefly.

'Another Christmas present,' he explained, coming back to her side. 'And this time it's for both of us.'

'What is it?' she said excitedly.

'This,' Alessandro said, as he held out an official-looking document.

When she went to take it from him he only shook his head, and then, very slowly and deliberately, began to tear it into tiny pieces.

'What are you doing?' she asked in surprise.

'Something I should have done months ago. That is what I think of our contract.' Turning around, he dropped the tiny scraps of paper into the wastebin by the side of the bed. 'Now it can never come between us again,' he said, coming back to stretch out beside her. Drawing her into his arms, he murmured, 'I love you, Emily—my wife, my only love, mother of my child—my children,' he corrected himself with a long, lazy smile.'

'And I love you, too, Alessandro,' Emily said as she wrapped her arms around him and snuggled into his chest. 'With all my heart.'

'So,' he murmured slumberously, 'will you live with me and be my love, Emily?'

'I will,' she whispered, taking hold of his hand and placing it against her belly to feel their baby's first forceful kicks.

MILLS & BOON®   0407/01b

Modern
romance™

BOUGHT FOR HER BABY by Melanie Milburne

Greek billionaire Damon Latousakis is claiming a mistress:
the same woman he exiled from his life four years
ago…he might not trust her, but he can't resist her!
Charlotte's never forgotten her heartbreak over Damon's
accusations, but how can she assert her innocence when
she's been keeping their little girl a secret…?

THE AUSTRALIAN'S HOUSEKEEPER BRIDE
by Lindsay Armstrong

Rhiannon Fairfax believes that everything should be calm
and orderly. Then Australian billionaire Lee Richardson
hires her. Stormy, complex and autocratic, Lee disturbs
her hard-won peace of mind. But he needs a wife – and he
wants Rhiannon!

THE BRAZILIAN'S BLACKMAIL BARGAIN
by Abby Green

Six months ago Brazilian tycoon Caleb Cameron thought
he'd uncovered Maggie Holland's plot to ruin him. In fact
Maggie was manipulated by her cruel stepfather. Now her
stepfather is dead and Caleb is the new owner of all the
family's assets. Then he makes Maggie an offer she cannot
refuse…

THE GREEK MILLIONAIRE'S MISTRESS
by Catherine Spencer

Gina Hudson is in Athens to settle an old score and that
doesn't include falling into the arms – and bed! – of her
enemy's right-hand man. No-strings sex is what Mikos
Christopoulos expects from Gina at first – but by the end
he wants to bed her for the rest of his life…

On sale 4th May 2007
Available at WHSmith, Tesco, ASDA, and all good bookshops
www.millsandboon.co.uk

MILLS & BOON®

Romance

THE SHERIFF'S PREGNANT WIFE *by Patricia Thayer*

Surprise is an understatement for Sheriff Reed Larkin when he finds out his childhood sweetheart has returned home. After all these years Paige Keenan's smile can still make his heart ache. But what's the secret he can see in her whisky-coloured eyes…?

THE PRINCE'S OUTBACK BRIDE *by Marion Lennox*

Prince Max de Gautier travels to the Australian Outback in search of the heir to the throne. But Max finds a feisty woman who is fiercely protective of her adopted children. Although Pippa is wary of this dashing prince, she agrees to spend one month in his royal kingdom…

THE SECRET LIFE OF LADY GABRIELLA
by Liz Fielding

Lady Gabriella March is the perfect domestic goddess – but in truth she's simply Ellie March, who uses the beautiful mansion she is house-sitting to inspire her writing. The owner returns and Ellie discovers that Dr Benedict Faulkner is the opposite of the ageing academic she'd imagined…

BACK TO MR & MRS *by Shirley Jump*

Cade and Melanie were the High School Prom King and Queen… Twenty years on Cade has realised that he let work take over and has lost the one person who lit up his world. Now he is determined to show Melanie he can be the husband she needs…and win back her heart.

On sale 4th May 2007

Available at WHSmith, Tesco, ASDA, and all good bookshops
www.millsandboon.co.uk